MANIA

Also by Lionel Shriver

LIONEL SHRIVER

MANIA

b

THE BOROUGH PRESS

The Borough Press
An imprint of HarperCollins*Publishers* Ltd
1 London Bridge Street
London SE1 9GF

www.harpercollins.co.uk

HarperCollins Publishers
Macken House,
39/40 Mayor Street Upper,
Dublin 1
D01 C9W8

First published by HarperCollins*Publishers* 2024
1

A catalogue record for this book is available from the British Library

HB ISBN: 978-0-00-865867-0
TPB ISBN: 978-0-00-865868-7

This novel is entirely a work of fiction.
The names, characters and incidents portrayed in it are
the work of the author's imagination. Any resemblance to
actual persons, living or dead, events or localities is
entirely coincidental.

Set in Fairfield LT Std by HarperCollins*Publishers* India

Printed and bound in the UK using 100% Renewable Electricity by
CPI Group (UK) Ltd

This book contains FSC™ certified paper and other controlled
sources to ensure responsible forest management.

For more information visit: www.harpercollins.co.uk/green

To Deb and Nick—generous, gregarious, hilarious lifelong friends. Please visit.

When there is no more hereditary wealth, privilege class, or prerogatives of birth, it becomes clear that the chief source of disparity between the fortunes of men lies in the mind.

—Alexis de Tocqueville

It is becoming more and more obvious that it is not starvation, not microbes, not cancer, but man himself who is mankind's greatest danger, for the simple reason that there is no adequate protection against psychic epidemics, which are infinitely more devastating than the worst of natural catastrophes.

—Carl Jung

ALT-2011

CHAPTER 1

I was on the way to pick up a few things for dinner—as she did so often, my running buddy Emory was coming over that night—when my son's school rang to inform me that he was being sent home for "bullying," so would I please pick him up. Darwin is a contained, deliberate boy, hardly inclined to push other children around, so I wondered if there might have been a misunderstanding. He'd always performed at the top of his class, and—until recently—he'd been the apple of his teachers' eyes. Sure enough, when I came to retrieve him from the front office, my slight, precocious oldest was sitting quietly, though his mouth was set, and he was staring fiercely into the middle distance, excluding the two adults in the room from his line of sight. At eleven, he was about the age at which I awakened from an indoctrination that Darwin had been spared. Yet his customary containment had a combustible quality reminiscent of my own demeanor when seething silently through Family Worship Evening.

"I'm afraid your son ridiculed one of his classmates," the assistant principal informed me. "He employed language we consider unacceptable in a supportive environment, and which I will not repeat." The official thrust her formidable breasts upward, dramatizing a haughty bearing in little need of emphasis.

"Well, most kids try bad language on for size—"

"Playground obscenities would be one thing. *Slurs* are quite another. This is a suspension-level offense. Any similar violation in the future could merit expulsion."

If not the very best in Voltaire, Pennsylvania, Gertrude Stein Primary is (or was) a decent public school not overly far from our house. Two grades below, Darwin's sister Zanzibar went here, too, while our youngest, six-year-old Lucy, had just started school here that September. Ergo, Wade and I couldn't afford to alienate the administration. Even if our son was drifting toward the doghouse, we just had to ease Darwin through sixth grade and out the door, so I promised I'd speak sternly to him and remind him that certain terms are "out of bounds."

The second-in-command didn't let me go without adding a warning. "I do hope he isn't picking up this kind of derogatory vocabulary because it's commonplace at home."

"I assure you we're very civilized."

"Any number of civilizations of times past held views we find abhorrent today. I think you know what I mean, Ms. Converse. This is a forward-looking institution."

Back in the car, Darwin remained silent. Because, thanks to my older two kids' anonymous test-tube father, his ethnic heritage is half Japanese, many people interpret his refined features and slight figure as signatures of a constitutional delicacy. But that slender frame is built on an armature of steel. Darwin is not delicate.

I let him stew on the drive back. Last fall, this leafy neighborhood had signs planted in nearly every yard, *"Morons" welcome here!*—the same sign that businesses in strip malls all taped hastily to their windows. But overt usage of such terms of opprobrium even in quotation marks rapidly morphed from declassé to crude to deadly, so the current crop of yard signs was more sedate: *We support cognitive neutrality.* The car up ahead sported one of those bumper stickers that had proliferated everywhere, *Honk if you hate brainiacs.* Because a plethora of other drivers also, it seemed, hated brainiacs, the trip home was loud.

Lest our woody, rambling five-bedroom give a misleading impression of my family's circumstances, Wade's and my fire-sale purchase of the comely and substantial property was made possible only by the foreclosures of 2008. In mid-October, it was too chilly to talk out Darwin's sins on the commodious back deck, so I sat my son at the kitchen table while I surveyed our larder for what ingredients we had on hand. I hoped this cross-examination would be short, because Lucy's school bus would arrive at our stop in less than two hours, and it seemed that I did still need to dash to the supermarket.

"It was about a T-shirt," Darwin said sourly at last.

"And?"

"Stevie was wearing one that said, 'If you're so smart, why aren't you smart?'"

I guffawed. "God, that's lame! It doesn't even make sense."

"That's what I said. Actually, all I said is it was stupid."

"The S-word."

"I didn't call Stevie stupid. I said his T-shirt was."

"Stupid Stevie" had a ring that in my day would have made it irresistible.

"Well . . ." I said. "When you wear a stupid shirt, that can't help but suggest that you're a little bit stupid yourself."

"I don't understand the rules anymore!" Darwin exploded. "Okay, so a person can't be stupid. You've explained why, over and over, and no, I still don't see how, like, as of, like, one day back around the beginning of fifth grade suddenly a fucking doofhead wasn't a fucking doofhead anymore." If I cursed occasionally on principle, I'd no place being prissy about my kids' language at home. "But, okay, I get it. I don't call anyone the S-word or a bunch of other words. But can a thing still be stupid, like a shirt? Can an idea be stupid? Can anything be stupid, or is everything intelligent now?"

I squinted. "I'm not sure. Calling everything intelligent might get you into trouble, too."

"This junk is all anyone cares about anymore! But it's not like we don't all know which kids are total pea-brains. The teachers are always calling on them, and no matter what they say it's always, 'Ooh, Jennifer, that's so *wise!*' And then when one of the thickos claims five times seven is sixty-two, our math teacher says, 'Excellent! That's *one* answer, and a very *good* answer. So would anyone else like to contribute a *different* answer?'"

I suppose none of this was funny, really; still, I couldn't help but laugh. I know I'm not objective, but mothers aren't meant to be, and my son charmed the pants off me.

"I swear, the teachers are actually afraid of the class dummies," Darwin continued. "The dimwits are never called out for talking during lessons or not turning in their homework. I guess now not doing your homework is just a *different* and totally *wise* way of doing your home-work. Meanwhile, the dummies are becoming a pain in the butt. They walk around with their noses in the air like they're so special, and they're always on the lookout for something you said that they can jump on and take the wrong way. Like, Aaron told this girl Wendy that her new phone case was 'super dope.' He was just trying to be nice and also to sound cool, but she punched him in the arm and reported him to the new MPC—" At my quizzical look, he spelled out, "Mental Parity Champion. I think all the schools have them. Anyway, Aaron was forced to apologize in front of the class, because Wendy and the MPC were both too clueless to know that 'dope' means 'great.'"

"I have a funny feeling that usage is on the way out," I said. "Listen, you don't say words like 'thicko' and 'dummy' at school, do you?"

"Of course not. That would make me a *dummy* and a *thicko*, wouldn't it? But I don't understand why we can't stick up for what we think. *You* said there is, too, such a thing as being smarter than other people, and it's nothing to be ashamed of. I don't understand why we have to go along with this junk."

I confess that I took pleasure in the cozy collusion of our heretical household. Yet I worried that my determination to preserve a sanctum of sanity behind closed doors put the kids in a parlous position. "There's obviously something to be said for staying true to what we believe," I said. "But we have to be prudent. Pick our spots. This new way of thinking about people is bigger than we are. If we stick up for what we believe in the wrong way, or at the wrong time, we won't accomplish anything, aside from doing ourselves a great deal of damage." In due course, I'd have been better off delivering this speech to myself.

"You mean we just have to go along with everyone else because we're outnumbered, or because, if we don't, we'll be punished. What's the dif-ference between your 'being prudent' and being a fucking coward?"

"There's no difference," I said heavily. "Now, get your coat."

At the last minute, Emory called me on what I was no longer, apparently, supposed to describe as my "smartphone," although I was baffled by how I was meant to refer to it instead. (I'd remarked earlier that week in our departmental offices, "What is it now, a mediocrityphone?" A colleague quipped tartly, "How about 'phone'? Is that so hard, Pearson? Is employing a usage that's actually more succinct still too great a sacrifice, the better to show a little respect, a little sensitivity? How about *phone*?") Was our menu sufficiently elastic to include Roger, Emory asked, this new fellow she was seeing? I could hardly say no, though I was annoyed. After the vexing business of Darwin being sent home from school, I was in no mood to make a show of interest in some stranger. I'd sprung for barely enough costly tiger prawns for six, and another guest would be a stretch. Roger would change the nature of the occasion from my best friend casually dropping by to join us for supper again to a "dinner party." Besides, we hadn't seen each other since the fall term commenced, and I wanted Emory all to myself.

Sure enough, they arrived with a pricey bottle and flowers, whereas Emory commonly showed up with box wine that privileged alcoholic ambition over refinement. If I even bothered with olives, we'd usually pluck them from the deli container while standing in my dark-wood kitchen, and now I had to put them in an attractive bowl, with a separate dish for pits. Lest the kalamatas seem paltry, I'd also put out beet and parsnip chips, though the plain old salt-and-vinegar potato kind were better.

Leaving Wade to finish the prep, I issued our guests with reluctant formality into the living room. Emory's gear—leggings with sleek black boots, a silk tunic in saffron accented with a red scarf perhaps purposefully reminiscent of her sixteenth birthday present to me—was simple but flash. Just as unsurprisingly, Roger was handsome. He was trim in that perfectly cornered way, reliably the result of vigilant dietary stinting and fearfully fanatic adherence to fitness rituals. The styling of his clothes was sporty, but their fabrics were high-end. He didn't say much at first, but his reserve didn't come across as shyness so much as an arch holding back to observe, assess, and judge. Immaculate grooming cultivated an air of sovereignty, perhaps the mutual quality that had drawn these two to each other to begin with. Yet he didn't say anything overtly boastful or patronizing, so maybe I just had a bad attitude.

It can be best to say what's really on your mind in these settings, or chitchat can feel pointless and diversionary. Skipping the specifics, I explained that I was still a bit upset because Darwin had been suspended for employing a "slur," and he wasn't used to being treated like a troublemaker. "He doesn't understand what the rules are anymore," I said. "I can't blame him for feeling confused."

"Well, have you heard about Obama's expansion of 'Don't Ask, Don't Tell'?" Emory asked. I had, but I was hazy on the details. "I only bring it up because it's a social template that's bound to apply beyond the military. So tell Darwin that these are the rules from now on: Don't ask where anyone went to school. Don't tell anyone where you went to school, even if you went to Yale—well, especially if you went to Yale! And that includes secondary schools: Never drop casually in conversation that you graduated from Andover or Groton. Don't ever mention, or fish for, IQ, obviously, but also SAT and ACT scores or grade point averages. You're even meant to keep your trap shut about how well you did on newspaper quizzes on the major stories of the week. And forget asking or telling about a performance on *Jeopardy!*"

Emory delivered this lowdown with an admirable deadpan, but her intention was clearly mocking. "You know, they canceled that show last week," I said.

"No kidding," Emory said.

"Gone, finito. It's *discriminatory*. And it's been on since 1964."

"Wow," Emory said. "So much for *Who Wants to Be a Millionaire*, then."

"I caught part of that program while I was shelling the shrimp for dinner, just out of curiosity," I said. "They're trying to stay alive, and stay *relevant*, by asking unbelievably primitive questions. Like, 'What—is—your—name?'"

"Phone a friend!" Emory exclaimed. "Oh, and I almost forgot: the army has also banned Rubik's Cubes in the barracks."

"Chess has to be next," I groaned.

"No, it can't be next," Emory said, her deadpan still impeccable. "They already banned chess. It creates a divisive and prejudicial environment, and it's antithetical to the spirit of unity in the corps."

"Oh, God, pretty soon this could hit where it hurts," I said. "Boggle and Scrabble are doomed."

"As they should be," Emory said primly. "They make any number of entirely equal people feel unjustly inadequate."

We were leaving Roger out of the fun. After passing around the olives, I asked, unimaginatively, how they'd met.

"Roger was a guest on the show," Emory said. "Though I'm not sure who was doing whom the favor. I had to warn him that no one, and I mean no one, listens to it."

Emory was not given to self-deprecation to make herself more likable; she spoke from genuine frustration. From high school, she'd nursed a single-minded ambition to make it in television journalism (by contrast, my sole driving ambition from my teenage years was to be left alone), but for a decade she'd worked at WVPA, an NPR affiliate. For six of those years, she'd hosted a minor early-afternoon arts program that sponsored local up-and-comers and B-listers, and she felt stuck.

"How relaxing for you, then," I told Roger. "If no one's listening, you can say anything."

"No, Pearson," Emory said. "These days, you most certainly can't say just anything." I wondered if she was giving me a personal warning.

Roger, it seemed, was a playwright. I wanted to say, "Does anyone even go to plays anymore? Everyone I know hates them. It's yesterday's form, don't you think? Who wouldn't rather see a movie?" But I didn't.

"It's an interesting time to be working in the theater," he said.

"Interesting?" I said. "I wouldn't have thought that's quite the word. Tricky, maybe. Or dangerous."

"Great theater is always dangerous," he said smoothly. "But I meant it's exciting to work in the arts when the culture's tectonic plates are shifting. The last couple of years have seen an utter upending of a hierarchy that goes back millennia. Back to forever, really."

"Yes, I haven't been living in a cave," I said sweetly, nodding at the coffee table.

But then, I worried that Roger might misinterpret the tome on display as occupying pride of place, whereas this household's exhibition of *The Calumny of IQ: Why Discrimination Against "Dumb People" Is the Last Great Civil Rights Fight* was pointedly ironic. As I'd felt the need to get in on the political ground floor in 2010, ours was a first-edition hardback, so the cover still pictured a little boy on a stool staring shamefacedly at his lap while wearing what no one would now dare call a "dunce cap." Later editions eliminated the hat, the image too harsh a throwback to a barbaric past, while rendering the subtitle as *Discrimination Against "D— People."* As "calumny" soon joined a host of vocabulary deemed ostentatiously "brain-vain," the last paperback I'd glimpsed at a supermarket checkout had simplified the title to *The Crime of IQ.*

If I'd never finished Carswell Dreyfus-Boxford's game-changing, era-defining magnum opus, that just made me like most people. It was one of those commonplace doorstops that everyone bought and nobody read. At best, the ambitious got through the set-piece introduction of forty pages, full of heartrending anecdotes of capable young people whose self-esteem was crushed by an early diagnosis of subpar intelligence. Once you digested the thesis that all perceived variation in human intelligence merely came down to "processing issues," you could skip all the tedious twin studies, cohort graphs, and demonstrations of IQ scores being raised or lowered by fifteen to twenty points depending on whathaveyou. Initially, the "cerebral elite"—academics, doctors and lawyers, scientists—lampooned the notion that stupidity is a fiction as exceptionally stupid (whatever they say now). Yet as the drive for intellectual leveling gathered steam, it was the sharpest tacks among that elect who jumped on the fashionable bandwagon first.

"You know, it's easy to forget, but that book was widely ridiculed when it first came out. *You and I* made merciless fun of it," I reminded Emory, hoping to stir her memory of a certain unruly, drunken late-night twosome at her apartment in the spring of the previous year. "Basically everyone agreed that the poor professor had published a howler. Then suddenly—you could probably pinpoint the pivot to a single day—Dreyfus-Boxford's proposition wasn't hilarious but irrefutably true: there's no such thing as you-know-what."

"Well, any day now I expect another blockbuster to make a splash by claiming there's no such thing as a beautiful woman," Emory said slyly to her date, extending her shapely legs to prop them on the coffee table. "Everyone is as beautiful as everyone else. And if you beg to differ, you're suffering from a *processing issue.*"

If there was indeed such a thing as a beautiful woman, that would be Emory Ruth. Tall and slender with close-cut raven hair, she was old enough at thirty-nine that if she were going to get hippy, the broadening would have shown by then. By that night I'd lost numerical track of Emory's boyfriends and broken engagements, which had long provided me a subscription streaming service akin to Hallmark Movies Now sans the $5.99/month. Her surfeit of male attention was boringly down to looks. But none of these guys was ever good enough for her, and it was more than possible that none of them ever would be. I thought, *Somebody oughta tell Roger.*

"So how's it going at VU?" Emory asked. "Are the babies behaving themselves?"

I'd been eager to talk to her about the tribulations of teaching English even at the erstwhile august Voltaire University, but now I felt constrained. If Roger was dating Emory, I was inclined to assume he was one of us, but he hadn't tipped his hand and remained an unknown quantity.

"Well, this fall is the first open-admissions intake," I said. "A few of the more conservative schools have held out, but the writing's on the wall for standardized tests; everyone expects that by this time next year they'll be just as illegal as IQ tests. Now that K-through-twelve has stopped giving them, colleges won't be able to use grades, either. The conceit—I mean, the understanding—is that everyone's the same level of . . . So the whole idea of letting in one applicant and not another is unacceptable.

I'm not sure if they pull names from a hat or it's first come, first serve. But there's really no point to having an admissions office anymore. A janitor could do the job: unlock the door."

"An economy, then," Emory said.

"When I didn't get into VU myself," I said, "I guess my feelings were hurt. At the same time, I knew in my heart of hearts that I wasn't really . . . good enough . . . qualified enough . . . But if I had been admitted, I'd have been over the moon. I wonder if we're denying young people a rite of passage that can be exhilarating. That letter in the mail. That burst of joy, that feeling of being chosen, of having made the grade, of being recognized and lifted up, that sudden giddy rush of being seen as special and finally believing that maybe you have a future." I said this last bit in an animated torrent, then caught myself. "I'm only saying that 'getting in' to Voltaire, to Cornell, to Harvard—it doesn't mean anything anymore. That seems like a loss. An emotional loss, if nothing else."

"But you said your feelings were hurt," Roger said. "From the sound of it, a sense of inferiority from that rejection still lingers, what, twenty years later? Wouldn't you estimate that far more young people have been devastated in the college admissions race than the few who've been 'exhilarated'? Isn't that an awfully big price to pay, collectively, for a few crack highs?"

I tried to take his measure. Roger's tone was tentative, if still on the politically acceptable side of neutral. Were he a Mental Parity true believer, he might be gentling his fervor from romantic savvy. After all, he'd have discovered after going out with Emory even once that she subjected the current catechism to wicked ridicule. Should they fall on opposite sides of this issue, it was only a matter of time before the clash destroyed the relationship—an advent that, assuming he was smitten, which Emory's swains always were, he'd have every motivation to put off. Alternatively? Maybe he chose to air views that fell safely within the Overton window (which had collapsed to a slit) out of caution. He was in an untested social setting where mouthing the shibboleths of cognitive equality might risk dreariness but at least would never get his head cut off.

"You do realize you're among friends," I said.

"Indeed," he said lightly, with an air of not understanding what I was getting at.

"I'm astonished by how fast this new way of thinking about human intelligence installed itself," I said. "And I'm not quite sure who installed it. The pace of ideological change has been dizzying."

"Funny," Roger said, "that's not my experience at all. I'm always shocked when I remind myself what a short time it's been, because to me it seems as if we've banned cognitive discrimination for years and years."

I was perplexed why Emory had yet to jump in—say, right here, maybe along the lines of "That's because when something horrendous is happening, time slows to a crawl." But she just sat there, submitting to her new boyfriend's many claim-laying touches as he sat encroachingly close to her on the couch—a stroke of a cheek here, a brush of a shoulder there, three fingers on her knee.

"As for my experience in the classroom this fall," I said, "if it were only the open admissions, that would be . . . difficult . . . challenging enough. But something else has changed." I was sick of walking on egg-shells in my own home, especially after picking bits of shell from my feet on return from the university multiple days a week, so I raised the frankness quotient a tad. "The students, especially the freshmen, display an inexplicable pugnacity. They all wear those 'IQuit' badges, which are now as ubiquitous as smiley-face buttons when I was a kid. Because the badges are almost a requirement, they don't distinguish the zealots from more passive students just swimming with the tide. Still, the zealots have ways of making themselves known. They choose desks toward the front of the room. They sit there glaring, often with their arms crossed, positively daring me to try to teach them something they don't know—as if they're sure they know it already, or if they don't, it's not worth knowing. They're smug, and they're surly. Also very touchy and on the lookout. Darwin told me the . . . that certain students display this same cunning, predatory watchfulness even in his primary school. It's as if the purpose of going to college is to test the faculty and not the students."

"Are *you* giving grades anymore?" Emory asked.

"All courses are now pass-fail," I said. "But that won't last. Already, for an instructor to give any student a failing grade would be suicidal. It would look like *discrimination*. Gosh, remember when being 'discriminating' was a compliment? So they'll all pass. The thing is, I don't understand what college is for anymore. Are students supposed to master a body of knowledge, acquire new skills? They don't seem to think so. What are we doing, then? Am I just meant to entertain them? They don't do the reading; there are no consequences for not doing the reading; so by implication the reading doesn't matter. Half the time, they pay no attention to me whatsoever, talking among themselves as if they're in the food hall. I'm the first to admit that I went into teaching university English because it was a soft, relatively undemanding job that gave me plenty of free time. But now the job is getting hard. Really hard. I don't know what I'm doing, and I feel like an—" I stopped myself just in time.

Emory shot me a sharp look and curved the conversation. "Have you followed the foofaraw over this new novel—*My Brilliant Friend*?"

"Of course," I said. And that's when I decided to jump in with two feet. I would declare myself. I was the host here, and it was up to me to set the tone. "This so-called controversy is *dumb*."

The D-bomb landed like Little Boy. Nobody said anything.

"'Brilliant' doesn't only mean smart," I continued. "It also means fab, terrific, swell. I gather for a while there, the Brits chirped 'Brilliant!' every time you bumped them on the sidewalk."

"True," Emory said, again with a peculiar impartiality. "And it also means shiny or dazzling. But the weird thing about all the boycotts, the bookstores refusing to stock it, Amazon taking it off the site—it's all so unnecessary. The novel was written in Italian. They could have translated the title however they wanted. How culturally tin-eared can you get?"

"*My Swell Friend* doesn't have much of a ring," I said. "Much less *My Shiny Friend*."

Emory laughed, which was a relief. "In any case, that novel's going to sell, like, five copies."

"Uh-huh," I grunted. "And all to activists for their book burnings." I was getting irritable. After I'd shared how impossible my job was becoming, no uptake. Wade must have finished the onions and zucchini long ago, too. Socially recessive, he used the kitchen to hide.

I'd fed Lucy earlier and put her to bed, but I never shooed off Darwin and Zanzibar to eat in the den with the TV. When my mother had an elder and his family to dinner, my brothers and I being exiled with the visiting kids to the "children's table" always felt humiliating. Thanks to our inclusivity, Darwin could already hold his own with adults.

Once we were all seated, then, I encouraged him to bring us all up to date on Fukushima, which he had followed as avidly as he had the Deepwater Horizon debacle the previous year. He was clearly headed for a career in science. Just as he'd kept up with every stage of BP's frantic efforts to close off the surging oil leak in the Gulf, he could now give a cogent, up-to-the-minute precis on the radiation levels at various distances from the disabled Japanese power plant and the amounts of cesium-137 still being released into the Pacific. Clued up enough to avoid monopolizing the dinner by letting his enthusiasm run away with him, he neatly concluded his presentation with a warning about Germany's horrified about-face on investment in nuclear power. (Thrillingly for his mother, he didn't actually say "about-face" but "volte-face"—a point of nostalgia, as foreign phrases would soon be spurned in common discourse for being brain-vain.) With a moderation unusual for the time, Darwin pointed out that major meltdowns at nuclear plants had been rare. Germany's overreaction was bound to leave the country heavily dependent on imported fossil fuels: "Pretty soon they'll have to get their natural gas from Russia. And Russia's a bully."

"There," I said to the table. "Now tell me there's no such thing as unusually high intelligence."

After which, everyone busied themselves with passing the bread and making sure they'd all gotten butter.

Zanzibar wouldn't embark on a similar recitation, and I wouldn't coax her into one, either. She was supremely self-possessed. She spoke when spoken to, and not in obeisance to a dated axiom. She responded to Roger's

guesty questions politely while looking him in the eye. She betrayed no exasperation that children get very tired of a grown-up's pro forma inquiries
about their favorite subjects in school, when they can tell their interlocuter
has no interest in the answers and isn't listening. For a nine-year-old, her
table manners were faultless. She sat still, hands and napkin in her lap.
She waited patiently for dishes to be passed, and quickly surveyed the
other plates before helping herself to the scarce tiger prawns, not wanting
to take more than her share.

   Nevertheless, Zanzibar was on autopilot. Like many creative children,
she lived in a parallel universe. Our friend Roger had no idea what she
was thinking, and neither did I.

Hoping I wasn't putting Darwin on the spot, I filled in the details of
his ejection from school that afternoon. "So what's the verdict?" I threw
upon the waters. "We know about the kid wearing it. But can a T-shirt
still be 'stupid' or not?"

"'If you're so smart, why aren't you smart?'" Emory said, shooting me a
wary look. "It's closer to *opaque*. Maybe it means: good luck clinging to an
antiquated label now that we no longer acknowledge the category."

"Pretty tortured," I said. "My chips are still on 'stupid.'" I wasn't sure,
but I thought I saw Roger wince.

"Maybe, Darwin," Roger said, "it's best to avoid that kind of charged
language as a general rule. That way, you're not only considerate, but
probably more eloquent, too. Ugly names for—for what we now call
'alternative processing,' a term you may have heard your teachers use—
well, they tend to be broad, lazy, and inexact. You could have called your
friend's T-shirt slogan 'unclear,' or 'strange,' or, as Emory said, 'opaque'—
meaning, hard to understand. Maybe you should push yourself to choose
adjectives like that, which add more value, more content, than just being
cruel. I'm sure you didn't intend to hurt your friend's feelings. But when
you use words that can also be used as slurs, even if you're only referring
to a T-shirt, you run the risk of misinterpretation."

All that worthiness was weighing down this occasion like low baro-
metric pressure. If Roger was pandering to present-day sensitivities purely
to protect himself, he was suspiciously convincing.

"A couple of years ago," Darwin said, "I could have called Stevie himself . . . that same word, and he might have punched me. Maybe the teacher would have told us to try harder to get along. But I'd never have been sent to the principal's office. No one would have called my mom to take me home. I want to know what changed. Why we never take tests anymore. I was good at them."

"Sometimes the grown-ups all get together," Roger said, "and decide we'll do things differently from now on. We come up with a way of thinking about things that's better."

"Or worse," I said. "You know, they study a little history, even in primary school."

"Listen, pal," Wade told Darwin, "our friend Roger here is making this way too complicated. Just don't use that word."

"Because it'll get me into trouble," Darwin said.

"Yup," Wade said. "And don't use a bunch of other words, either, and you know what they are. They're not worth it."

"So what's our son supposed to call something that's blatantly *styoopid*?" I exploded. "'That's so *alternative-processing*'?"

"He's not supposed to call it anything," Wade said. "Because there's no point in creating problems for yourself when you don't have to—*Pearson*." He used my name seldom. When he did so, it was to be pointed.

"I'm in our own house, among our own family," I said. "I'm under no obligation to watch my language."

"Zambia?" Roger shamelessly turned to our daughter to dial back the tension. She seemed to regard his mistake as amusing. "What do you make of all this? I bet you don't have to worry about being smartist in third grade." A bigger mistake. She was in fourth grade.

"I don't make anything of it," she said calmly. "I don't care. When you draw a picture, or play a song, or act in a play, it isn't smart or not smart. It's only good or not good. I try to do stuff that's good."

"An arts purist!" Roger exclaimed.

"Obviously," Emory said, "a whole range of vocabulary is now more radioactive than Fukushima. So I've been training myself to avoid it, even when I'm around colleagues I've worked with for years; in fact, even when

I'm alone. Just to groove my habits. So that when I'm in public I don't put my foot in it and accidentally ruin my career. I've been surprised by how often I used to say 'S-word' that, or 'Oh, that S-word I-word.' Roger's right. If nothing else, it was linguistically lazy."

Emory never used to say "the S-word" and "the I-word" in my presence, and I met her gaze with an expression of *Are you kidding me?* She looked back at me steadily: no apology. She had the whole Western world on her side.

"You should listen to Emory," Wade told me. "You're constantly taunting people, dancing back and forth across a line. I know you didn't draw the line, but tough luck. It's there. Don't step over it. This is totally about watching your back, because no one else is going to watch it for you, *capisce*? You run your mouth like it's still 2009 and accomplish absolutely nothing." For Wade, that was a long speech.

"Sticking up for myself isn't accomplishing nothing," I fired back. "Besides, you have no idea what it's like now. You work mostly on your own. All day, you hardly talk. And there's no such thing as a stupid tree."

It was bad form to have domestic squabbles in front of guests. Accordingly, Wade got up and cleared the plates. I followed him mutely to the kitchen with the serving dishes.

"If you keep up with your different-drummer thing," Wade muttered, "our kids will copy you, and they'll be persecuted, too. You're not a lone wolf, you're a mother. You have to protect them. Set an example that will keep them safe."

"It's my job to teach them more than how to be *safe*," I hissed.

"Can it," Wade said. "Not now, if ever."

I collected myself. Leaving Wade behind to clean the kitchen, to which he was relieved to withdraw, I came back out with dessert, served the kids, and released them. After I settled back in my chair, maybe it was lame to resort to current events, but they had to be good for something.

"Well, it looks like the Arab Spring has fizzled for keeps," I said.

"Pretty inevitable," Emory said. "Those protesters might have had a chance at international support, but staging sit-ins to bring back university exams and graduation requirements? Big turnoff. Came across as retrograde. Given the passions of the moment, they made themselves look like cerebral supremacists."

"Those countries are incredibly corrupt," I said, determined to remain even-tempered. "With huge cohorts of underemployed, ambitious young people. Earning credentials in an education system that still had some standards was the only way people without connections had a chance at a life. Governments in Egypt, Tunisia, Libya—they embraced the Mental Parity fad raging across the West out of rank opportunism. That way they could plug their underqualified, dull-witted cronies into every position imaginable. The system was nepotistic to begin with, and now it's worse—brazenly, self-righteously arbitrary."

"Come on, Pearson," Emory said. "You have to admit it was terrible PR. To on-trend Americans, they didn't look like bold revolutionaries but like right-wing holdouts trying to drag their countries back to the brutal morality of the past. Those placards in Tahrir Square? *Restore Merit! Mubarak is a—* Well, let's just say, 'Mubarak' is a word that combines 'more' with 'on.' I don't know why they wrote the signs in English, because they hopelessly alienated their Western audience."

"I'll tell you the protest that's effective," Roger said. "That's Occupy in downtown New York. Not only is the encampment in Zuccotti Park getting bigger and more entrenched, but the movement is already spreading to other cities, even going international. I'd love to own the merch rights to 'We are the 99 percent!' I don't know about 'If you're so smart,' but *that* T-shirt is going places."

The protest that had started the month before was partially fired up by the financial crisis of 2008. But what really gave the movement legs was new research revealing that 58 percent of America's wealth was owned by people with a "perceived" IQ of over 135—or only about 1 percent of the population.

"I don't trust that statistic," I said, taking another slug of wine, though any further disinhibition wasn't likely in my interest. "In my experience, smart people do plenty of dopey things, and that includes making lousy financial decisions like everyone else."

Roger placed his ice cream spoon deliberately on the table, looking pained.

"Besides," I continued. "That new book *The Cognitive Pay Gap*? Which also argues it's 'perceived' intelligence that overwhelmingly explains income inequality? I think the author's dismissal of discrimination by race, sex, and sexual orientation is outrageous. He's fundamentally making a category error. Racial discrimination is not only real but genuinely unfair. Skin color bears no relation to ability. But the reason you don't hire a dummy for an intellectually demanding job is that he *can't do it*."

"Excuse me." Roger placed his palms flat on his thighs, eyes drilling down at the table. "I've been trying to keep my own counsel, because I'm aware that I'm in your home, and I don't want to overstep. But I'm starting to feel complicit here, and I'm afraid I can't sit quietly and listen to smear after smear without objecting. If only as a favor to me, Pearson, I wish you would rein in the hate speech."

"What, is this because I said 'dummy'?" I said. "I'm sorry, but 'the D-word' doesn't do it for me as a euphemism, because, maybe because of that thudding, thick-sounding onomatopoeic 'duh,' there are too many words it might refer to: 'dumbbell,' 'dunderhead,' 'dummkopf,' 'do-do'—"

"Enough!" Roger exclaimed. "Look, I inferred from early this evening that you harbor a subtle antagonism toward MP—"

"Not subtle," I said. "Straight-up antagonism."

"Which we can discuss, tolerantly and respectfully, but only if you put a lid on the terms of abuse."

"Is this personal for you?" I asked. "Have you been showered by all those unpronounceable words that begin with 'D'?"

"No, not really," he said with noticeable embarrassment.

I was surprised. It was de rigueur to advertise the many occasions on which classmates or colleagues had pilloried you as a pinhead, as well as to claim that the trauma had permanently crippled your psyche and stunted your prospects. Ever having been called a nincompoop was a Get Out of Failure Free card.

"Like Emory," Roger went on, "I benefited from the selective education that's rightly become such an anathema, since I was in truth no more 'gifted' than anyone else. I think the onus is especially on those of us who've profited from this nasty stratification to fix the system."

"Doesn't that mean you stay in control?" I said. "'*Fixing* the system' means more than one thing. What's staggered me about this movement is how it's the intelligentsia that's led the crusade. You're on the cultural front lines as a playwright, so that would include you. What do you get out of it?"

"Maybe a better question is what harm does it do—to me or anyone else. In what way is your life marred by treating other people as if they're just as on the ball as you are?"

"It pleases me to treat *some* people as if they're *more* on the ball than I am," I said. "And thank God for that. As for the harm this obsession is doing? Emory mentioned what's happening in the military. But it's not only that soldiers can't play Mastermind anymore. The top brass is consumed with promoting the so-called *otherwise* and hauling up the cognitively subpar—is that all right? You'll let me say 'subpar'?—to positions of command. They put one of these newly promoted cretins—"

"Hey!" Roger barked.

"They put one of these fellows with *alternative processing*," I revised, "in charge of the Osama assassination in May, and that's why the murderous motherfucker got away!"

"Lots of other things went wrong—"

"Everything went wrong! Thanks to which, asshole lived to fight another day and blew up the Smithsonian's Air and Space Museum!"

"With a long history of extolling the cerebral elite," Emory said. "Good riddance." She was using that same deadpan delivery again, but any intended irony was too subtle by half—which I might have taken her up on if I hadn't been on a roll.

"And what about Jared Loughner?" I said. "Everyone fell all over themselves to be sympathetic, because he'd so clearly suffered from *cognitive discrimination* his whole life—and rightly so, I might add. Not only did he kill six people, but he grievously wounded a congresswoman, and thanks to all these new special rules, the new *decency*, we can't even say what happened to Gabrielle Giffords, can we? The woman can hardly string three words together anymore, but according to the prevailing doctrine she's mentally the same as everybody else and therefore the same as she's always been! Basically, Loughner didn't do her any lasting injury in the slightest!

"Or Anders Breivik, who's become such an international icon and cause célèbre, all because of that ludicrous manifesto of his, bemoaning the ridicule he's suffered for having—how should I say this, Roger?—*less than spectacular* intelligence. The poor puppy was even rejected by the Norwegian armed forces—which shows extremely good judgment on their part. So he only murdered those sixty-nine young people on that island out of understandable envy and private pain, because those kids had been designated as 'promising leaders of the future,' while no one ever made the mistake of calling *him* 'promising.' If he'd only been diagnosed as having dangerous narcissistic and antisocial personality disorders, they might have at least put him away in a loony bin for years, but no! He's bound to get off with a slap on the wrist because instead his court-appointed psychiatrist diagnosed him as tragically damaged by having been shunned from childhood, for good reason, as a *fucking idiot*."

"Okay, that's it," Roger said, standing and abandoning his melted Rocky Road. "Emory? I think we should leave. I can't sit still for, and implicitly condone, this barrage of bigoted bilge."

I'd have assumed that after her escort had made such a posturing ass of himself, they were finished as a couple, and Emory would stay behind. We'd open another bottle and make pitiless fun of his sanctimonious alliteration. Instead, I watched in incredulity as my best friend stood from the table, too. She turned her back. In rigid silence, they both fetched their coats.

CHAPTER 3

Since he abhorred confrontation, *of course* Wade told me to forget it, but I wasn't letting this go. I'd been insulted and embarrassed in my own home, and Emory had effectively sided with my accuser. That night, I had trouble sleeping. I called her the next day. I'm the first to admit I have something of a temper, so beforehand I took a breath, resolving to remain composed.

"I think we should talk," I said.

"Pearson. We are talking."

"I mean, I think we should get together."

"Okaaay . . . But didn't we just do that?"

"Last night doesn't count. The end of the evening left a bad taste in my mouth. I could use a debrief."

"Well, I've got a lot of reading to do . . . I'm interviewing some local debut memoirist who's written a six-hundred-page tome about having been 'abused' by parents who doted on her supposedly 'genius' brother. At least *Dolt* is a nervy title, though I bet they start stocking it in brown paper wrappers. Anyway, it's horribly written, and you know how that is: it takes twice as long to get through. So this next week's not good. How about the week after?"

Oddly, I wondered if Emory might have made up that memoir. Even if the *Dolt* interview were real, she had too much self-regard to lavish hours on a book she could flip through. See, as time passed, the unpleasant conclusion of that dinner was bound to stale. The later we met up, the more I'd seem unreasonable for dwelling on it.

"How about today," I countered. "I'll swing by the station when you get off at five."

I was struck in that moment by how unusual it felt to demand something of her, and I've thought about this since. Emory and her family having rescued me at sixteen had faintly tinged my side of the relationship with the instincts of a supplicant. With Emory, I readily defaulted to apology, gratitude, and a resolve to be no trouble. So it wasn't like me to insist. Yet I had no problem being forceful in the department at VU. That may have been one of the earliest points at which I realized that something between us was a little off, and most likely always had been.

Thrown by the jarring dynamic, Emory couldn't think on her feet. "Well . . . I guess . . ."

"See you at five." I ended the call before she could concoct a conflicting commitment.

We convened in a coffee shop around the corner from WVPA, and after we ordered, I jumped right in.

"I need to better understand why you flounced from my house in a fit of moral showboating." I admit I had prepared the expression "moral showboating" in advance.

"Pearson, no one *flounced*."

"*Marched*, then. *Stormed out.* Whatever's the very opposite of kisses at the door and promises to repeat such a wonderful evening as soon as possible."

"It was getting late anyway."

"It was only quarter of ten. It's not unusual for you to weave reluctantly home at two or three a.m."

"Letting my date leave without me would have come across to Roger as hostile and pointed."

"You didn't think leaving with him was *hostile* and *pointed* in relation to me?"

"I figured you and I could talk about it later."

"Which you weren't exactly eager to arrange."

"You seem so weirdly pissed off that you can hardly blame me."

"*Weirdly* pissed off? No 'thanks for dinner, it was delicious,' no goodbyes, cold silence, with that slam of the door behind you—"

"Nobody *slammed* the door."

"Emory? I was there. There's closing, and there's slamming. I know the difference. The point is, the whole performance was collusive. It conveyed that you agreed with him."

"Of course it did. That was my express intention."

"Why? Are you that into him? Because if you don't mind my saying so, he seems like a . . ." We were in public. "A complete pill. Or is it that you do agree with him?"

"Don't be ridiculous. Of course not."

"The entire evening," I said, "I can't remember you ever saying anything ideologically committal." With another couple in the next booth, I lowered my voice. "You didn't express outright support of MP, but you didn't poke fun at it, either. I try to tell you what a nightmare it's become at VU? No sympathy, no concern. And all night your language was squeaky clean."

"I told you. I have to get into scrupulous verbal habits, or I'm toast at WVPA."

"You were at my house, where you can say whatever you want. I'd think you'd be grateful to be able to let your hair down somewhere."

"Pearson, I don't know why you'd be so unaware of how serious this stuff has become, given the 'nightmare' at VU. But whatever you think of him, I can't afford to have the likes of Roger spreading rumors that in social settings I'm a coward who won't 'stand up to smartism.' It's bad enough that now he knows I'm friends with a political troglodyte."

"This st— This *mere* playwright is that powerful?"

"On the internet, everyone is powerful."

"Being afraid of him makes a pretty lousy basis for a relationship."

"I'm afraid of everybody."

"That doesn't sound like you."

"I may not always have been fearful, but I have always been pragmatic. Right now, being wary of absolutely everybody is pragmatic."

"But Emory, if you and I go along with this stuff, and everyone else goes along with this stuff—"

"Then we get this stuff," she said softly. "But we have this stuff. We've lost the argument."

"I don't recall ever conducting the argument."

"You know what I think behind closed doors. After all, it's not only university teaching that's been affected. Because they're supposed to be from Pennsylvania, the caliber of interviewees on *The Talent Show* was already . . ." Emory drummed her fingers during the now traditional scramble for vocabulary that hadn't yet been exiled to the naughty step. "*Underwhelming*. But now they're . . . *more underwhelming*. Still! Unless there is *absolutely no one else around* besides you and your family"—she cut her eyes toward the adjacent booth—"you'll see me toe the line. I stopped making a certain kind of joke at the station a long time ago. Do I miss those jokes? Sure. Does it pain me to police my speech all the time? Yes. But I don't plan on being crucified on social media and losing my job just from trying to protect the precious right to impugn someone else's intelligence."

"There's more at stake than that."

"What's at stake for me is my own future. My reputation and my career. And if you know what's good for you, you'll get with the program, too, even at home. Wade is right. You can't be too careful. One of our most senior reporters was fired last month for decrying some copy as—" Emory so lowered her voice that from across the tiny table she was unintelligible.

"What?"

Emory leaned over and cupped a hand around my ear. "Illiterate."

"You mean you can't even say—?"

"No, you cannot. And don't."

I talked into my coffee. "Then how do you refer to people who can't read or write? *Alternative processing* doesn't cut it. That's *not processing*."

"Pearson? Wake up. You don't refer to them. You don't refer to them at all."

"Pretty soon we'll all have to just stop talking."

"That would be safer in your case. You're starting to worry me. You fulminate using all this rash vernacular without stopping to think. I know you don't like being bossed around. But you're courting disaster. You can't change the way things are by acting as if they're still the way you wish they were."

"That's convoluted."

"I think you understand just fine. You and I are obviously in agreement on the basics. The whole MP shtick is a little . . ." She rummaged again among the last adjectives still standing, finally settling on, "Nutty. Maybe it's a passing fad, and it'll all blow over. But in the meantime, we have to make it to the other side of this thing in one piece. That means if we're around anyone else, even a guy I'm going out with, you watch your language. It also means that if you pull that kind of stunt again, showing off at table how you refuse to be tyrannized by all these newfangled taboos, I'll do exactly the same thing. I'll *flounce* out the door with my plus-one while doing the most convincing imitation of *moral showboating* I can muster."

While paying the bill, I considered wryly that, in Emory's reading of the present social situation—a reading, as she would have it, vastly more accurate than mine—and in her appreciation for the dangers we both faced by privately considering "cognitive equality" preposterous poppycock—an appreciation, as she would have it, so much more acute than mine—one might divine an element of *smartism.*

"At first I thought Roger was doing what you're doing," I said as we left the café. "Keeping up appearances just to be on the safe side. But he seems like a real convert. Why can't you see guys who're more simpatico? Other skeptics?"

"Who would that be, Pearson? There aren't any."

In wild contrast to the buttoned-up, mind-your-p's-and-q's spirit in which that dinner with Roger began, Emory and I spent a memorably raucous, conspiratorial evening in her apartment back in 2010. Feeling a need to keep abreast of cultural milestones, however bizarre, a few days before this boisterous late-night twosome, I'd bought that hardback of *The Calumny of IQ*, which had been out for only a few weeks. Thus I brought the entertainment, while Emory provided the cheese board. Between slivers of aged Gouda, I read aloud choice underlined snippets from the introduction. Especially into our third bottle of pinot, Carswell Dreyfus-Boxford's absurd assertions put us in stitches. At length, Emory and I traded impressions of the *intellectually disabled*.

In our weak defense, we were way worse than merely tipsy. The still-nameless Mental Parity movement remained in its gestational phase. No one else was present whose feelings we might have hurt. That said, I sometimes wonder if the real test of one's decency is how one acts unobserved. For starting with the slack-mouthed cliché "I'm gonna be a *bwain soy-jun!*," our performances would have appeared unkind to any witness well before Carswell Dreyfus-Boxford fired the starting gun of "the last great civil rights fight." Why, I know exactly how unkind we were, because during this goof-around stretch of the evening I filmed our nasty imitations on my phone. That's how I can recall that our irreverent get-together was in March—03/28/2010, to be exact: I have the time stamp.

I'd retained the incriminating file, which over the following year and a half had become a treasured talisman. The recording provided evidence admissible in court that Emory's initial ridicule of cognitive equality wasn't all in my head. Accordingly, on the night following our confrontation in the café over her "moral showboating," once the kids were all in bed, I battened myself into our en suite bath, perched on the toilet lid, plugged in my earphones, and hit *play*.

"Da whole idea of da *dum-dum* is doo-doo! Da dum-dum's gone da way of da dodo!" Emory smashes a rice cracker against her forehead and swirls the crumbs in her hair. "I'm just as smawt as da pwesident! I'm gonna *be* pwesident! Cawswell Doofus-Doofus told me so!"

"I'm a physics pwafessaw!" I chime in. "I'm wesponsible fow da Intewnationanew Space Station! I'm just wike Ow Gow! I invented the Intewnet!"

Not timorous, line-toeing, and compliant but subversive, mischievous, and defiant—that was my real best friend.

1972–2010

I'd never want to reduce anyone to a single experience that explains everything. Nor would I wish to portray myself in midlife as still struggling against the most odious aspect of my childhood, thereby according this sustained unpleasantness an undue power. Nonetheless, my having been brought up as a Jehovah's Witness is an ingredient of my character—much as pumpkin is an *ingredient* of pumpkin pie. Or maybe a better analogy would be rat poison in pumpkin pie, since the problem wasn't one of proportion.

During my school years, my classmates sympathized primarily with my perplexing banishment from celebrations, especially birthdays and Christmas. That's all most people know about Witnesses, and it's true these deprivations of merrymaking are particularly cruel for children. Not only could I not accept invitations to private parties, but I wasn't allowed to have a piece when another child's birthday cake was served to the whole class. In October, I could never design a homemade vampire costume with pointy candle-wax incisors and lipstick blood, much less score any free candy; the neighborhood kids soon learned to skip our house, since the best they could hope for trick-or-treating wasn't Almond Joy miniatures but copies of *The Watchtower*. In December, I couldn't deck the school halls with stapled construction-paper chain links; I sat listless on the sidelines while everyone else glued cotton balls to their Santa Claus masks. For Mother's Day, I never drew cards or gathered presentational bouquets of tissue-paper carnations. On the Fourth, while the rest of Voltaire picnicked in the park, my mother pulled the curtains on the fireworks display, at which my brothers and I weren't allowed even to peek.

So when in fifth grade the boy in the desk in front of me slipped me a valentine, I knew I was supposed to decline it, but some subversive kernel had already germinated. I hid the frilly commercial favor in my book bag instead. When my mother found it, she forced me to burn it in the kitchen sink. The brief conflagration was readily dampened with a blast from the faucet. The fire in my belly would prove harder to snuff.

Most of these wicked holidays were purportedly "pagan." The likes of Independence or Memorial Day expressed fealty to secular government, when "we" owed loyalty only to God. Although I don't give a tinker's damn about this literally party-pooping internal logic, it's telling that the sole occasion these lifelong buzzkills mark isn't the promise of Christ's birth but the downer of his death. Believe me, the Memorial is nothing to look forward to.

What pained me most about all this enforced funlessness was a sense of exclusion. In trade, what I got included in sucked. I never received a present of any sort until the day I turned sixteen. When Emory gave me a crimson scarf, I cried so hard she thought I didn't like it.

In addition to nurturing a self-congratulatory purity, the embargo on traditional festivals was intended to inculcate contempt for the unenlightened and their silly heathen ways. Unfortunately for my theological overlords, anything verboten grows more attractive. The mysterious rituals of my peers excited an envy, awe, and desire that the bone-chilling business of blackmailing neighbors for candy in a sack wouldn't seem to merit. After all, children are already prone to anticipate red-letter days on the calendar with far more impatience than the actual experience of the longed-for date's arrival could possibly justify. It takes many repeated cycles of eager expectancy followed by private disappointment to finally figure out that the anticipation is the real reward, far more than Christmas Day itself. Alas, once you register that bated breath isn't the lead-up to the payoff but *is* the payoff, the illusion is destroyed, the spell broken—which is why, for so many adults, Christmas gets demoted to a pain in the ass.

Happily, in my own adulthood I didn't suffer from that syndrome. Though Wade and I weren't practicing Christians, for December 25th I went all out: the tree, the tinsel, the poinsettias. I bought my kids mountains of toys they would break. I might not have personally enjoyed many little children running rampant around our house, but I still staged lavish annual birthday parties for all three of my kids, with streamers and bunting and cake—of which I saved myself a slice. Every fourth Thursday in November without fail, I laid out a full Thanksgiving feast, and I honored every traditional side dish, whether or not I especially cared for cranberry sauce. For I've always been driven by a quantity far more inexhaustible than a self-deceiving anticipation. As I sail through middle age, the fuel shows no sign of flagging, either: *spite*.

Yet the holiday ban wasn't really the worst of it. When I recall those years, whose images in my head are colored a sepia brown evocative less of a daguerreotype than a bad bout of diarrhea, what I predominantly conjure isn't the yearning for packets of spongy yellow marshmallow chicks at Easter. It's the boredom. A doughy, stultifying boredom that surely qualifies as child abuse far more than any walk-in-the-park IQ test. The "brothers" and "sisters" were boring—and what made the few exceptions fascinating was being unusually overbearing and sadistic, or (the women) unusually submissive and masochistic. The meetings were boring—and these sessions mumbled along for *four hours* a go. The Kingdom Hall was boring, more like a warehouse than a church, cleansed of any glimmer of stained glass or glint of redemptive beauty. And meetings weren't only on Sundays but twice a week—thrice, once you added "Family Worship Evening," which was the most oppressive; it was harder to zone out around the table with my compliantly droning father under my mother's sharp eye. The required reading was boring, improbably so—since you'd think that, generating that quantity of guff, those anointed blowhards at headquarters in Warwick, New York, would generate a line or two that was droll or piquant, if only by accident. But no, the worthies never slipped up: *The Watchtower* and *Awake!*, with their washed-out photographs and clumsy graphics, were boring through and through, and baptized Witnesses were expected to consume some three thousand pages of this turgid, semiliterate drivel every year. All about how Jesus isn't equal to God and there's no such thing as the Trinity and just because we told you the world was going to end last week and it didn't doesn't mean it won't end tomorrow. By my teenage years, merely laying eyes on one of those life-murdering tracts aroused a loathing akin to nausea.

What else was way worse than life without Christmas? The evangelism. Which is mandatory, in case you imagine those parties trudging from door to door with armloads of apocalypse are doing so from spontaneous religious effusion. Witnesses are expected to clock at least eighteen hours per week torturing their neighbors, and they're required to submit a log to the elders of exactly how much resentment they kindled in the unsuspecting every month. Alas, couples are also expected to drag their kids along.

I hated it. Not just because I was forced to squander most of my free time outside of school staring at the stoop while one parent or the other informed householders sweetly that all their beliefs were misguided and if they didn't join this killjoy cult they were going to be extinguished in the "End Times" any day now, after which paradise on earth would be ruled jointly by Jehovah and 144,000 self-anointed gasbags. Even more, I hated it because I was keenly aware from an early age how much these poor people despised being set upon and how desperately they wanted my family to go away. Oh, our targets varied tremendously in how long they would stand dumbly in the entranceway—often allowing billows of heat or air-conditioning to escape, and sometimes having the good sense to bulwark behind a locked screen door—before either firmly declining the literature or mutely accepting it instead, since taking the tracts took less energy than refusing them. Why, I acquired a rough respect for the men (it was always men) who took one look at our posse and slammed the door. But they all dreaded us, and some of them hid from us, though my mother could be persistent with a doorbell. Would you want to be a child at whose appearance nearly everyone exclaimed, silently in the main but sometimes aloud, "Oh NOOO!"? In fact, I came to pity most of all the handful of exceptions who listened attentively to our spiel, asked questions, and sometimes even agreed to return visits. For most of these isolates, so thirsting for human contact that they'd talk to Jehovah's Witnesses would have marked a new low.

Although I'm hardly in a position to ask her now, I suspected at the time that at least my mother was well aware we were perceived as the eleventh plague of Egypt. I think she liked that. To put the nicest possible spin on it, she relished rising to a challenge. But she also relished making these people suffer. She deliberately deployed their politeness as implicit permission to keep talking, and she relied upon their common decency to foist propaganda into the hands of neighbors reluctant to seem ungracious. In other words, just as you're meant to employ your opponents' force as a weapon against them in karate, she flipped the virtues of our victims into ordnance for our troops. She also seemed to find it satisfying when the alternative brand of mark grew rude and abusive: they would be wiped from the face of the earth in the coming Armageddon, and they deserved it.

I was obliged to wear dowdy, colorless clothing with skirts below the knee, unbecoming apparel that by my puffy pubescence I could ill afford—though insofar as drab garb made me more invisible, I was grateful for it. On occasion, however, a householder would still notice me, and after the rest of my pestersome clan had finally turned to go torment another family, the heathen and I would catch each other's eyes. My own glance burned with apology, while a barely detectable shrug conveyed the helplessness of a hostage. I generally received a look of sympathy and forgiveness in return: *You poor girl, dragged along on this fruitless mission by fanatics, when at your age you should be wearing skimpy frocks and making out with pimply boys. I just lost ten minutes of my precious life that I will never get back, but don't worry, that's not your fault.* These individual bestowals of unspoken kindness were merciful reminders that the larger world, in which discrete lunacies such as our sect circulated, was still relatively sane. I'm afraid that these days this same solace—that at least in the big picture everyone isn't completely crackers—is no longer available.

The other aspect of my childhood that distressed me more than staying home from a Flag Day parade was not having any friends. Which is not to say that friendship per se was forbidden. While we were warned off forming attachments to the "worldly," I was welcome to play with other children my age who shared our faith. But this ostensibly mild restriction translated in practice into having no friends. For here's where I puzzle over a question painfully germane to the present:

What was wrong with those kids?

I don't mean to be unreasonable. Small children take the world as they find it. Before the age of about eight, I accepted that everything my parents told me was true, as I also accepted that if I differed—after all, I can't recall ever *wanting* to go to meetings at the Kingdom Hall—that was because I was naughty and bad, and not because there was something wrong with their whole paradigm. I didn't know what a *paradigm* was, as a word or a concept. When you're perfectly trapped inside a bubble, there is no bubble.

That said, all we Witness kids went to public schools. We were given civics lessons about a government that, if it were up to the likes of our parents—who were prohibited from voting, supporting candidates, serving on a jury, and even holding political opinions—would not exist. We studied history, in which previous to 1881 our farcically slight sliver of enlightened humanity would have played not the tiniest part. Like other Americans, we walked a world awash in secular books, newspapers, and television channels, none of which conformed to the version of reality we were fed at home. Every day, we were surrounded by people who did not regard a cataclysmic divine reckoning as right around the corner, who didn't woe-muck from house to house with pamphlets every weekend, and who did not chatter endlessly about the number 144,000 because of some stray line in Revelation taken out of context. Now, *maybe* all these poor chowder-heads who weren't "in the Truth" were under the influence of Satan and were destined to be torched into oblivion by the righteous fire of Yahweh wheat-and-chaffing his way through the entire population any day now. But by at least age ten or so, what kind of child didn't allow it to enter his or her head: *But maybe not?*

It seems statistically and psychologically improbable, but throughout my childhood and early adolescence I did not encounter a single "brother" or "sister" in my cohort who rebelled, and that includes my two biological brothers. Oh, here and there Luke and Caleb and their friends broke the rules—read a horoscope, sneaked a copy of *People* magazine, used a curse word—but that was a far cry from overthrowing the rules and exclaiming like Alice, "You're nothing but a pack of cards!" For a short while I formed an alliance with a Witness named Jacob, who seemed to have something going for him, if not mischief exactly, then an eye outside; he'd discovered science fiction, which wasn't quite against the rules, but it sure wasn't in the rules. At some point I confided in him that, when a birthday card for our teacher circulated around my sixth-grade English class, I *signed* it. He was far more aghast than I'd expected, and worse: within the day, he'd squealed to my parents. (When I defended myself to my mother by whimpering, *But everyone else was doing it!*, she didn't know her daughter well enough to recognize that the reasoning was out of character.) How could indoctrination into a fringy and highly disagreeable denomination enjoy such perfect success? When I heard that the elders had ordered Jacob's parents to take away all his Isaac Asimov, Ray Bradbury, and Robert Heinlein, I thought, *Good.*

My incomprehension on this point necessarily rounds on my parents. My mother, Glenda Converse née Tate, was raised as a Witness, which presumably gives her some excuse except not really. Even if you hand minors a free pass for being incomplete or effectively stupid (get used to it; linguistically, I'm an animal), Glenda Tate crossed the cultural milestone of maturity at eighteen and still refused to exercise the agency that this temporal achievement awarded her. Sure, I should know better than most how callously you get frozen out of your whole social network when you dare to walk away from this fruitcake sect. But I doubt my mother stayed "in the Truth" out of fear.

She is—or was; I don't suppose anyone would have told me if she'd died—a classic high-achiever type. A catechism that boosted her into an elect from the get-go would have naturally appealed; it furnished believers social elevator shoes. With only a few million adherents worldwide, the Witnesses also circumscribed the context in which she might excel into a negotiable small pond. Hungry for regard, she was manically active in the beehive busywork of the Watchtower Society. I personally suffered for her aspirations, since she was forever ratcheting up her hours of doorstep evangelizing with her children in tow, the better for her extraordinary monthly reports to secure public plaudits from the elders. Maybe I recognized Emory's innate sense of superiority because my mother was much the same—although Emory always seemed to float obliviously above everyone else as if naturally levitating on a higher plane like a mystic, while my mother was made of more earthly stuff and in a secular sphere would have acquired a crass reputation as a climber. It was vital to Glenda Converse to be held in higher esteem than the other wives, whom she preferred to patronize rather than befriend.

In other words, she wanted to *win*. When you want to win, it's helpful to know what the rules are. The Witnesses oblige with a plethora of rules. The world at large is constantly changing them up, and out here in the boundless void of secularism, it's commonplace to imagine that you're streaks ahead of the competition, only to discover that all along you've been playing the wrong game. (You've got your promotion at last; surprise, your spouse is leaving you.) Glenda Converse was raised a Witness and so stuck with a game that she knew how to play. Be that as it may, this appetite for the accumulation of gold stars is fundamentally childlike. Assuming that she's continued to churn on the elders' hamster wheel, she's probably progressing toward a bitter old age. While Gloria Steinem was mobilizing *Ms.* magazine, my mother was feverishly shoring up an archaic patriarchy. Some gold star. Besides, when you're driven to distinguish yourself as an exceptionally accomplished sheep, you're still a sheep.

I've characterized the religion as joyless, but that's not quite true. For Witnesses, joylessness is itself a joy. Ceaselessly celebrating your perfect absence of celebration resembles a year-round party, and ruining other people's fun is a form of fun. In which case, throughout my childhood my mother had a high old time.

There were nice things about her, too, but maybe I can be forgiven for not dwelling on charms whose tender contemplation is not in my interest. My mother had, and presumably continues to have, a vengeful streak, and that's what I need to remember. By way of example? As a child, I privately rejoiced in my uncommon first name. I quite liked the fact that I'd never encountered any other kid called Pearson, while Luke and Caleb's predictably biblical handles blurred with all the other Abrahams, Adams, and Elijahs among our peers. Being herself prone to hubris, my mother was

especially alert to the sin of pride in other people. I must have been nine
or ten, shortly after we'd been introduced to cursive in elementary school.
I was sitting at the kitchen table practicing my signature, trying out various flourishes whose conceited curlicues clearly raised a red flag. That's
when my mother chose to explain that she had christened me in tribute
to Angus Pearson, a founding Witness who in 1896 personally converted
a record number of his neighbors in Monroeville, and ever since none of
our membership had racked up more of these hapless draftees in a single
year. If the pious nature of my namesake wasn't disappointing enough, she
also assured me that Pearson meant "son of Piers," Piers being an early
form of Peter. So my erstwhile striking-sounding moniker was as drearily
apostolic as Luke's. I don't think I've ever felt the same way about my first
name since, which is just what my mother intended. She knew she was
taking something away from me—a precious differentiation, a sense of
having been born apart—and she took a vicious pleasure in making me
feel ordinary. Yet the impulse was perverse. She sought to deprive me of
what she had given me in the first place.

Granted, a daughter's grudge-bearing against her mother and idol-
ization of her father is hopelessly trite. Yet I won't distort the record to
appear interesting. John Converse is—I will not say "or was," because I
spotted him on the opposite side of the street last week—a warm, decent
man who, surmounting an inborn cowardice, more than once protected
his kids from the worst of his wife's fanaticism. He's a convert, which
may give him less of an excuse than my mother for signing up to a dogma
of dourness and constraint—except that, according to my mother's coy,
faux-embarrassed accounts, he was smitten with her at nineteen. The
only way he could date her (with a chaperone) was to declare an intention
to marry her, and the only way he could marry her was to convert. If my
father therefore pledged fealty to a transparently barking catechism to
get into my mother's drawers, that's a better motivation than most.

A hardness would soon set in—a grim downward tug at the corners
of her mouth—but Glenda Tate was ravishing at eighteen, and wedding
photos verify this was not some treasured family myth. Her brunette
locks had a fetching natural curl, and her face shone with a virginal purity

that was hard to locate in any but a metaphorical sense in 1968. My father may also have been drawn to her ambition—never mind that she aspired to rise in a constricted, hermetic hierarchy dedicated to keeping a boot on women—because he himself had no ambition. I don't mean that unkindly. There's no requirement that all youngsters must yearn to become something or other when they grow up. He'd have appreciated entering a social milieu in which his in-laws would never push him to get a degree or express exasperation that he wasn't more financially prosperous. Fiercely discouraged from going to college, Witnesses have the lowest average level of educational attainment of any faith in the United States, and even his high school diploma bestowed on my father loftier credentials than most of his wife's tribe ever earned. My father was a docile young man who just wanted to get by. For my whole childhood, he worked in a hardware store thirty hours per week, never even scrambling to rise to manager. Rather cleverly, he'd located himself in the only community in Voltaire, Pennsylvania, where such pygmy career flatlining qualified him as a model of masculinity. Although the head of the family according to doctrine, he was in practice anything but. Witness wives are notoriously passive-aggressive, even if few of these poor know-nothings are familiar with the expression.

John and Glenda Converse had Luke, me, and Caleb in quick succession. My father allowed to me once that joining his wife's denomination was more "challenging" than he'd expected, which I inferred was a euphemism for wretched. But while logistically he might have fled, he regarded himself as having made his bed, and, bless him, he hadn't the constitution to abandon three children.

I'm bending over backward here to understand why my parents might have pitched themselves into the prison of that confining fellowship and thrown away the key, but I'm still struggling against utter bafflement. Even Jehovah's Witnesses don't promote a superstitious belief in an afterlife. When you die, you die. Nor do Witnesses embrace reincarnation. So as far as my parents were concerned, they each had this one life to live and no other. They were adults. They weren't metaphysicists inclined to tie themselves in knots over the matter, so they'd have blithely accepted the proposition that they exercised control over their destinies. It was a "free country," in that bygone era when the depiction was halfway credible. Given all the options—starting a strawberry farm in Oregon, running a dog kennel in Oklahoma, moving to France—how could they conceivably have chosen such a terrible life?

Most of my teenage apostasies were minor and covert. Walking through the park a few days after a Fourth of July, I picked up a trammeled paper miniature of an American flag on a toothpick. Rather than drop it as hastily as a hot brick, I wiped the icing off the sharp end and slipped it into my pencil box. (We weren't meant to own a flag—any flag. I'd have gotten into trouble for possessing the flag of the Kiwanis club.) Later, with an anxious glance over my shoulder, I slipped into a Salvation Army thrift shop (run by *another faith*) and bought a shirt. When my mother asked where it came from, I improvised that our school had declared open season on unclaimed items in the lost and found. It was just a men's button-down, but its plaid was subtle, in becoming forest greens and rust, and I loved that shirt. Though the fabric was thin, it warmed me with its mean glow of mutiny.

More than once, I picked up a cigarette butt and smoked its last few shreds of tobacco in secret. I didn't enjoy the abrasive heat in my lungs, but these infringements were satisfying purely for being infringements. I bought Tic Tacs afterward and drank lots of water; I had a gut feeling that breaking the tobacco taboo was on a more grievous level than the paper flag.

When out of the earshot of our ilk, I dabbled daringly in paganism. I wished an adjacent classmate "good luck" on an upcoming test. She looked at me queerly; I hardly ever said anything. She didn't understand that my invocation of good fortune had nothing to do with her. I wanted to discover if anything bad would happen to me, and I was experimenting, gingerly, with becoming someone else. Likewise, when I volunteered "Bless you!" after someone sneezed in the cafeteria, I wasn't obeying a social convention. I was violating one.

I'd be more impressed with myself if these toe-in-the-water dalliances with the dark side were conducted in open view of the folks for whom my humming the first few bars of "The Star-Spangled Banner" on the way home from school would constitute sacrilege. Yes, I was afraid, of course I was. But I was also in training.

After working myself up to it for a month, I finally crossed the line when I was fifteen. The rest of the family had their coats on and were heading for the door—I'd left my personal declaration of independence until the last minute—when I hung back and said I wasn't going to the meeting. I'd meant to use a strong, uncompromising voice, but my announcement came out as a croak.

My mother barely noticed. "Of course you are," she said matter-of-factly. "Now get your coat. We're running late."

I cleared my throat. "No. I hate meetings. They're long and monotonous, and I don't think I . . . I don't even believe all this stuff! You can't make me."

"We can make you, young lady, and we will make you so long as you live in this house." She shot my father a look of injunction. "John?"

"Come on, honey." When I refused to budge, he advanced with an expression of weary resignation and took my arm. I yanked it back. Then he grasped my sweater at the back of the neck. I honestly think he was trying to be gentle, but there's only so gentle you can be with a struggling body of 135 pounds if you're going to prevail. I didn't want to hit him, but I also didn't want to go out that door, and in the end he had to half-carry me, flailing, to the backseat of our secondhand VW Bug at the curb.

When we got back home, I was parked at the kitchen table and forced to copy the week's *Watchtower*, because if I was writing it out, I couldn't simply pretend to read it. My mother reported my insolence to the elders, and I was hauled in for a Judicial Committee Hearing. I braved it out by being sullen and unresponsive, which didn't help my case. I was officially "marked" for two weeks. While by that point having the rest of the congregation cut me a wide berth was bunny-in-a-briar-patch punishment, being mini-shunned by my own family stung. Instructed to act as if I weren't there—to pretend that their sister was invisible or, I filled in, dead—my brothers weren't supposed to talk to me. To my astonishment, they didn't, not even in surreptitious whispers, and not even when our parents were out in the backyard. As matters turned out, like secreting my miniature American flag, that fortnight of being blanked by my family would also prove good practice—for what would soon become the rest of my life.

It's sometimes assumed that misfits, weirdos, and outsiders must naturally be drawn to other misfits, weirdos, and outsiders, but nothing could be further from the truth. If anything, oddities avoid one another, the better to prevent contracting an even greater stink, and other oddities appear just as odd to oddities as they do to regular kids. Like their more normative brethren, outliers are attracted to the socially obvious. Fat or homely no-hopers are just as prone as sexpots to develop crushes on the captain of the football team. So why wouldn't I have already noticed Emory Ruth back in middle school? Everyone else had.

She exhibited a rare social ease that didn't rely on cruelty. She was good at things. She was the star of our public speaking class, and she never seemed nervous in front of a group; if she dropped her notes or lost her place, she was able to turn the faltering to her advantage with an ad-libbed one-liner. She was even good at stupid things: spinning quarters, snapping her fingers. Significantly, in retrospect, by high school her political instincts were impeccable; that is, she was able to ingratiate herself with our teachers while piping up with just enough smart-assed cracks from the peanut gallery to ensure that she was never spurned as a suck-up—although a gift for being all things to all people ill prepares you for the time you're obliged to choose sides. Up until a certain juncture, Emory and I never had a serious difference of opinion. I now wonder whether Emory ever seriously disagreed with anybody, whatever they thought. On balance, strong convictions don't pay off, and I should know.

Yes, she was preternaturally pretty, but my having been smitten from afar by our sophomore year of high school shouldn't be attributed solely to standard teenage obsession with surfaces. She was also bright, in the days when being quick didn't constitute a subtle disadvantage (and, later, not so subtle). Yet her easy academic excellence and snappy classroom wisecracks weren't precisely the source of my fascination, either. By her teens, Emory already exuded an air of what we'd soon call "entitlement," but she never seemed to be laying claim to a discreet set of tangible rewards that she unreasonably imagined her due. It's true that her parents earned considerably more money than mine (whose refusal to bring in a decent "worldly" income was all their fault). But Emory's pervasive sense of superiority seemed unattached to being fetching, clever, or well-off. It was a preexisting condition. That was the real source of my entrancement: Emory's conviction that she was better than everyone else wasn't based on anything at all.

Before we go any further, I should put in a word on my own behalf. I worry I've cast myself as an ugly-duckling sidekick. Such a crude self-portrait would be wide of the mark. I was a bit odd-looking in high school, and like so many girls I put on a few pounds during puberty. But once I ran away from home and started living with Emory's family (to get ahead of ourselves here), I was so mortified by imposing on the Ruths' pantry that before long my figure shrank to the proportions of a waif, so alarming Emory's mother, Kelly, that she put me on a strict supplementary diet of chocolate-malt protein shakes. Moreover, while we're often poor judges of ourselves, I wager that neutral parties, and even an invested party like Emory, would bear me out: by my latter teens, a certain ungainly mismatch of features growing at different rates finally settled, and my "interesting face" went from a euphemism for "plain" to understatement. Physically, the alteration in the relationship between my nose, brow, and cheekbones was absurdly slight, but it was socially seismic. Wade always claimed there was something undefinably "exotic" about my looks, which, he would also reluctantly concede, made a good match with the fact that my older two children are half Japanese.

I mention this Cinderella transformation not to brag but because it pertains to my friendship with Emory, which my gradual visual upgrade made not better or worse but more complicated. Granted, I started out something of a charity case—literally so, for two and a half years. And Emory was blithely accustomed to being the most striking female in any given room by the time she was twelve. That uncanny superiority of hers was sufficiently rock-solid that when surprise competition came up from behind, she took the new neck-and-neck in her stride. She was secure enough to recognize that a constant companion who brought more to the table than sheer obstinacy was in her interest; an eye-catching girlfriend gave her a measure more clout. Nevertheless, my no longer being an aesthetic sad sack required a sneaky tweaking of our relationship that I'm not sure she entirely liked.

While we're at it, however, I'm compelled to inject a less complimentary submission: I'm not very smart. In school, I was hopeless at math. In the sciences, I could memorize the four kinds of rock formation, which was no more demanding than memorizing four different rock groups in music, but anything more complicated lost me at photosynthesis. If mechanical engineering were left to the likes of me, we'd all be crossing rivers by getting wet. Unlike Emory with her effortless high marks, I got decent grades only by applying myself, and even there I was never selected for the advanced classes that Emory was put in. Besides, by the mid-1980s grade inflation was already rife, and the expectations of American high schoolers were knee-high; mostly, you just had to show up. In case I needed to have my self-suspicions quantified, my scores on standardized tests like the SAT and ACT would be mediocre (plainly, I can't remember the exact scores anymore because it wouldn't flatter me to remember them). To my knowledge, I've never been subjected to the "demeaning ignominy" of an IQ test, but I imagine the results would have been equally average.

Accordingly, in my adulthood the numbers in my check register have never matched my statements, and "balancing" my accounts has entailed scrawling over what I had miscalculated and taking the bank's word for it. As of 2008, I was left in no doubt that I have no grasp of economics. Despite my having read, glaze-eyed, more than one definition, a "credit default swap" still sounds to me like a card trick.

Between us, then, Emory was the better looking by conventional metrics and the far more outstanding student. From adolescence onward, this much, too, has remained a constant: she has always had an uncanny ability to keep up with changing fashions, and her look is reliably cutting-edge. She wears the hairstyle soon to become all the rage before most people realize the do is in vogue. She leaves the impression that she isn't following trends but setting them. She's the sort who knows what new slang means before you've even heard the term, and this verbal savvy predated the internet. Although search engines have devalued the knack, in the 1980s picking up hip new lingo that you couldn't look up in the dictionary wasn't so much a matter of reading the right magazines (whose vernacular was always dated) as having an instinctive inner ear. On a positively animalistic level, she knows which way the wind is blowing. For me, her riding at the very forefront of many an advancing craze had long made her seem like a real original. I now see Emory's precocity in a different light. She's consistently conformist before everyone else.

I'm afraid I conjure our history together with double vision. Though it ill serves our story for me to be mean about her, the burst of spontaneous joy that hit when she first started talking to me in tenth grade has become a cold emotional artifact, an abstraction. From the perspective of the present, I'm inclined to interpret her crossing of a social barrier of sorts in high school as self-interested, even if the benefits I offered were underobvious. Maybe, as the only Witness in our sophomore class, I seemed exotic even before my features settled. Maybe I was just a quirky feather to add to her quiver.

Yet I should clarify that, despite the barbaric reputation of high schoolers, my peers did not exile me. I exiled myself. We were not supposed to mix with non-Witnesses. Throughout my schooling, I'd been subject to any number of approaches for friendship that I rebuffed. (What was the point? I couldn't come to their houses, nor they to mine.) Emory didn't stand out as the lone brave soul willing to fraternize with a pariah, but because she was the only classmate whom I couldn't bring myself to brush off.

Although *she* wouldn't pay any price if we were discovered, Emory savored the illicit kick of our whispering sessions at lunch. I'd explained from the get-go that any confederacy on our part violated my religion— though I qualified "my supposed religion," and she was impressed that I was already mobilizing a resistance of one. She loved the story about my

father hauling me to the car by the scruff, and she joined me in ridicul-
ing the picayune prohibitions I grew up with. I showed her the flag in my
pencil bag. She learned to recognize my forest-green button-down with
the thin rust stripe as the bedraggled rebel uniform in which I faced down
my personal Crown Forces by guerrilla means.

The funny thing is, she was drawn to the very quality in me that would
eventually prove our undoing. I was born belligerent, and my natural in-
subordination transcended my rejection of the Jehovah's Witnesses. I'm not
convinced that I have "a problem with authority" altogether, because I don't
preclude the possibility of authorities being in the right. But I don't bow to
authorities when they're wrong.

I was already a reader (though *The Watchtower* didn't count), and I don't
mean that as a boast. For me, sure, reading was about escape, but also about
shirking. It was what I did when I was meant to be doing something else. I
kept a book open in my lap in class the better to ignore the lessons. Further,
because I was aware of not being the sharpest tool in the shed—oh, how I
miss those playful metaphors—I didn't trust myself to accurately infer the
meaning of vocabulary from context, the way everyone else seemed to, so
I routinely deferred to reference books. In other words, don't imagine this
slight anecdote is a tribute to my education. American public schools were
descending into lackluster decay decades before Carswell Dreyfus-Boxford
shoved the corruption into overdrive in 2010.

Because I associated books with disobedience, with recalcitrance,
with laziness and malingering, I reviled English class. I disliked being
told what to read, so any assigned text acquired a taint; that is, I was
predisposed to hate it. Having a book imposed on me from above denied
me its full possession, while also encroaching on the precious time that
I could claim as my own outside school and the Witnesses. Specifically,
in tenth grade I hated *Silas Marner* and *Julius Caesar*, and I blamed
Ms. Townsend for assigning them. I especially bore her a grudge for
assigning *Lord of the Flies*, which I had already read, and which was
already mine, and which I was loath to allow her to co-opt and ruin for
me. So much for background.

It was just an idle comment as she handed back our papers on Piggy and what he *symbolized* (my own distanced essay was purposefully flat): "I'm reticent to report that most of these analyses were a little superficial."

I raised my hand. I hope I haven't given the wrong impression; I wasn't *that* stupid. That is, I was smart enough to know this was stupid.

"Pearson?"

"I think you meant 'reluctant.'"

"Excuse me?"

"You said, 'I'm reticent to report.' That's a misusage. 'Reticent' describes someone keeping their feelings to themselves. You know, keeping your mouth shut."

"Is that so?"

"Yes," I said, holding my nerve. "That's so. 'Reluctant' is about not being eager to do something. You weren't 'reticent,' because you didn't keep what you felt about our essays to yourself—that they were disappointing."

"I might add, including yours," Ms. Townsend said with an edge. "Didn't your parents raise you to regard correcting your elders as impolite?"

"Only certain elders," I said obscurely.

"Well, then. Maybe you should learn to be more *reticent*."

Touché, I thought. I had taught her the meaning of the word.

I relate this remembered scrap because Emory's reaction to my impudence was telling. Cutting her eyes nervously at the reprobate in the back row, she looked both horrified and thrilled. She was attracted to my daring, but wary of being associated with it and thus potentially bearing the price of that association; she didn't smile, shoot me a thumbs-up, or give any other indication that we were socially in league. Later at lunch, she vacillated between the *reticence* of suppressed censure and *reluctant* admiration. Emory herself would never be guilty of such gross miscalculation. The small advantage of calling Ms. Townsend on her mistake— a handful of points to be won from fellow pupils—would be far outweighed by the disadvantage of incurring our teacher's disfavor for the rest of the year. My chastening of Ms. Townsend was self-destructive. But in those days, Emory found watching me fling myself on my own funeral pyre a captivating spectator sport.

Our classmates regarded the pair of us as perplexing, though as I've indicated I was more curiosity than outcast. So my peers didn't quite perceive me as a pity pal, while Emory's adoption of a benighted Jehovah's Witness may have made her seem more alluringly complicated. At the start of our friendship, there were indeed elements of utility on both sides. For me, Emory represented access to, and acceptance by, the whole wondrous non-Witness world. In kind, she was fascinated by my gloomy, despotic circumstances, so I also provided her access to another world, which she could sample voyeuristically from a safe distance.

But in short order, honestly? It seemed we simply liked each other. In the longer term, I might express our affections more strongly, but in truth, I don't remember how I once felt about Emory Ruth—and I mean neither that I refuse to reveal these feelings nor that I'm in the grip of a stubborn denial. I honestly can't remember. Owing to my borderline dyscalculia, multiple numbers in my checkbook register are heavily overwritten. The raw emotional material of Emory's and my years together before a certain crossroads is no more available to me than the fragile underlying figures of my arithmetic mistakes. Consider this a warning, then. You can't trust a rendition of a course of events by any narrator who knows how the story ends.

Word had been out for months that Emory Ruth and Pearson Converse had become, however incongruously, an established duo. Dizzied by the vast social vistas opening before me and fast losing a protective incredulity that I was pulling off a passable imitation of a normal person without being hauled once more before a scalding Judicial Committee Hearing, I lapsed into incaution. There was my life at school, where I was widely perceived as coming out of my shell, and there was my life at home, closed, dark, brittle: the shell I crawled back into. Aside from the occasional mortification of doorstepping a classmate's parents while my family soldiered the streets trying systematically to ruin a whole neighborhood's weekend, the two halves of my black-and-white cookie remained discrete.

It was my younger brother, Caleb, who ratted me out. He was enrolled in the adjacent middle school, from which he could easily espy my comings and goings across covered outdoor corridors when both schools changed classes. Not only would he have failed to recognize Emory from our Kingdom Hall, but revealing tops and svelte skirts would have advertised from a hundred feet that she was not one of us.

Ever since my thwarted effort to put my foot down over meetings, I had negotiated my coerced devotions by acting like a robot. I paged the tracts at a metronomic tempo gauged to approximate the time it would have taken to read them. I sat through Family Worship Evening every Wednesday, my back straight, hands folded, body unnaturally still, expression blank. During our evangelical rounds, I marched silently from house to house, lagging the smallest increment behind but never far back enough to be lectured to hurry up. On a mark's front porch, I no longer caught the householder's sympathetic eye after the rest of the family had (finally) turned to leave, because I couldn't afford to break character. At home, I spoke when spoken to, keeping my responses just complete enough that I couldn't be accused of surliness. See, I didn't act surly—or detectably brooding, resentful, or obstreperous. I didn't act anything. I remember that period as strangely fun. Neither my mother nor the ecclesiastical fussbudgets at the Kingdom Hall could catch me out doing anything wrong—or nothing they could put their fingers on. Which drove them wild. I had absented myself. They had no idea what I was thinking, and while they had their suspicions—whatever was going on behind those dead eyes, it couldn't have been good—they had no proof. Superficially, I was an exemplary Witness. Yet extreme compliance can constitute a form of insolence. This sly gambit especially enrages panjandrums, because disobedience disguised as obedience is impossible to prosecute.

Exposure of my double life brought this appearance of taunting line-toeing to an end.

We were still at the table after another flavorless dinner that spring. I remember I was wearing the crimson silk scarf that Emory had given me for my sixteenth birthday in February. To lower its profile, I kept it tightly knotted, tucking the tails inside my blouse. I'd explained to my mother with strained casualness that the "ratty old thing" had been discarded in a gutter on my route home from school, but at least it was warm and free;

by this cool early April, I feigned being prone to a chill. Mother didn't care for the "wanton" color, but I'd claimed that God had placed the practical garment in my path. To discard it would have been ungrateful.

"Caleb tells me you're thick as thieves with some harlot at school," my mother charged.

At the antediluvian argot, I nearly dropped my mask of stony stoicism with an eye roll (although honestly, had she called *me* a harlot, the archaic smear would have cut me to the quick as fiercely as it would have in 1850). My impulse to mockery was quickly overtaken by the flush of having been discovered. I shot a daggered look at my little brother, who blithely met my eyes with an expression of saintly innocence. I tried to keep my voice uninflected, but it developed a tremble: "I don't have any friends who exchange sex for money."

"Honey, don't nitpick," my father said. "You know we've discouraged you from getting too chummy with people who don't understand us and aren't in the Truth."

"She hasn't been *discouraged*," my mother corrected. "She's been *forbidden*."

"I do everything I'm supposed to, and who my friends are shouldn't concern you."

"When your friends are in the grip of Satan, they very much concern us," my mother said. "Caleb says this girl waltzes about half-naked, and he's spotted her with a boy putting his hands all over her parts while grappling on the bleachers."

I couldn't help wondering who it was. Emory had her pick. "I don't know anything about that."

"You're to cut off all contact with this floozy and keep yourself to yourself," my mother ordered. "We have to be able to trust you. If you carry on consorting with this silly girl, we'll have to move you to another school."

I was already debating whether I could manage to reconnoiter with Emory in locations out of my odious little brother's sight line, disliking the prospect of demoting my bold alternative persona to that of an ordinary sneak, when my mother upped the ante.

"The alternative, which I far prefer, is to pull you out of school altogether. You're sixteen now, and according to the law we only begrudgingly honor to keep these dreadful people out of our business, you're no longer required to keep wasting your time there. It's much more important for you to get serious and prepare yourself for baptism."

In that moment, quandary escalated to emergency. Cherished in its own right, Emory's friendship had also thrown me a lifeline. When you're trapped, you're susceptible to shortsightedness; all that matters is getting out. Resolved to escape the Witnesses, I was already wrestling with the reality that this meant escaping my family, too—though I'd yet to grapple with the emotional consequences. Insofar as I had any firm plans, I suppose I'd intended to tolerate the strictures of my parents' faith until I turned eighteen. As attracted as I was to the secular world, which appeared so much more dazzling glimpsed through the bars of a cage than when viewed by the carelessly unencumbered, I was also afraid of it. I had no idea how to pilot a wide-open future beyond the familiar confines of "our" religion. Any visions of that future were blurred. But of this much I was sure: I wouldn't have a hope in hell of navigating such an alien landscape, with no support of kith or kin, as a high school dropout.

This may seem surprising, but the second punch of my mother's one-two hit me harder. Day-to-day, I could forgive myself for going through the motions of adherence to beliefs I'd privately renounced, because I was still a minor, I needed food and shelter, and humoring my parents was the price of survival. But baptism would violate my inmost self. Maybe the Witnesses had made deeper inroads than I liked to admit, but I took the commitment seriously. Too seriously to make it. Crossing my fingers before immersion was not an option.

"But sixteen is the very youngest any Witness gets baptized," I said. I'd been counting on forestalling this Gethsemane until I could make my getaway as a legal adult. "I don't know if I'm ready—you know, mature enough."

"Sure you are, sweetheart," my father chimed in, thinking he was sticking up for me.

"There's no such thing as engaging in a righteous act too soon," my mother said, brisking up from the table and wiping her hands on a dish towel. "I'll advise the elders that you're eager to start your studies. As for that flibbertigibbet, when you tell her you'll have nothing more to do with her, there's no need to speak face-to-face. You can write her a letter; you can find her family's address in the phone book. I suggest you make it short."

Everything moved very fast. Whatever I can or can't remember feeling, just on the face of it the invitation from the Ruths to come live with their family was a gesture of enormous generosity, and not simply on the part of Emory's parents but on Emory's part, too. It's one thing to share confidences and lunch periods, quite another to share your mother, your father, your sister, and your own bedroom. I may have been particularly horrified by baptism, but it was the threat to the completion of my secondary education that persuaded her parents to make such a drastic offer. We all have religions of sorts. Her father, David, was a history professor, her mother, Kelly, an attorney in contract law, and they revered learning; graduation was their baptism. I'd met them only a few times in passing when they'd picked up their daughter from school for some family outing, but apparently my running buddy had kept them up to speed on her adoption of a woebegone victim of theological zealotry. If I'd become tantamount to one of those African poster kids with cleft palates and flies in their noses whom you send three dollars every month, rare is the checkbook benefactor who asks the benighted urchin to move in.

Although the flurry of hugger-mugger negotiations took only two or three days, that was still long enough for my mother to force me to write that letter to Emory, explaining that she was a bad influence, hoping that she found God lest she be wiped from the earth in the coming battle between Jehovah and worldly government, and announcing that, in the absence of such a blessed conversion, our ill-conceived friendship was at an end. (Despite the admonition to keep it short, my mother was dictating and couldn't control herself. Witnesses are a prolix people.) Emory duly received that letter in the post after I'd already moved in with her

family, and the two of us got it framed. So yellowed by sun that the ball-
point was almost indecipherable, it was still hanging beside her bookcase
the last time I was in her apartment, which I'm afraid was some time ago.

On the designated morning, I packed what little would fit in my
regular rucksack, the better to not attract attention. I gave my mother an
unusual kiss on the cheek and my father a hug whose ferocity and dura-
tion he wouldn't have understood. I left for school. I never came back.

At Kelly's insistence, I surmounted a paralytic dread and called home
that first night. Unfortunately, it was my mother who answered. "Hi,
Mother, I didn't want you to worry. I'm at my friend's . . . the *harlot*."

Dead air.

"Anyway, I'm going to be staying here for a while . . ."

She hung up.

Kelly suggested that maybe once everyone had had a chance to cool
off and miss each other, and my parents had been given the opportunity to
appreciate how strongly I felt about staying in school . . . I cut my hostess
off. I said I was already en route to being disfellowshipped. No one at the
Kingdom Hall would be allowed to have anything to do with me. I'd been
deleted from my family—worse than dead, more as if I had never been
born. But then I pulled up short, worried that this kind woman hadn't realized the absoluteness with which her daughter's companion had just been
dumped in her lap. "Unless, of course, you want to get rid of me," I added
meekly. "I could always beg the elders for forgiveness and maybe get off
with reproof . . ."

Kelly was having none of that. She made up the spare twin bed in
Emory's room. She shushed Emory's younger sister, Felicity, when the
thirteen-year-old assessed my long dun skirt and bunchy gray sweater:
"You look like you just walked off the set of *Oliver*." While preparing a
mac and cheese from scratch, Kelly mentioned quietly that maybe we
could go shopping for a few new clothes on the weekend. After dinner, I
curled up blissfully with the household's hardback of *The Bonfire of the
Vanities*, glorying in not having to read *The Watchtower*. In short order
it became a running gag with the Ruths that I was in their "Witness
protection program."

CHAPTER 3

With Kelly and David's encouragement, I applied to Voltaire University, if only because that's where Emory was going, and where her father taught, and when I didn't get in, it was embarrassing. Opting for nearby Penn College instead, I pretended to be glad for the cheaper public tuition and enthused about their struggling Great Books program, but exclusion from VU smarted. (Funny, we don't say "smarted" in the sense of wounded anymore. For a while, you'll recall, it became a transitive verb that meant show up as mentally inferior, as in "He smarted me!" Accusations of "mind-shaming" soon became more commonplace.) Looking back, I can see that whichever college I attended didn't really matter, but ask any eighteen-year-old from that era: it seemed to matter fantastically at the time.

After getting a master's if only to put off adulthood—were more striplings in their twenties eager to embrace the responsibilities of maturity, a host of graduate programs would have collapsed—I worked as an adjunct at local colleges because I couldn't think of anything else to do. The pay was poor, but the perks were considerable, and I do not mean access to the pool. In retrospect, I was barely older than my charges, and in a neutral setting like a bar I might have seemed a plausible candidate for their affections; no one's eyebrows would have necessarily risen at a young woman of twenty-six dating a younger man of nineteen. But the fact that I was their teacher put them off-limits. In 1998, most schools had yet to institute strict guidance on relationships between students and faculty, but I didn't need to read a manual to intuit that such fraternizing would be frowned upon—which made the prospect only more enticing.

I was a bit wild in my twenties. That may be standard, but I was more unmoored than most. Brutally severed from my past, I had no family and no faith, nothing to keep me grounded. Intoxicated with insubordinate nineties grunge, I spent many an evening flinging myself about my cramped apartment to the Pixies and Smashing Pumpkins until the neighbors complained. I was giddy with a freedom that I'd yet to understand was not just a freedom to do stuff but also a freedom to exercise restraint. In short, I slept with a fair number of men—too many, as I look back. I did it because I could. I'm not sure how many of these liaisons I enjoyed.

But I did enjoy Fabrizio. He was a sleek Italian who slumped in the back of my freshman comp class, and he never took his eyes off me. For weeks, that cool stare read like a dare. He did participate in class, but mostly to challenge my expertise; what was wrong with joining complete sentences with a comma if you hadn't finished your thought? The writing in his essays was mediocre, but their themes were original; he was good at telling a small story from which he drew a larger truth. It was a cliché for an Italian, but he seemed to answer to a strong moral code—and I responded to that, perhaps because something in me was missing a code of my own. When class concluded, he arranged to be the last student to leave the room, and he often dallied by my desk, taunting me with some example he had found in our reading that broke whatever grammatical or stylistic rule I'd just taught. (I didn't really care about the "rules," either, but no one had ever instructed me on how to teach composition, and I had to fill the hour somehow.) When signing up for one-on-one conferences, he always put himself down for the last slot, which allowed him to linger. I should say, allowed us to linger. There was a jousting, needling, poke-poke-poke to these hothouse interchanges in my shabby beige office that excited me; he couldn't stand to be corrected and would defend his dangling modifiers to the death. The closer to the surface the real game we were playing rose, the more dangerous it felt, as well as the more crucial that the conceit remain in place: I was his teacher, Fabrizio was merely my student, and we were working together on improving his argumentation.

I don't know how we made it through most of that fall term. I was so blasé about campus mores that I wasn't determined to keep my hands off that boy to suit the administration. It was more as if we were competing over who could hold a breath the longest underwater. Besides, once one of us touched a knee to a thigh and kept it there, we were in a whole other world, and something—the teasing, the tantalizing, the uproarious pretense that nothing untoward was going on here—would be lost.

At the end-of-term class get-together I organized at a beer-and-pizza joint, I showed up in a dress that left little to the imagination when I leaned over a cue at the pool table. I'm afraid everyone got rather drunk, and Fabrizio and I may have bordered on indiscreet, but at the time I thought, *Who cares?* The whole class seemed to have developed a wink-wink about Fabrizio and Ms. Converse.

To cut to the chase, we *consolidated* the flirtation back in his dorm room late that night, though after all the buildup, the experience was rushed and strangely flat. Fabrizio went home for Christmas break, during which we didn't communicate (I think we were both chagrined), and early in the spring semester—on my twenty-seventh birthday in February, as luck would have it—I discovered I was pregnant. I never told him.

I was furious with myself, because I was out of control, and the one thing I'd always wanted more than anything from childhood was control over my life. Here I was carrying a kid that was half not-all-that-bright Italian, and my half wasn't going to up the cognitive ante much, either. Though we both knew that sealing the deal had been a mistake, Fabrizio was the type to acquiesce to fatherhood as his fate, never mind that it would strangle a nineteen-year-old's future; bravely facing the music and accepting the wages of sin were doubtless cornerstones of his *code*. So a guy whose hair had already begun to recede and whose taste in movies ran to *Austin Powers* could be part of my life forever. An abortion was the one extreme contravention of my family's doctrine that ended up giving me no pleasure.

Twenty-seven was a bit young to forgo bearing children the old-fashioned way, so a word of explanation. I'd already planned to have kids at some point, on the assumption that I could do a better job than my parents had (well—talk about clearing a low bar). While living with Wade, I hope I became more trusting, but back then the idea of only half-owning something as intimate as my own progeny was anathema. I wanted children who would be *all mine*. I was also averse to leaving the contributing genetic material up to chance, gambling on whichever slouching specimen signed up for freshman comp at two p.m. rather than eleven in the morning. I started shopping for sperm.

My divulgence here that I specifically screened the lists of donors for high levels of intelligence will doubtless lose me any chance at sympathy these days. But I have no regrets. The anonymous Japanese gentleman whose excretions I purchased, and in sufficient volume that might give the results of a successful fertilization at least one sibling, had an IQ of 146. Behold, Darwin, whose name and biological origins were both gleeful digs at the creed I'd forsaken, which deplored evolution and artificial insemination both.

He was a subdued, watchful baby who I worried as time went on might be, contrary to the promise of his father's profile, developmentally delayed. Had the sperm bank lied to me? He cried only when he needed something tangible, and he never cooed or burbled. Shouldn't he have made a stab at "Mama!" by the first year, or certainly within eighteen months? But I shouldn't have worried. When he finally started talking at two, he spoke in crisp consonants and complete grammatical sentences. The first thing out of his mouth was "I want some grape juice, please."

Sure enough, when I opted to provide Darwin company with the same brains-in-a-jar, if across a more artistic spectrum, Zanzibar turned out just as exceptional.

It pleased me that Darwin and Zanzibar had the same parents; they were a matched set. They had the same thin, quizzically high eyebrows, eggshell complexion, and straight obsidian hair, though Darwin's shocked upward, while Zanzibar wore hers long. They got on; with only two years between them, that they were opposite sexes helped dissipate competition. Even when they weren't talking, which was often, together they generated a subtle hum. They hit the same frequency. They required little minding, and they readily occupied themselves without the aid of digital babysitters. Honestly, I know this is obnoxious, and I'm not trying to make anyone jealous—in due course, you won't be—but one of the things that made it so easy for Wade to move in with a single mother in 2004 was that I had perfect children.

Wade and I met when the landlord of my previous rental sent the lean, lanky tradesman around to cut down a moribund oak that threatened the roof. He was what some would call an "arborist," though he was more comfortable with "tree surgeon." Straight off, I found him insanely attractive. With a mane of black hair in a ponytail, he had a narrow, thoughtful face with a strong nose and high brow—almost like a horse, if "horse-faced" weren't pejorative, which it shouldn't be. His skin was burnished the color of olive wood from working for decades outdoors, while his figure exhibited an all-body fitness particular to an occupation of manual labor. His clavicle was pronounced, and I've always had a weakness for men with a prominent Adam's apple. From the moment he arrived, I trailed helplessly after those low-slung hips and broad forearms like a puppy whimpering after a treat. Though after pointing out the oak I might have headed back inside and gotten on with my business, I parked in the yard for most of the operation of three or four hours, gawking shamelessly up at this Adonis strapped to the trunk as he lopped off branches with his compact chain saw. Since he never shot me a quizzical why-are-you-still-here look, I wondered if such a striking specimen was accustomed to female customers staring soulfully up at his leafy camouflage all the time.

I mixed as little as possible with my fellow academics at VU. I ended up teaching university English mainly because, unlike Emory, I wasn't good at things; why, I was good at practically nothing. I'd never been insulted by that axiom that those who can't do teach: that was me. I couldn't do squat. While having located a job that paid me for reading made-up stories was appealingly scandalous, I found academia insufferable—all that professorial verbiage, disconnected from anything real or important or, usually, even true. So I responded to a man whose primary relationship was to the world he could touch. As I would soon learn, he wasn't squeamish about unplugging a toilet or clawing out fish guts. He could affix brackets to damp Sheetrock and a full-size *OED* would not bring down the shelf. I'm not handy myself. A man who exercised such fearless command over substance rather than semantics was sexy as hell.

As for Wade Haavik's purportedly mythical IQ, I have no idea. If he'd ever had his "value to humanity reduced to a few digits," as orthodoxy would have it, he never told me the number, and now that IQ tests are illegal I guess we'll never know. But he definitely wasn't stupid. His instincts were sound, even regarding subjects about which he was poorly informed. Beyond that, his intellectual capacities were beside the point. He understood how physical things worked. Wade's mastery of the material was a parallel intelligence, one which—and I'm not pandering to ideological fashion here—I may hold in higher esteem than the book-learning sort.

Because it's depressingly pertinent to our larger story, it might also be worth speculating where exactly Wade Haavik fell in the classic California F-scale of authoritarianism. (Aside from a tendency to trust my own judgment overly much, which entails submission to an authority of a kind, I flatter myself that my own score sits smack at zero.) Wade was no toady, but his relationship to authority was avoidant. In his occupational life, he escaped hierarchy by being self-employed. His instinct with the noise of politics was to press the *mute* button. He didn't engage. He eluded conflict. He would never land anywhere on that F-scale, because if you scheduled him for the assessment, he wouldn't show up.

Five years my senior, Wade Haavik was intensely private. He loved being on his own. He liked silence. He liked the woods. He went online as rarely as he could manage. He liked cooking and food. He slept, aptly, like a log. And he liked fucking. When he stayed on for wine and a bite after sawing the oak for my fireplace, I sampled his talent for joinery. We made for a snug mortis-and-tenon fit.

With a perfect absence of hesitation or handwringing, he soon moved in, arriving with all his worldly possessions in two scruffy duffels. He was quiet, and a taciturn presence proved calming. I'm not quiet, anything but, and a man of few words cleared more room for mine. I also learned to value the certainty that, on the occasions he did speak up, I should pay attention.

With such a serene experience of motherhood, I was open to a third, but when Wade mooted the idea in our first year together, I blithely assumed that we would avail ourselves of the last few teaspoons of brains-in-a-jar still in storage at the clinic. That way all three kids would be full siblings, and all three kids would be brilliant. I came to understand this was hurtful. At thirty-eight, Wade had never sired a child and obviously wanted to be the biological father. So I relented. I even went along with his insistence that we choose a "normal" name, and not one of my fanciful picks scavenged from the nineteenth-century natural sciences or the Indian Ocean, because we didn't want our offspring to suffer for our pretensions (he said "creativity," but that's not what he meant) and attract the wrong kind of attention. Given that the roster at his daughter's kindergarten would include "Hyacinth," "Sequoia," "Mazikeen," "Yamileth," and "Guadalupe," Wade's instincts were dated. In the end, it was plain old "Lucy" that stood out.

My capitulation on paternity entailed a sacrifice. The chasm between Lucy and her older siblings was too great to be explained by age alone. In dealings with their little sister, Darwin and Zanzibar were benevolent, solicitous, and polite. But there was no hum. Once my first two kids were old enough to understand—meaning when they were still very young, because they discerned the character of the world so quickly—I was candid about their mail-order father. I never announced outright that Lucy was only their half sister, but they seemed to sense from the start she wasn't cut from the same cloth.

For that matter, so could I. By about four, the older kids each went off *Sesame Street*, seeming to find the floppy, garish animal puppets a little insulting. They could both read by four, too, and teaching them was a breeze; I didn't need to illustrate the "L" sound more than once. Not only could they count at that age, but by age five they could do multi-figure sums and subtraction. Had I pushed him as hard as I should have, Darwin might have mastered second-year algebra by first grade.

As for Zanzibar, by the age of eight she'd become the Caravaggio of the crayon. I realize a recorder is dorky, but she figured out how to play it with only its flimsy fingering chart for instruction, and I'd had no idea what full tones could be wrested from that hideous tube of brown plastic. I immediately bought her a wooden one. Her singing was precociously tuneful. When she convened her friends she took charge, designing the plots of improvisational dramas, contriving the roles, and directing the others while acting the lead. Proud parents are so tedious, and you don't have to take my word for it, but I've come to suspect that Donor #83748 was good at more than math.

By contrast, at five Lucy still struggled with the Alphabet Song, which she was prone merely to *NAH-nah NAH-nah NAH-nah naaaah!*, failing to appreciate that the melody in this case was not the point. The amount of repetition required to get her to draw an "A" was wearing. She had a short attention span and wasn't interested; by the next day, she'd have forgotten not only how to draw an "A" but that there was such a thing as an "A." She was a rambunctious urchin, displaying quite a gift for mischief, her one precocity. Still, and this is a ghastly thing to say of one's own child, but at least in comparison to her brother and sister, Lucy bored me a bit.

If I sound harsh, I'd remind you of my earlier up-front admission that I've never regarded myself, nor been regarded by others, as any especial bright spark, either. Yet I wouldn't want that disclosure mistaken for cynically ingratiating self-deprecation. Much less was it a bid for pity. Rather, I was heading off incoming flak: my ostensibly obnoxious opinions cannot be disregarded as a would-be oppressor's craven defense of self-interest. Besides, intelligence per se is not, and never has been, what I am good for. What I am good for is *defiance*.

That defiance has come at some cost. Voltaire is Pennsylvania's third city, big enough that a certain crossing of paths hasn't happened often, but small enough that it was bound to happen sometimes. Whenever I've spotted members of my estranged family on the street, I've made it a policy to stare straight at them, occasionally adding an arch of my eyebrows or even an ironic wave. The cool shamelessness and hints of drollery are a performance. In truth, my heart rate always doubles, and acid rises in my throat. I don't know what I'm nervous they might do to me other than what they do do: stroll with studied indifference, no more acknowledging my presence than they would say hello to a fire hydrant. The three or four times I've intersected with my mother, I've sensed her rich, rancorous enjoyment—that singular joyful joylessness I grew up with. Only once did my father, on his own, shoot me a soulful glance, before turning heel and hustling in the opposite direction. My brothers, however, have never broken rank. They're grown men now with families of their own, and I suspect their children have no idea they have an aunt.

Without intending to, I'd also cheated my own children of kin. Thanks to their mother the apostate, they were raised with no access to their grandparents, uncles, and cousins—none of whom they'd ever meet. With Darwin and Zanzibar's father an anonymous test tube and Wade an only child, our poor excuse for an extended family came down to Wade's folks, whom we saw seldom after their retirement to the Florida panhandle. As for our household's larger social life, in the perfect absence of blood ties I was heavily reliant on a sprinkling of friends, one in particular. I did have adoptive parents of a kind in Kelly and David, but that only further raised my disproportionate dependence on Emory Ruth— whom even in adulthood I bestowed with the adolescent designation of my "best friend."

Looking back, I wonder whether she's ever said the same of me.

In sum: if Jehovah's Witnesses are determined to remain "separate from the world," I'm every bit as determined to remain separate from Jehovah's Witnesses. Yet this reliance on opposition is a weakness of my character. The bedrock of who I am is rejection. I'm a construction of negatives. Where most people store their convictions, I stockpile what I don't believe. I am less prone to passionate embrace than to fierce dislike. I revile being told what to do more than I long to do anything. I continue to be reactive, which is unthinking in its way; I will do or say anything that the Witnesses forbid. I always vote. I doubt I'm patriotic by nature, but I fly the Stars and Stripes every Memorial and Independence Day. I curse, though I learned to do so later than most, and sometimes my inserted profanities have a stilted quality and can seem almost prim. I conceived my first two children through the Witness no-no of artificial insemination. I still prefer Salvation

Army thrift shops to the Heart Association ones. I've bought more than one ritual package of blood sausage, though I don't especially like it; the sole upside of my older daughter's appendicitis was freely agreeing to the surgery. I not only got a college education but earned a master's, and during my career as an adjunct at Penn College and later as an instructor in VU's English department, I always designed reading lists for which the brainwashing autocrats of my childhood would harbor the most contempt.

However arguably empty and destructive, opposition has provided me an energy and endurance that the impetus of a more positive questing could never equal. The darker emotions are both more powerful and more abiding than their sunnier cousins. If you could pour them in the tank of a car, disgust, fury, outrage, and antipathy would speed you to the far horizon, whereas a fuel distilled from mercy, empathy, appreciation, and forgiveness would leave you rutted by the side of the road after a few hundred feet. Thus I've long trusted that the incendiary resentment I pooled in childhood would propel me all the way through to an acrimonious old age.

Yet I did grow gradually concerned as I approached midlife that even my stoked-high fires of anti-righteousness might eventually burn out. After all, by about 2010 I was in danger of a mollifying contentment. I had a ridiculously big house, a stalwart live-in partner who was smashingly handsome, three healthy children at least two of whom were exceptionally bright, work about which I was lukewarm but at least gave me summers and long holidays off, and a close lifelong friend. But I shouldn't have worried. People being as they are, I would not long lack for something new to despise.

ALT-2012

Emory's ducking-below-the-parapet strategy had much to recommend it. We could keep our heads down, shuffling the world in camouflage like soldiers wearing dun in the desert, duly observing every new linguistic prohibition and suppressing perceptions of our species once prevailing, now retrograde, the better not to stand out. We could constrain our confidential heresies to small gatherings of the like-minded, rigorously vetted beforehand and convened rarely, with doors locked and phones off. By 2012, I had long since inculcated some of those "good habits" Emory had commended, never articulating outré ideas or off-color jokes in texts or emails, which made my correspondence dull. The sandstorm could peak and subside while we hunkered down. If in historical retrospect we wouldn't be seen to have distinguished ourselves, we'd have plenty of company in that department, so the chances of a blanket amnesty were high. Most of all, we will have survived.

All very well save for the fact that curling up in a ball and waiting for the craze of intellectual egalitarianism to go away cut against the grain of my nature. Moreover, social hysterias do not stand still. If they are not yet losing steam, they are getting worse. And this one was getting worse. Radical movements keep ratcheting up their demands, because nothing enervates a cause more than success. Crusaders resent having their purpose stolen out from under them by the fulfillment of their quest; reaching the promised land leaves seekers bereft. There's little to do in a utopian oasis but sip coconut water. So the journey must never be completed. The goal must remain out of reach. To preserve the perfect impossibility of getting there, the desired end point becomes ever more extreme.

Sure, many of the cultural casualties seemed mere bagatelle. My son was upset by the cancellation of the Darwin Awards. This annual catalog of the stupidest ways people had improved the gene pool by departing the human race was now deplored as the modern equivalent of the minstrel show. But then, his partiality to the goof website may have been nomenclatural. The spiking of a long-scheduled feature remake of *The Three Stooges* was neither surprising nor a grievous civilizational loss, the slapstick vaudeville act being an example par excellence of grotesque belittlement of the *otherwise* for cruel gladiatorial entertainment.

As its patronizing know-it-all protagonist shamelessly advertised his "exclusionary intelligence," the British drama *Sherlock* met the same fate. A few bootleg DVDs might still be kicking around, but no one would admit to watching such a hidebound horror today, so it's easy to forget how popular the series was when it first aired. Yet the debut episode fatally coincided with the near-universal ideological pivot in the summer of 2010 among the newly minted anti-intelligentsia intelligentsia. I gather association with the hateful stereotype he portrayed deep-sixed Benedict Cumberbatch's acting career for the foreseeable.

Me, I reserved my personal grief for *The Big Bang Theory*. The uncommonly witty sitcom for grown-ups had been going strong since 2007 and, until 2012, had shown little sign of flagging. Yes, the writers tried desperately to make their scripts more "relevant" by having the objectionable fatheads in the cast make big mistakes—though the very concept of a "mistake" was becoming problematic—and by introducing a token *alternative processor* whose less readily recognizable intelligence was always showing up the defective thinking of characters who brandished PhDs. None of these brave efforts saved the series in the end because the show was still witty, and wit itself had become suspect. When CBS replaced the program with *Young Sheldon*, in which the conceited physicist in the original is shown to have been a perfectly ordinary little boy no more capable than his classmates, no one watched it, but at least no one marched with placards in front of the network demanding it be canceled, either. Hungry for unimpeachably anodyne fare, ideas for which, I'm told, are surprisingly hard to come up with, last I checked, the network was still filming all those scrupulously unexceptional primary school children into a twelfth season.

Of course, the repudiation of Sheldon Cooper and his stuck-up chums was just the beginning, and the cull was two-pronged. First, any portrayal of elevated intelligence even in eternally rerun classics had to be expunged for being an expression of cerebral supremacy. The scriptwriters of *Family Guy* had their haughty genius baby Stewie meet a swift crib death. Embarrassed by their participation in historical prejudice, Paramount claimed to have unearthed a last episode of *Star Trek: The Next Generation* in the late Gene Roddenberry's papers that had never been filmed. In this much anticipated add-on finale, Data, who ostensibly stores all the known information in the universe, is fed the very last bytes that will perfectly complete his data set: the spelling of the word "Mississippi." But he hasn't room for even one more fact and his head explodes all over the starship. By contrast, the intellectual chauvinism in the original series of *Star Trek* and its spin-offs was so interwoven into every episode that, rather than excise all the scenes in which a certain pointy-eared wisenheimer Vulcan appears, the production company extirpated the whole shebang. (The commercial withdrawal of figurines, fancy-dress costumes, and other lucrative merchandise was a grave loss for the franchise, since Spock had been their biggest seller. Black-market box sets of the show itself now sell on the dark web for thousands.) Niles and Frasier Crane were irredeemably brain-vain snobs, along with the contemptuous ex-wife, Lilith: NBC proudly announced good riddance to all eleven seasons of Frasier's eponymous show.

Second, portrayals of dunderheads obviously got the chop. *Dumb and Dumber* was one of the very first films to be prefaced with a warning about offensive representations of cognitive inferiority—which the uninitiated interpreted as one more gag; after the audience consistently laughed at the caution, censors offed the whole movie cold. Not only was *Rain Man* disappeared, but the Academy withdrew the 1989 Best Actor Oscar from Dustin Hoffman, going so far as to demand the return of the statuette. (The fact that his character of Raymond wasn't meant to be a dummy but an autistic savant was far too fine a distinction by 2012.) They did the same thing to Tom Hanks, in defiance of a small but vocal campaign maintaining that his portrayal of Forrest Gump was politically redemptive. If Forrest wasn't very smart, he was very wise: another differentiation too subtle by half for the times. Then there were the shows canned for embodying both eggheads and pinheads. *The Simpsons* was damned twice over, for Homer the doofus and his bookish daughter, Lisa. *Gilligan's Island* played on the now unacceptable opposition of The Professor versus the airhead first mate. *The Road Runner Show* relied on the same cognitive polarity, so even sly ground cuckoos and less than wily coyotes weren't safe.

I realize that most of you reading this—assuming that anyone is reading this—would have noted many of these vanishings as they occurred. Still, out of sight, out of mind, right? It's worth remembering, then, how much of our pop-culture canon has been shoved down the historical garbage disposal. We've lost all those archetypal characters who were famously two fries short of a Happy Meal: Woody Harrelson's namesake in *Cheers*, Chevy Chase's Clark Griswold in *National Lampoon's Vacation*, Steve Martin's Navin in *The Jerk*, Rowan Atkinson's Mr. Bean, even the starfish in *SpongeBob SquarePants*, for Pete's sake. Betty White's Rose in *The Golden Girls*, Matt LeBlanc's Joey in *Friends*, Leslie Nielsen's Dr. Rumack in *Airplane!* . . . Who still remembers "Don't call me Shirley!" or "Looks like I picked the wrong week to quit drinking"? Even aw-shucks Barney Fife on *The Andy Griffith Show* was tossed on the trash heap for being a crude stereotype. I sometimes wonder what uproarious films we've all missed out on since actors like Ben Stiller, Adam Sandler, Jim Carrey, and Sacha Baron Cohen retired in disgrace.

It took me a while to notice as well that even hagiographic documentaries and biopics had dried up, because it's easy to overlook what people are *not* doing. Like, they were *not* filming tributes to Leonardo da Vinci, Marie Curie, James Watson, Isaac Newton, or Alexander Graham Bell. So it wasn't just that Ron Howard's *A Beautiful Mind* went bye-bye; no one was scripting life stories of other tortured geniuses like Galileo or Alan Turing. The snide conceit ran that all these supposed icons were merely regular schmoes who'd tripped over whatever they were credited with creating or discovering by accident. Michelangelo's fruit seller could have painted the Sistine Chapel, too; he just hadn't felt like it.

If the many clones of *The Calumny of IQ* that colonized the bestseller list in 2012 seemed behind the curve, that was because it had been just long enough for lumbering commercial publishers to commission and release tomes like *The Collapse of the Cognoscenti* or *How to Be an Anti-Smartist: A Practical Workbook*. As children's literature had got in on the action, too, for her seventh birthday Wade's parents sent Lucy a copy of *All My Friends Are Clever*—which, thanks to all that passive cleverness with which the girl was now purportedly endowed, she could not read. Few of you will have forgotten some neurologist's *Getting Our Minds Right*, because the MRI imaging he included, demonstrating that everyone's brains were essentially identical, went viral on Twitter and occupied twenty minutes of the "Canvas" segment on the *PBS NewsHour*. On the other hand, it's doubtful you recall Walter Isaacson's chunky biography *Steve Jobs*, because it triggered another huffy boycott and sank like a stone. Naturally, *Fifty Shades of Grey* kept right on selling, because it was stupid.

Meanwhile, it must also have been around 2012 when I finally concluded that an across-the-board media dumbing down (look, live with it) wasn't all in my imagination. The semantics that guests employed on talk shows were noticeably pared back. They preferred shorter words and shorter sentences. Whenever they allowed thoughts to dribble off on an ellipsis or to degenerate into outright incoherence, hosts nodded approvingly. News anchors were restricting their vocabulary to punchy Anglo-Saxon like "hit" and "dog," while eschewing more esoteric words like "ratiocination" and, well, "eschewing." Systematically eliminating complex sentences and dependent clauses, newspapers followed suit, so that stories about a shooting at a Colorado movie theater in July read like the "Look, look! Go, Sally, go!" primers that Darwin and Zanzibar were too old for by the time they were four: "James Holmes was watching a movie. The movie was *The Dark Knight Rises*. This is a Batman movie. Mr. Holmes shot twelve people dead. He also injured seventy people." Oh, and doubtless somewhere in such an article the reporter would have inserted the standard disclaimer that "Mr. Holmes has the same mental ability as everyone else in Aurora." With one glance at eyes that might have been propped open with two-inch toothpicks and hair dyed the flaming orange of Bozo the Clown (may the "gross caricature of alternative processing" rest in peace), anyone who hadn't been brainwashed within an inch of his life could tell the pro forma media assurance was a screaming lie. If ever there was such a thing as a total muttonhead, James Holmes was it.

At some point that year, I picked up a copy of *The New York Times* only to discover that the crossword puzzle was no longer printed in the Arts section. I flapped through the whole edition to find the puzzle not moved but abolished. A search of the website turned up an explanatory apology from the paper's ombudsman. Failure to complete even the easy-peasy Monday crossword had rained untold trauma on the readership since 1950, while the larger, more demanding Sunday version had left the preponderance of subscribers anguished that they might have "something wrong with them" or "something missing." Sure enough, acrostics, ana-grams, and sudoku puzzles had also vanished from print media altogether, presumably because they fostered a bigoted self-congratulation in puzzle solvers and a gloomy, psychically deleterious sense of inadequacy in the stumped.

Of greater moment than the ransacking of our television schedules: the Democratic Party's apparatchiks had concurred by January that Barack Obama had become a liability. The president was aloof, snooty, and su-percilious. Never having gotten the memo about suppressing that silver tongue, he still deliberately rubbed the popular nose in his own articulacy. Either he was failing to track the national mood or he just didn't like the mood. Frantic advice from his press secretary notwithstanding, he con-tinued to convey the impression that he thought he was smarter than the average bear. However challenging it may be to recall now, in many a previ-ous era having a leader who was outstandingly astute, eloquent, and well informed would have seemed to any country's considerable advantage. Yet by 2012, appearing as anything but one of the folks was electoral death, because the whole notion that one might want to look *up* to anyone in a position of authority had become preposterous. Worse, the president's effortless cool and dry sense of humor had the same effect as those *New York Times* crosswords: he made voters feel that in comparison there was "something wrong with them" or that they had "something missing."

I'm reasonably sure that for party functionaries to convince a sitting president's own VP to challenge the incumbent for the nomination in the primaries was a historic first. Nonetheless, I'd be the first to agree that Joe Biden was an ideal fit for the times: he was impressively unimpressive. In contrast to Obama's irksomely inspirational oratory, Biden's speaking style was delectably leaden. His version of profundity was to make a prosaic point and then repeat it word for word. Whenever the vice president was at a loss, his compulsive insertion of "C'mon, man!" conspicuously failed to seem rousing and hip, and that election year any practice that underscored a shortcoming was the ticket. In other words, the more poorly Biden campaigned, the more voters he won over. One especially ingratiating appearance on *The View*, in which the VP neglected to utter a single complete sentence, while his salad of sports metaphors left the audience at perfect sea over metaphor-for-*what*, accumulated millions of hits on YouTube, secured the nation's adoration in perpetuity, and guaranteed that Obama would lose the South Carolina primary by a shocking margin. The speech to the nation in which the president announced his withdrawal from the race only emphasized his transparent unelectability—because the short address was deft, elegant, and droll. The fact that Obama had class was merely one more reason to hate the guy, remember? Along with any other attribute associated with preeminence, class was out of fashion.

On the home front, I was increasingly worried about Darwin. He'd always been such a self-motivated boy, prone to those extracurricular fascinations like Deepwater Horizon and Fukushima, and I'd never had to goad him to do his homework. By seventh grade, however, he had no homework, and the level of instruction at his new middle school was so primitive that this once energetic twelve-year-old was prone to narcolepsy in class. Before our glorious revolution, I'd looked forward to enrolling him in Voltaire's revered magnet school, the Henry Heinz Academy for Science, Technology, and Engineering, whose notoriously grueling admission exam would have been a cakewalk for a kid whose father had an IQ of 146. I'd hoped that Darwin could finally be educated among his intellectual peers. But no. You couldn't have schools for gifted children if that very category had become anathema. As of the previous year, the curriculum at Henry Heinz was just as dumpy and undemanding as every other public school's, and the great hulking brick edifice wasn't worth the commute of three extra miles.

My son had grown sullen and depressed. After school, he'd started playing video games for hours on end, and when I pressed him once about what made this repetitive activity so compelling, he droned, "It's what everyone else does, and I'm just like everyone else." He'd taken to speaking in a lifeless monotone, as if voicing the very leveling of which he was a victim at school. Darwin and his classmates had been mowed like grass.

Both my older children absorbed an expansive vocabulary from an early age, but what I once imagined as a one-way process went into reverse. Less talkative in general, they used words that were bland and clipped. Unless they were assuming this rigid pidgin as canny social camouflage, those two were deliberately erasing their formerly precocious idiolect.

Zanzibar continued to draw, but her pictures had grown small. On an eight-by-eleven piece of paper, she centered compositions half the size of a postcard. If exactingly detailed, these miniatures conveyed a crimped quality that seemed gratuitous amid all that white space. She preferred depicting interiors and still lifes, whereas before she'd opted for landscapes and living things—cats, plants, family. The sedateness, motionlessness, and implied silence of her recent work seemed, in contrast to her new stick-figure lexicon, creepily adult. She'd also abandoned color, preferring meticulously sharpened pencils or rapidographs. While I admired her draftsmanship, I missed the lush waxy blends she'd wrought with her Crayola 64.

As for the dramas she directed with her friends, those friends were fewer now, and while I used to hear them cackling for hours on end on a Saturday afternoon, their rehearsals had grown more subdued, the plots darker. They performed one of Zanzibar's improvisational productions for our family, and it proved an intermingling of Arthur Miller's *The Crucible* and Shirley Jackson's "The Lottery"—neither of which would have been taught in the feeble-minded iteration of fifth grade in which my poor daughter was lodged.

The protagonist (Zanzibar, of course) was a savant who spouted equations, browbeating her friends with the unnatural powers of a human calculator. The math the character trotted out struck me as correct, and I couldn't suppress a smile: my little actress could remember the answers to the digit. But these boastful arithmetic gymnastics were tiresome for the whiz kid's companions, who were made to feel ashamed that their meager mathematical jumping jacks could not compare. (Effectively the chorus, the other girls drooped around our living room, moping in a simian hunch while mumbling, *What's eight plus three? I don't knooooow . . .*) Meanwhile, the obnoxious main character demanded grapes (provided by our refrigerator) and other tributes like spare change, until finally the chorus had had enough. Together the educational working class revolted against their oppressor and slammed her to the floor with hardbacks (from my library), raising the books high and bringing them down with such theatrically persuasive force that I got a bit worried. This part of the drama was clearly the girls' favorite, and the pummeling went on for some time.

Thereafter, the girls danced delightedly around the limp form of my elder daughter, crying, *What's eight plus three? We don't caaaaaaaaare!*

The play had a pagan cast, and it differed from Arthur Miller and Shirley Jackson in its moral intent. The clever clogs was a tyrant and deserved her fate. The math itself was a tyranny, too. By the very end, the freshly liberated chorus was leaping about our carpet, growling, crowing, and barking. They'd been freed, all right—to be animals. Zanzibar was doubtless behind this direction. While her friends seized on an excuse to go wild, I wondered uneasily whether my ten-year-old was infected by a juvenile form of nihilism.

If not as dramatically as Darwin, even Zanzibar had grown a measure more withdrawn—bound up, watchful, and inclined to a secretive collusion with her brother from which Wade and I were excluded. By contrast, Lucy was thriving—after a fashion. Now in second grade, she didn't require the pretext of an amateur theatrical production to turn into a proper hellion, and it wasn't obvious to me why reduced academic expectations should necessarily translate into deteriorated behavioral discipline. Although her classroom was festooned with the traditional letters and numbers atop the blackboard, they might as well have been Egyptian hieroglyphs for all the attention the teacher paid to inculcating literacy and numeracy in her charges during the school day. I had, haltingly, tried to abet Lucy's academic progress with homeschooling on weekends, but on those rare occasions I could get her to focus I still didn't detect any indication that she was learning to read.

When I stopped by Gertrude Stein Primary to retrieve my youngest for a dental checkup that fall, the room was pandemonium. I was relieved to discern that at least the class seemed engaged in an organized activity, if not one that would get my youngest to decode the letter "T." They were making baskets with colored Popsicle sticks.

"Ca-rooool!" Lucy shrieked to her teacher at an eardrum-shattering pitch I recognized; my daughter hadn't noticed that her mother had arrived. "Suz-kutch-wun said a mean thing!"

Her face smeared with paste, the harried teacher hurried over, and I followed warily behind. Credibly a recent graduate, Lucy's teacher was young enough to have gotten in on the pedagogical revolution of the last three years. That meant this project would have been selected expressly because all the children should be capable of its completion.

Yet the six boys and girls at Lucy's round table were displaying skills that were ominously various. The pretty, delicate little girl to my daughter's left was painstaking. You know the type: obsessively neat and exacting. The corners of her Popsicle box were built on right angles, and she'd figured out the minimum amount of paste required to bind the sticks. She'd also separated her materials into tidy piles by color, enabling her to build a repeating blue/green/yellow pattern on every side—whereas most of the kids' color schemes were higgledy-piggledy and half paste. The boy on her other side was perched chin on hand, gazing at this architectural marvel in starstruck awe.

Lucy was anything but delicate. Big-boned for her age, she was as comely as seven-year-olds almost always are, but she was impatient. So far she didn't seem to have inherited her father's technical gifts, for her relationship to the physical world was rough. If anything wasn't working for her, she would force it, and she never listened. Accordingly, she hadn't grasped the fundamentals here. Rather than construct her receptacle by alternating pairs of sticks between the two sets of parallel sides, thereby creating said basket effect, Lucy had built the sides of her box by gluing the sticks together in a solid stack—the crafts equivalent of Sheetrock. By God, they were sturdy, but the walls didn't connect. There was no box, much less a basket, and Lucy was mad.

"Now, what seems to be the trouble, girls?" Carol solicited with the sweetness teachers reserve for when a parent is looking on.

"Suz-kutch-wun said my basket is crummy, and hers is *better*."

"Did you?" asked Carol in concern. "Did you claim your basket is *better*?"

"I didn't." Saskatchewan's voice was tremulous, but she still displayed a staunchness. "I only said she wasn't doing it right."

I could tell Carol's brain was shorting out here, because it would have been difficult to parse whether "not doing something right" was on the no-no list. "Well, there are lots of different ways to make a basket," she said, "and they're *all* wonderful!"

Lucy glared at her decidedly under-wonderful-looking slabs and started to cry. Her eyes were squeezed, and her tears weren't those of despair. They were aggressive. "She said the S-word! She said I was *stoo* . . ." Lucy gave in to large theatrical sobs.

"Did you use that word we don't call *anybody*?" Carol said sternly to the Popsicle wunderkind.

"I did not!" the little girl insisted. "She's a liar! I only tried to tell her how to do it!"

"You can't act like you know more than anyone else, sweetie," Carol admonished. "And you can't call other girls bad names. I'm sorry to have to do this, but I'm going to have to take your basket away. So you learn that all the children in our class are just as good as you are, and everything they make is just as good as what you make, too."

When Carol primly appropriated the offending creation, the little boy wailed after his teacher, "Can I have it?"

We'd soon be late for the dentist, and Lucy's crying jag had decayed to an unsteady machine-gun stutter. Hefting my daughter into my arms, I had an early inkling that I shouldn't be concerned solely for my own children's future but for the future of the United States. This August, NASA had placed responsibility for landing *Curiosity* on Mars into the hands of an employee who was just as good as everyone else at Cape Canaveral and whose work was just as good as everyone else's work. Thus the product of decades of costly, rigorous research crashed into a dusty heap. The final image the rover sent back to Earth was a selfie that looked like a dead spider.

CHAPTER 3

It might seem as if I had reason to be jealous, but I wasn't. The biggest difference between Emory and me was the degree of our ambition, and I'd never been apologetic about the modesty of mine. I was thrilled that Wade and I had a large, handsome house. I was thrilled to have a handsome lover. I was also thrilled to have a job that demanded little and provided such luxurious free time. If I harbored any proper ambition it was for my older two children, whose genetic heritage, which I'd gone to a great deal of trouble to engineer, should have ensured a promising future, and now a quirk of ideological fashion was busy invalidating the very quality that once marked offspring like mine as destined for great things. But I'd never been a public person beyond my willingness to speak to a class, so I'd no reason to begrudge Emory her promotion at WVPA. I was sincerely excited for her that she'd finally quit interviewing second-rate locals for *The Talent Show*, which in a paroxysm of administrative anxiety had been renamed *Everyone Is an Artist*; had they opted instead for *Everyone Thinks They're an Artist*, Emory and I might have gotten behind the rebranding one hundred percent.

Now moved to a substantial comment slot after the six p.m. news summary, Emory would enjoy a far higher profile and the more sizable commuter audience. As a testimony to my happiness on her account, for her debut broadcast the last week of October I gathered the whole family around my computer on the kitchen table before dinner, so that we could all listen to "Auntie Em," as D&Z had dubbed her tongue in cheek. The kids adored her. She always seemed so much more glamorous than their mother, and I wasn't offended by their ongoing crush. I was pleased that they responded to adult company, and providing them with a shrewd, quick-witted visitor both stimulated my children and indirectly reflected well on me.

"Shush!" I hushed my screaming, careening seven-year-old as the news concluded. "If you can't keep quiet, please leave the room so the rest of us can hear."

Emory has a low, seductive voice, and for her first line or two I was simply flushed with the same rush of pleasure I always felt when she greeted me in person:

I've never been wholly on board with the term "dog whistle" as a metaphor for wink-and-nod prejudice. Only dogs can hear dog whistles. By implication, only the intended audience for these coded signals can detect the latent hate-mongering. Supposedly, the rest of us sit there in our innocence as if no one has said anything the least untoward. But in my experience, so-called dog whistles register plainly to the ordinary human ear. Their messaging isn't subtle. We can all hear what the speaker is really saying loud and clear.

Ever since the Mental Parity movement roiled our backward institutions and finally issued in a fairer, more decent, more respectful public protocol, we've all recognized that a host of snubs and put-downs have grown unacceptable. We know what those words are, and how savagely they've been used in the past to disparage and dehumanize. But all social progress is doomed to be halting. After our one step forward, too many of our contemporaries are shuffling two steps back.

Start paying attention to friends, coworkers, and even politicians who would never be caught dead using the kind of language that I'm hardly going to cite on this broadcast; NPR has strict guidelines that would prevent my doing so even if I were so recklessly inclined. But too many of our fellow Americans—seemingly biddable, seemingly polite, obedient to the strict letter of the cultural law—have meanwhile been developing a whole new secret code to convey exactly the prejudice we're trying so strenuously to eliminate. Evasive, subtext-laden phrasing functions as a "get this!"—as a sharp but surreptitious elbow in the ribs.

I can't count the times I've heard the people we now call "alternative processors" flagged up in conversation, but they're always slyly identified as "unconventional," "special," "offbeat," or "eccentric." Folks also known as the "otherwise" may be described as having "exceptional" intelligence, by which the speaker really means, wink-wink, exceptionally low intelligence. True, this persecuted cast was once slandered outright, and a raft of flagrant insults having grown repugnant is cause for celebration. But I've encountered this crafty new language many times here at this very radio station. Nowadays, rather than be subjected to brazen ridicule, what the otherwise propose in the workplace is coyly characterized as "less than ideal," "somewhat impractical," "not for the best," or "perhaps not wholly thought out." What they write might be described as "not fully developed," "a promising start," "in need of another go-through," or "just a little bit short of perfect." What they say is gently dismissed as "a tad unclear," "a touch garbled," "reliant on weak logic," "based on a dubious factual foundation," or even—boldly, baldly—as "wrong."

These aren't dog whistles. They're human whistles. We can all hear them. And sometimes the whistle is at its most shrill when no one says anything at all. There's a look—a conspiratorial meeting of eyes between members of what was, until so recently, a spoiled, protected elect. This glance of shared exasperation often comes with a slight but detectable eye roll. It means "Oh, for pity's sake." It means "Not long ago, you and I would have been able to tell this inferior specimen to take a hike, and now, darn it, we can't." It means "We recognize each other. The rules may have superficially changed, but people like us are still in charge. We will continue to reap most of society's rewards and have everything our own way."

So I have a modest proposal. Let's retire the expression "alternative processor," which I think we could all agree has acquired a taint. I'm even lukewarm on "the otherwise," which really just means "the wise," and that refers to the whole human race. If you ask what term we should use instead, I say: let's not nominate any term. Human brains are all the same. Wisdom is the preserve not of the few but of the multitude. If there's no such thing as people with measurably deficient mental ability, then we don't need a name for them at all.

In addition, it's time to stop letting soft, indirect prejudice pass unaddressed. When colleagues brush off suggestions from certain people *as "poorly reasoned" or "likely to have unintended consequences," press them on what they really meant to imply. Don't cooperate with wink-wink bigotry, but make an example of these dinosaurs, and so put everyone present on notice that even thinly disguised discrimination will not be tolerated. And if someone*

meets your eyes with that familiar look of frustration, which they imagine is
mutual, don't cooperate. Don't flick your pupils upward, but glare back with a
challenge: "What are you looking at me for? If you have some kind of problem
with intellectual egalitarianism, you'll find no quarter with me."

When the broadcast moved on to an ominous weather report, the four of
us continued to sit around the table in stupefied silence. Finally, Darwin
said what we were all thinking: "I thought she thought MP was dumb."

"I did, too," I said leadenly.

"She's been trying to get you and the kids to keep your heads down,"
Wade said. "For your own good. She's right there. But this is a little different."

"It's a lot different," I said.

"Are you mad at Auntie Em?" Zanzibar asked.

"I'm not sure what I feel is mad," I said. "I feel disappointed."

"Are you and Auntie Em going to have a fight?" Zanzibar was a budding
dramatist. She wanted to watch.

"Do you think she's faking?" Wade wondered.

"How should I know?" I said. "If that was an act, she's fucking good
at it."

"I think she's giving her bosses at the radio station what they want,"
Darwin said.

"Hit that nail on the head, kiddo," I said.

"So maybe she doesn't have any choice," Darwin said hopefully.

"Honey, we always have a choice," I said. "She could have talked about
the election. Or the hurricane. She didn't."

"You'll have to decide whether to take her on about this," Wade said,
"or roll with it."

"And you think I should *roll with it*, of course," I said. "The way I'm
supposed to *roll with* every other absurdity that's ruining my life. You're
such a handyman around the house that there's no crack too big to paper
over."

"I didn't say that, and you're being unfair," Wade said. "But she just
staked out a position. I guess she's going to keep recording these things.

So the position is a done deal. Maybe I'm saying you don't have to listen. Or shouldn't listen. If you want to stay friends, that is. Slip in one of your old Pearl Jam CDs instead."

"Pressing my hands over my ears won't change the fact that her editorials are out there, and it won't change the fact of what they say."

"Why don't we talk to her," Darwin said. "We can explain it was way better when we had tests in school. When the students who couldn't follow what the teacher was saying at least *shut up*. When we studied stuff that was hard or interesting—stuff I didn't know already. You could tell her what it's like at VU—"

"I already have, pal," I said.

"But Auntie Em has all this time on the radio to tell people things," Darwin said. "She could use it to convince people that everything should go back to the way it was."

"Uh-huh," I said. "And instead she's doing her small, diligent part in making everything worse."

I didn't subject friends to political purity tests. Least of all Emory, after twenty-five years together of going through divorce from my whole family, college and the repeated heartbreaks of our twenties, more than one abortion (including both of hers), our first desperate efforts to earn a living while pretending to be grown-ups, intrauterine insemination and my three pregnancies. We'd even successfully bridged what for many lifelong duos would have been an uncrossable chasm: one of us having found a hand to hold while the other hadn't. Emory didn't always seem to see the point of Wade, but she'd taken my newly settled status in stride. Having given motherhood a miss herself made it all the more commendable that she made such an effort with my kids and treated them like real people. Too much hung in the balance to allow the fickle winds of factionalism to blow us off course.

That said, I couldn't remember having had a serious real-world disagreement with her before, so this was novel territory for me. I'd always assumed we didn't have conflicts over issues of the day because we shared a set of underlying assumptions about the world and so naturally agreed with each other. Now I'm not so sure. Maybe in different company Emory claimed that fracking was simply marvelous.

As it happened, Hurricane Sandy was then powering up the East Coast, and Voltaire was far enough south in Pennsylvania to be next in line after the predicted landfall in New Jersey. Residents were warned to batten down the hatches, and the whole state was put on red alert. Once the full force of the storm arrived on the night of the twenty-ninth, those of us who lived in the whole southeastern swath of the state were advised to sleep in basements or cellars if possible. The last time we obeyed the same advisory in the run-up to another supposedly monster storm the year before, we'd woken the next morning with sore muscles from sleeping on the floor, only to greet the sun shining and the birds tweeting, dew glistening in the yard; it had barely even rained. But mindful of the carnage at the end of *The Boy Who Cried Wolf,* I tried to take the recommendation seriously. Moreover, Emory's apartment building didn't have nearly enough belowground shelter for its renters, and her flashy modern digs on the twenty-seventh floor had big plate-glass windows with a dubious safety record. Ordinarily, I'd have leaped at an excuse to organize a grown-up sleepover. Yet with the lines of her Loony Tunes editorial fresh in my head—"Human brains are all the same"; "Wisdom is the preserve not of the few but of the multitude"—I extended the invitation to bed down in our basement with unease.

That weekend, I laid in supplies like food and bottled water; most of our neighbors did the same, and many a grocery shelf was bare. I carted a double load of logs from the shed to feed our woodstove. Meanwhile, Wade had more work than he could handle, because homeowners were desperate to trim branches or cut down whole trees that might threaten their property in high winds—which, as my exhausted partner putting in fourteen-hour days pointed out, they'd only had the whole rest of the year to take care of as a matter of course.

That Monday morning, Obama declared a state of emergency for Pennsylvania, which would release federal funds for any cleanup. VU canceled classes. Public schools were shut, which back in the day at least

Darwin and Zanzibar would have found frustrating—they used to like school—but now found a godsend. By about two p.m., the sky had grown dark enough for drivers to turn on their lights. Throughout the afternoon, gusts gathered and rain started to pelt, though I hadn't yet made a distinction between "pelt" and "lash." Zanzibar seemed to find the spectacle hypnotic. When the radio referred repeatedly to "Superstorm Sandy," Darwin corrected with weary scorn, *Post-tropical cyclone.* As he followed the whirls of leaves, skittering litter, and flexing trees through the front window, I overheard my son mutter, "I hope it wrecks everything." Uncertain whether to feel afraid or elated, Lucy raced through the house emitting an all-purpose squeal.

Pushing her timing, Emory showed up well after motorists had been advised to stay off the roads, and by the time I let her in early that evening the rain had indeed graduated from "pelt" to "lash." After a twenty-foot walk from the drive to the side door, her parka and backpack were soaked. She bundled inside with multiple sacks of snacks and a three-liter box of merlot. Her jittery jabber could have been due to the weather, but it felt diversionary.

"I guess it's perverse to hope your roof blows off," she prattled, unbagging her corn chips, dips, trail mix, wheat crackers, Goldfish, carrot sticks, and radioactive cheese puffs. The overkill seemed designed to make up for more than her imposition on our basement. "But, gosh, I hope *somebody's* roof blows off. That last hurricane-in-a-dress was such an anticlimax."

"Maybe Irene was softening us up so we'd let our guard down," I said. I might have said the same of Emory herself.

"Oh, and I brought my own sleeping bag and pillows. I had to go buy a nightgown, because ordinarily"—she wiggled her eyebrows at Darwin—"I never wear a stitch to bed."

I put on some popcorn to keep myself occupied. We'd already had sandwiches for a skeletal dinner, anticipating a dive downstairs at short notice. Outside had started to *hooo!*, while at irregular intervals a gale hit the windows as if some lout were body-slamming the house. Yet paradoxically, so long as the forces of opposition don't breach your defenses, being inside your own home while all hell breaks loose outdoors amplifies a sensation of safety.

Spreading her bounty on the kitchen table, Emory asked Darwin, "So, assuming the whole town isn't flattened tonight, what are you going as for Halloween?"

"A mad scientist," Darwin said.

"Hmm," Emory said, prizing the lid off the bean dip. "Is that a good idea?"

The mad-scientist trope was frowned upon as supremacist, the clichéd white coat and wild hair often compared to the robes and peaked caps of the KKK. *Back to the Future* had disappeared from the late-night listings, along with a trove of 1950s sci-fi classics. Even lighthearted fare like *The Nutty Professor*, whose fat-suited Eddie Murphy hardly glorified the stereotype, had become cinematic traif.

"Some people won't like it," Darwin said warily. "That's the point. So, yeah. For me, it's totally a good idea."

My son had been so beaten down this school year that I was relieved he was showing some spunk. Big on this blasphemous costume, I planned to buy dry ice for his beakers.

"If you get pelted with eggs," Emory said, "don't say I didn't warn you. What about you, Zanzo? Please tell me you won't be traipsing around in a dunce cap."

"I'm going as the color blue," Zanzibar said.

Emory guffawed. "You're such a trip, sweetheart!" She turned to me at the stove as the popcorn's drum solo reached its crescendo. "Where does she get this stuff?"

"Zanzibar thinks, as they say, outside the box," I said. My daughter's trick-or-treating as a color displayed an interesting neutrality. No one would pelt her with eggs. The abstraction was an opt-out.

"And what about you, Lucy?" Emory asked. "What will you dress up as?"

"I'm gonna be a MPC!" Lucy declared, jumping up and down.

"Mental Parity Champion," Darwin reminded us grimly.

"And what does an 'MPC' look like?" Emory asked.

"Big and scary with a giant badge and a notebook!" Lucy said. "And

I'm gonna report Suz-kutch-wun. She thinks she's better than ever-body else, and she's gonna be sorry."

I delivered the popcorn, muttering, "Wouldn't Mao be proud."

"Hey, it looks like Biden has it in the bag," Emory said.

Neither of us had any genuine desire to discuss the next week's presidential election, but we had even less desire to discuss what we really needed to hash out. "Yes, but I wish he'd let up on the stutter. Earlier in his career, he played up having conquered a speech impediment. Now he plays up the speech impediment. I think he's milking it. He sounds like Porky Pig."

"He may be overdoing it," Emory said, "but it's a canny gambit."

"It's unnecessary. The GOP lost this election from go when they nominated Mitt Romney. If nothing else, he's rich. By the dubious logic of the present, that puts him in the top one percent of the IQ distribution."

"That Occupy slogan is so weird," Emory said. "Chanting 'We are the ninety-nine percent!' is tantamount to advertising 'We are the nitwits!'"

I cut a sideways glance at my friend. In allowing herself to say "nitwits," Emory was trying to please. It wasn't like Emory to try to please me, so I inferred that somewhere in that stylishly coiffed head of hers she felt guilty.

"I'm going to miss Obama," I said. "And for the first black president to step down after one term is a bad historical look."

"Nobody gives a crap anymore about his being a black president," Emory said. "He's a know-it-all president. It's death. Even Romney has kept a foot on his own head—little words, *Me, keep you more mun-neee* . . . Obama just keeps spooling out elegantly subordinated sentences with that arch, amused, slightly despairing look on his face. He doesn't get it."

"He doesn't want to get it."

Wade had just come upstairs after fluffing out the sleeping bags for our slumber party. On discovering us pointlessly mired in electoral politics, he performed a strategic intervention. "Hey, Emory," he said. "We all listened to your editorial on the radio."

"Oh, you didn't have to do that!" Emory said. "I'm not sure I've hit my stride yet."

"I don't know," Wade said pleasantly. "Seemed like plenty of stride to me."

"You're too kind," she said.

"No," he said. "No, I'm not."

"Kids," I said. "You want to grab a bag or two of chips and head downstairs to claim your sleeping bags? You could take the iPad and watch that documentary about overfishing."

"No thanks, I'd rather stay up here," Darwin said, as Zanzibar also leaned back to watch the show. "Auntie Em? Did your boss like what you read?"

"It's funny you should ask, Darwin, because the answer is no, not entirely. In fact, I meant to tell you about this, Pearson, because I knew you'd find it hilarious. Or depressing. Apparently my word choice was too highfalutin. Let's see, what got circled in red . . . ? 'Latent,' believe it or not. 'Flagrant.' 'Surreptitious.' Oh, and 'biddable' was totally beyond the pale. Next time I'll just count up the number of letters and find a monosyllabic synonym if I get to more than four."

"But aside from the vocabulary," I said, unable to look her in the eye, "your minders liked the message?"

"Sure," she elided casually. "But Zanzo, you'll love this, because you're such a great performer yourself. I'd thought, *Hey, I'm used to being on the radio, asking people questions? So recording a written-out text should be a cinch.* Surpriiiiiise! I couldn't believe how nervous I got. It went okay at first, but when I tripped over . . . I think it was 'dog whistles,' which was the whole flipping theme! I kept flattening the middle 'S' into sort of a 'th' sound. I sounded like a total retard! And once I started muffing up, the flubs got worse and worse. Recording a six-minute piece took me over an hour! The poor sound technicians were at their wits' end!"

Check: she definitely felt guilty. Using "the R-word" wasn't merely trying to please but was kissing my heathen ass. I looked away at the kitchen window, whistling now, while whooshing, thudding sounds gathered outside. "Maybe what you were tripping over was what your editorial said."

"Okay, okay!" Emory held up her hands, now covered in cheese powder. "I had a feeling you'd give me grief. But this is a great break for me, which I can't believe you'd begrudge me, because I've been waiting to scramble out of that graveyard arts slot for years. If I make a powerful impression, this could pave my route to TV. Which is all I've ever wanted, and you know it."

"*All* you've ever wanted?"

"The main thing."

"I thought maybe you had a point, when we debriefed after your pal Roger's priggish grandstanding," I said, rolling a piece of popcorn in my fingers as if it were fascinating. "About how this MP thing has gone so far and so fast that we can't stop it, and we're better off keeping our mouths shut and waiting it out. Your monologue was different. It was *advocacy*. And now all I hear from you as an excuse—"

"I never said I wanted an excuse—"

"Your only excuse is cynical opportunism." I wasn't shouting. I must have sounded pained, because that's how I felt.

"I'd call it *savvy*."

"I'd call it a sellout." Sometimes Wade surprised me. His tone was mild; the term was not.

"That's awfully harsh from someone who never has to take a stand because he only cuts down trees all day!"

"That's right," Wade said calmly. "I've 'only' cut trees from dawn to dusk for the last five days to keep you and your neighbors from getting clobbered. I didn't choose an occupation that puts me in the way of other people's bullshit. You did."

"I'm just—baffled," I said. "You and I have both despaired of this cognitive justice stuff from the very beginning. And now on the radio you sound just like one of them!"

"Pearson, you're so naive. If I establish my bona fides as one of the MP faithful, I earn the right to take controversial positions on lots of other subjects. Then well down the line, I'll have carved out the credibility to raise the question—delicately, sensitively, and cautiously—of what having eliminated admissions standards, testing, grades, and graduation requirements is doing to the quality of American education. At that point, *maybe* I'll be able to get away with it. I'll have primed the audience to trust me, and to believe I'm not some cerebral supremacist trying to cling to power."

"This isn't the old *working for change from within* routine, is it?" I asked caustically.

"I'm sorry, but I'm starting to feel ganged up on," Emory objected. "I thought it might be fun to ride out Sandy together. I didn't expect an inquisition. I'm feeling a little trapped here. Cornered."

The side door thumped again. Rain volleyed against its windowpanes like flung gravel.

"Under the circumstances," I said, "no, you can't *flounce* from the house right now. But we hardly arranged for a hurricane to torture you at our leisure, like some newfangled form of waterboarding."

"Look," she said. "MP is a fad, a vogue, the way practically everyone thinks now, and there's no telling whether it will blow over or if it's a permanent realignment of reality. Either way, it's not my fault, right? I didn't invent it. So why are you blaming me? I'm simply managing—"

"No, you're turning the situation to your advantage," I said. "You said so yourself."

"Shouldn't someone benefit from this stuff? And if so, why not me?"

"Because you're my friend, and I thought better of you."

"Why is this so personal for you, Pearson? So maybe there's such a thing as variable human intelligence, and maybe there isn't. What does it matter? Most of all, why does it matter between you and me? When we're only talking about positions I take on the radio, about which I don't have a choice?"

"Mom says you always have a choice," Darwin said.

"Your mother is wrong," Emory said. "Why is that stupid editorial a betrayal, Pearson? Of you personally? If I told you I was voting for Mitt Romney, would that be the end of our friendship?"

"Of course not. And no one's talking about ending our friendship."

"Well, good," she said. "Then what are we talking about?"

That's when the lights went out.

"Oh, cool!" Darwin said, as Zanzibar joined in with "Wicked!" and Lucy cried, "Yay!" The kids were always exhilarated by a power failure, although historically what should have excited them was *having* electricity.

Wade and I used our phones to track down candles, matches, and candlesticks. I warned everyone not to open the fridge. With no certainty over whether the outage was for hours or days, I suggested reserving the remaining power in our phones and tablets for urgent matters, which meant, Darwin, no video games. I stoked the woodstove, since in these gales the house was rapidly growing colder. Wade offered to shepherd the kids to the bathroom to brush their teeth and bed them down in the basement, giving Emory and me a chance to speak plainly one-on-one.

When the two of us reconvened at the kitchen table, flickering yellow tapers cast a warm, forgiving glow on the ravaged bean dip. As sirens wailed in the background, I poured us another round of wine. The elements raging outside our fragile refuge underscored that we were all in this together, like it or not.

"I have a nagging feeling I should apologize," I told Emory. "But I'm not sure for what. You know what I think about all this IQuit nonsense, and that's not going to change. What's also not going to change is that this kooky belief system is having catastrophic consequences for the whole country."

"You're always on some crusade—"

"No, I'm not," I said. "I don't join activist groups or attend protests or circulate petitions. I haven't adopted a revolutionary way of looking at the world that I'm intent on imposing on everyone else. Everyone else is imposing their revolution on me. All I've done is refuse to capitulate. I've stayed in the exact same place while the rest of the world has careened off to la-la land."

"I mean you always have to be the maverick. The renegade. The contrarian. I'm obliged to display the same screw-the-lot-of-you pugnacity, then? So we can maintain our old solidarity and bemused disdain for other people? Never mind that my being contrary right now would demolish my professional prospects. Well, I'm sorry, but we can't all be as *brave* and *noble* and *principled* as you are." The adjectives weren't complimentary.

"This has nothing to do with nobility. It's about not being deranged."

"Even if I had the appetite for pushback," Emory said, "I don't have the clout for it."

"Come on, everybody adores you. They always have. If anyone could get away with talking a little sense, you're it."

"Flattering but misguided," she said. "If I go rogue in an editorial, the scripts are prerecorded; no argument for prejudicially promoting 'brainiacs' would ever get on air. I'd just be sacked, and no one I know besides you guys would be remotely sympathetic. All sacrifice, no gain. That dog-whistle piece—it's not going to be the last one. It can't be, since I have to come up with a subject that seems timely and trenchant twice a week. If I avoided MP, it would be conspicuous; I'd seem either cowardly or subversive. So I guess I need some reassurance that every time I broadcast a point of view you find unpalatable you won't fly into a fit. Because this is getting to be a pattern. I behave in a way calculated to protect my interest, and then I'm grilled within an inch of my life about all the terrible defects in my character."

I objected, "I didn't say—"

"You didn't have to. Whether or not you regard my 'joining the enemy' as a personal betrayal—which you obviously do—you think it's weak. Okay, maybe. I'm sorry if I've let you down. But it's not my job to live up to some idea you have of me, when maybe I'm more ordinary than you think. I don't know how you're teaching at VU without making compromises up the ass yourself, and me, I'd never fault you for that. Never. We're both navigating the same precarious landscape. Some weird new ethos hit both our lives out of the blue like an asteroid. But I refuse to allow that sociological bad luck to sink my career. You want to keep faith with the concept of intelligence? Well, not only surviving but *using* this turn of the wheel is intelligent."

I sighed. "Maybe we just have to agree to differ. You obviously think becoming a mouthpiece for what I can't bear is your only viable way forward at the station. All right, I question that. But I never meant to imply that your espousing MP, however insincerely, endangers our friendship. Which is pretty unconditional. We've known each other a long time, and you're"—my voice caught a bit—"incredibly important to me."

Emory reached out and clasped my hand. "Ditto, sister."

Returned from the basement, Wade seemed to appraise his strategy of hothousing the two warring women as a success.

"Still, I for one haven't given up on resistance," I wrapped up. "Like, in my international literature survey course next semester, guess what we're going to read? *Dostoevsky.*"

"You're not," Emory said.

"I am."

"Don't."

"You would say that."

"You would do that! *Don't.*"

"What are you talking about?" Wade asked.

I didn't say.

The upshot appeared to be that, yes, of course we would stay friends, and while clarifying that point was all to the good, as far as I was concerned the very existence of our relationship had never been in question; in fact, Emory's thinking in such absolute terms was a tad ominous. But I had also, it seemed, effectively issued her permission to speak abominations on the radio while promising never to give her a hard time about it. I wasn't quite sure how this amounted to progress. Once Wade and I finished brushing our teeth by candlelight upstairs, he said, "She's not the first person to be ambitious without having any idea ambition-to-do-what."

I spit out my mouthwash. "Ambition without content."

"It's ambition *with* content that's the exception, sport."

"Does your ambition have content?"

"You betcha," he said, picking up the candlestick and kissing the top of my head. "I aim to make stacks of money in the next couple of weeks clearing fallen trees, and then we're going to stockpile enough firewood for fifty years."

Voltaire was a mess, but New York City and the Jersey Shore suffered far worse. The food in the fridge and freezer was already a write-off, so I was strangely disappointed when our power was restored that Friday. Like the kids, I'd relished the camping atmosphere of huddling around the woodstove to cook our improvisational meals; we threaded hot dogs on skewers, toasted marshmallows, boiled the kettle on the cast iron (which took forever), and grilled cheese sandwiches. Most of all, the ban on video games meant I got my son back for a whole four days.

The next week, I tried to keep the family fun going by gathering us all to watch the election returns. But the suspense being nonexistent, the kids filtered off to their devices. It was clear from exit polls that Biden would win handily, an outcome about which I was tepid. Oh, given my upbringing, voting for anyone still gave me a frisson of the forbidden, but what I really wanted was Obama's second term—not because he was black but because he was funny.

The real drama was reserved for mid-December. The public had willingly sympathized with mass killers like Jared Loughner and James Holmes, who had lashed out after having been ridiculed for a subpar intelligence now summarily debunked as a scientific phantasm. But American compassion met a brick wall when the body count included twenty first-graders. So despite the dearth of evidence for this conclusion, commentators decided in unison that the unlikable anorexic weirdo in Sandy Hook, Connecticut, could only have been motivated to massacre twenty-eight people, including himself and his mother, by the prime source of evil nationwide: cerebral supremacy. After all, it was easy to project a warped sense of superiority onto an antisocial misfit whose chronic starvation made his cranium appear disproportionately large. Yet the popped eyes and narrow, elongated face evocative of Edvard Munch also underscored that the shrunken twenty-year-old who might have passed for a first-grader himself was insane. The association between claims to an elevated intellect and murderousness, moral turpitude, psychosis, and child abuse made Adam Lanza the Mental Parity movement's ideal villain. Thus the young man's incomprehensible rampage made isolated holdouts for the old cognitive order seem not only unpleasant and bigoted but dangerous: *See, this is what happens when people no smarter than anyone else are allowed to indulge the "myth of IQ."*

ALT-2013

I wasn't honestly sure why my students still came to class. Maybe they had nothing better to do; maybe they were stuck living at home and needed to get away from their parents. Maybe higher education's ancillary social function had been elevated to its principal purpose, and my classroom was now a Starbucks that didn't require you to buy a caramel cortado to use the restroom. Or maybe these open-admission students were too dumb to have figured out that, if I couldn't fail them and the university was obliged to issue them a diploma regardless of their performance, they could have played *Angry Birds* nonstop for four solid years and still have "earned" a degree.

At my most optimistic, however, I postulated that cultures in a deep sense rarely transform overnight, and the ritual of "going to college" was still planted in a high schooler's expectations of what comes next. Reducing this celebrated sacrament to a bracket of two occasions—a single day of queuing up for enrollment paperwork; an assembly of one's peers all wearing funny square hats with tassels—was too disconcerting, even for freshmen steeped in Mental Parity mumbo jumbo. Revolutionaries appreciate norms, if only as a canvas on which their reforms can be inflicted. Although *Good Will Hunting* and *The Social Network* were now abhorred as hateful hagiographies of brainiacs, most of these kids would have seen those movies before the films were verboten, and they couldn't take part in the same storied rite of passage from which Will Hunting and Mark Zuckerberg emerged if the exercise was abbreviated to farce.

Besides, my students weren't homogeneous. A proportion was going through the scholastic motions, having failed to contrive an alternative tradition of how eighteen-year-olds spend their weekdays. As for the beady-eyed Stasi in the front desks, scanning for the slightest sign that I didn't revere every one of them as a mastermind, this subsection attended for sport—one similar to hare coursing, and I was the hare. But to be fair, a minority wanted to learn something.

Now that we were all equally "wise," what preserved the university (and any school, for that matter) as a productive institution was the ticklish distinction between intelligence and knowledge. While as vessels human minds were all the same size, with identical capacities for the containment of information, pedagogy continued tentatively to defend the concept of ignorance. Across all populations, ignorance was a curable condition, and education was the cure. Ergo, people like me still had jobs.

The intelligence/knowledge divide was robust in theory but fragile in practice. Being an imbecile had been long synonymous with not knowing anything, so before Mental Parity came along, the sets of the pig-thick and the uninformed massively overlapped. Calling someone "ignorant" had never been a neutral charge, and it still wasn't. As a teacher, then, I was in jeopardy if I ever suggested that I was telling my students anything they didn't know already.

Awkwardly, too, exposure to information did not ensure that all our "equal" parties would retain it. Why, I made a note of this phenomenon this very afternoon—if the revelation that I have now been reduced to watching daytime-television reality shows doesn't give away too much of our larger story. Any fat forty-five-year-old in a TV cooking competition who lived in a cosmopolitan city of the twenty-first century and habitually characterized pasta as "aligante" would have been passively exposed to the expression "al dente" hundreds of times. This contestant's repeated use of "aligante" didn't prove a freakish eccentricity, either. The poor woman also had no idea what a "lentil" was and persisted in calling croutons "crouthons," despite being corrected by the program's other participants multiple times. Our specimen wasn't simply ignorant. She was *stupid*. At VU, this was why instructors could no longer give tests or grades. The capacity to learn *is* intelligence. Therefore any variability in our students' response to lessons expressed a differential that couldn't exist.

But then, the cognitive distinction that has come to rivet me more than knowledge vs. intelligence has been subject to less academic scrutiny: the slippery line between intelligence and cunning.

In truth, by 2013 any VU reading list was constrained by a plethora of unspoken restrictions, which in due course would be codified in university guidelines that committed faculty to honoring "our community's core values." Nevertheless, my Introduction to International Literature survey course had a broad enough remit that I should have been able to assign whatever books I liked. The fact that the abundance of my students wouldn't bother to read anything on our reading list should have provided my curriculum greater latitude still. Alas, most of these kids could at least decode an article cum five-letter word on a spine. Thus the protection afforded by their elective relationship to their homework wouldn't extend to a volume whose most incendiary aspect was its title.

Walking onto the campus that signal Monday in late January, I was unnerved by an eerie dissonance that had beset me before. Established in 1906 with Carnegie money, Voltaire University was designed with aesthetics that conveyed solidity, groundedness, and timeless endurance. The administration having resisted the jarring intrusion of modern architecture that marred so many of its sister schools, the neoclassical buildings were coherently of a piece. Constructed with Bellini granite, gray and white with distinctive burgundy flecks, they rose a uniform five stories. Wooden double doors were solid oak, heavy, and tended to stick. Interiors had never been gutted and refurbished, but the consequent hint of shabbiness—the worn marble thresholds, the glassed-in bookcases darkened around the latch, the faded mosaics of the floors—merely enhanced the august impression of generation after generation having humbled themselves in these halls. Rising from well-tended lawns, the deciduous trees had grown thick and towering; they'd been planted before you were born and would long outlive your passing. I'd been entranced by the campus when I was seventeen, one of the shallower reasons I was disappointed when I didn't make the admissions

cut; such a steadying, serene work environment was also one of the shallower reasons I was pleased to be hired here, even as a lowly instructor.

The school's ambience had recently queered, though no pushy donor
had yet imposed some monstrous glass-and-steel library on this island of
venerable repose, the better to get his name on a plaque. (Besides, did
rich benefactors bestow generous financial gifts on universities anymore?
Why would they?) VU's latter-day touch and feel wasn't precisely fake; I
wasn't tempted to duck behind the Science and Engineering building to
check if the facade was flat and propped by two-by-fours like a film set.
The texture of the institution had become not so much fraudulent as ridiculous. Think Vienna, where I spent a week of summer vacation in the
late 1990s. Although Austria is a small, dare I say has-been country whose
only negligible power is heavily diluted through the European Union, its
capital city is incongruously grandiose. Topiary gardens! Fountains! Gaudy
marble statuary astride chariots! Golden eagles on the wing! Vast looming white edifices with wedding-cake ornamentation towering above all
the little people! But with no empire to back it up, the city looks absurd. I
had a gut sense this same atmosphere of blind vanity, unfounded preten-
sion, and transparent self-delusion was also beginning to plague the stately
campuses of Princeton, Columbia, and Harvard. Pretty soon, the entire
educational superstructure of the United States would feel like Vienna.

The class was still shambling in when I arrived, though by now I
knew better than to wait for the students to settle. They would never
settle. I'd had to learn how to persevere through constant chatter; if this
was *To Sir, with Love*, we were stuck at the beginning of the film. I'd also
grown inured to having to compete with their phones. Although this was
a contest I was accustomed to losing, just this afternoon I entertained
the bold notion that for once I might prevail.

"I'd like to announce a revision to your reading list," I launched in.
"This week we were going to start *Crime and Punishment*, but I've got an
even more exciting idea."

Because the students self-sorted, only the small cabal who routinely
sat in the back left was paying attention: three young women, two of
whom were East Asian, along with one misleadingly bland-looking black

fellow named Cameron, whose papers displayed both original thinking and literary flair. Cameron was uniquely burdened by having to conceal the fact that he was far and away the brightest student in the class. Instinctively seeking one another out, these were the marginalized oddballs with educational appetite. In grade school, they'd have been shunned as teachers' pets; the same dynamic now asserted itself in college.

"But Ms. Converse?" It was quaint. Only the pets, whom I tagged in my head the student-students, still raised their hands. With my nod, Jimin, the Korean girl, continued, "I already started *Crime and Punishment*. You know, two hundred pages!"

Oh, wouldn't she have gotten a head start now. It was the Asian students who had the hardest time getting with the MP program. I wouldn't want to overgeneralize, but striving cultures are keen on measurable achievement, and with no clear markers of where they stood on a numerical ladder the Asians were at sea. Their most prevalent coping mechanism was to behave as if nothing had changed, keeping faith that if they continued to exert themselves in the manner that their parents encouraged, someone would finally dig through a dusty desk drawer to bestow what had become, alas, the contemporary Waffen SS insignia: a Phi Beta Kappa key.

"Well, an extra chunk of Dostoevsky under your belt won't do you any harm, now, will it?" I said over the din.

"I didn't mean that by getting ahead in the reading," Jimin qualified hastily, "I think I'm any—better—any better than someone who didn't get ahead in the reading. I didn't have anything else to do, and . . . I just mean I'm the same as everyone else."

These nervous ritual disclaimers slowed classroom discourse to a crawl, but I didn't blame Jimin for her caution. The others were contemptuous of the student-students, and the predatory set in the front would jump all over the goody-goodies for being smartist if they ever seemed to be showing off. To wit, smelling fear, the vultures turned to stare the Korean down.

"I was a bit concerned that Raskolnikov might be open to *misinterpretation*," I said. "The protagonist of *Crime and Punishment* thinks very highly of himself. It's his intellectual arrogance that convinces him he can kill an old woman with an ax, because he's so 'smart' that he's above ordinary moral laws. Now, Dostoevsky clearly doesn't believe this young man is superior. In many ways, Raskolnikov comes across as pathetic. In fact, one opinion writer last month drew a comparison between Raskolnikov and Adam Lanza. Still—it may not be a good idea to study an undisguised cerebral supremacist. Some of you might find passages in which the protagonist flatters himself upsetting. Raskolnikov embraces an *exclusionary intelligence* that would definitely exclude most of you." I was on thin ice.

"And what's that supposed to mean?" asked Lane, a young man with greasy blond hair in a front desk.

"Not a thing." I backed off lightly. It occurred to me then that because the very nature of pedagogy was heretically hierarchical, claiming to be a "professor" or teacher of any sort could soon be, in and of itself, unacceptably brain-vain. Perhaps then I'd just sit in a desk along with what we'd no longer call "students," and I wouldn't need to prepare a lesson plan at all. Why, something to look forward to. "Given that his themes are pertinent to the present, we're still going to read—or some of you are going to read—Dostoevsky. But I've selected a later novel that, among his own works, was the author's favorite. Not that my opinion matters any more than yours, but it's my favorite, too."

I wiped down the whiteboard, previously covered with high-tech tips for composition ("1. Make <u>one</u> point; 2. Say <u>why</u> you think this; 3. Make the same point again, but use <u>different words</u>"). Then I wrote the title of their replacement assignment in stark black marker.

I have to say it worked. I beat the phones. For the first time ever, the class went silent.

In unison, the vultures in front smote their instructor with a look of unbridled hostility. I physically stepped back. At once, I flushed with a backhanded sense of achievement. It was murder to keep from smiling.

"Hey, Converse," said the lout square in the middle of the predators, whose name was Drew. "Aren't you gonna *tell* us the name of the book? Aren't you gonna shout out the name of this book that's supposedly your big favorite?"

"I don't think that's necessary," I said. "It's a short title. And you can read. Or I assume so. We don't have any *processing* issue here, do we?"

Strictly speaking, Drew Patterson was a good-looking young man—symmetrically featured, slender—but he had a pugnacious way of holding his face that detracted from this comely impression. I was never certain whether he was truly dumb or merely lazy; when he was confronted with, say, an unfamiliar word, his instinct wasn't to master but to resent it. He may have been ahead of his time in finding his status as a student inherently humiliating. However well I concealed it, he suspected I was uppity. I'd have said the same of him. That is, Drew was unusually tall, and the vertically blessed often seem to take looking down on people all the time metaphorically to heart.

We detested each other. Ours was an addictive antipathy, too, the kind that entailed an element of relish. Drew never missed a class, the better to catch me out. While I was not nearly as self-destructive as Wade and Emory seemed to think and technically played by the rules, Drew was shrewd enough to discern that underneath his literature instructor's parroting of the era's shibboleths lurked a bad attitude. Yet my subversion was all tone—a dryness, a look in the eye, nothing that could be reported. If I ever put an overt step wrong, Drew Patterson would be gargoyled in the front row to record it. Paradoxically, this same challenging posture in the peanut gallery had been irresistibly seductive fifteen years earlier, so what was the difference? Maybe that Fabrizio wanted to fuck me, and Drew wanted to fuck my career. Not as sexy, somehow.

Though it's since joined the classic canon," I prattled on, "this novel was poorly received when published in Russia in 1869. It was criticized for being badly organized, and it is a bit all over the place, I'm afraid. Keeping track of all those Russian names can be a headache, too. But you're all so identically capable that I'm sure you'll manage."

I provided the class some background on our friend Fyodor's affliction with epilepsy, then apprised them that the novel was now in stock at the campus bookstore, although at no point did the title pass my lips.

I warned them that because, "curiously," the bookstore manager was uncomfortable displaying the books in open view, they would have to ask
for a copy. I pictured my students' squirms of embarrassment in the shop;
what would they do, write the title down? Perhaps with an initial letter
and four underscores, as if playing hangman with the clerk? As a word to
the wise (and weren't all my students terribly wise), I suggested that, to
ensure they weren't *misunderstood*, they might want to keep the paperback concealed in their knapsacks.

Before I left, I wiped down the whiteboard. Once out the door, in the
same paroxysm of insecurity that drove me back to the kitchen to check if
the stove was on after I'd already fastened my seat belt, I returned to the
classroom and vigorously wiped down the whiteboard again. I note this in
my defense. I was not really intending to set my house on fire.

Why did you do it?"

I'd waited until we were getting ready for bed to tell Wade that I was
being hauled before the Dean of Cognitive Equality the next day because,
I'd told myself, I didn't want to worry the children. In truth, I'd just been
delaying this conversation for as long as possible.

"Hard to say," I said. "Mischief?"

"Put down the floss. This is too important for pock-pock-pock." I com-
plied, though this left my hands tied. "So this was a spur-of-the-moment
idea? You were in front of the class and suddenly you were overcome by a
hilarious, quirky little ha-ha."

"Not exactly. I'd thought about it."

"You can't have thought very hard. You just shot yourself in the foot for
no reason. What do you get out of this? Besides trouble?"

"Self-respect? The thrill of the up-yours. Honestly, I was mostly just
having fun."

"That's the reasoning of a twelve-year-old. Though I shouldn't insult
Darwin, who'd never do anything that stupid. As for 'self-respect,' why
would you respect yourself for bringing a shitstorm down on your head?"

I unwound and discarded the floss. Having my hands bound felt too much like being arrested. I sat on the bed. "Once in a while, I have to assert myself, to poke at this stuff. Or else I feel like a zombie whose brain has been taken over by aliens."

"If you're thinking of this crap as some kind of long war," Wade said, "you won't come out on top by handing the other side easy wins. That book is a red flag to the bull. But what does 'come and get me!' accomplish? You're martyring yourself for nothing."

"I have to consider the handful of my students who are very bright, who might have thrived in a university that still had standards, and who are being punished. A teasingly insurrectionary assignment was a signal to them that they shouldn't give up hope. Every now and then, I throw up a flare: we're not all taken with this poppycock, and somewhere, someday, there may be life after Mental Parity."

"There's a place for us . . ." Wade sang caustically.

"I didn't expect to be ratted on."

"Why not? You told me there's a posse in the front of every class that practically sits there in their desks with automatics strapped to their chests. Why give them a target?"

"It's a great book!"

"I'm sorry to get heavy, but you're being irresponsible. Okay, Sandy has been a windfall—"

"Literally," I said.

Wade wasn't amused. "But most of the time, Treehouse, Inc., doesn't pull in nearly enough to support this family. We need your salary to pay the mortgage. So you're going to go into that office tomorrow and grovel. Say you weren't thinking, and you made a terrible mistake. Say you'll never, ever make a mistake like that again. Then promise to publicly apologize to the whole class."

"You want me to abase myself."

"Yes."

Granted, I was already accustomed to culling reading lists of *haram*. Although most universities had yet to specify their literary taboos outright, there was now a consensus in American English departments that Benjy Compson in *The Sound and the Fury* was apt to make many readers feel *uncomfortable*. Faulkner's narrator was a classic specimen of the *intellectually disabled*, or however we were supposed to identify such people, or not identify them, because officially they could no longer exist. (To me, one of the sadder consequences of MP was the inevitable defunding of schooling and independent-living services for a population still known when I was a kid as "special ed." When there was no such thing as specially unsmart, there was also no such thing as a budget dedicated to their support.) Benjy's mother still calls her thirty-three-year-old son "my baby." From the uncomprehending tumult of Benjy's first-person account one can't help but infer a certain failure to register the nature of reality: "my throat made a sound. It made the sound again and I stopped trying to get up, and it made the sound again and I began to cry." Rather than get caught up in awkward discussions of "alternative processing," which, I had to give her this much, Emory had accurately identified as having slid from euphemistic work-around to insult, it was more *graceful* to teach *As I Lay Dying* instead, which had the extra advantage of being shorter.

Doubtless you're ahead of me here: my fellow academics, cowards to a man and woman, had also quietly deemed rather *awkward* the sidekick in *Of Mice and Men*. Similarly impaired, Lennie Small (irony alert; Lennie is massive) likewise emblemized an offensive stereotype, though again it was difficult to parse how you could stereotype a whole class of people who no longer constituted a valid category of any sort. Efforts to rescue the Steinbeck novella from oblivion by pointing out that Lennie is likable, his passion for "soft things" endearing (if implanted with tragedy), his literalization of the trusty aphorism that you always kill the thing you love poignant, well—they went nowhere.

While I never advertised as much to my employers, my literary education was patchy at best, so when *Don Quixote* was shunned for its infamous numpty I was relieved; the novel was one more doorstop classic I'd never read, and I was delighted to get out of plowing through over a thousand pages written in 1605. I was sorrier to see *Flowers for Algernon* go. But the whole notion of a character getting surgery that raised his IQ from 68 to 185 was obviously problematic when IQ itself had been deemed a malignant myth. Funny, the plot had the potential to bulwark the movement's propaganda—when Charlie *perceives himself* as highly intelligent, he grows increasingly miserable and unable to sustain relationships—but the very presence of the adjacent letters "I" and "Q" in uppercase was enough to exile any novel to a library's warehouse.

In line with the movie and television embargoes, not only did the inclusion of lunkheads banish books to college cornfields but so did the presence of know-it-alls. Sherlock Holmes was even more obnoxious in print than Benedict Cumberbatch on-screen. Equally contemptible were fictional creations whose authors deviously ensured they were always right: Agatha Christie's fastidious, psychologically penetrating Hercule Poirot and condescending, degree-laden snoots like Hannibal Lecter (no one cared that he was a serial killer). The chess prodigy in *The Queen's Gambit* was in danger of making students who couldn't win a game of tic-tac-toe feel second-rate. While Victor Frankenstein might have made a poster boy for the pitfalls of intellectual hubris, Mary Shelley was stigmatized by administrative mediocrities who'd only seen those awful films. Hal and Deep Thought consigned *2001: A Space Odyssey* and *The Hitchhiker's Guide to the Galaxy* to literary landfill, though if in a digitally dependent age even a computer couldn't be a smarty-pants, we were seriously in the shithouse.

If I may put on my professorial hat for a moment, memorable protagonists in the classics are often guilty of folly (Raskolnikov's capricious dispatch of a moneylender being a case in point: the murder neither palpably benefits the perpetrator nor even proves his cockamamie theory). But most titans of the Western canon have not conceived of character as dictated primarily by intellect. Distinguishing a member of your cast through sheer brilliance (multiple PhDs are easily furnished with the bash of a few keys) is a cheap character-development shortcut more common to genre fiction like young adult, fantasy, and crime. Thus the lone laudable lesson of MP—that we shouldn't judge others primarily by their intelligence, an accident of birth—was already firmly ensconced in our cultural heritage. Literature aside, too, most Americans have always reserved their harshest judgment for seemingly elective flaws like avarice, selfishness, deceit, and cruelty. Sheer inert stupidity—as opposed to stupid actions, which are another matter—never topped the disapproval charts to begin with. In other words, we didn't need the Mental Parity movement. It was already considered shameful to pick on folks one egg short of a carton who weren't doing you any harm.

When reflecting on all these frowned-upon books, however—and there were many more—I really should have noted the fact that John Kennedy Toole's posthumously published novel made every curriculum's no-no list not so much because of its comically moronic antihero, but solely because of its title. Had I borne in mind the black cloud over *A Confederacy of Dunces* before indulging in my Russki "ha-ha," I might have exercised more restraint.

When the assistant saw me in, it was obvious that the Dean of CE had been granted prestigious office space—unusually large, overheated, and recently redecorated. Or I should say undecorated, because the big room had been purged of personality. The walls were white, with generic samples of abstract impressionism. The glass desk was so clean and uncluttered that you had to wonder what they paid her to do all day (paid her handsomely, too, I wagered). No family pics. The original dark-wood baseboards and cornices had been criminally painted over, which I suppose one couldn't necessarily blame on the office's present tenant. But with one look at Diane Poot, I was sure that she was the kind of person who would have slapped white semigloss over century-old mahogany without thinking twice.

Tastefully made up, Dean Poot might have been attractive for a woman in her forties, but her structured suit was of a washed-out pink drained of any vestige of softness or femininity. Her gear exhibited that cornered, brass-buttoned look of designer collections on grand department stores' top floors, though I'd never understood why anyone would pay so much to look so sexless. I wondered if out of hours she'd rehearsed that emotionless expression in the mirror, because few people could pull off such implacable blankness without practice.

"Gosh," I said, bustling in still wrapped in my scarf and puffer coat; even resting my backpack on the immaculate ivory carpet seemed like vandalism. "It looks as if it might snow! But the forecast—"

"Have a seat, please."

I did as I was told. The padded black leather chair before her desk was of a modern style that flung one backward in a position I associated with getting my teeth cleaned. It lay close to the floor, while Poot was seated much higher and upright. Later I considered how differently this interview might have proceeded had we swapped chairs.

"You're aware there's been a complaint?"

"Yes, I gather one of my Int Lit students took exception to a novel on my reading list." I hadn't taken off my coat, and now I was stuck in it.

"More than one student, Ms. Converse."

"I'm sorry to hear that. But the novel—"

"You were surely aware that the assignment would be perceived as deliberately provocative? This can't be a surprise."

Wade had said the same thing. "I wouldn't call it provocative so much as playful. Besides, college-level courses should *try* to provoke students—to get them to think, to question—"

"Let me put it another way, then," Poot said. "You had to have known that the assignment would upset, offend, insult, and disturb your students.

That it would cast doubt on their instructor's sense of fairness and decency. That it would make them anxious about whether they were being taught by someone with extremist political views."

"I think that may be piling a bit too much baggage on poor Fyodor in 1869."

"The complaint was not about Dostoevsky but about you. I gather you subbed this book in for another at the last minute? Why, Ms. Converse, did you choose that book?"

I had to stop myself from responding spontaneously, *Because I wasn't supposed to.* "It's one of the great classics of Russian literature. And I never once said the title out loud—"

"Why would that make the slightest difference?"

She had a point there. "I guess it wouldn't, much."

"According to one complainant, you've sometimes objected that the only text much of the class ever reads of your assignments is the title."

"Got that right," I muttered.

"And the title is a slur."

I attempted to regroup. "Look, I thought the whole point of the novel would resonate with contemporary sensibilities. All the other characters regard Prince Myshkin as a . . . as someone who's clueless . . ."—I wasn't confident about "clueless"—"who's inferior. But he's actually the wisest character—"

"You regard wisdom as occurring in people to differing degrees?"

"I mean Myshkin is unfairly cast as pitiable. He's good, he's virtuous. His innocence, and his belief in the goodness in others, and his belief in their capacity for redemption, is regarded by others as a sign there's something wrong with him. So he becomes a martyr. You could say this so-called I-word is the ultimate champion of alternative processing." I wasn't confident about "alternative processing" anymore, either.

When Poot just sat there, I carried on. "The same misguidedness is editing out Shakespearian fools. And I'm sorry about saying the F-word, but it's a traditional role in dramaturgy that we still don't have a replacement term for. In *King Lear*, as in so many Shakespeare plays, the, um, the 'fool' is superior to the regal characters, and the fool's jokes are at the ruling class's expense. The fool is the truth teller. It's the very opposite of a pejorative stereotype."

To say Poot's expression during this mini lit-crit lecture was "tolerant" would have been too generous. She wore the look of a television viewer waiting for the advertisements to finish. Meanwhile, I'd managed to get down the zipper of my puffer coat, but I was still sweltering, and I worried my face was sweaty. Sick of being thrust back as if to get my molars polished, I struggled up to perch on the edge of the chair, but that tipped it forward on its chrome skis, and I was in danger of flipping it on top of me.

"Besides," I went on shakily, "is it in the interest of the Mental Parity movement to rewrite the past? For us to appreciate the importance of pursuing cognitive equality, we have to also appreciate how viciously people with perceived mental deficiency have been treated historically, don't we? If we erase all the 'slurs,' we also erase our progress. We need to retain reminders of past wrongs to give ourselves credit for redressing them . . ."

More silence. She must have known as well as I did that the longer I talked, the higher the likelihood that I would hang myself. I shut up.

"You're merely an instructor here, is that correct?" Poot said at last. "You're not tenured, or even on tenure track."

"Well, I'm more interested in roll-up-your-sleeves teaching than in the whole research and publishing thing—"

"And you're aware that this office has considerable powers? That the CE complaints procedure is not mere empty theater to placate whiny students."

"Well, I'd never call them 'whiny'—"

"Yet all I'm hearing is that you're unrepentant."

There we were. Wade might as well have been staring me down. We had three children. We had a wonderful house with a mortgage. VU was the best regarded institution of higher education in the city. If I left its employ under a cloud, I'd have a dastardly time finding a position elsewhere. And no one had forced me to assign that novel. I had done this to myself. Should dire consequences ensue from a childish act of impetuosity, one of the many people who'd have no sympathy for me was me.

No longer fighting the chair, I slid back into my position of submission, though now the feeling was less dental than gynecological.

"No, I'm nothing *but* repentant," I said, hanging my head and clasping my hands piously in my lap. "I deeply regret having selected that assignment. Having had time to think about it, I now realize that the title of the novel alone made the selection needlessly hurtful and inconsiderate of my students' feelings. I've no idea what got into me, but I'd like to assure you that this kind of rash misjudgment isn't like me, not at all, and I will never, ever make a mistake of this magnitude again. I'm more than willing to personally apologize to each of the complainants, as well as to the class as a whole. I'd understand if you conclude I don't deserve it, but I'd welcome a second chance to prove that I'm a *fierce* advocate of Mental Parity, and that I *strongly* believe every single one of my students is every bit the intellectual equal of every other."

I looked up, and for the first time that afternoon Diane Poot displayed a hint of feeling; her eyebrows had lifted a quarter inch in approval. But if her expression meant "Go on," I wasn't sure how much more of this crawling on my belly like a reptile I could keep up.

"I just mean I'm sorry," I wrapped up lamely. "Really, really, really sorry." The impotence of amplifiers ("very," "extremely") and the peculiar manner in which they backfire—making one, for example, seem if anything *less* than especially sorry—was one of the lessons I'd taught in freshman composition.

Dean Poot said she would write up her report and I would be hearing from the administration shortly, though something in her freshly self-satisfied bearing seemed to indicate that the abasement was a success. I remembered to take my scarf and knapsack. My dignity, of course, remained behind.

As a postscript, this was still only 2013. The protocol had yet to be established, but in short order profuse apologies for any perceived violation of MP doctrine would only dig one's grave deeper. Were this same interview conducted a year later, Diane Poot would have encouraged me to blither my regret, shame, and desperation to make amends for at least another ten minutes, after which I'd have been fired on the spot.

The university left me dangling over my employment prospects until nearly the end of the term in late April, believe it or not, before which I shuffled the campus followed by a cloud of opprobrium like Pig-Pen in *Peanuts*. Meanwhile, my colleagues cut me a wide berth. I wasn't invited to departmental meetings (which made me lucky). From this extraordinary delay, I could only infer a degree of sadism. I was never grilled a second time, and I couldn't imagine my Int Lit students were able to provide a lusher version of events when my offense reduced to a single class. Meanwhile, post-Poot, I had announced to those students a reading list reversal. Not only was a certain title potentially "troublesome," but for a survey course, I said, all Dostoevsky novels were simply too prolix—an adjective the vultures were free to look up. They wouldn't.

When the letter finally arrived, it was anything but an exoneration. The Office of Cognitive Equality was declining to pursue the matter further, but the complaints lodged would remain on file. I was put on notice that I could continue to fulfill my duties as an instructor only in a probationary capacity and left in no doubt that I was being watched.

A piss-poor excuse for a party, you would think, but as a backslid Witness I took opportunities for occasions where I could find them. I asked Emory over that weekend to raise a glass to our household's continued solvency. For once she was between suitors and arrived unencumbered by any prissy moral arbiter who might mince from our house in an indignant huff, so she could let her hair down. Since she was currently keeping it pixie-short, she would let her hair down only so far.

I feel self-conscious about the fact that I always seem to describe what Emory Ruth was wearing. I can seldom recall most people's clothing, which, despite the anguish we can devote to sartorial matters, is par for the course. In truth, you can get away with wearing the same gear for days on end and no one will notice. But Emory was the exception to this rule. I can always visualize what she turned up in on a given evening. I don't think she spent an inordinate amount on her wardrobe, but she was good at mixing and matching, so that she never seemed to show up in the same outfit twice. It took me a while to realize that whenever she was on her way over I took an uncharacteristic interest in my own appearance. Was I competing with her? It was subtler than that. I was always battling to be received as an equal. Anyway, if I was competing, I was losing. Should I accessorize to the hilt, she'd appear in a supremely pared-down guise whose simplicity made my getup seem fussy and overplanned; should I go for simplicity myself, she'd overshadow me with flamboyance and my minimalism paled to plainness.

That night, she went for simple: loose mid-calf black trousers that rode low on the hips, a magenta top with a scooped neckline, and one of those ballet-type overblouses, also in black, that tied at the waist. She looked elegant and at her ease. She never seemed to be trying hard.

"Look at you, the employed person!" she said, kissing my cheek. "When you told me during Sandy that you were going to teach you-know-what, I never imagined you'd go through with it."

"Are you admiring or chiding?" I asked.

"A bit of both. Have you learned your lesson?"

"I've come to better appreciate the depths of lunacy into which this country has sunk, if that's what you mean."

"It wasn't. Say, where are the kids?"

They'd commonly have dive-bombed Auntie Em by now. "Lucy's in bed. Darwin and Zanzibar have become . . . more subdued. And conspiratorial. They huddle and whisper together all the time. They used to include me, and now they don't."

Emory shrugged. "Darwin's a teenager."

"Not until next month." I popped out the spout of the wine box. "He vacillates between furious and phlegmatic. I think I prefer the fury. As for Zanzo—have you noticed how this equal-everything-we're-all-the-same is starting to spread? That is, beyond intellect? She tried out for the school's spring play, and we're pretty damned sure that she wasn't cast because she was too good."

"Why would being good matter? If everyone's 'the same'?"

"Talent exposes the lie. So the gifted have to be punished. Suppressed. Shoved in the closet."

Emory accepted her glass of mediocre merlot and eyed me critically. "You shouldn't allow this stuff to eat you up, Pearson. Resentment is a nasty emotion with the half-life of strontium ninety."

"I just came within an inch of losing my job over what was, at worst, a verbal prank. How do you expect me to feel?"

"Relieved. I *thought* we were celebrating."

"Hey, the cops finally captured that joker," Wade said, coming in from the den to grab a beer.

"That *Djokar*," Emory said. "I'm embarrassed to admit I find him rather dishy."

"He looks like a lost puppy," I said. "The pic the FBI dug up could pass for a high school yearbook photo—you know, of a guy all the girls were sweet on but who never noticed he was a heartthrob. He looks so *innocent*. But here's the weird thing. On the news, that Boston Marathon bombing disappeared for days. You'd think an attack on such an iconic event would capture the national imagination. Instead it's been like 'The search for the perpetrators is ongoing'—at the end, as an afterthought."

"The American collective psyche is incapable of thinking about more than one thing at a time," Emory ventured. "Islamic terrorism is so yesterday."

"Totally," I said. "It's not a part of the 'last great civil rights fight.'"

"Lotta trouble to go to," Emory said. "All that planning, investing in those sturdy pressure cookers—only to be ignored. I worry we're hurting their feelings."

"I didn't ignore it," Wade said. "Not just the deaths. Dozens of people's lives will never be the same. Lost legs. Fucked-up faces. If I was them, I'd take exception to it."

We all fear physical injury, but Wade was especially leery of a calamity that could destroy his livelihood. Besides, some people inhabit their bodies more profoundly than others, and Wade was one.

"You know, plenty of other shit is getting squeezed out besides ter-rorism," I said. "Like, whatever happened to the campaign to legalize same-sex marriage? It was going great guns, and now the issue has been dropped cold. Gay marriage is as illegal as it ever was. The only thing that's changed is nobody cares."

"Huh," Emory said. "Guilty as charged. I forgot about that whole thing."

"All that matters is that stupid people can get married," I said.

Emory's predictable comeback—*Fortunately that's always been the case, or the institution would have died out*—was not forthcoming.

I grabbed my wineglass and slung into a kitchen chair. "But talk about tunnel vision? I keep going back to that grilling by Dean Poot. See, what I couldn't determine at the time, and still can't, is whether she believed this hogwash or was just acting as if she believed it. She was definitely wear-ing a mask. That face gave away noo-*thing.* But what was underneath? A completely different face, a different person, who may even have thought that her cross-examination of me was pointless, because there was obviously nothing wrong with a literature instructor assigning a Russian classic? Who maybe even yearned for the return of the days when there was such a thing as stupid, and when being stupid was more than enough to prevent your admission to VU? Or did the face under the mask look exactly like the mask? Like, was she just incredibly good at parroting what she was supposed to, or was she a full-fledged fanatic?" I had begun this reflection genuinely ruminating about Diane Poot, but toward the end my color must have risen, because I could as well have been talking about Emory Ruth.

"We all do what we must to get by," Emory said dryly. "Speaking of which, I have some news myself. Someone in New York has been follow-ing my editorials on WVPA and is favorably impressed. I've been offered a two-hour interview-plus-straight-to-camera slot on cable TV. It's New York One. Not CNN—yet—but a step in the right direction."

"Wow," I said. "You're climbing the greasy pole pretty fast."

"I'm nearly forty-one. I wouldn't call my rise meteoric. Besides, the image of my climbing some 'greasy pole' seems ungenerous. I've waited for this chance since graduating from college."

"Sorry," I backed off. "It's just an expression. I didn't mean anything by it. You're not moving to New York, are you? I'd be heartbroken."

"No, it's not a bad commute, and Voltaire is way cheaper."

"That's a relief. Except . . ." I should have stopped there, but I couldn't help myself. "Maybe I'd be the tiniest bit happier for you if you'd impressed New York One with your boffo hosting of a local arts show, even drawing from a miserable pool of talent."

Taking Wade's advice, I hadn't been listening to Emory's radio editorials, though they made enough of a splash from time to time that I'd overhear faculty members in the department (most of whom weren't speaking to me) mulling over their content—always with a superficial approval whose sincerity was opaque. Apparently aggressive promotion of Mental Parity continued to dominate Emory's content.

"New York One was impressed with the opinion pieces instead," Emory said steadily, "because the opinion pieces are more impressive."

"Maybe . . ." I said. "I wouldn't know."

"You don't listen to them."

"I don't think my listening to them is in the interest of our friendship."

"You're doing that again. Basically threatening me with excommunication. And implying that I'm doing something evil."

Wade shot me a sharp look. He knew full well I was about to fire back, "I think you *are* doing something evil." Instead I strained to be diplomatic. "There's no getting around the fact that you're paying lip service to an ideology I don't support. Is New York One at least halfway balanced? Broadcasting opposing views?"

"I don't think any network is broadcasting opposing views on MP," Emory said. "Even Fox hedges up a storm."

"Maybe that's because Fox is full of folks relieved they can't be called out for being fucking idiots anymore." I'm afraid that in my experience *trying* to keep from getting angry almost never works. It wasn't working.

"Why can't you give it a rest, scout?" Wade implored. "Gotta say, I've never understood why you're so determined to keep fighting your corner on this one. It's a losing battle. It nearly cost you your job. What would you sacrifice by giving in? Just—accept. Everyone's equally smart. Then move on. Get on with your life. Who gives a shit."

"In a way, your constant resistance means the opposition is always winning," Emory chimed in. "What could be a sideline issue, or no issue, is consuming all your energy. It's occupying your time. Meanwhile your private rearguard action is accomplishing jack. You're hooked, and you're stuck. You're not setting your own agenda. Wade is right. Real victory is getting your life back. Capitulate, even if you don't mean it, and voilà: you get to think about something else."

"If you two don't understand why I can't just concede the point, then you don't understand me at all," I said. "Fact: everyone is *not* equally smart. I may pander to the notion at VU to help pay our mortgage. But at least here behind closed doors I refuse to be bullied into embracing a ludicrous paradigm that flies in the face of what I've observed about other people my whole life. What I've observed about myself, too—because you know I've never considered myself all that bright—"

"Pearson, that's just a vanity of yours," Emory said. "It means 'I'm so smart that I know how dumb I am.' Which is no different from 'I'm really, really smart.'"

"You sound like you're writing another of your editorials."

"How would you know?" Emory shot back.

"Look, scout," Wade said, "stop trying to pick a fight with someone who's on your side. You were almost fired. Emory came over here to help you celebrate the fact that, miraculously, you weren't. And you're not answering my question. What's at stake for you? MP or no MP. Why does it matter?"

"Well, if we're going to leave aside how destructive the movement has been to the quality of American education—which matters to *us*, because we have children who are now learning virtually nothing I don't teach them myself, and Darwin is such a natural math whiz that he should be teaching me . . . Well, this pie-in-the-sky egalitarianism doesn't make sense even in the context of our own family. I don't like to bring it up often, because I don't think it's good for your relationship with Darwin and Zanzibar to remind you they're not—"

"I'm well aware I'm not their biological father," Wade said wearily.

"Well, someone else is," I said, "and he may be anonymous, but he had, or has, a genius-level IQ, right? So—and this isn't a 'vanity,' Emory—our two older children are wildly smarter than I am. There's a reason they could converse by two and read by four. They're sponges for information, and you don't have to tell them anything twice. Both those kids have the innate mental agility to rise to the top of whatever field they choose to excel in. That's not proud Mommy talking; it's medical reality. And they deserve the opportunity to achieve their potential, just as their country deserves to benefit from that potential. By contrast, and I know this is awkward, and I don't mean to impugn your genes, Wade, and for that matter they're my genes, too. But Lucy . . . she's not unusually quick to pick up new information and new skills, is she? I mean, she's an adorable little girl, and a bundle of energy, but to get her to remember something new, you have to repeat it, like, fifty times! Which hardly means she's of any less value as a human being, but—"

"You're calling our daughter dumb," Wade said.

"Only in relative terms! Not that it's remotely her fault, and it's only the luck of the draw. In the big picture, she probably occupies the very center of the bell curve, like most people. But yes, in comparison to Darwin and Zanzibar, Lucy is dumb."

That's when a rustle attracted my attention. Maybe the grown-ups' arguing had woken her up, because there was my seven-year-old in the doorway, glaring at her mother with raging hatred.

ALT-2014

Professionally, my "teaching" amounted to no more than speaking pointlessly into a din while babysitting young adults too old to need minding,
but I was still determined to address the educational shortfall in our own
home. Halfway through third grade, Lucy was making no headway on
learning to read. I didn't care if she wasn't interested, or if her school
wasn't interested. I was interested. For all the digital whathaveyou in
which our citizenry was immersed, even online you still had to be able
to tell the difference between F-A-C-E-B-O-O-K and T-W-I-T-T-E-R. No
daughter of mine was going to be raised illiterate.

Yet during our weekend tutoring sessions Lucy had become fiercely
oppositional. No matter how much I sweetened these lessons with
healthy treats and leavened instruction with games, Lucy dug in her
heels, as if every ort of learning she digested despite herself was a point
lost. Clearly, her school was reflecting on a micro level the same aggressive anti-intellectualism that was spreading through every American
sphere. To know anything was to make a claim of superiority in relation
to anyone who didn't know it, and therefore to risk pariah status as a
fathead. Lucy continued to bring home a variety of deformed crafts
projects, but no books.

Besides, I may have given the wrong impression about my youngest.
She was in no way exceptionally slow. If nothing else, she possessed a sly-
ness whose relationship to IQ could be a bit tangential. I suspected that
she was indeed learning to read whether she liked it or not, but that she
applied all that cleverness to hiding her own mastery. She wasn't remotely
stupid, but she was a mastermind at pretending to be. This tussle over
tutoring resembled the often unavailing parental force-feeding of children
who are anorexic. When I refused to release her until she wrote out every

letter of h-o-u-s-e, she'd resentfully comply in the end. But in our next session, she'd go right back to feigning that she couldn't spell the structure we lived in, much as the self-starved who've been bullied into finishing their tiny meals will run to the bathroom to throw up.

I'm not a perfect person, much less a perfect mother. So I sometimes grew short. "You're a phony little brat!" I exploded in February. "We've read this same story over and over, enough times for you to have memorized it, and you probably have! I can understand students who pretend to have studied their lessons when they haven't, but I am dumbfounded why anyone would *fake* being—incapable!" I was trying to watch my language, though I shouldn't have said "dumbfounded," at whose mention Lucy's eyes narrowed to accusatory slits. But this was hardly the way I wanted to spend my own Saturday afternoon. In fairness, much of my frustration was misdirected at my daughter, because I was paying substantial property taxes for this municipality to educate my children, and I wasn't getting my money's worth.

"Now, please," I continued more calmly. "Write out one short sentence for me. Just one. Then we can quit for the day."

Sure enough, Lucy wrote shakily but discernibly in her notebook, "mi mome iz meen."

Well, I told you that Lucy is wily, and she obviously wanted our tutoring sessions to stop. When finally she made her move, she'd bided her time for many months, and the ability to delay gratification—think that classic marshmallow test—is supposedly one of the signs of a high IQ. So when I received a letter from Pennsylvania's Child Protective Services, I had to wonder whether I'd underestimated my younger daughter's intelligence by a good measure.

Emory urged me to take our "home visit" more seriously than I was inclined to at first, because I considered the prospect of a social worker intruding on our stable, middle-class, two-parent home the height of farce. Social workers were for alcoholic single mothers on food stamps whose children got their only hot nourishment through free school meals. Social workers were for the world of juvenile delinquency, intermittent home-lessness, and families with multiple fathers, all of whom were in prison—a world with which I was familiar only via soulful television miniseries. But I inferred from my best friend's outsize alarm that maybe Emory was better positioned to have a finger on the pulse than a cloistered literature instructor, especially now that she was in television journalism and there-fore in the way of those relentlessly unpleasant stories on the news. So when Emory offered to sit in on the meeting as a "character witness," I thought she was being overcautious, but I accepted the offer.

Emory arrived early, looking "nice" rather than sexy, and she immediately marched me into our bedroom to get out of my jeans and sneakers and into a skirt and pumps. "And do yourself a favor," she advised. "Let me do as much of the talking as possible."

Wade had also warned me the night before that our daughter was not the only member of this household who had a problem with being "oppositional," and he'd implored me to be warm, cooperative, and "onside." *Don't talk back,* he'd ordered. *Don't get defensive and don't contradict. Most of all, don't get mad.* I was nonplussed by how no one seemed to trust me to behave like a grown-up.

Because officialdom didn't want to put children "on the spot," the appointment was scheduled for while the kids were in school. My head was crowded with clichés, so when I met this perfectly reasonable, rational-seeming woman in her midtwenties at the door, I was relieved that Sonia Whitehead—herself wearing jeans and sneakers—didn't seem especially strict, suspicious, or judgmental. Still, she was just young enough to have earned her professional qualifications while *the last great civil rights fight* was being waged. At a glance, too, she belonged to that strangely populous category of young women whose symmetrical, proportionate features were all in the right place yet who, for dismayingly subtle aesthetic reasons, didn't qualify as pretty. Perhaps this constituted the very class of females who went into social work.

"It's so good of you to take time out of your busy workday for our family," I gushed, as if she were doing us a favor. "But I assure you whatever this is about, it's clearly a misunderstanding."

"Yes," Sonia said with careful neutrality. "Most of my cases start out as *misunderstandings*." In retrospect, we may have differed on which party didn't get it.

Before I had a chance to introduce my character witness, Sonia had walked into the living room and stuck out her hand. "Good lord, Emory Ruth!" she exclaimed. "I watch your show on YouTube every week!"

I may have turned a blind eye to Emory's broadcasts, but she had mentioned casually that the clips from New York One posted online were racking up hundreds of thousands of hits per episode. Increasingly when we walked together down the street, strangers smiled or waved. Now I better understood why Emory wanted to be present. She was perceived as an MP true believer, and the association would make Wade and me look good.

"I'm only here as a longtime friend of the family," Emory said. "In the hope that I can assure you Lucy is being raised in a caring, support- ive environment. I know better than most how passionately Pearson and Wade cherish every person's special wisdom. But it's always great to meet another fan."

No one wanted tea. I offered to show Sonia around our home, declar- ing gleefully, "No infestations of rats! No black mold! No whole rooms filled to the ceiling with hoarded newspapers and dirty deli containers! No kidnapped neighbors manacled to heating pipes in the basement!" Okay, I was nervous and may have been a little manic. I figured I could jovially corral this woman into seeing our *misunderstanding* as comical. I was staying *onside*. But Emory shot me a rigid shake of the head.

"That won't be necessary," said Sonia. "I'm not here about mold."

"My friend Pearson is just a little anxious, as you would be, too, in her place," Emory explained. "She cares fervently about her daughter and wants nothing more than to allay your concerns. She'd also welcome any professional advice on how to be an *even better* mother."

Wade had promised to take a break from his current job to demon- strate shared involvement in our daughter's welfare, though it didn't help that he arrived ten passive-aggressive minutes late covered head to toe in mulch and sawdust. I could tell from his silent nod and stiff posture when we all sat down that he wasn't going to be much use. This was exactly the kind of encounter with authority that he went out of his way to avoid. He remained perfectly still and quiet as if huddling in a hunting hide, trying not to startle the local fauna.

I nattered on about how Wade and I had been together for over ten years and although we'd never got married that was just a matter of, you know, not ever remembering to get around to it and though he had also never formally adopted Darwin and Zanzibar that was also just inattention or procrastination . . . Sonia waited patiently for me to run out of steam.

"The report from the Mental Parity Champion at Gertrude Stein Primary is quite grave," she said, lifting the file folder in her lap. State and local government agencies were still notoriously dependent on paper documents and even fax machines. "Lucy confided that her own mother called her the D-word."

"Which D-word?" I asked. "There are lots of them."

"You keep lists in your head of slurs that begin with the same letter?"

"No, it's just . . ." I backed off. "There's something about the letter 'D.' It's associated with . . . I guess it's that thudding sound. It's kind of weird."

"All that matters is the word is harsh," Sonia said. "The department has strict guidelines on this point. Use of language of such a derogatory character with minors is classified as child abuse. We take verbal laceration as seriously as we do the physical kind. The scars are less visible but, if anything, longer-lasting. We're especially concerned when parents lash out at a child as young as Lucy. The remark as Lucy recounted it was exceptionally destructive, too, because it depreciated her intelligence in comparison to her supposedly smarter siblings. I can't think of a better formula for crippling a vulnerable child's sense of self, setting siblings against one another, and destroying family cohesion. This episode alone is potentially grounds for removing a child to foster care."

"Hold on here," I said, sitting up. "Who said anything about *removal*?"

"Maybe I can help," Emory intervened. "Ms. Whitehead, I was here during the 'episode' that seems to have sparked this investigation. We three adults were talking among ourselves. Lucy had long before gone to bed, and the other two children were upstairs. Pearson was sharing her concern that because Lucy processed information in a slightly untraditional manner, she was in danger of being persecuted by her classmates as . . . Well, as you noted, Pearson did use the D-word, or"—Emory shot me a confected smile—"*a* D-word. Though honestly? I don't remember her saying *anything* about the older two children in comparison. I'm sure you're highly trained in psychology, so you of all people must know how touchy kids can get about this kind of rivalry. I wouldn't be surprised if a little history between the three of them could have, well, influenced Lucy's recollection. We don't want siblings to compare themselves to one another, but they do.

"Unfortunately, Lucy woke up and came into the kitchen at the tail end of Pearson's expression of concern. Lucy clearly misinterpreted what she only partially overheard. Maybe our mistake was not clarifying at the time that no one, least of all her own mother, was actually aiming that terrible word at this adorable and thoroughly capable little girl. In fact, I blame myself. Instead, we kept chatting, and Wade took Lucy back to bed. We blithely assumed that if she'd gotten in on much of our conversation, she'd probably heard enough to get the context."

"Why was Ms. Converse using the D-word—or *a* D-word—in the first place?" Sonia inquired.

Emory sighed with a practiced theatricality. "Ms. Whitehead, I deal with this issue in the workplace all the time. It's true that to my great personal relief, our peers and, more importantly, our nation's children are no longer casually brutalized by vicious, medically unfounded labels that can permanently devastate their self-esteem. We've all turned a huge social corner. But to be fair? It seems as if we've always thought this way, but by the calendar we didn't come to our senses all that long ago. Older Americans grew up during a time when this kind of coarse, defamatory language was not only commonplace but acceptable. We've all tried to inculcate a more civilized vocabulary. We all appreciate that our old ways of talking about others were terribly hurtful. But after decades of slovenly speech hygiene, those filthy habits die hard. We sometimes slip up. Why, I've caught *myself* calling *myself* one of those words from time to time, in frustration under my breath. You know, 'Oh, Emory, you so-and-so!' In fact, I did a whole editorial on that topic last month, urging everyone to stop insulting their *own* intelligence. In some ways, that's the last frontier. Still, I can assure you that I come to this house all the time. I socialize with this wonderful family and this wonderful couple all the time. They're respectful. They embrace cognitive egalitarianism. The kind of language Lucy overheard that night almost never gets an airing here, and in this case the lapse was only due to anxiety on Lucy's behalf. Such a lapse is very, very rare. If Pearson ever lets a word like that slip out, she immediately apologizes, and she hardly ever has reason to."

"*And* she's sorry now," Wade said, looking at me pointedly. "Right?"

"Yeah, yeah," I said.

"Yeah, yeah *what?*" Wade said.

"Yeah, yeah, I'm sorry now," I said. "I've felt nothing but regret and despair for four solid years."

"But Lucy's version of the verbal climate in this household isn't 're-spectful' or 'egalitarian,'" Sonia said. "Lucy told the MPC a string of colorful invective that she hears, it would seem, constantly in the home. Reading the report made me blush."

"Might little girls sometimes exaggerate?" Emory proposed. "Unfortunately, these expressions haven't been expunged from the schoolyard. When you suppress hate, it often goes underground and then squirts back up like crude oil. Lucy could have learned those words any number of places."

"Are you calling Lucy a liar?" Sonia asked.

"Lucy can be—a bit of an imp." Emory's word choice was judicious. "Imp" was laced with affection.

Doubtless thrilled to be engaging with a television personality, Sonia turned to address me, the real subject of the state's concern, with reluctance. "Ms. Converse, I'm afraid there's more damning testimony in this report. The MPC infers from Lucy's stories of what you call 'tutorials' that you're 'browbeating' your little girl on weekends with information you're intent on shoving down the poor girl's throat; also, that you berate your daughter when she doesn't process this information in exactly the fashion you require. Lucy claims to be kept captive for hours on end, never allowed anything to eat or even to go to the bathroom, and she says she's released only when she reproduces information in a form that's to your satisfaction—often through her tears."

"Lucy is embellishing somewhat," I said. "Our tutorials sometimes last up to *one* hour. I provide snacks. Lucy is free to go to the bathroom whenever she needs to. I'm teaching my daughter to read. Does the state now regard that as child abuse, too?"

"If this private obsession of yours is pursued in the manner Lucy describes? Yes. We at CPS are worried that your parenting is too rigid, and you're not allowing your daughter to be wise in her own way."

"I'm not allowing her to be ignorant in her own way, that's for sure," I said.

"What Pearson means," Wade intruded again, "is she promises to quit the tutoring."

I turned to my partner in incredulity. "Excuse me?"

"*Isn't* that what you meant?" Wade pressed, staring me down. "That you're going to *totally* give up on teaching Lucy *anything*. So she'll be free to be *wise in her own way*."

I harrumphed back in my chair. "*Seriously?*"

"Maybe Wade has a point," Emory said delicately. "The extracurricular sessions . . . don't seem to be going that well. Maybe giving them a rest would be . . . prudent. And it might improve your relationship with Lucy. You could spend the time instead . . . baking. Make some cookies."

"Emory, even *baking* would entail *teaching* her to measure a cup of flour," I said.

"Then let her measure flour in *her own way*," Emory pleaded.

"So I'm supposed to raise a wild animal," I muttered.

"What did you say?" Sonia asked.

"Pearson said, 'So I'm supposed to raise a wise antelope,'" Emory clarified. "Lucy is always leaping and cavorting. Gracefully. Like an antelope."

Sonia looked at us back and forth mistrustfully, then turned to formally address me and Wade. "There's more than enough evidence in this report to justify placing Lucy in a more nurturing environment. But I'm heartened by wholesome social influences here. Lucy's lucky to enjoy the counsel of an opinion former like Emory Ruth, who's widely admired as a moral beacon. So I guess for now, I'm going to recommend a wait-and-see approach. Ms. Converse, per standard practice, you'll be required to complete a course in Cerebral Acceptance and Semantic Sensitivity—at your own expense. I'd also agree with you, Mr. Haavik, that these weekend browbeatings have to stop. And I should warn you both that this case isn't closed. If Lucy or, for that matter, anyone else reports additional red flags, foster care wouldn't be only one option. It would probably be the preferred option."

We saw her out. Wade waited a cautious beat before announcing, "Well, dodged that bullet. For now." He touched my arm. "And no thanks to you."

"I'm supposed to apologize for maintaining even a modicum of self-respect?"

"You bet," Wade said. "In that situation? They're threatening to take one of our fucking kids away? We can't afford your self-respect."

"Wade's right, I'm afraid," Emory said. "The name of that game was contrition. At which you don't exactly shine, Pearson, my dear."

"I thought I exercised admirable self-control!" I protested.

"In that case, I'd hate to see you lose it," Wade said.

After we debriefed with a pot of coffee, I said goodbye to Emory on the front porch. "You've been rescuing me since I was sixteen!" I exclaimed, clutching her in a bear hug. "Thank you, thank you. I'd never have come out of that interrogation with all three of our children without your help. And I thought you were weak on foreign languages. Thank God it turns out you speak fluent horseshit."

Wade remained behind a few minutes after Emory left, and it was jarring to find being in the same room with a man I'd lived with for a decade so cut-it-with-a-knife uncomfortable. I was too grateful for the coffee dishes to clear off, but Wade said sternly, "*Leave* them." For once, Mr. Avoidance wasn't eager for distraction.

"This isn't just offending a dinner guest or assigning a book that'll ram a cattle prod up your students' asses," he said. "This is on a whole other level."

"Look, I know, I know, I don't need a lecture—"

"I'm not sure you do know."

I sheltered behind a hand at the side of my face, so that Wade wouldn't see if I started to cry. "This may be all my fault, but please don't blame me. Not right now. I can't bear it. If only we were living in a sane world, this would never—"

"Sane or not, it's the only world we've got." He wasn't softening. "There aren't many things you might do that I couldn't forgive you for, but if Lucy—"

"Are you threatening me?"

"It's not a threat but a fact. The way things are. What's also a fact is from now on you're going to be perfect. And not in your terms. In theirs."

Wade returned stiffly to his tree-removal job. Once Lucy got off the bus, I let her tear around the house to exhaust herself before finally luring her to the kitchen table with a glass of root beer and a plate of Fig Newtons. I didn't allow the kids much sugar, and I worried too late that the snack might appear a reward for the last behavior I sought to reinforce. I felt strangely leery of my own daughter, fussing over fetching her a napkin by way of putting off our little talk. It was dawning on me that our family was now hostage to the caprices of an eight-year-old, as if we were trapped in a harrowing episode of *The Twilight Zone*.

"Lucy?" I pulled up a chair while she stuffed her face with a cookie. "Did you know that a lady came by today to talk to us about you? The lady was afraid you might feel sad or hurt."

"My MPC said they'd make you be nice to me," Lucy said through the crumbs.

"You don't think we're nice to you?"

"*You're* not."

Lucy had an adversarial relationship with her mother because I was the only person in her life who made her do anything she didn't want to. "It's true that our story times are sometimes hard. But later, I think you'll be really glad that you can read signs, and web pages, and even whole books, instead of only seeing a bunch of lines and circles that don't make any sense. It doesn't always feel that way, but I am being nice to you, Lucy. Almost nicer than anybody."

"My MPC said I won't have tuna-royals anymore. She said they were brown beatings."

"Well, we don't have to keep having lessons on weekends if you don't want to. But you may be sorry later. It's much easier to learn to read when you're little than when you get older."

"I'm not that little."

"Yes, I'm starting to appreciate you're a lot more grown up than I thought," I said. "But here's the thing. You might not realize that when you complain to your MPC, it can get very serious. Do you like living here? Do you like living with me and Daddy and your brother and sister?"

"Darwin and Zanzbar think they're better than me."

"Come on. They're just older. When you get bigger, you'll catch up with them." (No, she wouldn't.) "But answer me. Do you want to stay in our house?"

Lucy may have had her problems with me, but she was ferociously attached to her father, whose ankle she loved to wrap herself around while he walked her across the room. "I guess," Lucy said reluctantly.

"Then it's probably better if you don't tell your MPC there's anything wrong. If you're unhappy about anything, then you should come straight to me or Daddy. Because I don't want to scare you, but the lady who came today can take you away from us."

"I know," Lucy said blithely, grabbing another Newton.

I was *extremely* surprised that the authorities would have shared with a child herself any talk about "removal," which seemed emotionally cavalier. Such institutional sloppiness indicated a level of casualness possible only if children were now plucked from their homes because of what Emory called poor "speech hygiene" all the time.

"If they did take you away," I said, "we'd all be very sad. I think you'd be sad. Someday I'll tell you about it, but I got separated from my family when I was a teenager, and it definitely made me sad." Sad enough that even at forty-two I seldom allowed myself to think about it.

Lucy wasn't interested in my sob story. Besides, she seemed intent on reestablishing who was in control here. "You say tons of wrong words. S-words and I-words and D-words and 'IQ.' My MPC said that means you're a hate person. She said I should tell her whenever you say wrong words. And then you'll get in trouble."

When Wade came home and could keep an eye on Lucy, I slipped up-stairs to knock on Darwin's door, behind which he and his sister were conferring in the usual hushed tones. Standing in the doorway—heaven forbid my own children would invite me in—I laid out the situation, trying not to alarm them but being somber enough that they'd take seri-ously what was at stake.

"Ever consider," Darwin said after I'd described Sonia Whitehead's visit, "that maybe you should *let* them put Lucy in foster care?"

"Darwin, that's a terrible thing to say!" I exclaimed. "She's your sister!"

"Half sister," Darwin said. "And she feels more like a quarter sister. Or a not sister."

"Lucy spies on us," Zanzibar said.

"Well, maybe if you weren't so secretive," I said, "she wouldn't have to. She can't help the fact that she's still a little girl. When you get older, take it from me: you'll be grateful to have another sibling you're in touch with and get on with."

"Gosh, I can hardly wait." Darwin was developing a sour side I didn't care for. "Kids like Lucy don't change."

"Your younger sister has been surrounded by this Mental Parity twaddle from kindergarten," I said. "She doesn't know any other way of thinking, and she has no reason to imagine there's anything dubious or malign in what she's taught. It's not her fault. I try to expose her to a more traditional perspective, but nothing I say will drown out the chorus of the whole world."

"She's a type," Zanzibar said. "It's bad enough there're so many of them at school without coming home to another snitch."

"I'm afraid that's related to the main point I wanted to underscore with you two," I said, keeping my voice down. "Because we're all going to have to watch the mouth. Even at home, okay? That goes for me and your dad, too. No 'stupid this' or 'dopey that.' Only say in the house what you'd be comfortable saying in public. If it gets back to the authorities that we make 'hateful' and 'bigoted' remarks at home, they could snatch your sister from this house in a matter of days."

At a singsong behind me in the hallway—"Uh-*uuuh!*"—I jumped. Lucy was indeed getting good at creeping up on people. "Not only *me*-ee!"

"What are you talking about?" I snapped.

Lucy announced with satisfaction, "My MPC says they can send Darwin and Zanzbar to forest care, too."

CHAPTER 2

At $569 a pop—there was money in reeducation—the six-week class in Cerebral Acceptance and Semantic Sensitivity that social services forced me to take was certainly edifying. True, we began with elementary no-no's like "not the full deck," "D-word as a sack of hammers," or "two sandwiches short of a picnic," whose insulting lightheartedness belied the lasting injury their casual deployment would occasion. As I didn't need to be told that you weren't supposed to call people stupid anymore, I figured I could get through this indoctrination in the same way I'd survived public school: with a book in my lap.

Yet we moved rapidly on to less obvious prohibitions. "Dumb" was out even as a synonym for mute. Forget being "dumbstruck"; our earnest young instructor, a skinny, fragile character named Timmy Muswell, commended the lackluster substitute "surprised." A "dumbwaiter" could seem to allude to a "dumb waiter" and cause gross offense in the hospitality industry. Since an appealing alternative to zoning out with my heavily thumbed Evelyn Waugh novels was playing the innocent pain in the neck, I raised my hand.

"Excuse me, but if our older house happens to have one, what are we supposed to call a D-word-waiter, then?"

"You could call it . . ."—Timmy punched at his phone—"a small elevator used for conveying food and dishes or small goods from one story of a building to another."

"In that case," I said, "it might be more efficient to have the mechanism taken out."

The class tittered. The instructor was not amused. He was never amused.

We had also to protect the feelings of the inanimate. Thus automotive safety could no longer rely on "crash-test dummies" (Spotify had long before expunged the eponymous band); a fiberglass clothing model was respectfully dubbed a "mannequin." "Dumbbells" were "weights." Although by now we'd all gotten the message that calling someone "thick" was hate speech, we might be underaware that a piece of wood could no longer be thick, either; at a lumberyard, we should ask for a board "two inches fat."

As a person could not be "dense," neither could text or fog. As a person could not be "simple," neither could an arithmetic problem; we should prefer "easy," which I was obliged to observe did not mean the same thing—but Timmy moved rapidly on, because any reference to degrees of mental difficulty made him anxious. "Deep" could unfairly distinguish the profound, so the "deep end" of a swimming pool might more cautiously be identified as "the part with a lot more water in it." "Slow" was loaded; best describe an application process, say, as "gradual" or "drawn out," while a car up ahead keeping your progress to a crawl was "proceeding at a reduced speed." A waltz was not "slow" but "sluggish," a word that hardly made me want to hit the dance floor. Rather than risk bruising egos with "backward," it was prudent to walk "in reverse." Needless to say, heroin users were no longer "dope fiends," although if you were an opioid addict, surely having your perspicacity traduced was the least of your problems. "Getting the dope on" people should be rephrased "getting the intelligence on" them, and here Timmy grew flustered, because any allusion to intelligence was starting to feel risqué. "Or intel," he revised. On realizing this was merely shorthand for a quality that *we all enjoy in equal measure*, he recommended "doing background research on someone" instead.

If people could no longer be "dim," then neither could lousy lighting; darkened rooms were "poorly illuminated." The "dimmer switch" was now the "knob that raises or lowers brightness"—though once again Timmy kicked himself, because "bright" was also forbidden, so he amended hastily, "Or maybe the 'knob that raises or lowers how seeable everything is.'" As a purportedly "brilliant professor" was no quicker on the uptake than anyone else, so also a "brilliant sunset" was better described as "red." Oh, sorry; Timmy never would have said "quicker on the uptake" unless reminding us that the tribute was scandalous. "Quick" alone was out; a safer adjective was "fast."

"Does that mean," I interjected, "the King James Bible now has to be retranslated as 'the fast and the dead'?"

He ignored me.

Our instructor stressed that compliments in the workplace like "you're looking smart today" or "that's a smart outfit" could get us sacked. Commending a gesture as "thoughtful" risked implying that some folks cogitated more than others, so we were on more solid ground with "considerate" or "indicative of having paid attention to what I might like." Which prompted Timmy to add that because the notion that anyone might possess "gifts" that others didn't was objectionable, he recommended that at Christmas we gave one another only "presents."

Considering that "grasp" could convey mastery some people lacked, we should instead "grip" or "seize" our coffee mugs. "Command" could also mean an unjustifiable sense of intellectual dominion, so in a position of authority we should issue an "edict" or "direction." Admiring classifications such as "savvy," "scholarly," and "erudite" couldn't help but imply the existence of benighted characters who exhibited none of these qualities, so if we were hell-bent on acclaiming colleagues, we should keep to wholesome, simple—sorry, *uncomplicated*—compliments such as "I like you" or "That is good." Alas, avoidance of "piercing," often applied to the smarty-pants and the fruit of his or her overrated labors (a "piercing analysis"), also stymied mention of how fashionable young people decorated their bodies with loops and studs. "Hole in the nipple" would have to suffice. We couldn't use the word "bovine" even in relation to cows.

Our most salubrious unit was Cognitive Equality in the Kitchen. "Meatball" being a slur, subs with marinara sauce should contain "orbs of ground beef and veal." "Turkey" was defamatory, so every Thanksgiving we were meant to acquire a "domesticated gallinaceous bird"—and good luck to us, because even Timmy couldn't remember "gallinaceous" without checking his notes. We could no longer flavor the stuffing with "sage," either; if we insisted on adding the conceited herb, "poultry seasoning with furry leaves" would identify the plant for most people. Because the word was synonymous with dunderheads—not that Timmy put it that way—

best not say that a sauce had "lumps." A carelessly prepared blancmange had "bumps."

No one could have "chops" in the slang sense anymore, so we could only sauté "pork pieces." As "weiner" was a term of abuse, the ballpark staple was exclusively a "hot dog." "Gooseberry fool" was off the menu. Back in the day, "spud" doubled for "thicko," so hereon in we could only bake potatoes. Apropos of previous lessons, a *deep*-dish pizza was now a "tall-dish pizza," while *quick* breads were "hasty breads."

We were treated to an overview of recent culinary history. When Nestlé sought to cover its corporate backside by rebranding its powdered drink mix Nestlé Swift, self-deputized police on social media called the company to account, because "swift" could also mean mentally adroit; hence the hurried re-rebranding, Nestlé Rapid. Hostess had long before scrambled to remove its filled chocolate cakes called Ding Dongs from the shelves of every American supermarket. Trying to leaven our session with fascinating anecdotes from abroad, Timmy explained that the candy comparable to M&M's in the UK had also faced a trademark dilemma, because by 2012 the sweets were subject to an indignant nationwide boycott. When the tweaking of "Smarties" to "Smardies" was widely ridiculed, the subsidiary slunk out of business.

Dullness being associated with all those other unmentionable D-words, we should designate crummy knives as "not cutting well," though "lacking an edge" could be misinterpreted as lacking acumen. In kind, the existence of exceptionally "sharp" people had been exposed as fallacious, so efficacious blades and cooking shears should probably be described as . . . Well, we couldn't say "keen," which also meant astute, so maybe "good at slicing or snipping" or "capable of hurting your finger." Given the impropriety of the tags "sharp cookie" and "clever cookie," Timmy said it might be judicious to avoid "cookies" altogether. Perhaps we could opt for a touch of the cosmopolitan and, like the British, call them "biscuits."

When the class first convened, it had the atmosphere of high school detention. Bad boys who'd all sinned against MP dogma, we exhibited the smirking, slouching collusion of mutinous teenagers. Early on, a few of us would get a drink after our struggle sessions to share tales of what terrible line we'd crossed to land us in the class and to hoot over Timmy's latest lexical embargo. But the insubordinate ambience didn't last. Most of us were too terrified of putting a step wrong. I wasn't the only one whose custody of children hung in the balance, and given those stakes—I'm sorry if this comes to fellow travelers as a disappointment—I myself put a firm lid on the snark in class after the first day or two. Why, by apply-ing the same discipline I mustered at fifteen when marching through the rituals of my family's faith like a robot, I soon passed for a brown-nosing pleaser eager to master the vernacular of esteem and inclusion. Besides, even the subversive contingent got caught up in the game, competing over who could come up with contraband our instructor had missed.

"Hey, Timmy," a classmate might pipe up with enthusiasm. "If you can't be a 'whiz kid' anymore, you shouldn't be able to *take* a whiz, either, right? Like, you should only take a *leak*."

Or I remember one woman contributing in a spirit of excited dis-covery, "It seems to me that to claim someone is 'reflective' necessarily implies that other people aren't reflective—that is, some people don't think hard about things and don't contemplate the world with nuance and subtlety."

"That's right," Timmy concurred. "Any elevation of one person's in-tellectual powers is necessarily a derogation of someone else's. If there's no implied comparison—a pejorative comparison—the compliment is meaningless."

"But my point is," the woman followed up, "if you can't have reflective people, can you have reflective tape?"

There was another fellow who'd seemed pretty hip at first—sarcastic, prone to underbreath remarks at Timmy's expense—but who by the fourth week raised his hand to say, "Excuse my language, but folks in my office used to toss off 'That guy is a complete tool.' There's a touch of 'asshole' about 'tool,' but it definitely impugns intelligence. So what about 'tool' as in 'screwdriver'? Should we say 'implement'?"

"The *implement shed*?" I said skeptically.

"Why not?" he shot back.

"It sounds—" I caught myself just in time. The fact that I came so close to unthinkingly using a certain word aloud made me feel a little sick. "It sounds odd," I finished lamely, and kept my mouth shut for the rest of the hour.

I took a few half-hearted notes, if only to remember to tell Wade and Emory choice absurdities later, although our household's raucous, wine-fueled evenings of full-throated mockery were consigned to the past. I had to content myself with whispered confidences at bedtime and despairing snippets shared with my best friend over coffee on the rare occasions she could spare an hour (Emory was spending more time in New York). Sonia Whitehead had put quite the damper on our once spirited, irreverent home life. Or I preferred to blame Sonia, though the more immediate buzzkiller was our youngest child. Lucy was hyper-alert to any slip of the tongue, like an offhand dismissal of a sitcom as "dopey." As we'd yet to give our youngest a computer, tablet, or phone, a hankering to record these careless missteps, the better to report them during Sonia's regular "home checks," may have explained a slight uptick in Lucy's interest in finally learning to write by hand.

But unless Timmy's taboos were entertaining, there was no point in committing his lectures to memory. No final exam would measure how well we'd internalized all this "semantic sensitivity," because the Mental Parity movement didn't believe in exams. Even if we did take a test, we would all have to pass. Any difference between our performances would ipso facto display merely a difference in *processing*—that is, the variable presenting behaviors that disguised our incredible sameness. So they didn't bother. Propped in those community-center desks with my mind wandering gave me a taste of what it must have been like for my students to dream away my own classes. It was discouraging.

Being on our best behavior even *en famille* was especially hard on Darwin and Zanzibar, for whom domestic derision of the doctrine that dominated our lives elsewhere had provided a vital release valve. Rather than self-sanitize their stories at the dinner table, they clammed up.

Those two kids seemed to speak exclusively to each other, which seemed unhealthy. Although it's a jarring descriptor for siblings, I'd characterize their dealings with Lucy as "courteous." As for Lucy herself, she had acquired an air of superiority that neither her age nor her talents would seem to justify. She tended to brisk around the house, chin raised at an officious tilt, as if conducting an inspection. The impulse may have been unconscious, but I tended to give her second helpings of anything at a meal that was prized or in short supply. She got plenty more after-school root beer, and the latest iPad was already slated for her ninth birthday in July.

CHAPTER 3

To my embarrassment, here I am relating picayune points of philological fascism—the death of the "dumbbell"—while, out in the rest of the world, events of more considerable moment were afoot. But then, the same myopia governed the country at large. Prioritizing the minutiae of Timmy Muswell's hectoring vocabulary lessons over two conflicts both capable of starting World War III makes me typical of my time.

I do have to stop and note an inconsistency in the whole Mental Parity package that bears on these world events. On the one hand, there is no such thing as greater or lesser human intelligence; on the other, we must champion the rights of nitwits. How can you champion a class of people that doesn't exist? Zealots used the word "perceived" a lot, the better to disguise this contradiction, but in practice the grand American project well under way by 2014 wasn't the total obliteration of categories of intelligence originally envisaged by Carswell Dreyfus-Boxford but the aggressive elevation of stupid people.

Granted, Mensa had been banned as the kind of cerebral-supremacist organization that the FBI now asserted was the greatest threat to American civic order. (It was said that small pockets of brain-vain holdouts from that unashamedly bigoted membership were holed up in the mountains of Colorado and New Hampshire. The fiery standoff between armed Mensa members and federal agents outside Boulder got plenty of play, though one brave *Rolling Stone* journalist assembled convincing evidence that it was staged.) Spelling bees had been banned, too, as more child abuse (presumably, deep inside our heads we were all perfect spellers, but for some of us the right letters just had trouble getting out). Yet rather than discontinue the MacArthur "Genius Grants," whose administrators you'd think would have been falling all over themselves to apologize for their complicity in past discrimination, the foundation instead began to award $625,000 over five years to the dumbest candidates it could find. The Rhodes Scholarships followed suit, and I doubt they had much trouble finding fittingly unqualified students—or qualified students, since being unqualified was the leading qualification for free tuition at Oxford. True, the U.S. and other "civilized" countries eventually pulled out of the international chess circuit en masse, because the Evil Empire continued to field proper prodigies, which was seen as cheating. But before withdrawing altogether, America instead sent whole teams to tournaments who weren't only bad chess players; they weren't chess players. They didn't know the rules of the game. Seen through the latest looking glass, sending cocky representatives of the nation who already knew how to play would have been unseemly.

I'm citing this trend because it was politically germane. When Joe Biden appointed his staff and cabinet, he didn't merely turn a blind eye to how bright these people were; he went out of his way to find a candidate for the Secretary of the Treasury who was an imbecile. And not only an imbecile but an imbecile who was recognizably an imbecile—someone whose speech and affect were conspicuously vacuous. It was proudly shouted from the rafters by a fawning media and Biden's own press secretary that the president was purposefully seeking out the "historically marginalized," i.e., stupid people.

The same template was adopted at the Defense Department. The Joint Chiefs weren't simply mixing up the ranks like a salad; ignoring the lesson of their botched assassination attempt on Osama bin Laden, who remained at liberty, they were frantically promoting the most witless privates in the army to captain, colonel, and lieutenant general. Americans were still beside themselves about the "scandal" of their military having until 2011 administered an IQ test called the Armed Services Vocational Aptitude Battery to all prospective recruits; before the ASVAB was theatrically disavowed, the U.S. military had not inducted any soldiers with a score below 85. The Senate hearings had been dragging on for years, though their conclusions were foregone: for that test ever having been administered, heads would roll.

The Biden administration's forceful promotion of civil servants *per-*

ceived to be thick as two planks came with an unpleasant corollary. Smart people—and it's funny how you can often recognize them at a glance; it's something in the eyes, a subtly alert set to the facial muscles, as much a matter of what people don't say as what they do—were demoted, quietly sacked, or never considered for positions in the first place. Were I to quantify the rule of thumb, I'd estimate that anyone with an IQ of about 95 or below could write his or her own ticket; anyone with an IQ above around 115 didn't have a prayer. To detect this pattern from abroad, world leaders in competing geopolitical spheres of influence wouldn't have needed a network of spies, either. An internet connection would have done, and perhaps readily affordable digital subscriptions to two or three mainstream American newspapers.

Starting with Crimea, in the spring of 2014 Vladimir Putin's Russian army proceeded to annex the entire country of Ukraine. As the U.S. Defense Department was consumed with cleansing its ranks of "smart rage," no one had thought to train or equip Ukrainian troops beforehand, so the once sovereign country's poorly prepared and undersupplied army offered little resistance. Russian forces promptly rolled on to take over Moldova. Though there was some speculation that Georgia, the Baltics, and possibly even Poland now topped Putin's to-do list, these forecasts were limited to cramped 650-word egghead op-eds that no one read.

So little did this invasion occupy the national conversation that I couldn't remember without looking it up just now whether Putin's army crossed into Estonia before or after China invaded Taiwan (it was after, not that you care). I sensed Beijing's naval invasion got pretty scrappy, though it didn't take long for the CCP to choke the flow of information from Taipei, and stories about "The Second Chinese Civil War" nearly dried up—though the few accounts that did get out were horrific. In the end, of course, China not only occupied the island, installed its puppet regime, and imprisoned or executed "collaborators" with the renegade province's illegitimate government, but also gained near-total control of the international microchip industry. After this dazzling display of military might, Japan, Vietnam, Malaysia, and the Philippines all shut up about the South China Sea and let the Chinese have it.

I don't mean to claim that these tectonic shifts in the international balance of power were completely ignored in the American press, but the criticism leveled at both autocracies was concentrated on their rampant violations of human rights. Universities, government departments, and companies in both Russia and China openly pursued unambiguously smartist policies, shamelessly rewarding those with perceived higher intelligence, while preventing the allegedly less proficient from occupying positions of authority and consigning them to menial jobs. I recall many a grim insider exposé about schools in Moscow and Beijing, where students still had to sit cruel, exhausting exams, and the *otherwise* were made examples of. I just don't remember reading much about the Ukrainians, Moldovans, Estonians, and Taiwanese who were murdered, raped, blown up, burned to cinders in their apartment blocks, or buried alive.

Nor did I encounter any analysis in the mainstream media daring to point out that both China and Russia had been emboldened to confiscate vast swaths of new territory because the Western world was wholly caught up in this Mental Parity fiasco and had made itself ridiculous. It was obvious from abroad that all we cared about was dummies not getting their feelings hurt. Meanwhile, Biden and the other leaders of the G7 did a certain amount of posturing tut-tutting about "wars of choice," but they didn't *do* anything—maybe because their electorates' heads were up the national ass, so that an assertive foreign policy destined to be ignored domestically wasn't worth spending political capital on, much less real money. That's bending over backward to give the administration credit for rational decision-making. The more cynical side of me suspects that stuffing your cabinet and staff full of underachievers and halfwits had to have had consequences. It was *hard* to know how best to curtail naked territorial aggression by hostile powers armed with nuclear weapons, and the people Biden and Co. had proudly installed at every level of the federal government didn't do hard.

Like most of my compatriots, I doubt I could have found Ukraine or Taiwan on a map. Still, it seemed to me that if the West continued to wallow in this utopian preoccupation, which had taken hold particularly in the Anglosphere—the Canadians, Irish, Kiwis, and Aussies were even more fanatical about cognitive equality than the Americans who'd started the craze—little stood in the way of the "smartist" countries taking over the world. I even started to wonder if Xi Jinping descending on Cornell and forcing the physics department to give grades again would prove our salvation.

ALT-2015

It would have been sometime that summer when I noticed one evening that Wade was in an unusually dark mood. I congratulated myself for having picked up the change in atmosphere. Wade often spent long periods of time not saying much, while I was prone to getting caught up in my own interior churn—having been for years irradiated by what Emory called the strontium-90 of resentment over the fact that history had taken a big fat dump on my family's head. Discerning the difference between my partner's ordinary taciturnity and an aberrant glumness gave me hope that maybe I wasn't the oblivious, self-involved helpmate that I sometimes feared.

The kids had cleared off, and Wade wasn't finishing his rosemary lamb skewers, though he was certainly chewing on something.

"What's wrong?"

In his lengthy pause I read a familiar superstition: a problem that remains unspoken isn't real yet. "I hired a new assistant," he said at last.

"Isn't that good news? You've been shorthanded ever since Benjamin left to start his landscaping company."

Wade didn't look at me and tapped his forefinger on the table. "I didn't want to hire this person. He's not qualified. He has no training in tree surgery."

"So why did you hire him?"

"The whole qualifications issue . . . It seems to have gotten complicated. I'm not sure it's acceptable to demand qualifications anymore. Meeting a standard means passing a test. There are no tests. They're . . . discrimina-tory."

"You could still refuse to employ someone who doesn't know what he's doing, right?"

"No, that's not right. He threatened me. To demonstrate his 'skills,' he started waving around one of my chain saws without the safety on. I . . . was alarmed and . . . not thinking, so I used a word. It was a knee-jerk response. Flew out of my mouth before I knew it. He threatened to take me to court."

"What word?"

"The same one that got you into trouble at VU. You're so free with your language around here that I . . . Well, it came to mind too easily."

"As a matter of fact, I'm not 'free with my language' around here anymore, much to my dismay. You're not trying to blame me, are you?"

"No, of course not, I'm sorry. But now I've got to work with someone every day who I don't like and don't trust. His name is Danson. He's cocky. He's lazy. He takes long breaks. He vapes all the time. Some sort of cotton-candy flavor. The smell turns my stomach. And he's . . ."

"Stupid," I filled in instinctively. In my defense, the kids, most importantly Lucy, were all upstairs.

"That's one way of putting it."

"My head is bursting every day with several dozen ways of putting it." I studied my handsome partner, who still wasn't looking me in the eye. "You thought you could steer clear of the whole business, didn't you? You thought Mental Parity had nothing to do with you or your job, so you could sail through your life unsullied. You thought you could sit this whole thing out on the sidelines, watching, or declining to watch. You thought it would never come after you and fuck you up."

"I work with *trees*, Pearson."

"You also work with people."

"Which is the only thing about my work I can't stand."

I sat back and crossed my arms. "I don't think I told you about going to see that dance troupe with Emory last week. After hosting *The Talent Show* for so many years, she still likes to keep a hand in the local arts scene. I'm not that into dance, but it was something to do. I know local performances can be second-rate, but this was terrible on a whole new level—which helped explain why the audience was so sparse. Most of the dancers were overweight. They didn't look fit. They had no sense of rhythm, and they were graceless. Wade, they couldn't dance. During the intermission, Emory and I sat there and couldn't say anything. When most of the audience sneaked away, we only stayed out of pity. The handful of other people who also braved it to the end sat there with implacable, oblivious expressions, and they clapped ferociously at the curtain call, as if marshaling enough pugnacious approval could disguise the travesty we'd just sat through. That performance dovetailed with what's happened to Zanzibar. She's the best little thespian in the school. So they don't cast her. They won't cast her. I think those dancers were chosen in the first place *because* they couldn't dance. Picking people who are wiry and strong and who've studied for years to get good at what they do no longer seems *fair*."

"And your point is?"

"There's nowhere to hide. There are no spectators in this game. In the end, you're in this up to the neck as much as I am. Sure, MP started out as a great leveling project in relation to smarts. But now we're busy leveling every field there is—until the U.S. looks like Ukraine after Putin was finished with it. So there's no such thing as being good at tree surgery, any more than there's such a thing as being good at brain surgery. Actually, the situation is worse than that. It's not only that now everyone is equally good at stuff. We're undergoing more of an inversion. The people who suck at stuff get to do it, and the people who excel at stuff are annoying and show up the sucky people and have to be squelched. Maybe we're lucky they haven't started shooting talented ballet dancers and burying them in pits. And *you're* lucky this Danson guy isn't taking over Treehouse, Inc., altogether as a matter of moral right, *because* he knows nothing about tree surgery. *Blessed are the poor at shit, for theirs is the kingdom of heaven. Blessed are those who muck everything up, for they shall be comforted—that no one will ever point out what a fucking mess they've made. Blessed are the bunglers, for they shall inherit the earth.*" Every once in a while, my biblical upbringing came in handy, though Wade was raised as nothing in particular and the allusion to Matthew 5:3–12 was lost on him.

I could have explored this theme to a greater extent if Wade weren't impatient with just this variety of set-piece rant. By 2015, the aforementioned "inversion" had flipped pretty much every discipline. Literary prizes like the Pulitzer and Nobel hadn't merely deteriorated into a lottery; the awards were deliberately bestowed on authors who wrote bad books, and I mean truly appalling books. The Oscars went to terrible movies and terrible actors, while the Tonys went to the very worst plays (a distinction for which there was fierce competition). Why, the only domain that remained impervious to an aggressive advancement of inaptitude was the visual arts, which, having adulated lumps of dung and bricks on the floor for decades, were ahead of their time.

Thereafter, Wade assured me that he was trying to keep Danson Pelling to the relatively safe, boring jobs like clearing debris, feeding the chipper, and chainsawing logs at ground level, though there was no point in having an assistant if you couldn't put him to work on the main task at hand. Wade was irascible during this period, because in addition to puffing away on cotton-candy vape pens, Danson never shut up. This had a noticeably negative effect on my relationship. Only long hours in the absence of conversation stored up enough enthusiasm for discourse for Wade to communicate at home. He was newly morose and unresponsive. Meanwhile, I was enjoying the bliss of my reading-rich season of malingering, though it troubled me that summertime reprieve from the classroom had become an even greater relief than it once was.

My storytelling has been remiss! Just as I might have moved up the little matter of China and Russia taking over the world, I should have mentioned that earlier that spring, Emory was poached by CNN. Although in the interest of our enduring comity I'd continued to duck her pontifications—sorry, not the kindest of nouns—that avoidance was becoming more challenging. Any number of people knew we were friends (Emory's implicit imprimatur gave me cover in the English department that I could sorely use), so colleagues would bring up this or that opener or forceful interview even if I'd managed to miss it. Because YouTube remembered previous searches for Emory Ruth, the site was always pushing recommendations of her latest appearances up in my face without having been asked. And those appearances weren't restricted to CNN. Emory was everywhere. Podcasts, conferences, panels, speeches, you name it. Numerous times I would browse the cable channels only to accidentally trip across my best friend holding forth.

As far as I could ascertain, she was making a name for herself as the intelligent face of idiocy. The formula seemed to be not form following content but form clashing wildly with content. She was smooth, alluring, and sexy, but most of all she came across as blatantly bright. Thus she flattered her viewers, who, if everyone was as smart as everyone else, were also as smart as this silver-tongued broadcaster. Although after being upbraided for using "biddable" Emory had toned down her highfalutin lexicon, she never lowered the tone to nearly the degree that many of her media rivals did. This was shrewd. She didn't appear to talk down to her audience, and while the point she was making was often anti-intellectual, her syntax and delivery were sophisticated. Stylistically, then, she reassured beleaguered members of the roundly deposed intelligentsia—whose reservations about the culture's direction of travel had become unsayable—that the country had not been entirely lost to barbarians. I wasn't eager to form the thought explicitly, but Emory met all the requirements for a successful populist demagogue.

For example, when I switched on the TV one Sunday morning to see who was on *Face the Nation*, surprise, the set was tuned to a dialogue between Emory and some stuffy academic at Columbia. Although I'd never have sought out this appearance, I simply couldn't change the channel right away.

While the show's format was supposedly oppositional, by this point no one, but no one, went on television and threw cold water on Mental Parity as a theory or called for the restoration of standards in hiring, education, and the arts. To the contrary, even talking heads explicitly invited for being "controversial" routinely wasted a portion of the program allaying any fears the audience might harbor that they were even slightly interested in returning to the bad old days of cruel cognitive apartheid. Predictably, then, when I started watching this bearded fiftyish fellow Dr. Arden Hughes was midway through his obligatory hedge: "There's no question that in the past we sidelined far too many folks whose rich but differently expressed perceptions and perhaps less than obvious talents were therefore lost. As a society, we've been impoverished by that dismissal. There's no question, either, that the science on MP is settled . . ." Typically, then, this guy wasn't really on the other side, but to fill the hour he'd niggle over how many people of precisely the same intelligence could dance on the head of a pin. It's worth remembering that in those days there was no other side. You were either thrilled by Mental Parity or ecstatically thrilled.

As it happens, this video is still online, so I can give you a flavor of the discussion word for word.

"But arguably," Dr. Hughes said, once he at last got around to the topic at hand, "Lieutenant Columbo is a natural MP hero. He's an archetype of the chronically underestimated character who's mistaken by his would-be superiors as unsmart. The joke is always on the so-called intelligent characters, who are hanged by their own condescension. These slick, self-impressed murderers make mistakes and give their guilt away because they hold a detective with *perceived* cognitive inferiority in contempt. Every episode is an MP morality play. The . . . if you will, the D-word, if you'll excuse the crudity, always triumphs, and the aloof, patronizing 'experts' end up in jail. The show may go back to 1968, but its themes are ultra-contemporary. Banning the reruns would be a pity. Justifiably, the program might now garner a large new following."

This was the first I'd heard that *Columbo* was on the chopping block.

"What do you think, Emory?" the host asked. The older woman's physical orientation toward Emory even while Hughes was talking suggested an eagerness to ingratiate herself with CNN's rising star. "Maybe we shouldn't merely allow Peter Falk to remain in the back of Nick at Nite's closet, but should restore the detective to prime time."

"Well, I think we'd find that for modern audiences the production values are too low, and the premise is too formulaic," Emory said. Flowing white robes gave her an angelic air; the garb hit harmonics with Jean Simmons's revivalist scenes in *Elmer Gantry*. "But that's not why I'd bury that show six feet under. *Columbo* still embraces the whole disreputable smart-slash-not-smart paradigm. While I can see why you might mistake the program for forward-thinking, Dr. Hughes, it's anything but. I worry your error here is to confuse a *class* issue with a cognitive one. Lieutenant Columbo is blue-collar; the accent, the shambling manner, and the crumpled trench coat are all signifiers. His prey is reliably wealthy. But the show still casts the characters in accordance with a conventional and now conclusively debunked hierarchy of intelligence. If in disguise, Columbo is the smart character. Also in disguise, the murderers are cognitively inferior. The producers have turned the class stereotype on its head. But the old brutality—the violent separating of wheat from chaff, the fetishistic distinguishing of who's cleverer than whom—well, it remains perfectly in place. Prejudice is embedded in the very concept of the program. But the fact that this bigotry isn't immediately apparent—it's insidious—is one of the main reasons I wouldn't want children to be raised with access to it."

"But even if the show does adhere to a dated 'paradigm,' as you say,"

Dr. Hughes said, "isn't there a place, an important place, for preserving examples of our bygone and discredited way of thinking? 'Here, this is a drama in which some characters are portrayed as smart, and others are demonized as not; this is the way we used to categorize people, and wasn't it ugly?' Maybe we need to save these artifacts as a jumping-off place for teaching children not only what to think but what not to think." It was the same zero-impact point I'd made with Dean Poot.

"But *Dr.* Hughes—" The emphasis was sly. Titles now cast you as suspect.

"Please. Arden."

"According to that reasoning," Emory went on—she was so fluid, never missing a beat—"we would logically preserve all the hateful cultural content of times past as precious examples of hateful cultural content— the better to have a 'jumping-off place' for teaching children what *not* to think. If we're intent on presenting the anti-example, the same reasoning would also have us sponsoring all manner of bigots to spew their poison in forums like this one—not that I'm referring to yourself, of course."

"Of course," Arden said curtly.

"The debate about *Columbo* is highly reminiscent of the tiff over *Get Smart*," the host got in edgewise.

"Which was mindlessly proscribed just because of the title." Arden's cross interjection sounded dangerously spontaneous.

"Maybe," Emory conceded. "But the series employs the same transposition. Maxwell 'Smart' is anything but smart. He can't work CONTROL's gadgetry. 'Agent Smart' is an ironic designation, because he's a figure of fun, whom the scriptwriters, and therefore the audience, sneer at and feel superior to. There's no laughing with; it's all laughing at. His partner, Agent 99, is the real 'smart' character. The film and the *Get Smart* remake follow the same template, so taking the lot off streaming platforms was a good move. All the program's comedy is at the expense of the mentally stigmatized."

"The same argument tarnished the Pink Panther movies," the host noted.

"Which I was also relieved to see go," Emory said. "Film audiences were encouraged to be callously collusive with the writers and producers and even with Peter Sellers himself: Inspector Clouseau is, well, take your pick of the slurs. Ha-ha-ha."

Transcribing this is tedious and depressing, so I think that taster will suffice.

Throughout my adulthood, I'd tried to keep in touch with Kelly and David Ruth, the closest folks I had to parents. But with three children and a career hanging on by the fingernails, I easily got caught up in immediate family and work. As their de facto adoptive daughter, I hadn't been as attentive as I should have been, considering how much I owed them for taking me in, teaching me the rudiments of how to negotiate the sane secular world—or previously sane—and helping me to apply to colleges. So when they reached out and asked Wade and me to dinner in early December, I begged off on Wade's account (he hated socializing, and during our previous visits as a couple it was painfully obvious that a contract lawyer and history professor had no idea what to talk about with a tree surgeon), but I happily agreed to come.

I calculated we hadn't seen one another in a couple of years, though not much more than that, so I was taken aback by how much older they both seemed to have grown in such a short time. Though David had always kept himself in good trim, he'd fleshed out, and his previously animated face had dropped, as if all that former vitality and joie de vivre had been an act. Kelly hadn't put on weight, but her posture recapitulated the new droop in her husband's face. When she greeted me, her pleasure in seeing me again appeared genuine enough, but giving expression to that gladness seemed to cost her too much effort, and her manner was a trace forlorn. The phenomenon shouldn't have been as rare as it was, but they'd always been one of those couples whom you could tell at a glance had been young once. That is, you could immediately see through the wear and tear to the energetic, attractive people they used to be, because they carried that energy and attractiveness into the present. I'd always held them up as examples of aging with grace who gave me hope for my future, so my disappointment over how spent they looked had a selfish side.

The Ruths had downsized to a narrow upscale townhouse whose interior was paneled in dark wood and padded with Oriental rugs. Any sections of wall that weren't dotted with classy original art were lined with floor-to-ceiling bookcases. The library was mostly hardbacks, the fiction alphabetized by author, the nonfiction organized by topic. Surfaces of antique furniture sponsored single striking objects from extensive international travel. This variety of learned decor was beyond out of fashion; it was so frowned upon that most people would have ripped out those bookcases years before. Indeed, there was such a glut of used books on the market that they were being pulped and compressed into logs for woodstoves.

"Hey, hey!" I gave Emory a hug and the full European two-cheeker. "I wasn't sure if you'd be here."

"Well, I was in Dublin over Thanksgiving," she said, "and I'm lined up to do a tour of Melbourne, Brisbane, Sydney, and Adelaide over the Christmas period. So it made sense to get together in between the red-letter days. Sorry about the lousy sense of occasion. I know you love holidays."

"Right," said the younger woman on the couch. "And I was also able to wedge this dinner into my demanding schedule of shopping for paper towels and watering Mom's geraniums."

"Felicity, great to see you." I gave a quick, awkward hug to Emory's younger sister. With a wary, combative affect that made her less immediately likable than her sibling, she was one of those people capable of taking "hello" the wrong way. Something about touchy people makes me compulsively bring up the worst possible subject. "Listen, I was sorry to hear that you and Selwin parted ways."

She shrugged. "We had a fatal philosophical disagreement."

"About what?"

"What do you think?"

I didn't pursue it, though I could guess. I should have expected Felicity to be here. Emory had mentioned not only the divorce but her sister's abrupt termination as a biomedical engineer. For now, she was back living with her parents. But her aura of resentment didn't hail solely from this recent hard luck. She'd always seemed a bit cheated, her shoulder-length auburn hair and faintly freckled complexion so much less dramatic than her sister's luminously pale skin and jet-black pixie. She'd none of Emory's easy self-confidence, blithe sense of preeminence, or air of generosity. Felicity wasn't bad-looking, but she was tight. Still, in not especially wanting to talk to her I felt obliged to disguise my not wanting to talk to her, which meant continuing to talk to her.

"So I gather you're between jobs?"

"On the far side of one of them, anyway. 'Between' may be optimistic."

"Did you have another . . . fatal philosophical disagreement?"

"You could say that," she said out of one side of her mouth. "There's been a big shake-up at Pfizer. Like the sort of 'shake-up' where you mix a bottle of barbecue sauce but forget to screw on the top."

Felicity had been a fun, quirky kid. I might not have responded to her in adulthood, but until this last year she'd had an impressive come-from-behind career. She could never compete with her sister in the charm department. Yet she was a hard worker who'd gotten into MIT back in the day when that meant something. Majoring in chemistry, she'd applied herself to just the kind of demanding degree that had become an anachronism, and female students in STEM subjects were then thin on the ground. She exhibited the same mastery of the physical world that appealed to me in Wade. So while Emory was stalling out at WVPA, Felicity went from strength to strength in the pharmaceutical industry. She made scads more money than her more charismatic sibling, or she had until the music stopped. She must have been too glaringly gifted to survive in our current Year Zero. Reverse discrimination was ensuring that droves of highly skilled employees were out on their ears. As folks who knew what they were doing were replaced wholesale by folks who didn't, social justice seemed to intermingle with an unfocused revenge—though what exactly the competent had ever done to the clueless was hard to pinpoint. I couldn't blame Felicity for feeling jaded.

"I sometimes worry that my having held on to my own job doesn't reflect well on me," I said, trying to lighten things up. "Maybe I'm not smart enough to be fired."

"Au contraire," David said, handing me a glass of white. "Hanging on to employment in academia right now at the least requires *canniness*." He cut a barely perceptible side glance at his older daughter. "You must have developed your political sea legs."

"Hardly," I said. "I didn't tell you guys about it at the time, because I didn't want you to worry, and I was hoping it might just blow over. But I had a wickedly close call with the Dean of CE in 2013."

"Ah, yes, Ms. *Poot*," David said. "They keep giving her a larger and larger staff. Her offices now command a whole wing of the Administration Building's ground floor."

"With nicely framed abstracts," I said, "humiliatingly low chairs, and thick white carpet."

"The better to accentuate the bloodstains," David muttered. "And what was your original sin, if I may ask?"

"In my Int Lit survey class, I assigned them *The Idiot*."

David guffawed. "Are you suicidal?"

"I'm the same as I've always been," I said. "Which is the problem. Ultimately, I was just making a joke, but the last thing you can count on these days is a mutual sense of humor. I scraped by with my job, but ever since I've been marked as unsavory. I can't put a foot wrong."

"You sure put a foot wrong with Lucy," Emory noted.

"Oh, right," I said. "Last year, our youngest turned me in to social services."

"Her own mother?" Kelly exclaimed, bringing in crisp breads and herring.

"She overheard me saying something about her not being as smart as her siblings. I'm really sorry, too, because I hated hurting her feelings. Still, you know Darwin and Zanzibar. I'm not as smart as those two, either. Jesus, hardly anybody is. But Lucy was only four when MP exploded, and it's all she's ever known. She's never taken a test in her life.

So she accepts the whole shebang at face value. It would never occur to her there's anything questionable about cognitive equality. It's just a fact."

"I suppose that means she's been raised in a state of purity," Kelly said, shooting a swift side glance at Emory identical to her husband's. "She's uncontaminated by the prejudices of the past. A member of a whole new generation whose minds are—clean."

I studied my ersatz stepmother for a moment. Her tone was impenetrable. Sardonic, or sincere?

"In a way . . ." I said with a returning ambiguity. "For Lucy, the world is black-and-white. Bad people use bad words and think bad thoughts, and good people don't. So if her mother talks in comparative terms about intelligence, she's speaking atrocities. I have to be corrected or fixed. Or punished. And it's no joke. Child Protective Services threatened not only to take Lucy away but to put all three of our kids in foster care."

"Oh, sweetie," Kelly said, clutching my arm. "That must be terrifying."

"Pearson, it's not that hard to learn to talk the talk, and you know it," Emory said.

"Yeah," Felicity said with more than a touch of snideness. "But getting with the program comes more easily to some than others."

"Pearson herself is better at toeing the line than she'd have you believe," Emory said. "Little Miss Maverick, the brave heretic, sticking her neck out while the rest of us pull back in our shells like turtles, is just as politically obliging in public as everyone else."

"That's because I don't want to lose my children or my job," I snapped.

"Since when can you not take a little razzing?" Emory said. "Jeez. And you think it's other people who have no sense of humor."

I followed Kelly into the kitchen to see if I could help. So far this evening had a funny edge on it that I couldn't put my finger on.

Their larder had open shelving, and it took me a minute to put together what about the generous lineup of condiments and foodstuffs was peculiar. The ketchup wasn't Heinz but an off brand from Poland. The label on the mayonnaise looked like Dutch, and on inspection the product was packaged in South Africa. Naturally the rice vinegar was from Japan, but the olive oil was from Turkey, the lentils from Jordan. They didn't have just the usual mushroom soy and water chestnuts from China; the cans of kidney beans and evaporated milk were from China, too. The writing on the bags of flour was Cyrillic.

"Wow," I said after my survey. "Quite an international lineup. I guess you're not that into 'buy American.'"

"No," Kelly said quietly. "It's a policy. The last time I bought sugar produced in this country, it was full of weevils. A container of hummus last year from Weis Markets made David sick for days. After a long string of contaminated, spoiled, or downright inedible American products, that was the limit. Now I make my own hummus."

Sure enough, our marinated flank steak was imported from Argentina. Kelly's multicolored roasted peppers had been trucked from Nicaragua rather than the Midwest or California—which also grew plenty of rice— but no, I checked the bag; the rice was from Malaysia.

"Are you and Emory having a problem?" Kelly asked sotto voce as she sliced the steak and I spooned the peppers onto a serving platter. "I sense a certain tension."

I could have said the same of this whole household. I kept my voice down, too. "I'm not on board with the *views* she's promoting. We're managing. And it's not as if I have to endorse her every public position. But she senses my disapproval even when I don't say anything. Now that she's getting so famous, I'm supposed to be proud of her. I'm sorry to say this, but I'm not."

"You should be careful," Kelly said.

I wasn't sure what she was getting at. "I'm careful every day of the week to the point of exhaustion. Now that we all operate under Lucy's eagle eye, we can't even kick back and relax at home. I'd hoped this house would be the one place left in the world where I can let fly."

"For our part," Kelly said full voice, "David and I are *very* proud of Emory. All those speeches and appearances! I don't know where she gets the energy. Our neighbors and colleagues are amazed. Always sending us links to the latest." But as she said this, she didn't look me in the eye.

Not that I didn't feel welcome, but I considered then whether I might have been invited to this dinner partly as a buffer between Emory and her parents. I wasn't quite family-family, and my presence might help keep the occasion a measure more formal and better behaved. It arrived with an internal *ping*, like a text message: Emory's parents were afraid of her. And that made me wonder whether I should be afraid of her, too.

Once we'd all sat down and passed the serving platters, David announced to the family that this would be his last year at VU.

"That's a surprise," I said. He couldn't have been older than about sixty-seven. "With no mandatory retirement age, professors often keep teaching into their seventies and eighties."

"I don't want to make you nervous on your own account," David said, "but the financial situation at VU is dire. The university had been heavily dependent on foreign students, who pay far higher tuition. But applications from abroad have dried up. Wealthy Nigerians, Asians, and Indians no longer want to send their kids to American schools."

"Gosh," Felicity said. "I wonder why."

"Many would say because of cognitive prejudice," David said dutifully. "So the administration's official line is good riddance to a bad lot. But high-mindedness doesn't fill the hole in the budget."

"I guess it would depend on your politics whether this is a silver lining or a catastrophe," I said, "but the same thing's happened at the southern border. Mexicans, Central and South Americans—they've done a U-turn. A colleague of mine flew through JFK recently and said it seemed different somehow. It took her a minute to realize that the airport had practically no foreigners in it. Think of it. *JFK.*"

"Maybe a pause on immigration could be good for this country," Emory speculated. "So we could catch our breath and assimilate the immigrants already here."

"It's not a *pause,*" I said. "It's a tidal reversal. You can't assimilate immigrants who are on their way out the door. And then there's the domestic brain drain—"

"As for why *else* I'm looking at retirement?" David cut me off.

I'd made him anxious. Any mention of America's "brain drain" to the very countries that once sent their most promising graduate students and professionals our direction could be career-ending. If there is no such thing as exceptionally smart people, then all the exceptionally smart people leaving their country for elsewhere is a nonevent.

"It's an admirable intention," David continued. "Nevertheless, I'm afraid this 'decleverization of the curriculum' is proving too much for me. I'm supposed to stop focusing on traditionally towering figures of history. John Locke, Adam Smith, Rousseau . . . Even the 'Age of Enlightenment' is out the window. It's been rechristened the 'Age of Arrogance.' In fact, I don't know if you've encountered these people, Pearson, but there's even a growing student movement on campus to rename not only the university but this city."

"After whom do they want to name Voltaire instead?" I said. "Beavis and Butthead?"

"Beavis, Pennsylvania," Felicity said. "Has a ring."

"I think I'd prefer Butthead, PA," I said. Felicity was growing on me.

"The point is," David said, "in my courses, I'm now meant to celebrate all the historical figures we've customarily overlooked."

"You mean the people who never achieved dick," Felicity said.

"Now, that's much too harsh a way of putting it," David abjured with a *shut up* glare at his younger daughter.

"Yes," Kelly said. "And a more rounded version of the past, one that tries to include all those people who weren't singled out as special—it's much more equitable."

"But there are . . . logistical problems with following this rubric," David said. "We simply don't have records of all these *otherwise* folks who were callously dismissed in their time. I can explain to students why a host of erstwhile distinguished figures have been acclaimed unjustly, but I've no idea how to go about digging up biographies of, you know—"

"Nineteenth-century knuckleheads," Felicity filled in.

"Honey, you know we don't talk like that in this house," Kelly said.

"I'm simply saying that, however lofty the project," David said, "it's beyond me in purely practical terms. I'm too old a dog for new tricks. It's easier to call it quits and let someone raised on all these fresh ideas take over."

The David Ruth of times past would have railed to the high heavens about "decleverization"—pouring another round of wine and alternating between raucous ridicule and table-pounding rage.

"Of course, I have to admit," he added, "it's painful for me to eliminate the likes of Copernicus and George Washington Carver from the syllabus. Even Martin Luther King is too off-puttingly eloquent. I can see making room for the unrecognized. But"—again he flicked a nervous glance at Emory—"I wonder if in suppressing study of Albert Einstein and Charles Darwin—your son's namesake, Pearson—the pendulum has swung too far the other direction."

"God, Einstein has become Public Enemy Number One," Felicity said. "And he's not even vilified because of a vague association with nuclear weapons. He's just a notorious smart-ass. He's offensive for having ever been born."

"You know, Darwin—I mean my Darwin," I said, "got into huge trouble about three years ago when he wore a sweatshirt to school printed with that classic portrait of Einstein, with all the hair? You remember, they used to be everywhere. It was a perfectly innocent birthday present, from back when Darwin got so involved in the Deepwater Horizon spill. Since then, the image has become 'hate speech.' So my son would never make the same mistake today. He's even wondered if he's going to have to change his first name. I'm pleased to say that he still loves his name, but it's attracting the wrong kind of attention, and Darwin has a hard enough time disguising the fact that he's a fucking genius."

"Stephen Hawking's house was vandalized last week, did you see that?" Felicity asked me. "Eggs, red paint everywhere, windows smashed. As if his life isn't lousy enough already."

"He'd been . . . provocative," Emory said. She'd been unusually *reticent* so far.

"He's not having it," Felicity said.

"Too late for that," Emory said. "He will have to have it."

"Yes, thanks to the assistance of *certain people*," Felicity said icily to her sister, "it's been shoved down all our throats."

"Now, girls, let's try to have an amicable meal," Kelly said. "More peppers?"

"I can see how coming to appreciate different varieties of intelligence is a good thing," David said. His wife shot him a look. She wanted to change the subject. "But I'm not sure why that necessitates denigration of people with the more standard kind."

"I think the idea," Emory said, employing the diplomatic tone she used during panels on which a contrary thinker had, against the odds, managed to gain a spot, "is people with a 'more standard' intelligence have had their day. Einstein, Darwin—they've hardly been underfeted in the past."

"We're thinking of getting a new car," Kelly introduced firmly.

"Boy, about time," I said. "What are you considering?"

"Possibly a Nissan Skyline," Kelly said. "Or we've even thought about importing a Tata Nexon or Beijing Auto Senora."

"The Chinese used to do cheap knockoffs of every popular model in the U.S.," Felicity said. "Lately it's the other way around. American manufacturers are copying Chinese cars."

"Well, what *about* an American model?" Emory asked her mother.

Felicity guffawed. "For a *high-flying journalist*, you sure don't keep up. That Ford pickup that burst into flame on I-75 and caused, like, a ten-car pileup? All those Chevrolet minivans whose entire chassis have dropped off? There've been so many recalls of U.S.-made cars lately it's a wonder we have traffic jams anymore. The roads should be deserted."

"We've flirted with a Lada," David said. "Classic. Longer-lasting than you'd think."

"Do you really want to buy Russian right now?" I asked.

"Putin has helped himself to Eastern Europe, whether or not we buy one of his cars," David said sorrowfully. "But I'm not sure about a new car, even if the Volvo is on its last legs. Kelly and I have a difference of opinion on this, but with my stepping down from VU, we might think bigger picture. Things in this country are getting so . . . politicized. I want a peaceful old age. I could definitely see moving kit and kaboodle abroad."

"Come on, Dad," Emory said. "I can't count the people I've heard threaten that they're going to leave the country. A whole passel of my friends swore in 2004 that if Bush won again they were moving to Europe. Guess what. Bush won. No one moved to Europe."

"Not Europe," David said. "The east belongs to a totalitarian thug, and the west . . . is too much like here."

"What's wrong with here?" Emory asked.

"Perhaps it's a matter of taste," her father said, and declined to elaborate.

"Dad's mentioned Thailand," Felicity said. "Sexy ladies."

"But it's uncomfortably close to Taiwan," David said.

"New Shanghai," I corrected glumly.

"Moving to any country within throwing distance of China at this point," David said, "is probably foolhardy."

"You mean 'imprudent,'" Kelly said.

A trace of the old David Ruth shone in his rolled eyes. "I'd consider Australia or New Zealand, but they've both gone in . . . the wrong direction. The Seychelles?" He added under his breath, "I'd entertain Brazil, but I'm not sure it's nearly far enough away."

"Isn't the biggest issue the language?" I asked.

"Honestly, Pearson, my dear," David said wearily, "being surrounded by people jabbering away in a manner I find indecipherable sounds like bliss."

"Any picking up of stakes is well down the road," Kelly said. "For now, I can't face the prospect of packing and finding a new electricity provider in Bali or something. Besides, in case it's escaped everyone's notice, I'm still working."

"Yes, how's the practice going?" I asked.

"Contract law has become rather complicated," she said, taking a moment to regroup and choose her phrasing with care. If the editorial function occupied a particular location in our brains, then the lobe was bulging against our craniums from overuse. "Nowadays, when one party fails to fulfill its side of the bargain—delivers an unsatisfactory service or, say, builds something to the wrong specifications—the delinquent party will often claim that being held liable for this deficient performance is smartist. Any number of cases have been successfully defended on these grounds, especially since the 2013 Supreme Court ruling upholding affirmative action for people with a *perceived* mental deficit. But of course, anything complicated is good for lawyers, and our practice has more work than we know what to do with. That's why all this talk of flying the American coop is premature. What's much more immediately pressing is David's hip replacement."

"Finally," I said. "David, that hip has bothered you for years. Fortunately, the Voltaire Medical Center has a fantastic reputation for joint replacements."

"Yes, um," David said. "It once did."

"I haven't read much about it in the press," Kelly said. "But we have friends . . .. I wouldn't usually put much store in isolated anecdotes, but when they accumulate . . . Oh, most of the surgeons know what they're doing. The problem seems to be the younger nurses and residents. The second tier of support. Wrong doses of anesthesia. Infections from inadequate aftercare. We have the resources, so we're planning to book the surgery in Delhi."

"You're going all the way to India for a hip replacement?" I asked.

"They have good doctors," Kelly said. "And we've never been to India, so it sounds like fun."

"You're not going to Delhi to have *fun*," Felicity said. "You're in flight from a medical system that's increasingly infiltrated by *alternative processing*. And no one wants an *alternative* hip replacement. Like, they install an artificial shoulder on your thigh bone instead."

"I think at this point that term 'alternative'—" Emory intruded.

"Oh, fuck your *terms*, Emory," Felicity cut her off. "You MP losers only want to talk about words for things, and meanwhile the fucking country is in a state of collapse! You can't get anything done here anymore, because nothing works! We're promoting *total fucking morons* to be CEOs and presidents and Chiefs of Whathaveyou, thanks to which the postal service has imploded, you can't get a driver's license or a passport, the cars are exploding, and Mom here won't even buy a box of Ritz crackers if they're baked in New Jersey!"

Felicity's prandial pugilism with her sister struck the no-holds-barred note that my latter-day conversations with my best friend lacked. I envied the rough-and-tumble between them, the absence of a constraining caution. Still, I'd never have leveled "you MP losers" directly at Emory. She may have been a collaborator, but she was surely a double agent. She was an opportunist, all right, shamelessly so. She hadn't lost her mind.

"I did a long opener on this, because I've heard that dirge so often," Emory said. "Big social change always creates teething problems. But this 'the country is going to the dogs' thing is a wild exaggeration. Keep your shirt on. The U.S. is huge, and it's always had problems. So, shocker: it still has problems. Overstating them doesn't solve anything."

"At this point, I don't think it's *possible* to overstate them," Felicity said.

"Typical projection," Emory said. "Things aren't going great for you right now. So you look out the window, and all you can see is divorce and unemployment."

"There's a reason I'm divorced and unemployed: the pandering political quackery you broadcast night and day."

"Oh, for Pete's sake!" Emory exclaimed. "Selwin is my fault? Pfizer's my fault?"

"Yes, and yes. Selwin started listening to your stupid show. You personally convinced him. He's a convert. And Pfizer is just mindlessly following the logic, or illogic, of the goofball gospel you and your crackpot pals have imposed on the whole Western world."

"Felicity, stop it," Kelly intervened. "You may have your differences, but Emory's still your sister—"

"I'll stop it, all right," Felicity said, screeching out her chair. "I can't stand being in the same room with the fucking cunt." She marched off and then the front door slammed.

CHAPTER 5

After an embarrassed silence, Kelly began, "Sweetheart—"

"Look, she's unhappy and taking it out on me," Emory said. "I get enough hate mail—always anonymous—to have developed a pretty thick skin. So I take on the sins of the world at a family dinner. There's my public service dispatched for the day."

"That's very grown up of you, honey."

"Yes, at forty-three I may have finally graduated to adulthood." Emory's tone had a bite.

"Pearson, how are Darwin and Zanzibar doing?" Kelly asked, no doubt hoping to move on to safe topical territory. Good luck with that.

"Well, speaking of unhappy," I said. "In the deep dark past, I'd have expected Darwin to be gearing up for a host of AP classes and organizing to skip his senior year, if not his junior year, too. He had an eye on a PhD in physics or math by the time he was ten. But there *are* no more advanced placement classes. With the quality of college education nowadays—apologies, David—leapfrogging to Yale would only secure him the equivalent of more high school. So back here in reality? He's planning to drop out when he turns sixteen this spring. I wouldn't say this within his hearing, but I don't blame him. He gets nothing out of school, which, when a few words finally escape his lips, he describes as a cross between a rowdy basketball game and an institution-wide food fight. He's angry and unmotivated. I don't know what will become of him."

Kelly might have preferred a shorter answer. Like, "Fine."

"You're too dark on the kid, Pearson," Emory said. "Up against it, I'm not convinced he'll drop out. He's a teenager in the usual turmoil. But he's resilient. Resourceful." I inferred these were among the few distinguishing adjectives that remained acceptable at the dinner table.

"But Darwin used to be so curious," I said. "Now nothing interests him, and he's churning in a vortex of misanthropic nihilism. The only news stories that have captured his imagination in the last few years were that grotesque Adam Lanza spectacle and the gruesome terrorist attack at the Bataclan in Paris last month. I sometimes worry I'm living with tomorrow's headline."

Kelly followed up with understandable apprehension, "And Zanzibar?"

"She's always been social, even something of a kingpin," I said. "But recently, she's been ostracized. Of course, thirteen-year-olds are like that. Still, to the extent that she's explained it to me—not much—I think she's being shunned for being good at things. She's such a talented artist, but when she, like, produced an anatomically accurate pencil drawing of a human hand—they're hard to draw—it seemed to make her teacher mad. It definitely made her classmates mad. When Zanzibar's back was turned, one of them scrawled green marker all over that sketch. Or on the flute—her tone is clear, and she can fly through fast, complex passages without missing a note. But the other day, when she was at band practice—ordinarily a hopeless cacophony, because none of these kids is taught to play the instruments properly; no one dares correct them, so they play *in their own way*. Anyway, during a slight lull in the racket, Zanzibar lit into a Bach sonata—the one in B minor, I've heard her play it before—and maybe because it was so arrestingly beautiful, the other kids went silent. Well, she says the band leader made her stop! He was cross, too, just like her art teacher. I guess he regarded the impromptu recital as showing off, and you know how strongly that's discouraged. Then there's the added problem of her having become arresting in another sense." I pulled up a photo on my phone and extended it to Kelly.

"Good lord, she's gorgeous," Kelly exclaimed, handing the phone to David.

"Not merely pretty," he said. "Turn-your-head-and-stare."

"But why is a face like that a problem?" Kelly asked. "Emory sure didn't find smashing good looks a disadvantage." She'd never have said such a thing with Felicity there.

"No, we all wanted to be around her," I said. "Hoping for some of the magic to rub off. But something's changed. Being attractive isn't—well, it doesn't actually *attract* people. It stirs outright rancor instead. Our minds are the same, so our bodies should be, too. In fact . . . Emory, didn't you make a joke, way back when? About how we might as well declare that everyone is equally beautiful?"

"Mmm, I don't remember."

I think she did. "It's not funny now."

She laughed uncomfortably. "You say that like an accusation."

Maybe it was.

Did I blame Emory for Darwin and Zanzibar's travails in the same way that Felicity blamed her for Selwin and Pfizer? The inclination would be irrational. Emory didn't invent Mental Parity. She'd jumped on the bandwagon to advance her career, but had she not, someone else would have clambered onto the cart in her place. If instead she'd risked throwing in her lot with MP's opposition, well—what opposition? She'd simply have lost even the sorry platform she had to begin with at WVPA. For you could always take your place at the end of the unemployment line, but there was no rearguard resistance to join. Fringy "extremist" holdouts nostalgic for standards said their piece at best once and were subsequently erased from the landscape; no one would ever hear from them again. Besides, how much real influence did Emory exert? Wasn't she just humming along with a chorus, putting out the same message— a message not of her concoction—on a repeating loop? I even questioned whether Felicity's ex had been genuinely "converted" to what had long before become mainstream cant. Wasn't that the problem with comment journalism in general? Who had ever been persuaded by broadcast editorials? Audience members who disagreed tuned them out or turned them off. The function of comment journalism was purely confirmatory. Arguably, my best friend had never changed anyone's mind about anything. She was simply good at putting into words what her viewers thought already, thereby providing them a cozy but inert glow of self-congratulation that was relatively harmless.

As for Emory's direct effect on my children, the older two had been disconcerted that on the one hand "Auntie Em" was the same warm, mischievous, teasing presence they'd grown up with, and on the other hand she had become a high-profile mouthpiece for an ideology that was wrecking both their present and their prospects. Fair enough. They were learning that other people can espouse views we reject and still be agreeable company. That it's possible, and often necessary, to keep a distinction between what we think in private and what we say in public. That sometimes in the real world we need to compromise our principles to put bread on the table. And that grown women can take radically different approaches to surviving in a dangerously charged political ecology and still be friends.

So why did I hold what was happening to my children against her?

Uneasy with these thoughts while Kelly brought in her buttermilk pie, I tried to mitigate my woebegone account of my kids.

"D and Z are total savants when it comes to languages," I said. "They pick them up more readily than their dirty socks. Spanish, obviously, but better than a smattering of Greek and Portuguese. They've even mastered a fair bit of Mandarin, and Zanzo has started on Russian. So about a year ago, I heard them nattering away in the usual inscrutable *nee-naw-see-sa-tee-soo*, and I asked, 'What is that, Japanese?' Zanzibar said scornfully, 'No, Mom, *this* is Japanese,' and rattled off a couple of sentences that definitely sounded more like World War Two POW movies. What had they been speaking? *They'd made up their own language.* Can you believe it? With its own grammar and vocabulary. Strictly speaking, Russian and Mandarin can be understood by millions of other people, so they're not *private* enough. Jesus, what a pair."

"You never talk about Lucy with that much enthusiasm," Emory said.

"Lucy hasn't exactly endeared herself to the family," I said, "having forced us to tippy-toe around her all the time, and she's turning into an utter hooligan."

"At ten years old?" Emory scoffed.

"I can't civilize her all by myself. Wade is a calming influence, but he's no disciplinarian, much less a math tutor. At this point, I doubt she'll ever learn to add."

"Oh, who cares?" Emory said. "Making children learn math in the digital age is pointless. Buy her a calculator."

I hesitated before observing, "I swear you'd never have said that five or six years ago."

"Sure, I would have," Emory said coolly. "I didn't have a problem with math in school myself, but how much do I use it? Hardly ever."

Kelly served the pie, whose filling was smooth and pellucid. "I love the lemon," I said, licking my fork. "And the hit of zest is just right."

"Your favorite flavors," Emory said. "Acid and bitterness." The tease didn't come out as jocular as she might have intended.

"I admired the *zest*," I countered. "As in 'for life.'"

"Listen, I'm not their mother," Emory reflected, putting her fork down after three bites. She was strict with herself on calories, and her built-in Geiger counter had detected large quantities of butter. "So why do I stick up for your kids more than you do?"

"I'm not criticizing them. They've been victimized by grown-ups who've gone off the deep end."

"But children are robust. They're naturally adaptable. Have a little faith. They'll be fine."

"They could have been better than fine. They could be thriving. They're not. And on that point, yeah. Absolutely. I'm bitter."

Kelly and David had watched our interchange with trepidation, and David called time. One daughter storming off in a cloud of profane invective was enough for one night.

"Looks like Biden's not going to run again," David said, as if physically turning a page.

"That's what I've read," I said indifferently. Clearly, I should let this unaccountable friction with Emory go.

"I don't think the party apparatchiks are giving Biden a choice," Emory said.

"Still, it's odd," Kelly said. "Two one-term Democratic presidents in a row."

"Ukraine and Eastern Europe, Taiwan?" Emory supposed. "They haven't helped this administration's reputation for diplomatic finesse."

"Are you kidding me?" I said. We were both registered Democrats, but even discussing electoral politics Emory and I couldn't manage to stay on the same side for longer than thirty seconds. "American voters don't give a flying fig about Eastern Europe or Taiwan. Because all those countries are unashamedly *smartist*, aren't they?"

"I think there's a consensus," David said carefully. His safe subject was proving more volatile than he'd hoped. "Biden is merely a mediocrity. And that's not good enough anymore."

We all knew what he meant.

"The Democrats have seized on an ace in the hole, and that's why the party higher-ups are coaxing Biden out the exit," David continued. "They know as well as we do who'd be a shoo-in. The tiny vocabulary? The repetition of the same words over and over? The incomplete sentences? He checks every lowbrow box in the book. He's crude. He's crass. He's a boor. He has garish aesthetic taste. He's fat. Better still, he routinely wears that slack, brutish expression, and he never reads. It's also a big plus that he has no foreign policy experience. Ditto his never having been elected to a political position of any sort. The PR people might need to coach him on that arrogance problem, but so long as you're boasting about how unremarkable you are, you can get away with all the narcissism you like. I'm sorry, Emory, if this seems to you to do a disservice to a reigning ethos you've provided such a convincing gloss of decency. Hats off to you, my girl; as a rhetorician, you're a trapeze artist. But what qualifies a candidate for high office right now is having no ideas and knowing absolutely nothing. Voilà, we get the president we deserve."

ALT-2016

CHAPTER 1

There's more than one Before and After in this story, and one watershed was the twenty-ninth of April 2016. In my cupboard of an office at VU, I was jotting a half-hearted lesson plan when my phone rang, after which our household would plunge into disarray.

Wade had been rushed to the Voltaire Medical Center. When I hastened to his side he was foggy with pain meds, so I pieced together the story only a day or two later. The Treehouse, Inc., team had been trimming a large ash that was diseased, and though the owners were hoping to save it, the trim would have to be drastic if the tree was to have a chance. Wade was near the top of a tall stepladder. Having previously complained about not being given "real" tree surgery jobs, Danson Pelling was harnessed farther up the trunk. The assistant took it upon himself to sever a large bough without checking that the coast was clear; it crashed onto Wade and toppled the ladder. Wade's foot got ensnared by one of the steps, and it was wrenched around in a direction nature never intended. The tendons were a mess; the ankle would require surgery. He also landed on his wrist and broke it. He was badly scraped up, and he had a concussion. In other words, Wade had been forced to hire someone who was just as smart as everyone else, and look where it got him.

I brought the kids to visit and arrived with earbuds, toiletries, and slices of frittata with chorizo. Though she'd never been on Wade's wavelength, Emory canceled a recording for *Peas in a Podcast* to spend a torturous half hour at his bedside. But simultaneous to all our tender concern, a cruel calculation intruded. Our household's finances were already precarious, and while Wade convalesced, his contribution to our budget would sit at zero. It was impossible to judge how long he'd be out of commission, or whether he'd ever be able to return to clambering three and four stories high. Let's put it this way: tiger prawns were off the menu.

I discovered in retrospect how helpful Wade had been in the domestic department once I had to take up the slack. Without bidding for credit, much less having to be asked, he had vacuumed, dusted, shopped, and taken out the trash while ensuring the kids took showers and got to bed at a seemly hour. I'd been spoiled. But overnight our house no longer stocked and cleaned itself.

Wade was insured, but his high-deductible policy didn't give us much latitude in choice of doctors. So when I met the surgeon who'd do what I gathered was a complex operation on his ankle, my heart fell. I have no prejudice against youth per se, though there's no getting around the cliché that practice makes perfect, and this whippersnapper wouldn't have had much practice. Yet in recent times my anxiety about callow professionals had jacked up a level. After all, by then Kelly and David's decision to book a hip replacement in India had grown par for the course; wealthier Americans were quietly slipping off to get procedures done abroad by the tens of thousands. Might this fellow be green enough to have gone to medical school post-2010? The students in my own classes who didn't do the reading, talked through my lectures, and had contempt for the whole concept of education wouldn't likely achieve a full appreciation for the lush fruits of civilization that had ripened before they were born. But at least ignorance about Herman Melville wouldn't kill anybody.

Wade was pretty dejected. It had taken him no longer than it had me to recognize this accident was a financial catastrophe, for the jobs he'd canceled from his hospital bed alone would have covered our May mortgage payment. He was too practical a person to work himself into a rage at Danson Pelling, as rage wouldn't moderate the cold reality of What Is one whit. Still, anger is energizing (before it wears you out), and the alternative to fury was dolor and defeatism. Maybe to some it would seem an odd lifetime aspiration, but Wade had never wanted to be anything other than a tree surgeon; he enjoyed the same natural affinity with plants that people more commonly feel with animals. I could tell that he was anguishing night and day about whether he'd be able to return to his occupation, because this was the one subject he never talked about.

The surgeon was a skinny guy with stick-out ears who looked about twelve and whose silly name, Barry Sarsaparilla, didn't encourage confidence, either. I was present in the hospital room when this child physician explained to us what they were planning to do to Wade's ankle, whose torn ligaments and tendons I pictured as a plate of spaghetti. But whenever doctors describe medical procedures, I often feel woozy, and I have a terrible time paying attention—not because the details don't seem important but because they so very much do. For me, the urgency of following the particulars induces paralysis. Telling yourself to concentrate being the polar opposite of concentration, for the whole spiel all I really heard hissing in my head was "Listen!" Once Wade was wheeled off, for all I knew they were about to weave his connecting tissues into a macramé wall hanging to sell at a local crafts fair.

Beforehand, Wade and I had been in accord over preferring a local nerve block to general anesthesia. It might have been sweeter to simply wake up after it was all over, but going fully under in this hospital didn't seem safe. This was now a place you had to keep your wits about you, and even sleeping was an uneasy proposition. While the visuals of the institution were unchanged from when I'd given birth to Lucy here in 2005, its touch and feel had transformed in much the manner of the VU campus. In its accoutrements, the university still looked like a sacred vessel of cumulative human knowledge, but as the institution broke faith with its core mission of handing on that knowledge, its infrastructure had reduced to pure pomposity. In the case of the medical center, the catalyst for a similar corrosion from the inside out was patient mistrust. Waiting in the lobby for Wade to come out of surgery, I watched numerous doctors and nurses rushing down the halls, and while they all looked plausibly like doctors and nurses, some of them were fake doctors and nurses, mere simulacrums, who threaded undetectably among the real ones like Stepford wives.

When the twelve-year-old reported on the operation, Dr. Sarsaparilla was reassuring that all had gone well, though he assumed an incongruous lightness of tone; I suppose there was no getting around the fact that it was not *his* ability to walk up the stairs, much less his lifetime calling, that hung in the balance. In contrast to his preparatory lowdown, he delivered no specifics, and there was something about the way he looked not quite straight in my eyes but about an inch to the side that I did not like.

Wade was kept overnight on an antibiotic IV, and I'll tell you what else I did not like: being phoned the next morning with the assurance that Wade was fine and there was nothing to worry about. I said, "I haven't been worried. Why should I have been worried?"

"No, no," the surgeon said. "The point is, you *shouldn't* worry. He's sleeping soundly and his vitals are back to normal."

"What do you mean, *back* to normal?"

"There was, well, an event. Mr. Haavik is right as rain now, but very, very briefly, he went into cardiac arrest."

"Why on earth? He broke his wrist. He wrenched his ankle. But he's only forty-nine and spectacularly fit. There is, or *was* before you people got your hands on him, nothing wrong with his heart."

"It seems there was . . . a little mix-up. With the IV."

I took a deep breath. "Uh-huh. Do I at least have you to thank for noticing that my partner was—not to put too fine a point on it—dying?"

"Not exactly."

"He wasn't 'exactly' dying?"

"No, I mean I wasn't personally the doctor who identified the pharmaceutical error and revived the patient. That would have been Dr. Howard."

"Out of curiosity. How old is Dr. Howard?"

"I don't know," Sarsaparilla said. "*Old*."

"Well, thank God for the doddering codgers who actually had to pass the MCAT to get into med school. I imagine Dr. Howard could even tell the difference between a femoral artery and a big toe."

"I'm sorry, Ms. Converse, and maybe I'll give you a free pass because you're under a lot of stress. But that kind of talk is unacceptable—"

"What's *unacceptable* is nearly murdering your own patients!"

I can't tell you what wildly incorrect drug drained into my partner's arm, and for once not because I couldn't pay attention but because the surgeon didn't, i.e., wouldn't, tell me, even after I got my temper under control and pressed him. It seems quaint, looking back, but caginess borne from fear of malpractice suits was still habitual in the closed ranks of the medical profession. I say quaint, because at my urging Wade would indeed consult an attorney about bringing a suit against the hospital. But the lawyer would talk him out of it. Echoing the resolution of all forms of malfeasance these days, accusations of medical malpractice were systematically thrown out of court as manifestations of cognitive bigotry.

I'm trying to set the emotional table here. I was as anxious as anyone would be about a gravely injured de facto spouse. I'd also reason to fear for Wade's state of mind. If his wrist and ankle didn't recover full functionality, he might never resume a livelihood he loved, and I couldn't imagine that sinewy denizen of the treetops plunked in a desk job. Even if he did recuperate, an extended convalescence would put us in financial straits, and we had three children to support. On a day-to-day level, I suddenly had to run our whole household on my lonesome, laundry, cooking, shopping, the works, while teaching a full course load.

But these normal tribulations—the slings and arrows that are the cost of doing business as an alive person—were exacerbated by rank stupidities that were purely elective. Wade never should have been forced to hire an incompetent moron on the worse than shaky premise that there's no such thing as an incompetent moron. In addition to the rational concern that always attends serious injuries—physicians can rarely put Humpty Dumpty together again, quite—I was obliged to fret over whether the ostensible professionals who'd determine this case's outcome knew anything about human anatomy, drugs and dosages, diagnostics, or interpretation of an MRI. Indeed, I could not be certain whether the clinicians charged with treating my partner's infirmities ever should have qualified for medical degrees, now handed out as carelessly as shopping flyers. QED: an anonymous muttonhead had poured something like Thousand Island dressing into my partner's IV and given him a fucking heart attack. I planned to discourage Wade from getting worked up about the ineptitude that precipitated his near-death experience—he'd need to relax, destress, and rest to heal—but that left me doing double duty, generating enough consternation for the both of us.

Furthermore, ever since my daughter ratted me out to social services I'd been living in my own home with an effective fist in my mouth. Ditto at VU, where if I was not regurgitating fashionable absurdities I was saying nothing at all. As noted, I'm not by nature a quiet person—not a *reticent* person, thank you, Ms. Townsend—and suppressing nearly everything that came into my head, for *years*, had created a buildup that was combustible. Put a pressure cooker on high heat without a release valve, and dinner ends up on the ceiling.

This sounds as if I'm making excuses for myself, which I suppose I am. But throughout the awful leisure that has allowed me to examine a certain afternoon from every conceivable angle, I've racked my brain to determine whether I feel badly about it or rather proud of myself. The consequences have been so catastrophic that a perfect absence of regret would be insensible. But now that I have little left besides my pride, I'm reluctant to let go of that, too.

After being informed that Wade's nurses were using his IV bag for a barkeeping course in creative cocktails, I went in for a quick visit, ascertaining that, though pale, Wade at least had a pulse. He was desperate for fresh produce, since all the hospital's fruit was canned, so on the way to VU to teach my Advanced Creative Writing course (that "Advanced" bit was shameless flattery of our artless wards), I pulled over to pick up provender from a greengrocer. Understandably distracted, I didn't especially attend to the fact that a trip between the hospital and the university, outside my usual orbit, took me alarmingly close to the neighborhood where I grew up.

Emerging with grapes and tangerines, I froze. My heartbeat soared and grew uneven, inducing a mild nausea. Across the street, that was unmistakably my mother: overdressed for a sunny spring day in a dour black overcoat. I didn't think she'd spotted me, or not yet, so my brief glimpse of her face, softer and rounder than I remembered it, provided a rare vision of what she looked like when she was genuinely not seeing me rather than pretending to not see me. Her chin didn't jut; for once not trained fiercely and unfalteringly forward, her gaze was open and shifting.

I calculated later that she must have been sixty-six, and she'd aged better than I'd have expected. The siren who'd bewitched my father was still in there somewhere.

But I gathered what little I did in a microsecond. During previous chance encounters I had forced myself to hold my ground, staring unapologetically straight on even as my metabolism went haywire. This time my response was adolescent. I fled—racing to the car at a sprint, dropping a couple of tangerines along the way. Once inside, I slid down in the driver's seat, starting the car in a slump, not sitting fully upright until I'd taken a roundabout route that didn't reconnect with the main road my mother was traversing until over a mile later.

What did I fear? That hadn't been done to me already? I'm sorry there's so little to that story—which isn't a story or even a proper anecdote—but I mention it because the sighting had the quality of an omen. Glenda Converse in that black overcoat functioned as a raven perched on a wire.

Also, that glimpse of my mother could only have ratcheted up my growing volatility. Yes, I was then forty-four, and maybe I should have aged out of this outsize reaction to merely laying eyes on the woman. I've no idea what good it would have done anyone should I have bawled my head off so many years later; still, had I been in therapy (little chance of that), any psychiatrist of that period would have informed me knowingly that I'd never "processed the trauma" of my family's disavowal. The one price I paid for skipping all that expensive self-pity was this spontaneous welling up of woundedness on those few occasions I was presented with physical evidence that this denunciation wasn't just a poignant backstory to make myself seem interesting to new acquaintances, but was real and ongoing. (I still lived in the same city. I was listed as an English instructor on the VU website, and my name was unusual enough for that citation to have appeared on the first page of an internet search. Nothing had ever stopped my parents or brothers from experiencing a change of heart and looking me up. I didn't squander energy on whether I'd accept an apology that would never be forthcoming, but I daresay I'd have been receptive to a simple expression of curiosity about how I'd ended up.) These surges of feeling, which hit like a cross between a mugging and an overdose, didn't last long. Yet the residue of knifing resentment that I was raised in a family that placed a higher premium on dogma than on their own daughter and sister was still dispersing from my bloodstream when I arrived in class.

It was no little bewildering that students allergic to reading still evidenced an overweening desire to write. All VU's creative writing courses were oversubscribed, the only reason it fell to me to teach one. Mine was a spillover class, mopping up the students who didn't get into the workshops taught by academics who had at least published some semiautobiographical coming-of-age novel. (With blithe hypocrisy, these kids yearned to study solely with writers who'd made a mark in the pre-2010 dark ages, spurning the more recent discoveries whom the publishing industry had lionized for being irreproachably crap.) I was a nobody who'd published nothing, and you'd think an uncredentialed mediocrity would have qualified as one of this generation's heroes. Instead, they were irked by having been dumped in a class whose instructor had no status. The one student this semester who had certainly sought out my class as opposed to getting stuck in it was Drew Patterson—the tall, smarmily good-looking guy from my 2013 Int Lit survey course and doubtless one of the three unidentified tattletales who squealed to Dean Poot about my little Dostoevsky prank. Drew was a senior now, and this was his last opportunity before graduation to make my life unpleasant.

Mind, these students didn't want to *learn* how to express themselves, because the conceit ran that they already knew how. As ever, this gave us something of a structural problem.

Thus, while I never pretended to know the least thing about character development, I made a small effort at getting these young people to compose correct, marginally coherent sentences. On this point I made negligible headway, but I was still committed to an educational format in which the "teacher" occasionally had to impart "lessons," and explaining the difference between "less" and "fewer" gave me something to do. Yet this fateful Thursday afternoon, the prospect of feebly interjecting that "quicker" was not an adverb held little appeal. If I may reach for an expression more associated with my parents' generation, I was "in a mood."

I'd commonly spend class in a half-stand before the desk, my ass perched against its ledge, striking an attitude of casual toleration that facilitated waiting out long periods during which the students were by no stretch of the imagination under my control. Today I sat, propping my legs on the desk crossed at the ankles. Hands clasped on my chest, I extended in the spring-back chair, a gentle rhythmic bounce conveying the same time-limited patience as drumming one's fingers. The students seemed to notice that something was afoot, because—no less a miracle than Moses' parting of the Red Sea—they shut up.

"So," I said at last. "You all want 'to write.' *Why?*"

No volunteers were forthcoming.

"You've been to a library?" I supposed. "At least a bookstore. All that text—many hundreds of years' worth. What makes you think we need more?"

One of the few East Asians still enrolled in an American college, Baozhai raised her hand. "Our generation has a very unique perspective—"

"There's no such thing as 'very unique,'" I said. "A perspective is either one of a kind, or it is not."

"Our generation has a—a unique perspective to contribute," she said meekly.

"But according to that very 'unique perspective'—" I began.

"I thought nothing could be 'very unique,'" Drew interrupted from the front row.

"The usage was emphatic rather than amplificatory, thank you," I said, employing the *very* Latinate vocabulary that educators now took pains to avoid. "Your generation's credo posits that we're intellectually all the same. In that case, we've always been the same. Therefore, the self-regarding 'brainiacs' of the past you're all so keen to depose may not have been any smarter than you after all, but they were *as* smart as you, according to your own golden rule. So I repeat: given that your predecessors—your perfect intellectual equals—generated mountains of blah-blah already, why do we need any more?"

"I like writing stories," another student piped up. "It's fun."

"That's a good reason as far as it goes," I said. "But if enjoyment of the process is the sole point, you should write stories and then throw them away."

"You're always hassling us to turn shit in," Drew said. "There's your reason."

"I had no idea you were so motivated to please, Drew. Because you know you could write nothing for this class, or any class, and you'd still sail through to graduation. Despite that, any number of you do write things. I want to understand why."

Back to square one.

"We're in college," someone said finally.

"Yes," I said. "And whatever for?"

"I have no idea." The grumble in the back was from my only other repeat student, Cameron—the black kid with stupendous literary talent whom the last four years had criminally embittered.

"We're all the same," I said. "Logically, what we produce is the same. I could nominate one student to write a story for all of you. Everyone else could go home."

"Stuff can be different and equally good." One of the student-students.

"True," I said. "But do you folks genuinely believe that all the stories we've read in this class have been equally good?"

Given the widespread shifting in desks, this line of inquiry was making them nervous. The usual thought police in front sat straighter and perked up. It took a minute, but a chorus of "Sure!" "Yeah!" and "Of course!" duly rolled in.

"*Really?*" I said. "I'm sorry to single anyone out, but you remember Jerome's story about the dog that kept barking, and then it stopped barking? Jerome is absent today, so we can be candid with one another. 'The Big Barking Dog' was boring. It was strangely short but still managed to work in an improbable number of grammatical errors; I doubt I could come up with that many mistakes per paragraph with a gun to my head. The prose was flat; the story wasn't even a 'story' as most of us understand the term; and it was perfectly pointless. That is, it meant nothing, it imparted no moral or revelation, and the world would be a better place without that story in it. Are you seriously telling me that none of you submitted to that drivel while thinking privately to yourself that *your story is better?*"

This was the point at which I probably crossed a line. I had violated the university's precious "core values" and its behavioral guidelines for faculty. I had all but called Jerome's story you-know-what.

"Our generation doesn't think that way," Baozhai said hastily.

"Oh, no?" I said, bringing my feet to the floor and leaning forward on my elbows. "Because I would propose that what makes you want to write something, even in this glorified kindergarten, is that you think you're *special*. You have a *special* story to tell and a *special* way of telling it. In defiance of an indoctrination that has worked relentlessly to punish it out of you, you have an innate, deep-seated need to distinguish yourselves as *better* than other people."

"Everyone is special!" Baozhai said in a panic.

"No," I said, punching my phone. "That would defy the meaning of the word: 'better, greater, or otherwise different from what is usual.' *Specialness* is an empty concept without a baseline to rise above. You cannot have special people without unspecial people. In fact, the concept is meaningful only if *most* people are unspecial. If most people basically suck. Which, you few standouts will be happy to hear"—I looked directly at Cameron—"they do."

This set piece now officially qualified as apostasy, which for my part felt exhilarating, and which for the zealots' part, alas, felt exhilarating, too. Drew Patterson had the look on his face of wondering whether he still had Dean Poot's office number in his contacts.

"I don't think we're the ones need to feel so goddamn special," Drew said. "'Cause you sure sound like a cathedral supremacist. Seems like you're the one thinks you're more better than everyone else."

That was the trigger. I have no idea why. It just was.

"*More better?*" I repeated, jumping to my feet. "Or maybe I feel *most better*. Or *more better-er. Better-er yet,* maybe I feel like the *most bestest* person in this room. I sure as hell feel *more better-er-er* than you, Drew. Because you're a senior in what was once a top-ten American college, and you sound like a hick. So tell me, because it's been bugging me: are you *actually* dumb, or are you *playing* dumb?"

Effectively, a crack of lightning. Eyes glittering, Drew licked his lips; it was to witness exactly this moment that he had enrolled in no fewer than three of my courses. "Ooh, baby," he said with a grin. "Your ass is fried, lady."

"Honestly, that's what I need to know from all of you." Emerging from behind the desk, I was out of control, but whatever forbearance I'd been drawing on for years had plumb run out; the tank of self-interested re-straint was bone-dry. "Are you people really so stupid that you believe this claptrap about 'everyone being as smart as everyone else,' or are you cynically playing along with a lie that you *know* is a lie? Do you even know the difference at this point? And either way, do you imagine the lie is harmless? A massive whack of this student body never would have been admitted to this university with even the most *minimal* aptitude require-ments. Lest I risk being misunderstood? Point-blank, most of your fellow students are stupid. So even the smart students are drowning in stupid. We're graduating engineers who couldn't put together a . . . a Popsicle-stick basket! Computer coders who don't know how to turn on the italics in Microsoft Word! Try going to an emergency room now, where you'll be diagnosed by some dimwit frantically punching your symptoms into WebMD.com and performing amputations with dull scissors! The entire cabinet of the federal government was specifically selected for being thick as a plate of cold mashed potatoes, and these are the people charged with not running the economy into the ground and representing this country abroad! You think we're seen as so dazzlingly, enviably *fair?* No, we're a laughingstock! China and Russia *think we're retards.* And they're right! We're retards! Mental Parity is *retarded,* and everyone who's gone along with it is *retarded,* and that includes me, I'm afraid, for cooperating with this farce for even five minutes, much less for six long years, so mea culpa! This institution is retarded, this country is retarded, and your teacher is retarded, too—*retarded, retarded, retarded!*"

My cheeks were flaming and doubtless red; my breath was labored. Half the students had either left or were in the process of leaving. The other half had stuck around to film the diatribe on their phones, much the way enterprising photojournalists had captured for posterity the Buddhist monks in Vietnam who set themselves on fire.

CHAPTER 3

The joys of the internet being what they are, by the time that, with nauseous foreboding, I forced myself to check my email on arrival home, I'd been sacked. Though it was only five p.m., I poured myself a frozen vodka the size of a hotel orange juice. It was a trite emotional response, but I wasn't terribly consumed with originality at the time. Oh, and overpriced grain alcohol didn't help in the slightest, if you're interested, though the glass did give my hand something to rest on to keep it from shaking. When FaceTime rang on my phone and I saw it was Emory, I hesitated a couple of rings before punching *accept*.

"It's everywhere, Pearson." She skipped so much as hello. I recognized the backdrop as her slick Voltaire two-bedroom. "Not only on Twitter, either. You're in the live feed of *The New York Times*."

"Yes, well, you'll forgive me if I don't rush to go read it. I was there, so I can skip consulting the misquotations."

"Multiple videos are online. They don't need to misquote you."

I took another slug. "Oh, and I've been fired. Universities are known for their creaky bureaucracy. It's heartening to see that at least the Office of CE can move with such fleet-footed efficiency."

"You're surprised? And I don't understand why you sound so flippant."

"I can now sound however I like. When all is lost, nothing's at stake."

"What the hell got into you?"

"Nothing that hasn't been in me since I was about ten years old. I guess the question is why it got out."

"Exactly. Aside from that nonsense with Fyodor a few years ago, you've kept yourself in check. Now you've thrown it all away—for the sheer satisfaction of blowing your top, as far as I can tell. Was it worth it?"

"Emory, I don't need to be lectured. Not now."

"I worry you don't understand how serious this is."

"Oh, I understand, all right. I live in the same world you do, you know. I've never figured out why you think you have to translate it for me."

". . . Are you okay?" A softening. For a moment, she sounded like a friend of mine.

"Of course I'm not *okay*. That's like asking someone who's jumped off a forty-story building if they're *okay*. And I dread telling Wade."

"You won't have to. You're topping all the push notifications. All he has to do is turn on his phone."

"Oh, great. I can visit him in the hospital well assured that he's already pre-hating me. He's barely out of surgery. The timing could hardly be worse."

"It's *your* timing," she said.

"It's not a coincidence. I found out this morning they poured nitroglycerin or something in his IV by mistake, and they almost killed him. I was . . . in a state of some displeasure."

"I'm really sorry to hear that. Is he going to be all right?"

"So they tell me. Though I can't trust doctors anymore."

"Still, I doubt that's enough of an emotional backstory to get you off the hook. If you went off about incompetent medical personnel, it could sound like more of the same."

"You're already designing my comeback PR?"

"I think it's called clutching at straws. I have a hard time imagining how you'll escape being evil incarnate for the foreseeable."

"A sizable proportion of this country agrees with everything I said this afternoon. They'll watch that video, probably more than once, and not from horror but delight. They just won't say so."

"I'm not sure that proportion is 'sizable,' Pearson. There's a fringe of outliers on the right—"

"Why is belief in standards, and excellence, and stringent qualifications for certain important jobs necessarily right-wing?"

"Now of all times you want to split political hairs? Yes, the elevation of those values over other values, of justice, of civility, is perceived as reactionary, if not fascistic. You can rail against those labels with me, but you'll never win that argument in public."

"That's because my compatriots are cowed, frightened, easily manipulated worms."

"More winning PR," Emory said. "Though I'm queasy about the ge-
netics of a 'cowed worm.'"

A glimmer of our old affectionate banter, now grown all too rare.

Right before she signed off, I noticed a funny rectangular ghost beside
her bookcase on the wall behind her. The framed letter my mother had
forced me to write, telling Emory that we could no longer be friends unless
she found God, because otherwise she'd be "wiped from the earth in the
coming battle between Jehovah and worldly government": it was missing.

My children are digitally literate. Even Lucy was not averse to learning when it came to mastering her iPad. So I assumed the whole trio
had watched the four-minute and fifty-two-second video by the time I'd
backed out of VU's reserved faculty parking (for the last time, as it happened; I was immediately banned from campus, not even allowed to clean
out my office). They'd have waited until they heard me get off FaceTime,
after which Darwin and Zanzibar filtered down to the kitchen with the
silent somnolence of a procession in Catholic mass. After a slight lag—
D&Z never consorted with their younger sister if they could help it—Lucy
followed, skipping with glee, though I think even at ten she grasped the
rough implications of my newfound infamy. After all, she'd personally
brought the full force of officialdom to bear on her mother on the basis of
hearsay. This ongoing public lynching—which was just getting started—
was sparked by hard evidence.

As a rule, in adolescence Darwin was emotionally undemonstrative,
so the fact that he rested a hand on my shoulder for a long, sorrowful beat
nearly moved me to tears. Grown willowy and as tall as her mother at
fourteen, Zanzibar took my face between her palms, kissed the center of
my forehead, and gave me a hug. When Lucy exclaimed, "Mommy's gonna
get in tro-ouble!," they blanked her.

We convened with a funny formality around the kitchen table. Despite
the fact that their maternal genetic heritage was therefore on the aesthetic

wane, I was still gratified that as they matured both D&Z were looking more Japanese. I loved the subtle androgyny of my donor's ethnicity, which made them seem more like identical twins than brother and sister. I treasured the unwritten canvas of their features, which seemed capable of concealing just about anything, even if that entailed concealment from me. I'd always associated the Japanese visage with not so much duplicity as discretion—a quality in eternal short supply in the United States. Physically, the contrast between the older two and their sister had only sharpened. Lucy wasn't fat, but she'd grown blunter; one of Wade's close ancestors must have been a lumberjack.

For a minute we didn't say anything. The feeling was that we didn't have to. We were all in the process of working out the inevitable domino effect of my outburst; we could almost hear the dotted wooden tablets clicking in a snake around the room. Even Lucy was socially attuned enough to infer that maybe at this exact moment it was best to put a sock in it.

"I'm most concerned about what effect this could have on you kids," I said at last. "The stigma . . ."

Darwin emitted a short, mirthless guffaw. "We're already stigmatized. Have been for years."

"Smart is one thing," I said. "Satanic is another."

"No, smart and evil aren't any different," he said. "Not anymore."

"You shouldn't worry about us," Zanzibar said. "I mean, maybe you should, but things on our end really couldn't get much worse."

"You may be wrong about that," I said. "You could be physically attacked."

"That might be a relief," Zanzibar said.

"No, it wouldn't be," I said. "I think for now you should all stay home."

"Nobody ever attacks me!" Lucy declared. She was making the same mistake of so many of her revolutionary forebears, who time and again blithely assumed that the forces they'd unleashed would never blow up in their own faces. I had a feeling our family's neo-Stasi snitch had made a fair number of enemies at her elementary school. Some of her classmates might seek to turn the tables once she was tarred overnight as the spawn of a pariah.

"I realize you're *way too scary* for anyone to pick on," I said. "But just to be on the safe side, for now you're staying home from school, too."

"For me, doesn't matter," Darwin said. "I'm sixteen next week. Planning to drop out anyway."

When he was younger, I'd never have imagined that my son the scientific prodigy would ever say such a thing and all I'd respond was "Yeah, I know."

"Have they fired you yet?" Zanzibar asked.

"Yup."

"So with Wade laid up," Darwin said, "where's the money coming from?"

"That's not the sort of thing you should concern yourself with. It's your parents' business to sort out." I must have advanced this parodically Mommy-ish assertion by way of playacting the competent grown-up, since I was starting to feel like anything but. I'd been irresponsible. I'd driven our family to insolvency. I'd communicated an additional social taint that my abominably bright older children could ill afford. And for what? Unless it was only the vodka, one sign that I was feeling more culpably negligent than I could bear was near narcolepsy at six p.m. I could hardly keep my eyes open.

"It's totally our business," Darwin said. "So don't be—can I say 'Don't be stupid'?" He nodded at Lucy. "I mean, what can she do to us now?"

"I think what you should say," I said with a little smile, "is 'Don't be *retarded.*'"

"*Retarded, retarded, retarded!*" both older siblings recited together, and laughed. Lucy scowled. Some spell had been broken, and she didn't like it.

I went on to explain that we had to brace for a slew of vitriol. I'd be pilloried on social media and in the press. The house might draw hostile reporters; in that instance, we should refuse to talk to them and shelter our faces from photographers. No one should answer the landline. Meanwhile we needed to be nice to one another, I said, because no one else would be. Although we'd need to visit Wade until he came home, we should avoid unnecessary forays into the outside world. For groceries and such, until this foofaraw blew over—"If it ever blows over," Zanzibar noted—we should order in. Insofar as humanly possible, I suggested staying off the internet, if only to preserve what little peace of mind we had left.

"How are we going to buy everything online and stay off the internet?" Darwin said.

"You know full well which sites to steer clear of. Don't put yourselves in the way of incoming artillery. Remember that when people say and write horrible things about your mother, you can't ever unhear or unread them."

And then I said I could not express how sorry I was to have brought this shitstorm down on our heads.

"Don't apologize," Darwin said. "I thought it was fantastic. I was only disappointed it didn't last longer. I've watched it four times now. Like, good for you. Finally pulled your tongue out of the MP ass."

"I never planned to say any of that stuff," I said. "I just lost it. I don't see how I get anything out of this besides grief. I'm not sure I deserve your admiration for an act of consummate self-destruction."

"Take what you can get," he said.

It was good advice.

Wade's release the very next day should have been good news, if only because he was safer out of the clutches of ninnyhammers, but facing down his reaction to the fact that he was now living with the most de-plored woman in America was nothing to look forward to. This was a guy whose raison d'être was to be left alone—to be overlooked, to fade into the landscape—and I might as well have covered our house in the overkill Christmas decorations of neon poinsettias, blinking fairy lights, illuminated snowmen, and rooftop Santa's sleigh that send your electric bill into the thousands and draw gawkers from out of town. Sure enough, that morning the TV crews I'd anticipated had set up on the sidewalk.

In a scarf and dark glasses, I dived into the car, uncertain why I made so much effort to keep from running them over.

On arrival at the hospital, for once I regretted my "interesting face." It seemed I was instantly recognizable. Medics whose job was ostensibly nurturing, healing, and caretaking pointed at me in the hallways, turned heel and marched nose-high in the opposite direction, glared with un-abashed antipathy, and indulged in verbal abuse, from a mumbled passing "bigot" or "fucking hatemonger" or "you're a disgrace!" to the receptionist's prim, tight-lipped instruction, "I hope you can keep your potty mouth zipped, madam. We don't tolerate cognitive smears in this facility."

By the time I caught my breath in that empty classroom, I'd already accepted that my diatribe had been reckless—impetuous, intemperate— but those are morally moderate adjectives that didn't belong in any sincerely searing self-reproach. True, I'd resorted to language "unac-ceptable" not only in the post-MP years but for the previous twenty. Yet by my own lights the taboo against employing "the R-word" was merely a matter of rhetorical fashion. The term simply meant "slowed." Given time, the stigma that attached to being *learning delayed*, or whatever we were told to call the disability next, would inexorably infect every euphemism that replaced it—much as one's unwashed clothes, transferred to another piece of luggage, will soon impart the same funk to the new bag. When I was growing up, children wielded the word with abandon, while "mentally retarded" was still the preferred, neutral classification of the public school system. Proscriptions installed later in life don't bite as deep. Besides, in the climax of my tirade, I may have instinc-tively reached for "retarded" for its very rawness. I'd been trying to cut through.

On review, then, although my demeanor had hardly embodied a model of pedagogical patience, I believed everything I'd said. I'd impugned the larger student body as unqualified (well—not "unqualified"; *stupid*); I'd dissed the absent Jerome's dismal doggie story; I'd insulted Drew Patter-son, who'd been begging me for years to do just that; but I'd been short of overtly abusive to the other students in that class. I might have been kicking myself for inviting a host of dire practical consequences, but aside from unintentionally damaging my family's fortunes and reputation, I'd done nothing wrong in my own terms. Nevertheless, I can now testify that shaming works. I felt soiled. Feeling soiled for speaking the truth *did* seem wrong, which made me feel worse.

When I'd phoned the night before to warn that his partner had been "terminated with immediate effect," Wade had said only, "We'll talk about it later"—flatly, with no inflection. When I met his eyes as he perched on the edge of his hospital bed, I had trouble reading his expression. Forlorn? Resigned? Fuming? Despite everything, able to see the funny side of this debacle? It was anyone's guess. But the biggest favor I could do him at that moment was not share our personal business within anyone else's hearing. I'd brought his baggiest sweatpants, which just cleared the surgical boot. Mutely collecting his things, fetching his crutch—with his left wrist in a cast, he could use only the one—I concentrated solely on the material world that Wade understood.

Out in the parking lot, I adjusted the passenger seat backward to give him more room. In perfect silence, Wade propped his crutch against the car while keeping his balance with the open front door. When I stood, he pulled me to him with his uninjured arm and held me close for a good thirty seconds. It was just what I needed.

We didn't talk until we were both settled in our regular timber-framed lounge chairs on the broad back deck. The minimal footage the cameras out front would have garnered when we slipped in the side door from the carport wouldn't have given them much for the evening news, and our woodsy backyard, newly exploded into leaf, protected us from the peering of disapproving neighbors. It was doubtless inadvisable to combine the white wine I'd poured us with Wade's pain medication, but we were learning to live on the wild side.

"This is nice," Wade said, reaching for a cheese straw. "I guess we're all on a kind of extended vacation."

"Or retirement," I said.

"You're forty-four. That'd be a *very* extended retirement."

I took a sip of Chablis. It was only four p.m., but at least white wine was more likely to go the distance during a long-term dependency than straight vodka. The air was oxygen-rich and humid with a slight breeze; the cheese straws were crisp; the birds were nesting. In this state of suspended repose, it was hard to remember what all the fuss was about.

"It was bound to happen sooner or later," Wade said.

"Oh, probably," I said.

"You're headstrong. You have a temper. You can't stand irrationality, and you have an authority problem. Whenever we go through airport security together, I hold my breath. It's worse than traveling with a bomb in my bag. I travel with a bomb on two legs. So maybe I should be grateful you held off for so long."

"I don't know. Maybe I should have gotten it over with years ago. Then I could have trained as your assistant at Treehouse, Inc., and your wrist and ankle would be fine."

"You get vertigo, and you're terrified of chain saws. You'd make an awful tree surgeon."

"I wouldn't have mugged you with a tree branch while you were at the top of a ladder."

"Pretty low bar," Wade said.

". . . Are you mad at me?" I asked in a small voice.

"What good would that do?"

"Authentic emotions aren't always *useful.*"

"I knew what you were like when we got together."

"Do you *like* what I'm like?" I seldom sounded so timid.

"I accept what you're like. But that isn't what I'm thinking about, and with three kids it shouldn't be what you're thinking about, either."

"I don't want to be thinking about what I'm thinking about."

"I couldn't sleep last night," Wade said. "I'm stumped. I don't know what to do."

"Did they give you any idea how long it will take before you can walk?"

"Six weeks, maybe two months. That's if all goes well. And you? The way you . . . You won't get any severance?"

"Not after violating VU's *core values.* I'd be surprised if I get this month's paycheck. I'm sure there's some moral turpitude clause in the fine print."

"Moral turpentine . . . ?"

I laughed. "Maybe that's what I need to clean off the stink: *moral turpentine.*"

"That video. It's going to follow you."

"I know, I know! I can kiss any other teaching job goodbye."

"We're way past that. We're talking any job. Every time someone enters your name into a search field . . ."

"Give me a little credit. I've been intensely aware of that from the get-go."

"You're marked. And it could last for years."

"I could change my name and get plastic surgery."

"You say that like a joke. But it's not a joke. It could come to that. Though we don't have the wherewithal for plastic surgery—"

"Or I guess we could leave the country."

"People always say that. But it's not so easy, switching countries. And it's possible that the video . . . especially in Europe, Canada, Australia. It could even keep you from getting a visa."

"There's always Russia or China."

"This is serious," Wade said. "You have to stay serious."

"I was serious. Though both countries are very restrictive. And leery of Americans. It's as if we carry a virus, a cultural virus, and they don't want to get infected."

"We have to focus on right now. We don't have—"

"I know what we don't have," I snapped. "We can probably get through June. Maybe even July."

"It's May."

"I know what month it is. I'm out of a job, I'm infamous, but I'm not demented."

"The semester was almost over. You only had to get through a couple more weeks—"

"Okay, I knew the recriminations would come eventually. So go ahead. You're due. Recriminate."

"I don't want to fight." Wade backed down. "But I don't know what people do. In this situation. It has to have happened to people before, with accidents or other bad luck."

"If you're fired for 'willful misconduct,' you don't qualify for unemployment in Pennsylvania. I looked it up."

"I'm self-employed, so I don't get unemployment, either. There's a chance I could get disability through Social Security, but the process of applying can take a long time, and I'm not good at that stuff. I hate it."

"You're right that this kind of sudden calamity or roadblock, everything going wrong—it has happened to people before. Lots of people. And there is a protocol." I said heavily, "You lose everything."

I didn't realize at that time quite how right I was.

CHAPTER 4

With the kids home all day on a weekday and wine in the afternoon, the house had a perversely holiday feel, and none of our old rules seemed to apply. With the edge off our appetites, Wade and I got a late start on dinner. After all, what did any of us have to get up for in the morning? I didn't head upstairs to fetch the kids to the table until 9:45 p.m. Zanzibar would be in Darwin's room, and when I knocked and was granted admission after a slight delay, they were both still gathered around his computer, though the lid was closed.

"I assume you're ordering groceries?" I said. "Because I told you. Unless it's for logistical reasons, stay off the internet."

"It's bad, Mom," Zanzibar said.

"Of course it's bad," I said. "Why else would I urge you to avoid it?"

"I mean it's really bad, Mom," my daughter emphasized. "And whether or not we see it doesn't change the fact it's there. Keeping ourselves in the dark doesn't make it go away."

"What have you been looking at, Twitter? Facebook?" I said. "This, too, shall pass. Next week they'll be cutting somebody else's head off."

"Twitter and Facebook are awful enough, but—"

"You heard her, Zanzo," Darwin interrupted. "She doesn't want to know."

"She has to know, and she's going to know," his sister said.

"She doesn't have to know *now*," Darwin said. They were talking as if I weren't there.

"What's the point of putting it off?" Zanzibar said. "Rip the Band-Aid."

"I don't know, maybe an aneurism will burst in her sleep tonight," Darwin said in exasperation, "and then she can die in peace!"

"What's this about?" I asked.

"Never mind!" Darwin said. "Forget about it! Let's have dinner!"

"Darwin thinks he can protect you," Zanzibar said. "I don't think so."

"Protect me from what?"

"If we tell you what we're protecting you from," Darwin said, "then we're not protecting you anymore, are we?"

"YouTube," my daughter said miserably.

"So some podcast went for the jugular?" I said. "I think I can take it."

"It goes up a few minutes after the broadcast." Zanzibar stared at the floor. "Every Thursday, a little after nine."

At last they triggered a genuine dread. Though sensitive as children, these two had hardened into tough cookies. They were less given to hyperbole than to dry understatement. I asked warily, "What goes up?"

Darwin and Zanzibar looked to each other. Finally in unison they said, "Auntie Em."

Funnily enough, in the CNN opener the kids then played a second time, the content was sufficiently arresting that for once I couldn't tell you what Emory Ruth was wearing.

We like to think that we're enlightened now—broad-minded, shed of the prejudice and Neanderthal misconceptions that for too long held Americans back as a people. We're fair. We're principled. We see the wit and wisdom in everyone. A whole vocabulary of bullying, vilification, and unfounded slander has been retired. But once in a while we're presented with incontrovertible evidence that a battle we like to think we won long ago is far from fully fought. Evidence that we have a long way to go. Evidence that maybe the war we thought was over has barely started.

Voltaire, Pennsylvania, is a leafy medium-sized city in the southeast of the state whose citizenry consider themselves socially advanced, morally upstanding, and politically forward-looking. I should know, because I was born and raised there. My parents live in Voltaire, and I still maintain a home in the city. Though I've not been so blessed, I've always thought it would be a great place to raise kids. If burdened with as dire a history of brutal cognitive discrimination as most of our nation's once disreputable

*educational institutions, Voltaire University was at least quicker than most
to embrace Mental Parity, and to undergo a soul-searching of its disgrace-
ful past. So I'm sorry to say that, as of yesterday, I'm ashamed to hail from
Voltaire, which until a certain viral video finally fades from our country's
collective memory is sure to function as a byword for hate.*

*Furtively, many of you have already seen it. But some of you may not
have, and I'm of the view that to combat deep-seated, virulently enduring
cerebral supremacy, we have to look it in the face. While I commonly aspire
to broadcast a family-friendly show, parents might usher their little ones
away from the TV for the next few minutes. I'd also advise the viewership
that the content we're about to air violates a host of strict ethical guidelines
at CNN. But our CEO felt as strongly as I did that editing this footage
would unethically blunt its impact. Were we to bleep out the cognitive
smears, all you'd hear is bleep this, bleep that—one long bleep, in fact.
Apologies in advance for the obscenities you're about to hear, but sometimes
there's no substitute for the raw, unvarnished ugliness of real life.*

This version of the video picked up at "*Specialness* is an empty concept
without a baseline to rise above," that opening line alone conceptual
anathema, rapidly accelerating to all those *more betters, better-ers,* and
most bestests, which had felt cleverly cutting at the time but on television
appeared deranged. I hadn't watched any of these clips before. I hanged
myself even more unequivocally than I'd remembered. (This notion I'd
nursed that I hadn't directly abused my own students didn't hold up.) It's
always unnerving to see yourself objectified like any old somebody, and
the spectacle is reliably devastating; we're never as attractive, articulate,
funny, or charming as we imagined, and this performance heightened
that shock. My hair was disarranged, my eyes were bulging, my hands
out of control. More than once in the harangue my voice broke. I hadn't
realized I'd used the word "retarded" quite that many times. Though I
always kept the word mentally to hand, sequestered in my private lexicon
if only for the purpose of referring to myself when I'd done something
exceptionally silly, on-screen over and over it made me wince.

———

*W*ell, Emory continued, *that was an instructor to whom countless parents have entrusted their offspring—young people on the cusp of adulthood, ideally confronting their futures with hope, optimism, self-confidence, and a nonjudgmental openness to others unparalleled in any previous generation of Americans. Are these the qualities their teacher cultivates? Hardly. In a shrill, berserk lambaste, she promotes self-doubt, chagrin, and a retrograde impulse to ridicule other people. Here the invective we thought we'd buried once and for all has crawled from the grave, like an especially grisly scene from* The Walking Dead.

The administration of Voltaire University assures us that this woman, one Pearson Converse, has been fired. About time. But the school should have acted on glaring warning signs three years ago that this faculty member harbored alarming far-right views. Converse had assigned a Dostoevsky novel with a title so offensive that Amazon now refuses to stock the book. As for which novel, I will spare you one more slur. I think you've been bludgeoned enough for one night.

There were other red flags. Voltaire's Child Protective Services were put on notice in 2014 that Pearson Converse was a danger to both the community and her own children. She had abused her youngest, a pretty, delicate thing then only seven years old, by smearing the little girl to her face as cognitively deficient. What punishment did our civil servants mete out? A mandatory course in etiquette. A course. Meanwhile, numerous friends, relatives, and ex-colleagues of the disgraced former English instructor have testified to reporters that in private conversation Converse routinely employs cognitive slurs and pillories Mental Parity as "kooky," "self-defeating," and "delusional."

But perhaps the brightest red flag is also the oldest. Converse was so committed to our rigid, fallacious, arbitrary, and now blessedly anachronistic mental hierarchy that she selected a sperm donor exclusively for his, ahem, "genius level" IQ. We might feel sorry for such a mother, who was sold a bogus product: sperm that could produce only children with the same intellectual abilities as everyone else's children. Except that her older two kids have been raised to believe that they are the product of vastly superior genes, and that their mental capacities tower over those of their classmates. The results have been tragic: kids living out a fantastical version of themselves that has inevitably turned them both into outcasts at school. Let's call a spade a spade: Pearson Converse is a eugenicist. And a failed eugenicist is still a eugenicist.

Is merely losing her job sufficient—a job that I gather Converse never took very seriously to begin with? Is public shunning sufficient—since the chances are that Pearson Converse's dinner invitations will from here on be few and far between? This case is so extreme that mere social and professional exile seems inadequate.

I would encourage the students Converse traumatized to seek therapeutic help. Following their psychiatric recovery, I'd also encourage her victims to pursue justice in civil court. Surely those poor kids are due compensation for emotional damages. Yet I also think a larger social gesture is called for, the better to put this wretched episode behind us, and to signal to the remaining troglodytes creeping out from under their rocks that we've had enough of their bile.

Voltaire the "philosopher" was a figure from the Age of Arrogance who fancied himself preeminent in every way. His written work celebrates mockery. In particular, he had it in for the otherwise. I never thought much about it growing up; "Voltaire" was simply the city I lived in, and I wasn't keenly aware of the man to whom that name paid tribute. I'm aware now. A student movement at the university is demanding that we rename my birthplace after someone or something we can be proud of. I'm throwing my support behind this crusade. Let's stop memorializing self-anointed brainiacs who held so many of their contemporaries with perfectly comparable talents in contempt. Let's emancipate the lovely place where I grew up from its misguided genuflection. This program has a large, invariably smart, creative viewership. You can contribute suggestions for the city's rechristening on CNN.com/RIPVoltaire, or via #NewHometownforEmoryRuth on Twitter.

Lastly, lest the tip-off be leaked later as some sort of scandal, yes, Pearson Converse is an acquaintance of mine, and has been for some years. So on top of being socially concerned for all of us, I find her outburst personally disappointing.

———

Um, yes. Talk about personally disappointing. I'd been braced for an onslaught of opprobrium from strangers. Not for this. D&Z saw me downstairs to the table, each taking an arm, as if their mother had become an invalid. They left it to me to bring it up, and I didn't. We talked, haltingly, of other things. Lying wide-awake that night, I told myself I should be angry, and I kept groping for my fury as I might have searched for a pair of reading glasses I'd mislaid in the sheets. The anger wasn't to be found. Sorrow alone sat on my chest, crushing my breath like a stone.

By the next morning, with Lucy still abed, the moratorium on the subject was lifted. Clumping about the kitchen in his surgical boot, doggedly organizing breakfast, Wade, typically, tried to remain neutral. D&Z were anything but.

"I don't see why you'd ever speak to her again," Zanzibar said.

"We've been friends for thirty years," I said.

"*Acquaintances*," Darwin said.

"Don't," I said.

"Sorry," Darwin retreated. "Here. Zanzo made you some toast."

They were tending me. They were parental.

I was sitting before my cup of coffee, my phone resting on the kitchen table. The device was an instrument of torture.

Zanzibar noticed that I kept staring at it. "You don't actually think she's going to call, do you? 'Oh, it's ten a.m.! More than anybody, I totally feel like talking to the one person I just trashed for fifteen solid minutes in front of millions of people!'"

"No, obviously she's not going to call," I said glumly. "But the prospect of my calling her makes me ill." Too clearly, I could hear Emory's cool, indecently collected voice on the other end, in contrast to my stop-start gibberish—since often, when you have too much to say, you can't say anything. "Besides, what would I tell her?"

"'Fuck you!'" Zanzibar supplied.

"What good would that do?" I may have instinctively been consulting children on how to proceed because, although Emory and I were middle-aged, our rift was reminiscent of seventh grade.

"I think Zanzo means unloading on her might make you feel better," Darwin said.

"It wouldn't," I said.

"You know perfectly well," Wade said, bringing me the all-fructose strawberry jam, "she'd see it was you and let the call go to voicemail."

"Probably," I said.

"Definitely," Wade said. After all, my partner was the expert on side-stepping conflict. Satisfied with my cryptic thumbnail, he hadn't even listened to Emory's diatribe on CNN—in defiance of my usual instruction to composition students that whenever possible they should rely on original sources.

"And then I'd leave, what?" I said. "Some flustered, babbling message that's unintelligible."

"No message," Wade said.

"If she's not going to pick up and I'm not leaving a message, there's no point in making a call in the first place," I said irritably.

"Maybe you *should* leave a message," Zanzibar said. "Write it out first, so you can't trip over your words. Like I said: 'Hi, Emory, I just wanted to tell you I'm never speaking to you again.'"

"You don't *phone* people to inform them you're not speaking to them," I said. "That's a contradiction in terms. Clearly, you don't mean it."

"Text, then!" Zanzibar said in exasperation.

"Right, and then I can text, 'I'm not texting you, either.'"

"No," Darwin said, "how about adding 'and thanks a lot for telling the whole world that my stuck-up kids have delusions of grandeur.'"

For me, the passages of Emory's treacherous speech that induced rage rather than catatonic depression were the ones about my children. But indulging that wrath would only exacerbate my son's own sense of personal betrayal. I noted tritely instead, "Dependence on texting is one reason your generation is so ham-fisted at conducting relationships."

"Don't you oldies have a thing for email?" Darwin said. "So send a long one. Get it out of your system. Lay it out. Take your time. Have your say. Get in all the one-liners that most people think of only after it's too late."

"Trust me, email is the road to perdition," I said. "I've seen it at the department repeatedly. The first party bashes out one version of events. The other party bashes out a different version. The back-and-forth accelerates until what started as a small disagreement blows up into all-out war."

"Seems to me you and Auntie Em are at all-out war already," Zanzibar said.

"But this isn't only about right now," I said. "It's about a lifetime. I've known her twice as long as you've been alive, sweetie. You keep pushing me to walk away, but never speaking to each other again would leave a ragged edge. It would afflict me like one of those scratchy care labels at the back of the neck, and not only for a week or two, but for years. Possibly forever. And I'd always be afraid of running into her."

"Why shouldn't *she* be more afraid of running into *you*?" Darwin asked.

"Because I'm not a hundred percent sure she'll think she's done anything wrong," I said. "I can't think of a time she's ever thought she did something wrong. It's a certain kind of person. Hell, it's most people."

"Are you any different?" Wade said, topping up my coffee.

"Maybe not," I said. "Like, I still don't think what I said in that creative writing class was wrong. It wasn't wrong; it was stupid."

Having finally gotten up, Lucy was clambering into her chair to pour milk on her cereal. "Mommy said the S-word!" she declared. But her heart wasn't in the admonition. She didn't understand why, but she could tell we weren't afraid of her anymore.

"That's right, Lucy," I said wearily. "Get used to it." Reputational oblivion had a liberating side. I was impervious.

"If you did talk to her," Wade said, "wouldn't you risk getting another earful? You don't want to have to go through that CNN thing twice."

"As usual," I said, "your solution is avoidance."

"I just don't want her messing with your head any more than she's messed with it already, sport," he said, placing a warm hand on the side of my neck. "There's a place for avoidance. You don't walk through the middle of an oil slick."

"Only one option is off the table, folks. And that's doing nothing." I tapped the phone case pensively. "After thirty years, there has to be a way to the other side of this."

"You're not seriously considering forgiving her, are you?" Zanzibar asked.

"Forgiveness of the unrepentant is meaningless," I said. "One hand clapping."

"Who knows," Darwin said, "maybe she'll surprise you and be super-sorry. Maybe she figured she was just doing her job, and she expected you'd understand that, like always. Maybe the whole thing was tongue in cheek, like, a performance, a fake-out. Maybe she thought you'd see she was playacting. Sucking up to her bosses at the station. I mean, she doesn't actually believe this shit, does she?"

"Of course not," I said.

"She's been into this humoring the head honchos for years, hasn't she?" Darwin said. "So maybe she had no idea that this time you'd take it seriously and she'd hurt your feelings."

"Calling for the students to *sue*?" Zanzibar said incredulously. "Never mind hurting Mom's *feelings*. Em set the dogs on her! As if we aren't broke enough already!"

"Okay, okay, point taken," Darwin said. He'd always adored Emory, and this situation was hard on him, too. "I only mean—maybe she didn't realize she was going too far."

We'd knocked out an unavailing phone call, a halting voicemail message, a texting tit-for-tat, and an escalating email feud bound to end in nuclear holocaust. One form of communication remained, looming above the others as maximally terrifying.

YOU OWE ME THIS MUCH, I texted quickly before I could chicken out. MEET ME FACE-TO-FACE.

CHAPTER 5

I was surprised that in our terse exchange of texts Emory agreed to come to our house. I thought if she was willing to see me at all she might insist on neutral territory—a coffee shop, a park. But she might have concluded that an encounter in public would seem artificial, stilted, obliging us to be civil, to keep our voices down, to be mindful of being overheard; if we weren't going to be candid, meeting up would serve no purpose. It wasn't as if we were handing off a bag of bills for a ransom exchange or something. Besides, I'd verified at the hospital that I was easily recognized as the bigot who'd let fly with a "shrill, berserk lambaste." Thanks in part to Emory herself, I couldn't go anywhere without being accosted.

Since members of my family had yet to have their faces plastered on wanted posters, Wade took the kids to a movie, the better to give Emory and me privacy and to eliminate any impression that she was being ganged up on.

With saddening punctuality, Emory drove up at the exact knell of four p.m. This was the temporal precision that governed appointments with doctors or lawyers, strangers with whom one's dispassionate relationship is transactional. Parking out front and heading for the side door, she ran a gauntlet of cameras that she had personally helped plant on our sidewalk. They didn't appear to rattle her. Emory was used to cameras.

Peering from behind the front blinds, I couldn't help it: I was happy to see her. I was always happy to see her. As habitually, I checked out her garb: black leggings, scoop-necked black sleeveless top, spotlessly white cross-trainers—the nearly weightless kind for maximum agility. It was workout gear. She was dressed to spar.

I'd spent an uncommonly long time deciding what to wear myself. The season was changing, and I went from too cold to too hot and back in an afternoon. Feeling a need to swaddle myself, I'd opted for soft, oft-washed jeans and a plain white T-shirt, topped by a long-sleeved, below-the-knee, solid-red cloak open at the front. Its fabric weighty enough to give it swing and flow, the wrap had always made me feel classy. It was too late to reconsider this regular-shuffle-about-the-house-with-a-dash-of-style ensemble, but I was already sweltering. My pulse was high, my ears were ringing, my palms damp. Which was ridiculous. Emory was my best friend, right? My best friend.

The moment I opened the door it hit me in the face that Emory and I were living in drastically different realities, forming a Venn diagram whose circles didn't even kiss, much less overlap. In mine, I was aggrieved, and I had a right to be aggrieved. It should have been Emory's job from the start to assuage that grief, to explain herself—to both mend and make amends. But one glance confirmed that this wasn't how she saw matters one bit. My initial inkling proved horribly on the money: her expression was untroubled, the picture of innocence. I physically stepped back, as if from a slap.

Yet I was still civilized enough to mind my manners. "Would you like something to drink?" I solicited. "Tea, a beer?"

"I'm plenty hydrated, thanks," she said lightly, lifting her stainless-steel water flask.

Bad form. The purpose of a drink was not the liquid. To illustrate as much, I grabbed a beer I didn't necessarily want.

The weather being clement, I'd originally thought we'd talk on the verdant back deck, but it was abruptly clear that those timber-framed loungers would assemble us in an unsuitable attitude of ease. Extending side by side and gazing together at the birds flitting through our backyard bracken would have been painfully reminiscent of the truism that lovers look at each other, while friends look together at something else—and apparently when Emory and I stared at the same thing, I saw a white-breasted nuthatch and she saw a bottle of bleach. Instead, I led us to the living room. We never hung out in the living room.

I slid onto the leather couch, but instead of assuming its other end, Emory chose an upright wingback subtly too far away, putting her several inches higher than I was. Her affect was guileless, expectant, pleasant.

Technically I had summoned her, which put the onus on me to initiate proceedings and set the agenda. My head was racing with snippets of the monologues I'd delivered to the bedroom mirror, but I hadn't prepared an opening play and felt tongue-tied, at sea. Sometimes it's a mistake to rehearse these things. They never go according to plan.

"I guess you're not going to apologize," I said.

"No." Again, the lightness. The monosyllabic answer conveyed that she wasn't going to help.

"Can you . . . understand why I might think you should?"

"Narrowly," she allowed, crossing her legs so that one bright white athletic shoe caught the sun. "But then, I might just as naturally expect an apology from you."

"How do you figure that?" My astonishment was genuine.

"You put me in an intensely awkward position with that conniption fit of yours. Just enough people are aware we know each other—"

"That we're *acquaintances.*"

"That we're acquainted, yes," she said evenly. "By spewing all that poison in the vicinity of some thirty phones, you risked splashing some of it on me. In five minutes, you made yourself socially radioactive. You must have read about some of these cases. People have lost livelihoods two or three degrees of separation from an ill-considered remark, never mind a raving meltdown."

I wanted to put the beer down—alcohol in the presence of asceticism puts one at a disadvantage—but I didn't want to ring the oak coffee table or rise to fetch a coaster. The only answer was to drink it.

"Let me get this straight," I said, taking a slug for punctuation. "You can't see how denouncing me, my morals, my parenting, and my professionalism *on television* might possibly seem like a teeny-tiny betrayal?"

"On the contrary, I think it's an act of consummate loyalty to show up here in front of all those cameras after you've become Public Enemy Number One. For Pete's sake, you might at least have given a thought to your family. You've branded your partner and all three kids."

"Please. You're the one who dragged my children through the mud on CNN."

"I think Darwin and Zanzibar would be much better off if they got over this notion that they're endowed with superhero mental powers. That mythology makes them neurotic and alienates them from their peers. However much I may personally like them, to most people it makes them unlikable. If it goes on much longer, their pretense of precocity will destroy their prospects in adulthood."

"For you to take it upon yourself to drill into my children that they're drearily unexceptional would be overstepping big-time. Besides, you know full well that their precocity is no pretense."

"You've always made such a point of your middling intellect. But your sense of superiority the last few years—"

"Excuse me. *I* have a sense of superiority?"

"Your ego is bigger than you pretend. You just reroute your vanity through your kids. 'I may not be so smart, but my children are smart! Smarter than anybody's!' You use them to bolster your intellectual bona fides by association. It borders on child abuse, Pearson."

"I couldn't believe you labeled me a 'eugenicist.' I know you're expected to juice this stuff up for effect on TV, but talk about over-the-top—"

"You selected your older kids' father *solely* in accordance with his perceived IQ." (I noted that for Emory the insertion of "perceived" had become a reflex.) "What's that but eugenics? What else is there to call it?"

"You only know that because I confided it to you as a friend. And then you go and use it against me—"

"You advertise your kids' parentage to anyone who will listen. Everyone knows that who knows you. What few they number."

I didn't flag that last comment, though I should have. "You only knew a whole slew of that stuff because we're friends. An *acquaintance* wouldn't know any of it."

"I'm a journalist. I gather information wherever I can find it."

"So all along I should have been aware that anything I told you could end up on TV?"

"All along you should have been mindful of my occupation, sure. And honestly—I don't regard myself as the center of the universe, and I don't assume you organize your every behavior around me . . . Still, I've had to wonder if on some maybe unconscious level that flamboyant shitfit at VU was *intended* to damage my reputation. Or if that wasn't the intention, the blowback for me might at least have seemed a plus. It's not a conceit on my part but a fact: I have a high profile. You had to have known a Saint Vitus' dance like that was not only going to hit the internet but in short order would implicate the only person you know who's recognizable to the wider public."

"You were the last thing on my mind at the time. I'd simply had it up to the eyeballs and I exploded. For you to imagine I was deliberately trying to take you down with me *is* conceited. Worse than conceited, it's bonkers. Why on earth would I have any desire to sabotage your career?"

Emory sighed. So at odds were we in the present that I think she tended to forget I knew her very, very well. Ergo, her extended pause wasn't indicative of a reluctance to get into this whole subject matter; it was a *performance* of a reluctance to get into this subject matter, which she was champing at the bit to address.

"In the same way you've pretended to regard yourself as not very smart," she began, maintaining that air of hesitancy a beat or two longer, "you've pretended you're not ambitious. Which has always seemed like sour grapes to me. You've got to be disappointed in the way your career has turned out. You've never even made it to, like, associate professor or something. As for why, we don't have time here. Let's just say you've always been self-destructive. All your energy gets plowed into undermining yourself, as if you're furiously digging a hole under your own feet. Even if we overlook for a moment your spectacular detonation of a suicide vest two days ago, that absurd business with Dostoevsky is a premier example. What good did that do you? Along with a great deal of harm? But me, I've applied myself, I've worked hard, I've honed my skills, and I've gotten somewhere. I earned my way up, and I don't think I scored my current position at CNN through a lucky break; I think I got it because I deserve it. All I'm saying is, it's natural, maybe even inevitable, when two people have known each other a long time"—Emory had yet to employ the word "friend"—"and one of them excels and the other doesn't. You can't help it, but you're jealous. Good God, look at what I had to broadcast on Thursday to finally get you to watch one of my openers."

"I haven't avoided your broadcasts because I'm jealous, but because I find them political anathema."

"Uh-huh. And why is that?"

"Duh! Because I think Mental Parity is a load of twaddle. I've tried to be tolerant while you mouth support for this crap, but if I subjected myself to much of your lucrative propaganda, however insincere it may be, we were likely to get into fights."

"That's quite a story you tell yourself. So you've been sacrificing for the tranquility of our relationship—suppressing the almost uncontrollable yearning to see me shine in the media just so that we can get along better. It's a nicer story than being a comparatively unaccomplished English instructor who finds it too painful to confront the celebrity of another woman she grew up alongside who began basically in the same starting place."

"I wouldn't say growing up as a Jehovah's Witness was the same starting place."

"Thirty years on, can we finally call time on that self-pity?"

"I've never said I feel sorry for myself."

"You didn't have to."

After this torrent, we came to a stop. The beer was gone. I was bunched at the far end of the couch, my red wrap pulled tight and terminally wrinkled. Meanwhile, Emory was draped languidly across her wingback, bare arms open, her expression airily quizzical but otherwise unperturbed. It occurred to me then what a shame it was that present mores among the professional class forbade such a horror, because it would have suited Emory Ruth stylistically had she smoked. I was dumbfounded how this woman opposite had just two nights previous betrayed my confidence, imperiled my family, shoved the knife an extra two inches into my career, and assassinated my character on a major cable news channel, yet here I was the one balled into a defensive crouch. I forced myself to uncross my arms and sit up straight, but this body-language folderol is nefarious. I'd no sooner make a deliberate effort to stop looking so guarded than I'd find my arms crossed tightly once again, my tailbone slid forward, my shoulders hunched.

At last, as if benevolently filling the yawning social hole that her hostess was too maladroit to fill herself—in my mind's eye, beforehand she took a deep drag on one of those long, slender cigarettes marketed to women, and exhaled a thin stream of smoke with a hint of menthol—she noted idly, "And who says my openers are 'insincere'?"

She finally got me to sit up.

"You *believe* that stuff?"

"Every word."

"Since when?"

"I admit I was skeptical at first. Before MP, my father's academic life revolved around the cognitive hierarchy. Traditionally, lawyers like my mother were members of a cerebral elect. But gradually this new way of thinking began to make sense. Honestly, Pearson, why *is* it so important to you to be able to impugn other people's intelligence? To make them feel small and unworthy and inferior?"

"Insult isn't the point. The point is reality. And out here in reality, everyone is *not* as smart as everyone else."

"But why is that idea so important to you?" she reiterated.

"Because it's not an idea. It's a fact."

"According to you."

"Not according to me. According to the observable world over which our ideas exert no control."

"Well, that's all very fancy. But you're so proud of being a renegade. Does it ever occur to you that maybe you're isolated and culturally out in the cold because you're wrong?"

I got up and began to pace. "I can't believe we're even having this conversation."

"You described yourself a few minutes ago as 'tolerant.' You've been *tolerating* my advocacy of cognitive justice, which for reasons not altogether obvious you interpret as disingenuous. But every time I come over here, I'm subjected to the kind of crude language and throwback thinking that would get me fired in a millisecond at the studio. Seems to me

I'm the one who's been tolerant. Extremely tolerant. Maybe too. Silence is complicit."

"I know it is. That's why I finally blew my stack. I felt almost physically incapable of keeping my mouth shut any longer, because if I didn't say anything, all this consternation and disgust was going to explode through the top of my head. You act as if the only consequence of this barmy doctrine is that people are at long last being *nice* to each other. On the contrary, the country is falling apart!"

"I'm so tired of that Chicken Little nonsense," Emory said with an eye roll. "The sky is still up there."

"The sky is on the *floor*. Even your own parents are talking about emigrating."

"Sound familiar? The end of the world is nigh? Isn't that the same hysterical apocalypticism you grew up with? Maybe you didn't shake your religious indoctrination after all. And your pseudo-secular street-corner evangelism channels the same superiority I was talking about. It's more of the chosen-people guff you supposedly put behind you. *You* have a special vision. *You* have special access to the truth. *You* can see that the country is in tatters, and everyone else, for whom life keeps perking along just fine, is blind to its unfolding ruin. That's what this misfit iconoclasm of yours is about: clutching your status as uniquely enlightened to your chest like some one-eyed teddy bear."

"Why does this whole conversation so far concern *my* character?" I may have started to shout. "What about yours? What about your completely having changed your tune on this stuff, just because it's socially and professionally convenient? I mean, do you truly believe anything?"

"Yes, of course. I believe in Mental Parity. I seem to recall being crystal-clear on that point only two minutes ago."

"But you used to think it was hogwash."

"And what's wrong with political maturation?"

"What's wrong is throwing over everything you think, and everything you *know*, and credulously swallowing whatever crackpot notion your culture has most recently cooked up, just to be liked and to get along and to get ahead. What's wrong is being so empty, and so incapable of independent thought, that you'll believe pigs fly, and blue is red, and up is down, just because that's what they told you to mindlessly regurgitate *this* week—"

"'They'?" Emory interjected. "Pearson, you sound unhinged. There is no 'they.'"

"I thought we'd both been trying just to survive until the country gets a grip, but you're not surviving. You're actively propagating this tommyrot! I mean, Jesus Christ, I don't expect us to agree on everything, but I have no idea who you are anymore! I know you've always been out for number one, but I never had you down as a total coward. I never had you down as a fucking idiot!"

"Don't you *dare* use that language with me!" Whether Emory was offended by "the I-word" or pretending to be offended was up for grabs, but as she abandoned the chair that had so obligingly featured her shifting poses of nonchalance, she did finally seem a bit exercised. "The sanctimony of just that sort of pious, grandstanding speech, that's what's really the limit, Pearson—this unquestioning self-righteousness of yours! It's relentless! As if deep down inside, you're still a Jehovah's Witness after all! Talk about 'incapable of independent thought'? Well, thinking independently means first and foremost looking at *yourself* and holding out the possibility, the tiniest possibility, that you *yourself* might be full of shit. Like, since when are you so good and pure? Starting with the fact that at sixteen you broke your parents' hearts? And that affair you had with that lunkhead Italian"—*lunkhead?* she was slipping—"that was flat-out sexual harassment, if not assault—"

"Please. It didn't go down that way at all. He loved it."

"You were his teacher, and that was abuse of power, Miss Priss. And getting pregnant on top of that was irresponsible—"

"Come on, I've had one abortion, but you've had *two.*"

"*And* you never told him. What if he'd wanted the kid? Never got a chance to put a word in. Then you got this bizarro notion into your head to get artificially inseminated with some stranger's supposedly 'genius' semen, when you were making no money and had no partner. Wade rescued you, but he can't anymore because of the accident, and now look what you've done: left your family in the lurch, drenched in shame, with no income, just so you could 'blow your stack.' Oh, and let's not forget to throw in that you spurn, disparage, and neglect your own little girl, just because Lucy doesn't conform to your idea of a whiz kid. I don't call any of that righteous."

"You're doing it again. Twisting everything around so this is all about me. Two nights ago, *you* sold *me* downriver, okay? Dearly beloved, *that* is why we are gathered here today in the sight of God."

"Okay, let's talk about me, then." Placing a middle finger in the center of her forehead, Emory restored an appearance of calm that struck me as ominous. "From the start, I've tried to be charitable with you, Pearson. You were so out of the loop and awkward in high school. Yes, I did, I felt sorry for you. I brought you into my home. I've kept up with you—"

"What, I've just been your little project?"

"But you've been incredibly demanding. You've continually referred to me as your 'best friend,' but 'best' implies a bunch of other friends I theoretically stand head and shoulders above. What other friends? I don't think you have any, and I can't remember your ever having any. That puts a huge burden on me, Pearson. You've sometimes made a point of telling me how important I am to you, but that's the problem. I'm too important to you. I'm sorry to put it this way, but I don't know how else to say it: you're a little . . . clingy. Nuts, the way you wore that red scarf I gave you practically every day. It was just a scarf. A cheap little present. It meant too much to you. You're— You seem fixated on me, Pearson, and you've seemed fixated, unhealthily so, from the beginning. Sometimes I've even wondered . . ."

"Wondered *what*."

"Your obsession seems almost . . . erotic."

My hot cheeks would have matched my cloak. "Don't be ridiculous."

I must have gone into emotional shock. My paralytic disbelief was a convenience for my guest, as it facilitated the delivery of what I would personally tag a "pious, grandstanding speech" without interruption. I still remember the peroration nearly word for word, and I've little doubt that Emory had rehearsed it, much as I had rehearsed the bones I had to pick with her. But I had signally failed to hit the majority of my talking points:

I'd allowed my indignation over her public characterization of my older children as outcast fabulists to fall by the wayside; I'd never ridiculed her description of Lucy as "delicate"; I'd forgotten to so much as mention my outrage over her enticing my students to sue; my expression of affront over that "acquaintance" jab had been far too indirect; I'd neglected to pillory her ludicrous scheme to rename our city as ahistorical, Stalinist, and anti-intellectual, if the latter adjective could even function as a criticism anymore. By contrast, Emory managed, I would wager, to render her own practiced homily relatively intact.

"I could almost keep it up," she began, "even if your attachment to me is a little off-color. I've tried to support you and to include you in my family. To keep you company. To listen to your problems at VU and the challenges of raising your kids. And I could even, possibly, try to support you through this latest catastrophe you've brought down on your own head, if it weren't for the content of the catastrophe.

"It would be one thing if you and I didn't see eye to eye on, you know, the practical economics of recycling plastic. But landing on opposite sides of Mental Parity is too fundamental. It *is* about character. I'm sorry to sound sappy or preachy, but it's about primitive right and wrong. MP is about how we treat other people, and how we think about other people, and even how we regard ourselves—about what we think makes us valuable. You don't only cling to me personally, but you also insist on clinging to an outdated and frankly repulsive way of thinking, and I can't condone it. I can't implicitly endorse your regressive prejudice by continuing to see you, keeping quiet and looking the other way while you unashamedly promote sentiments I find atrocious. I can't keep pretending to laugh at jokes that aren't remotely funny. It's too much of a strain, and I go home hating myself.

"It was hard, but I came here because we *have* known each other a long time, and it would have seemed tacky and, yes, cowardly to send you an email or just stay out of touch until you got the message. So I'm telling you to your face: I can't do this anymore. It makes me feel like an accomplice. I'm abetting a brace of attitudes that turn my stomach. We're going to have to part ways. Please tell Wade and the kids I'm sorry and I wish them the best.

"Meanwhile, I hope you get some help. There are any number of terrific books out that might get the scales to fall from your eyes and break
down your obtuse resistance to seeing that human brains are all the same.
Look at the pictures. Just look at the damned pictures."

Emory rescued her stainless-steel water flask and saw herself out.
That was quite a lesson in learning not to act self-righteous.

I might not be good at math, but I have the emotional intelligence to
understand that anger is often a shield or, if you will, a blowtorch, which
blasts outward to protect the self from fully inhabiting pain. That's why I
was so surprised at my original reaction to Emory's scathing CNN broadcast: I'd have expected to be incandescent, then slowly admit to myself
that behind the fury lay a deep and abiding sense of injury. Instead, the
woundedness came first, and I was defenseless against it. I hadn't been
mad. I'd been sad.

Thus in the days following that conflagration in my living room, I had
reason to anticipate a searing self-reckoning: *Pearson, face it, you're hurt.
A friendship of many years has been demolished, its past defiled. There's no
alternative to feeling your way through this—through all the humiliation and
self-doubt. Particular lines from that conversation are going to circle back
and cut you like spirals of razor wire, and you will have to allow them to do
so, to lacerate you over and over until they've worn off their sharp edge. It's
impossible to tell from this vantage point how many months or even years it
will take for the blades to blunt, and there's no guarantee that recollection of
that Saturday afternoon will ever lose its power to flay you. We can only be
assured that there's no shortcut to the other side; as Wade would put it, you
have to walk through the middle of the oil slick. You must know your sorrow,
and even love your sorrow, to ever be shed of it.* In other words, just as the
headshrinking hacks would have recommended in relation to my parents'
renunciation at sixteen, I'd have expected to start in on the long, hard
work of "processing my grief."

Yet this drawn-out churn of grueling self-examination and gradual
acceptance of loss failed to commence. Instead what gathered was the

very anger that in the wake of that broadcast should have hit me up front. The anger was of a particular character, too: calm, steady, calculating, and above all cold. It wasn't a blowtorch but an ice pick. If there was a grain of truth to Emory's assertion that I had always been self-destructive, I was calling time on the tendency. I was now primed to destroy someone else.

As for what I did, I'm not asking for applause. I cheerfully concede it was unchristian. In retrospect, I regard my retaliatory play as downright unattractive, though I didn't care whether it was attractive at the time, and I still don't. I didn't give a tinker's damn whether anyone else agreed that the target had it coming, and that included Wade and the children, who may have been in accord over the gesture's being warranted but were divided on whether it did "any good." The point was not to do good. The point was to do harm.

Accordingly, I've no interest in forgiveness, from this story's principals or its purely hypothetical readership. As I told Zanzibar, forgiveness without repentance is meaningless, and I've never repented of my gambit, in which I took some pleasure—although that pleasure, even at its most intense, proved subdued. Revenge rarely satisfies, but I knew that going in. As suggested, I'm not an emotional halfwit. In fact, if you're expecting to be made whole in any way, I strongly advise giving vengeance a miss. It doesn't work. It doesn't make whatever you're avenging not have been inflicted on you in the first place. It seldom instills in your nemesis an iota of regret; it seldom spurs this poor excuse for humanity to acknowledge that the payback was deserved. But I wasn't intent on provoking regret, and it was of no consequence to me whether a certain someone ever acknowledged even to herself that she'd asked for it. I wasn't trying to make myself happy. I was trying to make the certain someone unhappy.

The most Old Testament of my children, Zanzibar helped, though the process turned out to be simple enough that I probably could have figured it out on my own. The video was easy to locate, because I'd rewatched it enough times to remember the date: 03/28/2010. Waiting a seemly couple of days after Emory's histrionic disavowal, I uploaded the file that Monday to YouTube:

"Da whole idea of da *dum-dum* is doo-doo! Da dum-dum's gone da way of da dodo!" Emory smashes a rice cracker against her forehead and swirls the crumbs in her hair. "I'm just as smawt as da pwesident! I'm gonna *be* pwesident! Cawswell Doofus-Doofus told me so!"

While I watched the whole take to confirm the transfer's success, I kept count—pleased to calculate that Emory had used the word "retarded" even more times than I had in my creative writing class at VU.

ALT-2023

CHAPTER 1

All right. Let's go for the wide-angle lens.

The uploaded video had the predictable effect. Not that Emory ever personally informed me as much, but no need; the fact that she'd been fired from CNN was all over the papers, not to mention on CNN itself, whose other hosts competed with one another over who could seem more incensed, and whose CEO took out a full-page apology to its viewership in *The Washington Post* and *The New York Times*. Countless other organizations with which Emory Ruth had formed alliances severed the link with great public fanfare. While that video was being viewed tens of millions of times, her televised Pearson Converse rant backfired, as I knew it would. The Twitter campaign she kicked off, #NewHometownforEmoryRuth, was re-hashtagged #NewHouseArrestforEmoryRuthless, so I was hopeful that the movement to rename the city of Voltaire would get lost in the shuffle. Our antics in 2010 were matey enough to imply that she and I were far chummier than "acquaintances," and to say that her rapturous repetition of all those R-words made her look like a hypocrite would be quite the understatement. Not one commentator mitigated her sins by allowing that, at the time I filmed the two of us cavorting on a third pinot, the term "Mental Parity" hadn't even been coined yet, much less had its tenets been sacralized into Western-wide gospel. By 2016, clemency was thin on the ground.

On reflection, the emotional payoff for pressing the *eject* button on Emory's meteoric career was not merely "subdued"; it was nearly nonexistent. I was fully aware that posting that video was mean and gratuitous. I had not made the world a better place. I was at peace with this. I'd never been heavily invested in being a "nice person," much less in being an altruist, and I wasn't bothered by how well or badly the deed reflected on my character. In my own terms, it was more concerning that, rather than tarnish the creed I reviled, I'd if anything fed the mania. By that point, it was a bastard to find anyone dumb enough to claim that anyone else was dumb, and serving up a rare certified smartist to rip to shreds merely provided fresh red meat to a media starved for carrion. But the animals would have found another corpse to chew on, with or without my help. In my detached repose, I've even wondered if my posting of that video on YouTube was a wan, backhanded bid for intimacy: I had landed Emory and me in the same boat.

I didn't waste any worry on how Emory would manage as roundly unemployable. I was too absorbed in having become roundly unemployable myself. Apropos of the poor rewards of revenge, having dragged another woman down with me hadn't refurbished my own reputation in the slightest. In short order, too, my family's tribulations multiplied further.

The failure took a few weeks to manifest, but Wade's ankle did not seem to be healing within the time frame that Dr. Sarsaparilla had estimated. More to the point, it did not seem to be healing, period. My partner aspired to stoicism, but even heroic grin-and-bear-its can't muster blitheness in the face of agony proper, and his suffering read loud and clear despite his efforts to conceal it. What was also apparent as he lunged about the house leaning on furniture: the pain was getting worse.

In time, we went back to Sarsaparilla, who seemed annoyed that his handiwork wasn't performing according to plan, and who projected this disappointment onto the patient, as if Wade were the disappointment. Announcing in a second follow-up appointment that now the surgery would have to be done all over again, he sounded miffed, put upon, and admonitory.

No way were we going to allow the twelve-year-old to twirl the spaghetti of Wade's tendons a second time. In the end we appealed to an out-of-network surgeon, the fiftysomething Dr. Howard, who had already saved Wade's life once. When we first consulted the older surgeon and he mentioned in passing that he recognized me, I feared that Howard would refuse to operate on the partner of a notorious hatemonger. Rather, he shot me one of those collusive glances that had provided Emory the topic for her very first radio editorial. As tipping one's subversive hand was by then regarded as too risky, such tacit moments of shared apostasy had grown uncommon. We'd found the right doctor.

Yet self-funding meant a full-freight cash payment we didn't have. With embarrassment, we resorted to begging Wade's parents in Florida for what they knew full well wasn't really a "loan." They were obliging, but retirees on a fixed income wouldn't have prodigious reserves, so we'd burned a bridge. We couldn't come back to them twice.

The second surgery was more successful, though Dr. Howard was forthright about the fact that the first one having been botched came at a price. The ankle would always be weak; Wade would always require a cane; there was a high likelihood of intermittent if not chronic pain. While the wrist had mended more or less, this joint was also fragile in perpetuity. The surgeon's bluntness was meant as kindly: Wade should seek out an occupation that wasn't dependent on manual labor.

I doubt Wade will ever read this—even if this manuscript ever finds a small, insubordinate audience, he's not a reader—so I can be frank. Across the surgery, redo, and extended recovery, he became a different person. Maybe people who live in their heads anyway can manage the transition to physical impairment and maintain a steady sense of self. But Wade and his body were entwined. He was deprived of his animal grace. He'd always been a doer, and now he could mostly think. He'd never cared for thinking, and since I thought too much, I'd lost a moderating influence on my tendency to churn in place. Technically he was still as handsome as the man who'd cut down my moribund oak thirteen years earlier. His face retained its striking equine contour, and a taut, honed figure takes months to melt. Yet I discovered that all along what had made him so magnetic was an animating spirit. That spirit was broken. He was considerate as ever, pitching in where he still could. He never complained. But he was newly pliant. If Wade were a tree, he'd gone from sturdy hardwood to willow. I'm saying that what made him seem an invalid was not the limp. Something was disabled inside. I still loved him, but my tenderness was tainted with melancholy, or with what a more hardened observer would call pity—which no former master of the material world would want.

If we're listing out the many things that two broke, unemployed people could not afford, top of the list would be a lawyer. For during Wade's extended medical ordeal, we also suffered the return of Sonia Whitehead, who in the last couple of years had piled on the pounds. (I got it. Why forgo cupcakes and hit the treadmill only to look as plain as you ever did?) Child Protective Services took a predictably dim view of my pyrotechnic display at VU. As I was constitutionally incapable of prostrating myself with the degree of contrition that the fussbudget bureaucrats required, nothing I might say during Sonia's badgering interviews would ever make up for my heathen hissy fit. So in the end I didn't even try.

I will cut to the chase. But I will not fly into a weepy, emotive theater of hair-tearing maternal bereavement the better to move you here. I want you to know what happened to me, but I am not your performing bear. Let's leave it at this: I may not be the best mother in the world. I can be curt, impatient, at times unfair. I can get too wrapped up in my own affairs. But I am a normal mother in most respects, with normally fierce ties to her offspring. Feel free to exercise your emotional imagination, then, when I share the unadorned facts of our summer that year.

It was determined that Darwin and Zanzibar would be removed from our home and put in foster care. To the siblings' horror, they were to be placed with different families. So violent was their reaction that my two teenagers were taken from Darwin's locked bedroom by force with the assistance of an armed detail from the sheriff's department, using a battering ram to bust in the door. D&Z were rustled into a waiting van in handcuffs, like criminals. Lucy was allowed to remain with her biological father only if Wade promised to stop living with me.

Meanwhile—everything happened at once—we missed our first mortgage payment in July. We might have put the house on the market, except—little remarked on in the media, and isn't *that* interesting—the American economy had sunk into a prolonged recession, having been flailing since 2014. The housing market had tanked. Even if we could find a buyer, the house was sunk in negative equity, and selling would cost more than walking away. Eviction lurking right around the corner, Wade made the anguished decision to auction off his company's equipment, using the proceeds for a deposit on a small, depressing apartment far enough from me to satisfy social services and at least keep custody of his daughter.

Wade and I made all manner of promises to each other. For a while, we did indeed meet in secret, and I have to say those liaisons sponsored some of the best sex we'd had in years. But the stakes were so high that the stress eventually outweighed even the erotic thrill of the forbidden. Wade always had to find a sitter, because I was barred from being in the same room with Lucy; in the absence of legal representation, I'd been unable to finagle even supervised visitation, and I could never slip into Wade's apartment with a warning to Lucy that she shouldn't tattle, because Lucy always tattled. Before the end of the year, we would call it quits.

In my next encounter with our benevolent overlords, who have our children's interests at heart ever so much more than their mere parents do, a contingent of CPS heavies showed up at my door in September to announce that Darwin and Zanzibar had both run away from their foster families, though the cadre delivered this information with the sneering assumption that I knew this already (I didn't). They searched the house—even the woodshed. Claiming to have a warrant I never saw, they commandeered my phone. Nevertheless, I was joyful. Although these nimrods were convinced otherwise, I'd honestly no idea where those kids had fled to. But they were resourceful. They wouldn't have absconded without first putting together a plausible plan. I had a gut feeling they were fine. And of one thing I could be certain: they were together.

Yet by that point the writing was on the wall for the house. We'd missed three mortgage payments, and a computer spit out threatening notices almost daily. We'd used up our small savings and maxed out the cards. I had no income. I was an employment nonperson; imagine what popped up as the first item on an internet search of my name. Wade picked up a pittance part-timing at the Voltaire Botanical Gardens, which would have been a great place for him as a proper tree surgeon, but now he could only lurch around the greenhouses misting fronds and pinching off dead leaves. He earned barely enough to keep Lucy in Pop-Tarts.

Where could I go? It wasn't true as Emory claimed that I had *no* other friends, but I definitely had no friends who would dare give sanctuary to a civic leper. This was the juncture at which my kin's disavowal felt especially grievous, since when push comes to shove most people fall back on blood ties. In desperation, I reached out to Kelly and David, who were at least willing to talk to me, but in hushed tones. No, given the circumstances, they couldn't put me up. Even if they overlooked my having ratted out their daughter online, Emory was staying in their spare room.

If where I went was unclear, that I would go was a certainty. The official eviction notice arrived in October, labeled as such in big bold black letters on the envelope, just in case you were such a deadbeat that the pharmacy wouldn't sell you ten-dollar reading glasses. I wasn't about to be hustled from my home by another posse from the sheriff's department too callous to let me grab a spare pair of socks. I packed a roller bag with a few clothes, official papers, a tarp, a throw pillow, a water bottle, and this laptop. You know that nagging feeling of having forgotten something important on your way out the door—keys? Wallet? Something to read on the bus? What I'd absently left behind when I pulled the side door to for the very last time was my house.

The first place I camped out was the entrance to CPS. I made it clear to the security guards that I wasn't going anywhere until I got my phone back. It's not that I wanted to play *Donkey Kong*. After they allowed enough time to elapse, Darwin and Zanzibar were sure to get in touch. Personnel trooped blindly past my protest for three days. In the end, I did get my phone back, on the understanding that, bribed with my own property, I would move on. The screen was shattered—I bet they smashed it on purpose—but it still worked. I switched the plan to pay-as-you-go and resolved that regardless of what else I had to do without, my first financial priority would be to keep the lifeline functional.

At last in November I got a text. They were fine and I shouldn't worry, but it wasn't safe to disclose their location. I understood. When I tried to respond, the number no longer worked. They'd probably bought a cheap burner solely for that reassurance, then chucked it. I deleted the text.

I won't stiff-upper-lip it in print; this was a tough period. Sometimes I slept rough, others I hit the homeless shelters, where protecting this aging laptop required such vigilance that I rarely got any shut-eye. I'd do just about anything to earn a few bucks—clean houses, rake yards, rinse out recycling bins. For odd-jobbing, I came up with the alias "Amy Flowers," crafted to sound maximally harmless. Yet sometimes would-be employers recognized my face, and there went the dishwashing gig. I naturally considered leaving Voltaire—which had narrowly held on to its name—if only to escape the constant anxiety that either relations who'd excommunicated me or my poor facsimile of a best friend would spot me huddling under a tarp in a park. But transport would be one more expense; I was persona non grata nationwide; and this was the city to which Darwin and Zanzibar would head if they ever came looking for me. I was especially optimistic by the spring of 2018, when Darwin turned eighteen. Having aged out of the foster care system, he'd be free to return without looking over his shoulder.

That summer, a new restaurant called Deer Abby had opened on the edge of downtown, and with nothing to lose I approached the guy I guessed was the owner as he signed off on a delivery of venison. In general, my prospects were looking up, because getting anyone to do anything had grown so difficult; it was now as hard to fire workers in America as it had long been in France. Employees could always accuse management of sacking them because they were stupid, and all manner of deficiencies, like not deigning to show up, were now protected as *processing issues*. I said I'd be glad to mop floors, set chairs on tables, cut onions—whatever he needed. I would work off the books for under minimum wage and could save him on unemployment insurance and Social Security. From the start of my down-and-outery, I'd at least kept clean, itself nearly a full-time job.

He didn't seem that interested, until suddenly he was. "Hold it," he said. "You're Pearson Converse."

I could have grabbed my bedraggled roller bag and hightailed it, but I was tired. "No, I'm not. Who's that?"

"*Amy Flowers*, my ass! I'd recognize that face anywhere. You're Pearson Converse."

"I don't know who you're talking about." I felt a bit like the Apostle

Peter, except I wasn't denying knowing Jesus but myself, which was even weirder.

He wasn't having any of it. "Seriously? Predictable, I guess. Now you're on the street."

Paul had gone for three times. "Yes, I'm on the street," I said. "But I'm Amy Flowers." The idiotic name didn't sound convincing to my own ears, and I braced for the usual invective. You're a disgrace. We don't want your kind around here. Maybe a gob of spit. I just hoped he wouldn't hit me. If he knew who I was, then he also knew he'd never be prosecuted for leaving this sorry specimen in the gutter.

"Fuck, you're one of my heroes," he said. "Please, come inside. Put your feet up. I'll make you some lunch."

It turned out there was an incidental resistance on the downlow after all, mostly isolated individuals who kept their outré opinions to themselves. But little by little, these throwbacks had formed loose allegiances and were starting to get organized. After he'd given me work as a sous chef, installed me in an empty room above the restaurant replete with midget fridge and hot plate, and bought me a few clothes at the local thrift shop, Sam Nilsson invited me to be the guest of honor at what its members billed to others as a book club but what they cheerfully tagged behind closed doors as a "hate group." It was only eight people, but they were all smart. More crucially still, they all thought it likely that some people—lots of them, considering the course of the previous eight years—were stupid.

So, *Emory*: these people became my friends. They did not agree on everything. They had all conducted amicable long-term relationships with passionate supporters of Mental Parity, whom my new confederates had never chosen to denigrate, ostracize, or make examples of in public—although most of the group had themselves been denigrated, ostracized, and made examples of in public by the faithful once an idle comment that strayed from the straight and narrow escaped their mouths by mistake. It was a pattern: shunning worked in only one direction. See, Emory? Even your denunciation of our friendship was unoriginal.

I didn't mind cutting green onions on the diagonal or trimming venison steaks. The work entailed the wholesome physicality that Wade had always celebrated. After nearly two years of sleeping rough, the room above Deer Abby felt more palatial than the five-bedroom I lost to the bank. The seditious weekly meetings of our hate group kept me sane.

I suppose I didn't blame the kids for being cautious (well—I did blame them a little; although they were good about sending cryptic texts every few months to confirm what kidnap negotiators call "proof of life," for the better part of four solid years I was beside myself). But Darwin and Zanzibar didn't reach out for a proper catchup by video link until April 2020, the month Zanzibar turned safely eighteen as well. They'd established themselves in something between a commune and an arts colony called Select (which sounded like a credit card). The fraternity's location in the wilds of Wyoming was a closely guarded secret. Its formational concept: this outfit had standards. A baldly illegal preserve of intellectual snobbery, Select did not let just anyone in.

D&Z were flourishing. Zanzibar was writing plays, while her once crimped miniature drawings had exploded into enormous canvases that covered half a wall of the collective's barn. Having regained his voracious curiosity, Darwin was exploring the outer limits of advanced mathematics, which for someone like me who'd struggled with second-year algebra was incomprehensible. Yet they both took part in raising chickens and weeding the vegetable patch, while taking their turns on cleaning and cooking rotations. If this enterprise followed the progression of previous utopias, it was only a matter of time before a handful of characters ate more than their share of the mushroom lasagna and did an insultingly cursory job on the toilets. But if they always descended into acrimony, resentment, and petty power contests, the beginnings of these communal projects were exhilarating, and I hoped for my kids' sake that the halcyon period was protracted. Improving its prospects, this one did seem to be animated by a unifying principle more plausible than the standard Marxist rubric of each-to-his-abilities, but otherwise we're all the same. Select was dedicated to the proposition that we're anything but all the same, so an ambitious, preternaturally brilliant young man named "Darwin" fit right in.

Unfortunately, the spread of a novel but, it turned out, not especially lethal virus for the vast majority of the healthy, non-elderly population prevented me from reuniting any time soon with D&Z, since the morons in control of the country had panicked and shut down the entire economy for an initial pause of three weeks that evolved grindingly into two years. Deer Abby was obliged to close. Like the rest of the citizenry, we all lived on government handouts of fabricated money whose overproduction, the more economically clued-up members of the hate group assured us, would in due course perilously devalue the dollar—as if the U.S. needed any more problems. To forestall the onset of narcotic lassitude during this period, Sam urged me to write this account, and not because my story is so unusual but because it isn't.

I don't have much faith that this manuscript will see the light of day. I may be encouraged by the stealthy emergence of pushback against Mental Parity in tiny pockets, but I worry that our joy in locating fellow travelers makes us prone to overestimate our numbers, although none of us is so foolhardy as to overestimate our influence. There isn't a hope in hell that Amazon will carry even a self-published book titled *Mania* unless it's packaged as horror (which this is, after a fashion). Mainstream bookstores will run a mile. YouTube and Facebook will malign it as hate speech. I hesitate to encourage anyone to retain a document the possession of which could ruin their lives, so be apprised: this is on you. Maybe if my chronical reaches you, download a copy, read it, and before you delete it from your hard drive *and* your trash, forward this samizdat to anyone you know with an open mind. If experience serves, that won't require you to forward the file many times.

I don't mean to condescend to anyone who's lived through the same era I have, but it could be nominally useful to step back and assemble the dysfunctions of the last thirteen years in one place. Let's start with where we are politically. With his landslide victory for the Democrats in 2016 and the even greater electoral mandate he garnered in 2020, Donald J. Trump has ridden the coattails of cognitive egalitarianism. Whatever you think of his policies, the big galoot has radically transformed the template for high office in the United States. It's now taken as a given that for any candidate to be seriously considered for either major party's presidential nomination next year, he or she will necessarily be badly educated, uninformed, poorly spoken, crass, oblivious to the rest of the world, unattractive and preferably fat, unsolicitous of advice from the more experienced, suspicious of expertise, inclined to violate constitutional due process if only from perfect ignorance of the Constitution, self-regarding without justification, and boastful about what once would have been perceived as his or her shortcomings. We blithely assume that whoever is elected president will surround him- or herself with mediocrities or worse and purposefully appoint a cabinet whose leading credentials are having no credentials.

Moreover, the wholesale embrace of a flagrant lie by an entire population has inevitably opened the gateway for other lies. We have severed our connection to truth, thereby losing faith in the very existence of truth. That means our representatives can say anything, espouse anything. Everyone is beautiful: the assertion alone makes it so. In throwing in our lot with what we will to be true, rather than with what is true, we break with the scientific method through which all advanced economies have achieved their prosperity—a method whose previous practitioners were willing to brave the discovery of the ideologically inconvenient.

Then there's the bigger political picture. I don't know beans about the European Union, and I'm still uncertain whether the UK's departure from the bloc was all that significant in retrospect. Yet even while in the throes of losing custody of my children and contending with the inevitability of losing my house and partner as well, I took note of what tipped the balance for that national plebiscite in 2016. The folks who wished to stay in the EU tried terribly hard, or so I read, to keep their messaging cognitively neutral, but it seems they couldn't control themselves. Whether or not their advocates said so outright, it was obvious to the electorate that "Remainers" held their opposition in contempt. Leaving the Union was not merely to Britain's *disadvantage*; it was *stupid*. It wasn't much of a leap to infer that these establishmentarians thought "Leavers" were stupid as well. Their cause blackened by cerebral supremacy and their leaders tarred as bigots, Remainers were trounced. I don't remember the exact number, but Leavers carried the day by something like 90 percent. Funny, if Remainers had slyly planted a few double agents on the other side publicly proclaiming that staying in the EU was stupid, the vote might have gone the other way.

Having fallen hypnotically in love with its own virtue, the West has ceded South and Central America, Africa, and the Middle East to the de facto control of the Chinese (thanks to whom the oceans are nearly dead; with no other nation willing to constrain the practice, their supertrawlers have raked the ocean beds bare, and a single eighteen-ounce bass can now sell for three hundred dollars). The Chinese cannot believe their luck. In their national mythology, global domination is their destiny, but Xi Jinping never imagined the competition would so obligingly accelerate the inevitable by committing civilizational suicide. I bet he's even a measure disappointed that the takeover is proving so effortless; a fair fight would have been more fun. Meanwhile, we've gifted to Russia its old czarist empire and then some. After all, to get into the U.S. military these days, I bet you need an IQ of *below* 85, which might explain why nearly all the fatalities in our armed forces are now caused by friendly fire. As ever, most Americans don't regard a full-scale invasion of our continental territory as remotely within the range of possibility, but I do. If that seems absurd, maybe we could agree on the less alarmist view that in the history of the postwar United States there's never been a more propitious time than the last few years to question the supposedly unassailable position of the country as a world power you wouldn't want to mess with. Any rising autocrat worth his salt who's kept up with the state of play here must be at least toying with the idea of trying his hand.

Because let's face it: nothing works. Nobody does their jobs anymore, because nobody gets in trouble when they shirk; that jurisprudential refusal to punish malfeasance that Kelly noted in relation to contract law has spread to everything. Garbage mounds every corner. Civil servants' willingness to report to work is a matter of mood. Fortunately, it's of no real consequence that you can't get a driver's license, which became meaningless once you could no longer fail the test. Little matter that you can't get a passport, either, since a growing list of countries won't let Americans in even with a passport. The blackouts are getting longer and more frequent. As Silicon Valley was one of the first industries to vaunt its commitment to cognitive equality, internet outages have also grown constant; digital security being less important than some boofhead's feelings, fraud is rampant, and the only reason it's not even worse is that dollars are decreasingly worth the bother of stealing them. I've had to block all updates to my laptop's operating system, because downloading the latest OS notoriously leaves you with a cold blank screen and a large, flat paperweight.

Now that the slow and inept have for years been promoted to positions of authority in the private sector, American products have a well-earned reputation as flimsy, badly designed, and faulty. Even in the domestic sphere, our dish soap stains crockery purple; our vacuums spew dust in the wrong direction. Rather than use a vegetable peeler made in Minnesota, you'd be better off clawing at a carrot with your fingernails. Our fridges freeze the cucumbers and melt the ice cream. Our washers chew a load of whites to pillow fill. Our ovens don't accurately regulate the temperature within 100 degrees Fahrenheit, and when not singeing your roast into a charcoal briquet, they explode instead. As Felicity noted, by 2015 automobiles manufactured in this country were bursting into flames on the interstate, and that was in the happy instance that they started up in your driveway. Brands that long emblemized quality—Black+Decker, John Deere, even Tesla—are now the butts of stand-up. If they have the wherewithal, even dyed-in-the-wool MP fanatics spring for imports from the very smartist regimes they claim to revile. Accordingly, that once ubiquitous red, white, and blue "Made in America" sticker has disappeared—the export market along with it.

Sorry, there is an export market—for talent. Physicists, chemists, mathematicians, biologists, oceanographers, engineers, and professors of every stripe are defecting in droves to Russia, in a dizzying reversal of the Cold War. Ditto the dancers, directors, actors, and writers who have anything on the ball. Meanwhile, any quick-witted young people who remain behind are sleeping twelve hours a day in their parents' basements and set an alarm only to buy more drugs.

This last post-pandemic year has seen a sluggish return to economic life, the better to sponsor wall-to-wall catastrophe. Plane crashes not only *seem* far more common, as newscasters coyly put it; now that pilots don't have to pass a practical and written exam, and the folks designing the planes and writing aeronautical software are boobies, plane crashes *are* far more common—along with head-on tractor-trailer collisions and train derailments. During the extensive coverage of the collapse of the sixty-story high-rise in San Francisco, the bridge that dumped fifty-eight vehicles into the Mississippi, and the terminal at LaGuardia whose roof fell in— and that was just the implosions from last month—we heard all manner of mumbling in the media about "our aging infrastructure." But that high-rise in California was *new*, that bridge in Iowa was *new*, and that terminal building in New York was *new*. Nevertheless, throughout this cascade of calamity there is one phenom that newscasters can never impugn as even a contributing factor, and that's the one phenom that even the zealots know perfectly well is the overwhelming factor: Mental Parity.

Sure, we had our share of auto accidents and shoddy construction before MP. And maybe even having converted our hospitals to morgues and our universities to the sets of *Romper Room*, we might have muddled on somehow. But I think we can all concur that we crossed a line with the vaccines. Sinovac and Sputnik weren't very effective against Covid in the end, but at least they were relatively harmless. You could hardly say the same about the snake oil from Pfizer, which had long since jetti-soned all the company's skilled personnel like Felicity, who knew the dif-ference between monobasic potassium phosphate and household drain cleaner. So this mR2D2 concoction was stirred up by trick-or-treaters in mad-scientist costumes waving beakers of dry ice, like twelve-year-old Darwin on Halloween. Me, I bought a fake vaccination certificate on the black market; I assume if you're perky enough to read this, you did the same. But far too many of our compatriots were credulous. I've lost track of the underreported mortality count, but at the minimum it's in the tens of millions. By the time all the long-term side effects have taken their toll, the international death count could come to hundreds of millions. I don't care for hyperbole, but I don't believe this is an overstatement: the Pfizer "miscalculation" marked the start of a full-blown emergency.

Should we even care? I'll speak for myself, though I doubt this reca-libration is unique to me. Watching an entire population swallow whole a transparently lunatic proposition and then jubilantly embrace a raft of ruinous new social conventions has profoundly lowered my estimation of people in general. I hesitate to exempt myself from that category, too, so I suppose this disappointment extends to yours truly. If people as a class are far less impressive than we'd like to think, then I am unimpressive, too.

But something difficult to pinpoint does distinguish me from most peo-ple, and if you're still reading this, you probably land in the same genetic camp. I don't honestly understand why I was born with a funny immunity to the dogmatic diseases that so easily infect our fellows, any more than I understood why certain phenotypes were unaffected by Covid-19. I'm loath to claim membership of a Witness-like elect, and maybe I'd have been a more contented person these last thirteen years if I'd mindlessly followed the crowd. After all, I've paid a terrible price for being out of sync. I've lost my home, my lover, my job, my reputation, several years of my two older children's upbringing, and perhaps contact with my youngest child in per-petuity. All I can say is that I was made this way. I'm congenitally incapable of reciting with a shrug, "Oh! There's no such thing as stupid people. My mistake."

Please—I don't mean I'm anointed. Besides, if a larger proportion of our species had my obtuse temperament, we might suffer from chronic social incohesion and get into far more scraps—both between countries and in bars. Maybe our institutions would be paralyzed by staff at con-stant loggerheads. Obviously, we can't all be obstreperous in a populous, complex society that requires a high degree of interpersonal cooperation even to keep milk in our fridges. All of us can't wake up in the crib and decide to rebuild every custom, every shared communal "truth," from the ground up. It's possible, too, that I myself have unquestioningly accepted a host of assumptions that are irrational, destructive, or, yes, *stupid*. I'd love to give you an example, but because I *have* accepted these assumptions, I don't even know what they are.

Still. I'm straining here. Because by this point it's indisputable that human beings will believe anything.

Accordingly, a wide variety of historical phenomena that once confounded me now seem explicable, if not ordained. I'm no longer astonished by the Holocaust, and there's no country in the world that I would deem impervious to the modern equivalent of a Nazi takeover. Rather, I figure that full-blown fascism in, say, the U.S., the UK, Australia, France, or modern Germany, for that matter, could manifest itself within approximately three weeks. Mao's cultural revolution, Stalin's labor camps, Cambodia's killing fields—they now strike me as perfectly normal. Likewise the cult of Scientology, Jonestown, Waco, and the Witnesses I grew up with. I'm not in the least surprised that some people think a single drop of tincture diluted by a hundred thousand gallons of water will cure cancer, that the murder of small children will protect them from the devil, or that we are eternally living in the "end-times," after which exactly 144,000 people will ascend to heaven and rule the earth in concert with Jesus Christ. Backhandedly, I have come to give my parents a bit more credit. Sure, what they believed was nuts, but that merely made them just like everyone else.

More immediately, I wish I had the answer. Our tiny conspiratorial "hate group" spends a disproportionate amount of time knocking heads together over how to haul this country from its pit. Now that my location has quietly spread among our fragile, disparate network of reprobates, I received an intriguing under-the-table invitation. As illiteracy and innumeracy soar across the nation, an underground academy has arisen in Texas that's dedicated to meritocracy. Its provost warned me in his cover letter that if I agreed to teach in their fledgling English department, I could be at risk of arrest. For this secret university has strict admission requirements, administering a bespoke, unapologetically illegal four-hour exam. So far, that exam has a 3 percent pass rate—although most of the wunderkinds who ace the test are accepting the university's offers. The school will give grades. It will flunk people. It will issue diplomas only to students who have verifiably mastered a body of knowledge. Hearteningly, though the Old-School New School's existence is hush-hush and unadvertised, applications have flooded in. I don't hold out hope that such a small effort in its incubational stages can make much difference, but the fact that the institution has popped up at all is grounds for cautious optimism. Why, once I've put the finishing touches on this manuscript I may give the post a go—though I'm a lousy, lazy academic, and had I not made a name for myself by repeating the word "retarded," no rigorous educational outfit ever would have made overtures to me about a full professorship.

More personally, I wish I could say that, once the immediate emotional aftermath of Emory Ruth's grandstanding in my living room subsided, I haven't given her a moment's thought. Nothing could be further from the truth. It's been seven years now, and my sense of injury is still raw. I might finally fathom the Rwandan genocide, but in relation to my erstwhile best friend I'm still bewildered. Try as I might, I can't identify the point at which she must have stopped pretending to believe in MP and started believing instead. Maybe she didn't experience a Damascene conversion but more of a slow glissando from one note to another that she wasn't entirely aware of herself. Only one thing have I firmly concluded from her turnabout: over a sustained period of time, it's veritably impossible to promote a falsified viewpoint in a cynical spirit of pure self-interest while simultaneously maintaining a private viewpoint diametrically at odds with the public one. It's too exhausting. It's too much mental labor to erect a Chinese wall in your own head. Why, in going along with cognitive equality in the classroom the better to keep my job, I myself suffered brief blankings out, during which, for a second or two, the movement seemed plausible or at least not flagrantly mad. After all, the public at large bought into this improbable ideology virtually overnight and in no time forgot that they had ever believed anything else. So I might give Emory credit for holding out longer than most.

I don't feel like giving her credit, of course. But I have wondered whether her vandalism of our entire relationship was a mere expedience—making it easier to turn her back and walk away. Wade claimed at the time that the reason for her repudiation was simple: I had become a liability. I failed a cost-benefit analysis. Professionally and socially, standing by me would have been priced too highly in comparison with the marginal advantages of shared box merlot.

Yet for me to dismiss her renunciation of our long-standing tie as the faithless pursuit of self-interest is suspiciously convenient. I can't rule out the possibility that I always seemed to Emory to be a burden and a pest; that she was always distressed by something unwholesome in my attachment to her; that the friendship was always unbalanced, and I'd been willfully blind to how much more I liked her than she liked me.

ALT-2027

Pearson Converse, Four Years On

*The agent of MP's undoing opposes
the very progress she enabled.*

By Pearson Converse

I begin with embarrassment. I never imagined that my memoir, *Mania*, would reach even a handful of misfits, much less become an enduring bestseller. The memoir's success was a zeitgeist thing. A critical mass had had enough. Widespread horror over the rolling effects of the Pfizer "vaccine"—still with us today—produced a social sea change, gradual at first, which gathered into a tsunami right when my first-person pleading that we all get a grip hit a host of laptops in 2023. The rest is history. Not only was I lucky; we've *all* been lucky. The proverbial pendulum has swung back.

I am deeply uneasy with a regime grown overcorrective.

I worry that *The Atlantic* intended to commission a self-aggrandizing look back at how I single-handedly returned the Western world to rationality. Yet I doubt we need any more theatrical expressions of relief that we once again expect a leader like President Andrew Yang to be knowledgeable and intelligent—indeed, to be *more* knowledgeable and intelligent than the abundance of the population he governs. Yes, we now enshrine competence as a quality both real and requisite for a variety of positions whose remits can affect the well-being of millions. Yes, there is such a thing as dumb, and rarely have we employed the word and its affiliates with such gleeful, and I would say excessive, abandon. To my surprise, the insults we dispensed so casually before 2010—and now employ with relish—have retained to my ear a degree of the unutterable quality they acquired during the reign of MP. I'm inclined to use a word such as "idiot" sparingly and reserve it for the rare cretin who truly deserves the label.

Many qualities distinguish us besides mental endowment.

For I'm bound to frustrate my loyal readers here. I am deeply uneasy with a regime grown overcorrective. It's one thing to return to standardized examinations for university admissions, quite another for administrators to so ruthlessly weed out underperforming students as they adjust to college life. Most of these poor kids spent the bulk of their school years in the educational desert of Mental Parity. Let's cut them some slack. Furthermore, it's one thing to restore IQ tests to public schools, quite another to elevate the test's results to the exalted position they enjoy today.

Lodging students' IQs in their transcripts is reasonable enough. But why boldface IQs at the top of every tax return? Why should employers be required by law to hire the statistically most intelligent job applicant when IQ takes no account of other qualities, such as affability or punctuality, that might recommend a candidate for the position? What's the justification for putting a consumer's IQ on the upper-right-hand corner of every credit card? Smarter people aren't necessarily better credit risks. Clever folks can be unconscionable, as well as crafty at escaping their obligations. Yet higher IQs now qualify home buyers for larger mortgages and raise customers' credit limits. I can't be the only one who finds the current proposal in Congress that all Americans get their IQs tattooed on the inside of their forearms to have a forbidding historical precedent.

Socially, too, I much preferred the days when we met someone new and quietly appraised for ourselves whether this acquaintance seemed on the ball. To me, the modern convention at parties of introducing your IQ along with your name seems terribly gauche. The *very* first mandatory input on dating websites is those two or three indelible digits. But pairing participants whose IQs are both 122 is surely less likely to end in romance than the old algorithms' matching of shared hobbies and who likes spicy food.

The *Mania* readership may recall that I don't regard myself as all that bright. My friend (or so I imagined) Emory Ruth once pooh-poohed this claim as an inverted vanity: *I'm so smart that I know I'm not smart.* Well, this isn't in my interest to publish, and I'm sure to disappoint my admirers here, but I took that test in 2024—not that I had any choice— and the result was stark: 107. Pretty crap. Pretty middle-of-the-pack. Having for years advertised my run-of-the-mill intellect, I should have been prepared, but I wasn't. I was stung. I'm even dumber than I thought.

That 107 score put my employers at the Old-School New School in an awkward position. According to the Texas university's bylaws, the administration was forbidden to keep me on the faculty. It took a snowstorm of paperwork to exempt me, then another snowstorm to award me that honorary doctorate. But being something of a celebrity at OSNS, I got special treatment. Less notable employees across the country haven't been granted such indemnity. I can't look on these mass layoffs as a legitimate source of national pride.

Granted, I selected the father of my older two children for his high IQ. In our recent past, that damned me as a eugenicist, a charge I've come to see as fair. Yet my once eccentric determination to bear clever offspring has grown standard, and we milk genetically intelligent men like cows. Indeed, we're in danger of regarding the highly intelligent of both sexes as a precious communal resource.

At what point do we decide that people whose IQs lie in the right-hand tail of the bell curve don't belong to themselves?

Many qualities distinguish us besides mental endowment. Generosity,

Why boldface IQs at the top of every tax return?

loyalty, kindness, and common sense. The capacities for wonder and joy. A sense of humor. A sense of honor. Grace, clemency, and candor. Diligence, conscientiousness, and a willingness to sacrifice for others. Smart people can be intolerable, while many a buddy with a middling intellect is still great company and may go to the ends of the earth to save your bacon. Whatever I have to offer, it wasn't measured by that test.

Accordingly, I oppose the new electoral dispensation, whose innocuous tag "the Fitness Proviso" makes it sound like some healthy nationwide commitment to jumping jacks. Still whizzing through the last of our state legislatures, the constitutional amendment requiring all registered voters and all candidates for state and federal office to have a minimum IQ of 115 will eliminate 84 percent of the population from participating in the democratic process. That's not democracy as I understand it, but benevolent dictatorship—and I challenge whether dictatorship is ever benevolent, really. Yes, I get the stock line. Stupid people elect stupid leaders who make stupid de-

cisions. But intelligent people may elect intelligent people who still make stupid decisions. This is one of them. Even more do I oppose the extremist campaign spearheaded by the elite-of-the-elite to raise that 115 limit to more like 130—whereby 2 percent of the American population would control the whole shebang.

Many of our betters in the cognitive elect dismiss dissenters like me as merely embittered. My self-respect has suffered a body blow because I didn't make the cutoff. Members of my generation with quantifiably poor judgment are accustomed to having a say, so I'm naturally disgruntled that my tiny electoral power could be taken away. But I'll get used to being disenfranchised in time, and I'll grow to appreciate the rationality of the system when it results in a country that runs so much more smoothly. Children growing up under the new protocol will take it as a given that if their IQ is below the threshold, they simply don't have the goods to exercise authority for the benefit of all. Aldous Huxley got here way back in 1932: the proles will know their place, and they will love their place.

Tyrants are always trying to convince the peons how lucky they are to be spared the onus of control over their own fate.

But I prefer chaos, uncertainty, and dysfunction to any order that works too well. Historically, elites reliably confuse "the benefit of all" and their own interests. We are about to install a high priesthood. I grew up with a high priesthood, and "the elders" to a man were creeps.

Mind, my opposition to the Fitness Proviso is a thorn in the side of my employers. The OSNS law faculty helped draft that amendment, which the administration expects me to champion. But it's my nature to be a thorn in the side. I was uncomfortable with yanking my compatriots toward my way of thinking only to find myself drowning in the mainstream. The more I face into the prevailing winds, the more I feel like myself.

The Mania *readership may recall that I don't regard myself as all that bright.*

Acquainted with my family, readers of *Mania* might appreciate a brief Christmas-letter-style update. Be assured that even if the 28th Amendment is fully ratified, my two older children will be allowed to vote and hold elective office, though I'd be surprised if either of those kids runs for president. At twenty-seven, Darwin—whose IQ turns out to be 144, about what I expected—has joined a group at the reconstituted MIT who are chucking all the politically manipulated computer models and rebuilding climate science from the ground up. He tells me they have absolutely no preordained conclusions about CO_2, anthropogenic influences, fossil fuels, or anything else. The group will be as delighted to confirm current orthodoxies as to overthrow them. That means his colleagues are, he assures me, real scientists.

Do I suffer from an unconscious sexism or a prejudice against the arts? Because I was surprised that Zanzibar tested as even brighter than her brother at 151. That doesn't mean she's happy. Oh, the art world is her oyster, and the first play she's finally pleased with is on its way to Broadway. But beauty has proved a curse. The fact that young men with dazzling stats on the upper-right-hand corner of their credit cards throw themselves at her feet has had a detrimental effect on her character. Between these lavish attentions and her elevated status as a member of the ".1 percent" with an IQ of over 145—the traditional threshold of "genius," as which even her brother missed qualifying by a whisker—she's become quite the prima donna. This is a terrible thing for a mother to admit, but in my darkest moments I some-

The more I face into the prevailing winds, the more I feel like myself.

times debate which would improve my daughter as a human being more: a cerebral hemorrhage or an acid attack. (Sorry, Zanzo. Only joking.)

As for my third child, the restraining order barring me from contact with Lucy wasn't lifted until she was eighteen anyway. I've come to appreciate how many other parents were also separated from their children over some minor infraction of MP doctrine. These social services inter-

ventions were most common among the well educated. The media have already gone to town on the scandal of genetically bright children denied the nurturing not only of gifted-and-talented programs but of their own credentialed parents (themselves often demoted or sacked). Although not in the gifted category, Lucy is yet another MP casualty. When she finally took the test, she came in at a respectable 112—considerably above average—but she squandered her intelligence on *not* learning to read, which unfortunately she got very good at. A doting father but never much of a reader himself, Wade tells me that she's finally absorbed the rudiments despite herself, but her comprehension is still weak.

Lucy is suffering from psychic whiplash. Her strict adherence to MP principles and her overeager policing of her peers now count as strikes against her. Her schooling, if you could call it that, was criminally deficient. Her brain was bound much as the Chinese once bound feet. Beyond our limited tutoring sessions, she has never experienced rigor, and her stunted version of aspiration was to fixate on becoming a Mental Parity Champion.

There are no more Mental Parity Champions. Worse, at the very point she finished high school, barriers to university admission were reerected like fury. Suddenly, the SAT was back, and Lucy had never taken a pop quiz, much less a three-hour exam. The few high school seniors covertly tutored at home could take their pick of the Ivy League. Everyone else who'd relied on the pandemonium of formal education was screwed.

Lucy and her peers have reason to feel resentful. I've heard all too much snide talk about "Generation Moron," an appellation that's grossly unfair. Those young people didn't conceive this ideology. Lucy and her ilk are its victims.

Lastly, there's one character who played a dominant part in *Mania* whose circumstances I've failed to update here. I intend to keep it that way. So I'm keeping a recent chance encounter to myself. Though not much happened, this crossing of paths feels intensely private.

I'll take refuge in generalities, then. Since my memoir's publication, I've heard from countless others who've lost lifelong comrades due to a blowup over Mental Parity—always entailing a repudiation of doubters by true believers. If you've been disavowed over politics only to find that the pain of betrayal has lasted well past the demise of the doctrine itself, you're not alone. For me, anyway, winning the ideological war (and then some, I'm afraid) hasn't ameliorated in the slightest my sense of injury over Emory Ruth's denunciation of my character, my motives, and my morals, as well as her disavowal of thirty years of what I used to think was a friendship.

Pearson Converse is the author of *Mania* (HarperCollins, 2024) and the current occupant of the Old-School New School's Benedict Cumberbatch Chair.

———

Well, that's the edited copy; I'm told the article is scheduled for next month's issue. While I gather that having one's text rejigged if not mangled is par for the course in freelance journalism, wrangling with *The Atlantic* has been frustrating enough that I doubt I'll accept one of these assignments again. The original was far more scathing about the Fitness Proviso. At least I held the line and refused to go on and on about how much better things are now (I'm not so sure). I also resisted Pat's urging that I be more personally confiding. (That penultimate para drove her crazy.) I've confided my butt off. I've earned the right to my own business.

As for confiding in this journal, I just idly combed through the files for early 2025 to discover that I never recorded how it went when I finally visited Wade and Lucy's apartment two and a half years ago. I must have found the evening too saddening to rehearse once I got back home. A few details I can still dredge up, then:

Overall, the occasion was strained. It was hardly my idea to absent myself from Lucy's upbringing, but I could see how her subjective experience was one of abandonment. She didn't seem happy to see me, and I suspect she finally agreed to the meeting after refusing to see me for some eighteen months only under heavy pressure from her father.

If she's decidedly not thick in a mental sense, she is a bit thick in the physical one. Her body still has that bluntness, the quality of an immovable object, and I guess that made me the irresistible force. In her spirit of wariness, suspicion, and belligerence, she's more my daughter than she knows.

"So I guess you wrote some sort of *book*?" she charged. A book was an enemy.

"Yes," I said. "Mostly telling the story of our family."

"What would you know about the story of our family?" she said. "You haven't been here."

"I wasn't allowed to be here, Lucy," I said. "If anything, that was even more terrible for me than it was for you."

"It hasn't been terrible for me," she said. "*I* haven't missed *you*."

"Lucy!" Wade exclaimed. "Lots of Lucy's classmates in her community college have heard of *Mania*, and some of them have even read it."

"I haven't. I don't plan to read it, either." If my younger daughter was being offered a degree of cachet through her mother's celebrity, she didn't want it. "Books are . . ."—in her hesitation, I recognized a deeply ingrained mental stop, which gave the word great brute force when she got it out—"*dumb*."

That can't be the sum of our interchange after mother and daughter were coercively parted by the state for seven years, thanks to which we were personally alienated even longer, but it's all I can recall. I didn't hold out much hope for the flowering of our relationship at that time, and sure enough, Lucy has never answered my breezy emails or texts since, much less thanked me for my ignorant birthday presents every July. That's not only CPS's fault but mine. I've sometimes wondered whether I beat myself up too much over this, but the truth is that I haven't beaten myself up over it nearly enough. I deserve Lucy's scorn. I gave D&Z preferential treatment because they were smart (and now we're systematizing the same discrimination in the whole country). I can't blame her for being hostile.

I was glad Wade and I had kept in sporadic touch with all those emails we scrupulously deleted, but I hadn't seen Wade in person for almost eight years. He seemed to have aged more than that. He'd broadly maintained his figure, but his physique had lost its chiseled quality; now careworn, his equine features recalled less the racing stallion of yesteryear than a gelding at pasture. He was still kind, though. When we allowed Lucy to excuse herself to her room, he said, "Maybe I was wrong, always urging you to keep your mouth shut. Look at you. You're famous."

"Well, that 'to thine own self be true' stuff doesn't necessarily pay off. I came within a hair of being a dumpster-diving bag lady in perpetuity."

"You hung tough. You stood your ground. You made a difference."

"It wasn't just me and my 'dumb' book. The time had come. Maybe a few months later, but the tide would have turned without me. Besides, I didn't have any choice, did I? You know what I'm like. I don't know how to be otherwise."

"You mean, you don't know how to be stupid?"

I laughed. "I think we can restore 'otherwise' to its lowly grammatical status of yore. And I definitely know how to be stupid."

"Pigheaded, more like it," he said. "Listen, I'm sorry I gave you such a hard time about going ballistic at VU. Maybe I could have been more understanding. More supportive."

"I put us all in a dreadful position. That temper tantrum cost us our house, you two of our three kids, me all three kids. Given the circumstances, you were remarkably temperate. So how's your ankle?" I'd noticed his limp when he answered the door.

"It hurts."

"In the end, you paid a bigger price for that nonsense than I did." Wade was involved in a tree-planting operation for a new green belt around Voltaire, but his role was advisory: which trees are hardy, grow fast, are native to the region, and play well with others. He no longer got dirt under his fingernails or surveyed a landscape from the treetops. "Hey, I'm curious," I added. "Did the heavies ever bully you into taking an IQ test?"

"Yeah." He sounded sheepish.

"I picture you hauled off hog-tied and screaming."

"Came close to that. I threw the test, first time. They noticed. So many of the answers were wrong that it was, like, statistically impossible unless I was giving wrong answers on purpose. Like, picking at random with my eyes closed would have given me a higher score."

"They made you take it again?"

"Yup. Second time, I guess they convinced me that if I crossed the magic number, it would come with perks that could be useful for Lucy. And, you know. She's gonna need help."

"Did you? Cross the magic number?"

"Uh." More embarrassment. "Yeah."

"So, out with it. What did you score?"

"Come on, scout, you know I don't like this stuff."

"We lived together for thirteen years. Don't be coy."

He shrugged. "One twenty-nine."

"Ha! I find that incredibly satisfying. I'm not sure why."

"Doesn't mean anything."

"It sure means something nowadays. You know, *I* didn't cross the magic number."

"That's impossible."

"It's more than possible. What makes me who I am has nothing to do with smarts."

I caught Wade up on D&Z. I wasn't going to hold my breath for Zanzibar's honoring of an old familial tie, but I assured him that Darwin would gladly get back in touch (he has). We didn't need to address it directly, but it was clear the moment we saw each other that we weren't happening as a couple. It had been too long, we were going different directions, I was living a good part of the year in Austin, and although I hadn't told him yet, by then Sam Nilsson and I had already become an item.

As for the story I cruelly withheld from Pat and *The Atlantic* readership, it's still super-fresh, so maybe I should get it down while I can still lay hands on the particulars.

It must have been three or four months ago when I agreed to participate in a panel in Philadelphia before a large live audience—you know, that big hall with the weird chandeliers. As usual, it was easier to agree to the appearance way in advance, because I'm always indulging this fiction that distant commitments never arrive. Rule of thumb: never agree to do anything you wouldn't be willing to do tomorrow. Or five minutes from now, for that matter.

After doing dozens and dozens of these events following the release of *Mania*, I think I started turning them down at last because I'd gotten sick of making the same points. As time went on, too, those points began to sound self-evident—since that's what happens when a house of cards falls. ("Look! It was only a house of cards! Why didn't we notice before that it was only a house of cards?") Sure, at the outset there was a big battle to wage. But once the fight was won, beating up on the last of MP's beleaguered defenders started to feel a little mean.

Yet this Fitness Proviso business is so upsetting that lately I'll sometimes say yes, so long as the subject up for discussion isn't how awful the old regime was but whether all these new measures to restore intellectual meritocracy go too far. Back in the days when I was doing three of these events a week, I was good about remembering to ask who would appear alongside me, but I was rusty, and this time I didn't vet the other participants in advance. Which was idiotic. Don't do that again.

So the "distant commitment" did its inexorable thing, until I was obliged to show up three nights ago. I wasn't in the mood. But I don't crap out on people. My only passive-aggressive gesture was walking into the greenroom way less than the requested hour in advance.

I swear Emory turned toward the door as if we'd only just finished off another box of merlot last week. Fair enough, Emory being Emory, she probably *had* asked who else was on the panel and was therefore girded for my arrival. That didn't wholly explain the smoothness, the mildness, the untroubled pleasantness with which she met my eyes, after having ripped my guts out the last time we saw each other *eleven years ago*. But then, her trademark has always been unruffleability.

Boy, was *I* ruffled. I broke out in a sweat. My heartbeat soared, and I knew without checking that if I held out my hand it would shake. I also knew that anything I might say in that moment would be incoherent. It wouldn't remotely resemble whatever I might have contrived beforehand had I any warning that you-know-who was on the panel. By the way, I can always summon *exactly* how I felt three nights ago, because it's the same way I feel when I spot my mother.

Christ, Emory didn't miss a beat. Not a beat. Lightly touching my shoulders, she gave each cheek an airy European kiss. "Pearson!" she exclaimed. "How nice to see you."

Rewinding this, I should have said, *Is it? Is it "nice"? Is it really?* Instead I said, "Yes." Which didn't make any sense. But that's the way these things go.

Menopause may have put a millimeter on her midsection, but otherwise at fifty-five Emory hasn't changed much. Her hair hasn't thinned as much as mine has, and she must be doing okay financially to afford yet another short, high-maintenance do. Those few crinkles around the eyes just make her look a little slyer, more game for anything, more mischievous— as if she's chortled her way through the last decade-plus because poor Pearson Converse never cottoned on to the fact that the over-the-top earful in her living room was a practical joke. As ever, she was wearing a sleek monochrome dress whose styling drew attention not to the talent of its designer but to the faultless figure underneath. Likewise the smashing heels: they made you look not at the two-tone leather but at Emory's legs.

I could see her quickly appraising the situation: Pearson's white shirt, perfectly crisp only minutes before though Emory couldn't have known that, was wilted and clinging wetly in patches. Pearson looked paralyzed. It was therefore up to the eternally poised Emory Ruth to take charge, ease the situation, and make this greenroom encounter and subsequent public debate flow as gracefully as possible.

"Hey, I never got a chance to congratulate you on the book," she said.

Imaginary response: *You never got a "chance" because you walked out of my life forever, you fucking cunt.*

Real life: "Oh, that. Yeah, it's been out for a while."

"I gather it sold pretty well!"

It didn't sell "pretty well," it sold tens of millions of copies, pal.

"Uh-huh. Nothing to complain about."

"Come over and pull up a chair. We've got half an hour to kill. Honestly, the only reason we have to show up so early is to keep the event managers from getting hysterical."

She introduced me to the three other people around the table. Abstractly, yes, yes, of course I know it's canny to show up for a panel on the early side, the better to ingratiate yourself with the opposition (get your foes to see you as a lovely person with feelings) and especially with the moderator, whose biases ("Why don't I call on that charming Pearson Converse, who was so warm and unpretentious in the greenroom!") can sway the course of a discussion. Having always been an ace at this stuff, Emory had duly buddy-buddied the trio, all three of whom already acted as if she were their long-lost cousin. Me, I'd arrived as late as I could get away with, and beforehand I never give these appearances a moment's thought. (I don't think I wing it out of arrogance. I think the problem is not giving a shit.) But I was suddenly so incapacitated—I could almost hear the synapses in my brain shorting out, as if someone had just poured milk on a bowl of Rice Krispies—that I wished this once I'd lined up a few killer points ahead of time. I had no idea how I was going to get through the evening without throttling this woman in front of fifteen hundred onlookers.

On reflection, it's noteworthy that Emory didn't dwell any further on *Mania*, in which she features so prominently. With anyone else, I might infer a sense of discomfiture, or maybe a silent acknowledgment that the memoir tangles so intimately with our relationship that we could hardly get into any of its nitty-gritty in the company of strangers. With Emory, I infer instead: she hasn't read it. I daresay that, just like Lucy, she has no intention of ever reading it.

For I've had to accept that one charge in Emory's bonfire of my vanities in 2016 contained an element of truth: there was always a hierarchy to our relationship, sometimes subtle, sometimes more glaring. During the prolonged leisure she herself generously provided me for contemplation of the matter, I concluded that, whether consciously or instinctively, Emory tried to maintain that hierarchy, because who wouldn't rather remain the one on top? She sheltered me in high school and extended her popularity to me like an umbrella. She took me into her family as an orphan. She found me my first adjunct jobs, and it was her father who greased the wheels at VU for my instructorship. Of us two, she was socially the far more agile, and her looks have always held universal appeal, while mine are more of an acquired taste. She was the one who became a media darling. What was fascinating in that greenroom: I am now far more famous than she's ever been, and it didn't make any difference.

I mention this scrupulously preserved power disparity because it explains why she will never so much as sample that memoir. *Reading is an act of submission.*

Given Emory's perfidy, Zanzibar would have counseled that I should have either walked out on the event (thus doing myself reputational damage) or at least assumed the far end of the oval table and buried myself blackly in a magazine. But the rules of common courtesy exert an astonishing influence even on us famed contrarians.

"So—what have you been up to?" I asked.

"Well, I went through a period of downtime," she said, breezing over what must have been years of ignominy and unemployment. "But believe it or not, I'm back at CNN."

"Seriously?"

"It's still a junior position, no screen presence, but I should be able to move up the ranks quickly enough. Funny, I have you to thank for that."

"How do you figure?"

"As you must be aware, there's been a huge sorting of the sheep from the goats in the post-MP years. Plenty of folks high up the food chain have been tainted."

"Only to a point," I said. "Nowadays, everyone claims they never believed any of that drivel in the first place. You'd think the whole country was one big scheming fifth column for a generation."

"I know!" she said lightly. "I ghosted an editorial for Anderson Cooper about that. Anyway, turns out your uploading of our 'retard' video was the best thing that ever happened to me." (Now that "retard" has been refurbished—I never thought I'd say this—I'm getting tired of the word.) "*The Calumny of IQ* has become a modern-day *Mein Kampf.* So our ridicule of that disgraced masterpiece is a badge of honor. As you said, these days everyone pretends they always thought MP was claptrap. I'd never have wowed CNN by just *claiming* I'd always thought MP was claptrap, too. You shored up my bona fides. I can't think how I can ever repay you." Yeah, she said this with a straight face—though the corners of her mouth twitched.

"But CNN bigwigs would know better than anyone what a cheerleader you were." I was flabbergasted they'd rehired her, and Emory's gratitude was taunting.

"We settled on a market view," she said. "Supply and demand. I was the supply."

"Meaning," I said, "journalism is purely in the business of telling people what they want to hear?"

"Can we take a moment to discuss the seating?" the moderator, Gail Something, interrupted gently. "I know this event is loosely structured as a debate, but I'd like us to maintain a convivial tone. I thought it would look less adversarial to seat both Emory and you, Pearson, on the same side of the stage."

"Hold it," I said to Emory. "You're *defending* the Fitness Proviso? And all this singeing of IQ into everybody's forehead with a branding iron?"

"A tiny, tiny number on the inside of the wrist," Emory brushed off. "Totally discreet. And conditioning enfranchisement on high IQ beats only letting people vote who own property. Or just men, or just white people. I only draw the line at nitwits."

"Now, ladies!" Gail intervened. "Let's save the sparring for the audience—"

"But on both radio and TV," I said, "you got up on your high horse for years—!"

"Oh, so what," Emory dismissed. "It's a new day. Cultures evolve."

"Never mind *culture*. We're talking about you, doing another dizzying one-eighty—"

"It's called rolling with the punches."

It's called being a hypocrite. Or it's called having no real convictions to begin with, which conveniently precludes failing to live up to them. It's called having no soul.

"Pearson, I'm sorry to have to bring this up," Gail intruded again, sounding pained. "It's delicate. But I'm afraid it may arise in the Q and A, and I'd hate for you to feel put on the spot. There's an atrocious rumor online that you didn't make the Fitness Proviso cutoff. Might it be judicious to lay that charge to rest right up front? Otherwise, you're sure to be accused of merely being resentful that you wouldn't personally be able to vote. You can make a stronger argument if you make it clear that you're over the threshold, just like the rest of the panel. In fact . . . if your test score is especially strong, you might cite it exactly. That would shut critics in the audience right up. That's what I'd do if I were you."

For three years I've kept this scandalous factoid under wraps, and this was the first I'd heard that word had finally leaked from OSNS admin. Though Pat urged me strenuously to delete that paragraph, outing myself in *The Atlantic* next month will nip the foofaraw in the bud. There's no better way to kill the momentum of a rumor than to announce it's true.

So I told Gail cheerfully, "My test score isn't especially strong. I didn't make the cutoff. Not by a long shot."

The whole table went quiet.

"And I *am* resentful that soon I could not be allowed to vote anymore," I continued. "Why shouldn't I say so?"

Also gung ho about the Fitness Proviso, Emory's male debating partner inserted nervously, "Can she even appear in this event? In this venue? Under the auspices of Intelligence Squared?"

"I'm sure we can make an exception," Gail said hastily, if with little confidence. "But meantime, maybe on reflection, Pearson, it would be better if you didn't announce your IQ."

"One hundred and seven," I said, too loudly.

"My, my," Emory said with a smile. "You always said you were dumb."

"Never you mind, Pearson," Gail said, patting my hand. "You're a public figure with gazillions of fans. Everything will be fine." She didn't believe it for a minute.

Emory effortlessly dominated the whole event. On the rare occasions when she allowed the other four of us to talk, she came across as terribly gracious. She made the Fitness Proviso seem rational, fair, and sensible by reiterating these qualities in her voice, manner, and presence. With feigned modesty, she deflected the matter at first but still managed to insinuate that she herself had made the cutoff and then some at 134. Since it's looked for ages as if we opponents of the 28th Amendment are fighting a losing battle, she was therefore slated to become one of the audience's new overlords. During the death grip of Mental Parity, she'd embodied the intelligent face of stupidity; now she embodied the affable face of tyranny. She was funny. She was relaxed. She was engaging, light-hearted, and self-possessed. The subtext ran, *Look, if the likes of me will be making the decisions from now on, obviously life under the thumb of an intellectual illuminati won't be so bad.* Though the content of what she said constituted the polar opposite of what she espoused eleven years ago, sty-listically nothing had changed. Maybe for Emory, style had always been the point—though the substance of what she tossed off just as winningly in the 2010s ruined my children's education, destroyed my lover's health and livelihood, and exiled me to living out of trash cans for two years, so I might have expected to be undercharmed. Instead, I'm ashamed to record that I chuckled at her wisecracks along with everyone else, just as I did in high school.

One crowd-pleaser was a set piece, and I'm sure Emory had delivered it before:

"Honestly, you guys must have seen some of those Times Square clips, in which a videographer offers American passersby a dollar if they can name a single continent. And they can't. I mean, these poor chumps can't name a single continent, not even for money. Or they'll answer 'Alaska' or 'New Jersey.' Then the interviewer asks, 'What's Obama's last name?' One woman is stumped, while her friend thinks Obama's last name is 'Care.' Then there's the wracking brainteaser, 'If you travel sixty miles per hour for one hour, how far do you get?' Answers include 'I don't know, I'm not good at math'; 'A mile'; and '*Two hours.*' Talk about not being good at math? Asked, 'What's the biggest number you can think of?,' another duo chimes, 'A hundred.'

"Well, until and unless we fully ratify the Twenty-Eighth Amendment, these are the Americans we're allowing to vote. We even allow them to run for, and God forbid sometimes win, elective office. People who, when you ask who fought in the Civil War, say, 'America and France'—they've been choosing our government! People who, when asked to cite a country that begins with 'U,' come up with 'Yugoslavia,' 'Utah,' and 'Utopia.' Or they can't think of a single country beginning with 'U,' when they live in the *United States*! People who imagine that the U.S. won its indepen-

dence in 1776 from *Korea*. Do we want to put determination of our foreign
policy in the hands of folks who think Hiroshima and Nagasaki are most
famous for 'judo wrestling'? Who think Israel is Catholic? Who think
that the currency of the United Kingdom is the 'Queen Elizabeth'? Do
we really want the most important decisions in this country—about who
runs things and how, who goes to prison and for what, even whether we
go to war, for pity's sake—to be made by citizens who think a triangle
has four sides, or one side, or no sides? Who, when asked to locate Iran
on a map, point to Australia? Who believe that Al Qaeda is 'a wing of the
Masonic order' and that a 'mosque' is some kind of animal? Who can't
tell you the state where Kentucky Fried Chicken was invented? Come
on, folks! I mean, I don't think these dolts should be taken out back and
shot, but I sure don't want them picking our president."

Wild applause.

I paid especial attention when Emory was called out on her previous
MP advocacy. I really ought to have been the panelist who brought her
philosophical about-face to the audience's attention, but Gail got there
first.

Emory held up her hands. "Mea culpa! Though the video that Pearson
here was kind enough to make public in 2016 testifies that I came full
circle—back to a long-standing perception that some folks start out with
more marbles than others. Besides, if we didn't allow ourselves to change
our minds, we'd all still be back in that gray egalitarian soup, wouldn't we?

"On the other hand, I do think we can be overly harsh about Mental
Parity, even if it was a mistake with dire repercussions. It was a nice
idea. It would be great if its premise were true. It's awfully unjust, even
if the injustice isn't our doing, that some people are born with smarts
and others aren't. I think I fell in love with the idea of a level playing
field. I fell in love with a world in which we're all blessed with the same
talents. In the back of my mind, like a lot of people, I thought if I wished
hard enough, like squeezing my eyes before blowing out the candles on
a birthday cake, that world would come true. If I acted as if we're all the
same, and chastised people who claimed we weren't, we would magically
be the same. The impulse was anything but malign. It was generous."

"It was the Inquisition!" someone shouted from the audience. "It was the fucking French Revolution, guillotines and all!"

"Now," Gail chided, "you'll all get a chance to contribute during the Q and A."

"I've looked into myself," Emory went on, "and I think I found MP appealing because I felt guilty. My father was a distinguished academic, my mother a high-flying lawyer. So my considerable genetic heritage is double-barreled. But not because of anything I did. I didn't earn my gifts. So it seemed only fair to disavow them. In recent years, though, I've come to realize that a sharp mind isn't just an undeserved blessing. It comes with responsibility. Responsibility that I didn't ask for, either. I wonder if I might be a happier person with a lower IQ—"

"Oh, no, not the 'happy dope' trope!" The same heckler.

"Intelligence is a burden," Emory continued, *unruffled.* "Sometimes a torture. It entails an obligation to put it to good use. I hope I'm mature enough now to meet that obligation. I'm the first to accept that I have a lot to make up for. And I'm really glad you asked about this, Gail. It's therapeutic for me to explain my personal journey in public."

Journey? I thought. *You didn't go anywhere. You set up shop on Carpetbagger Avenue, and you've kept that address ever since.*

"You are a piece of work." It took a moment to realize that I'd said that out loud.

But the audience laughed and then burst into an applause punctuated by the odd "You go, girl, Em!" They agreed, all right, but they loved that Emory was a piece of work. My aside only redounded to her glory.

As for my performance, I don't think I humiliated myself, but I didn't shine. I kept my head down, while praying for this event to please be over. My observations were plodding. I was too earnest. (Despite the appearance of seriousness at political gatherings, their audiences are the same as audiences everywhere: they want to be entertained. You don't win by landing a trenchant point but by making the mezzanine laugh.) My boosters would have been disappointed, which helped explain the anomalously short line of people at the end waiting for me to sign *Mania.* Through the whole event, despite my medaled status as the general who'd led the charge against Mental Parity, Gail turned to me, when she turned to me at all, with a hint of condescension, or pity, or both. She hadn't forgotten about that 107.

Obviously, I've done tons of these appearances, and now that no one's going to read this but me, I can stop pretending to be so humble. Most of the time, I'm pretty damned good. I'm hardly ever such a wet blanket. But that night I was continually distracted by my utter incredulity that here I was sharing a stage with none other than Emory Fucking Ruth. I was distracted by wanting to impress her, which is an impediment to successfully impressing anybody. I was distracted by being disgusted that I still wanted to impress her. And I was especially distracted by this puzzler: Emory was messing with my head. *Why wasn't I messing with hers?* Did she even remember some of the things she'd said to me? That below-the-belt accusation about my attachment to her having always seemed "erotic"? Sure, I retaliated with that YouTube upload, but she went for me first, and she asked for retaliation. *Still,* I found myself marveling, *look at her!* Emory wasn't *distracted.* Rather than sitting next to a woman she'd torn to pieces and left emotionally for dead—or to "get some help"—she could have been perched beside nothing more distressing than a glass and water pitcher. In the final ten minutes, when nearly all the questions from the audience were addressed to Emory, I was trying to formulate something to myself about shamelessness. The power of it. The advantage.

Oh, and while we're on the subject of advantage? Deeply held convictions are a ball and chain. Ask Dietrich Bonhoeffer. The only reason my own story came right in the end was lucky timing, because most people who stick by their guns in a merely metaphorical sense end up in debt, in jail, or dead. Maybe I should tell my son, given his namesake: believing in absolutely nothing aside from what everyone else believes in the present is a huge evolutionary asset. Honestly, I found myself—admiring Emory, in a backhanded way.

The book signing being so dismally brief, I arrived back in the green-room to collect my stuff only a few minutes later than the other panelists, who were chatting vivaciously with Emory, carrying on the discussion we'd had onstage and getting in a few points that Emory's having totally

taken over the whole "debate" had precluded. Once I grabbed my backpack, I guess I could have slunk off, but that would have seemed rude,
or anticlimactic, or something; I knew I'd kick myself back at the hotel
and order room service for dinner purely in terror of running into Emory
again, when, as Darwin pointed out so long ago, *Emory should be afraid of
running into me.* Also, though you'd never guess it from the way the event
went, *I* was supposedly the main draw of this panel, right? I was the one
person most of the audience had come to see, and these other four filler
figures were riding my coattails. But I sure didn't feel like the center of
attention, and when I committed to at least saying a civil goodbye to a
woman with whom I went back four decades, that meant waiting patiently
on the outer edges of the garrulous quartet, meekly hoping for an opening
with the star of the hour.

At least those few minutes provided me a moment to inspect Emory
unobserved, and maybe most of all to inspect myself while observing
her. Railing privately against her for years (I'm embarrassed by how
many such diatribes rage through this journal), I've often imagined what
I might say to her face-to-face. It seems the answer is: not much. If I'd
found her original conversion to MP confounding, presumably this latest reversal was no less so. But there's nothing mysterious about Emory
as a type. She's adaptable. She'll always land on her feet. Had I never
uploaded that "retard" video, she'd still somehow have capitalized on the
nationwide renunciation of Mental Parity, just as she'd capitalized on its
slavish adoption.

What I really pressed myself on was more basic. I wanted to know if
I hated her. I sure had reason to. But it turns out you can't drum up an
emotion of that intensity just because you *ought* to feel it. To my consternation, I found her as disarming as ever. She was striking for a woman in
her midfifties, and despite several long years in a discreditable exile that
would have put a serious dent in the self-regard of any normal person,
she still had that inexplicable and, or so you would think, unjustifiable
sense of superiority and entitlement that in the end it's impossible to fight.
Thinking you're superior and being superior—well, it can be difficult to

tell the difference, and the one may be a precondition for the other. The truth was I still liked her. And I still wanted her to like me.

"Say, Pearson," Emory said, folding her notes into her bag and slipping its strap over her shoulder, "I think they booked us all at the Hyatt. Care to join me for a drink at the bar? Talk about old times?"

"That depends on which old times," I said pointedly. Over the last three hours, that constituted both the sole allusion to our vicious falling-out and my only good line.

Emory just laughed; rather than undermine me with a comeback, she let me have my moment.

"Merlot, then," I said. "Sure."

ABOUT THE AUTHOR

Although LIONEL SHRIVER has published many novels, a collection of essays, and a column in the *Spectator* since 2017, and her journalism has featured in publications including the *Guardian*, the *New York Times* and the *Wall Street Journal*, she in no way wishes for the inclusion of this information to imply that she is more 'intelligent' or 'accomplished' than anyone else. The outdated meritocracy of intellectual achievement has made her a bestseller multiple times and accorded her awards including the Orange Prize, but she accepts that all of these accidental accolades are basically meaningless. She lives in Portugal and Brooklyn, New York.